Anna Abney is among ~~~~~~ family, former residents ~~~~~~ Hall, a lost house of Derbyshire. The Measham Hall series is a fictionalised account of her ancestors' lives. An academic who teaches English and Creative Writing at the Open University, she wrote her PhD on the seventeenth-century writer Margaret Cavendish. Anna was born and raised in London, and lived in Northern Ireland and the Republic of Ireland for thirteen years before returning to England. She now lives in Kent with her husband.

Praise for *The Master of Measham Hall*

'It's rare for a historical novel to feel so timely'   **Jo Baker,**
Sunday Times-**bestselling author of** *Longbourn*

'A taut, fraught, stylish and important novel… drawing upon the facts and fictions of an oft-neglected moment in history'
Eley Williams,
award-winning author of *The Liar's Dictionary*

'Impeccably researched and wonderfully atmospheric, with a heroine you can't help rooting for'   **Frances Quinn,**
author of *The Smallest Man*

'Exciting and immersive. It took me straight into the heart of Restoration England in all its rich and vivid detail. I was gripped! Anna is a stunning new talent'   **Nicola Cornick,**
author of *House of Shadows*

'A thoroughly engaging romp through Restoration England as Alethea makes her way from the plague-ridden streets of London to her father's estate in Derbyshire. By turns entertaining, surprising and thought-provoking, this is an impressive debut'   **Jane Johnson, author of** *The Sea Gate*

'A gripping depiction of what people will do to survive, the long-held beliefs and scruples questioned and cast aside as well as the unexpected kindnesses and unusual alliances made. In elegant prose, this enthralling novel puts a human face to the trials, terrors and enduring hopes of the plague years'   **Catherine Meyrick, author of** *The Bridled Tongue*

'Dazzling... brilliantly merges the past and present and keeps you guessing till the end'   **Emily Bullock,**
author of *Inside the Beautiful Inside*

'By turns humorous and heart-wrenching, impeccably re-searched and beautifully written throughout, this is a haunting and original debut that demands to be read'   **Lianne**
Dillsworth, author of *Theatre of Marvels*

The
MASTER
of
MEASHAM
HALL

ANNA ABNEY

DUCKWORTH

In Memory of my mother, Denise,
25 May 1942 – 14 February 2015

First published in the United Kingdom by Duckworth in 2021
This edition published by Duckworth in 2022

Duckworth, an imprint of Duckworth Books Ltd
1 Golden Court, Richmond, TW9 1EU, United Kingdom
www.duckworthbooks.co.uk

For bulk and special sales please contact
info@duckworthbooks.com

A catalogue record for this book is available from the British Library.

Typeset by Danny Lyle

Printed and bound in Great Britain by Clays.

1 3 5 7 9 10 8 6 4 2

Paperback ISBN: 9780715654507
eISBN: 9780715654361

'As long as you don't deprive them of property or honour most men will be happy enough'   – Niccolò Machiavelli

Part I
London

✦ Chapter One ✦

It was coming closer. She could almost smell it in the air. As the warm breeze touched her cheeks, she felt the poisonous atoms battering at her flesh, finding entrance through her lips and nose. How to fight an enemy that creeps unseen through the city streets, slipping silently under doors and over lintels? All they could do was watch and wait as it advanced, praying like the children of Israel that their houses would be passed over.

'Come away from the window Alethea, for mercy's sake. You will bring the pestilence into this house.'

Lady Margaret swept into the bedchamber, accompanied by clouds of acrid smoke that blew in through the open doorway, making Alethea cough and splutter.

'What's the matter? Are you feeling unwell?' Margaret peered anxiously at her.

'It's just the smoke, My Lady.'

'Pitch and resin, Alethea, I'm trying to keep the house free of contagion. Pull those curtains closed, will you? We should be burning brimstone but My Lord won't allow it. "Are you trying to summon up the devil himself?" he says.' Margaret paced the room, vigorously shaking perfumed water out of a silver censor. 'The devil doesn't need summoning, he is here already. I'm doing my best to keep him from our door.'

Alethea was not sure whether Margaret was addressing her or merely talking to herself. With her smell of frankincense and her special water she reminded Alethea of a popish priest. How shocked she would be at the idea, her a good protestant. The thought made Alethea want to laugh.

'Don't stand there smirking, go and fumigate the corridors.' Margaret thrust the perfuming pot into Alethea's hand. 'Where's my daughter?'

'She's with the dancing master.'

'Who let him into the house? Goodness knows where he's been. And why aren't you with them?'

'Lady Jane asked me to fetch her shawl,' Alethea lied.

She'd grown tired of watching Jane play the coquette with her French dancing teacher and slipped out of the room knowing her absence would go unnoticed.

'Well go back and tell him he is to leave at once and not to return until further notice.'

Alethea began to make her way slowly through the smoky house. Jane would not be pleased to have her sport interrupted. When she'd been told she was to go to London with Jane Calverton as her gentlewoman, Alethea had not expected to be treated like a maid. She'd been bred to better things.

Just before she reached the drawing room Lady Margaret called down to her.

'Wait, Alethea, I have an errand for you. Come up to my chamber.'

Alethea turned and plodded back up the stairs, she was getting accustomed to her Lady's capricious nature.

'An Italian gentlewoman has lately arrived in town,' Margaret continued airily. 'I have it on good authority that this lady, a Signora Pozzuto, has an infallible remedy against the current sickness. You are to obtain a vial of her plague water.'

As she turned to face her, Alethea noticed how the doughy flesh that hung in folds from the older woman's jaw trembled as she shook her head.

'His lordship doesn't look kindly on what he likes to call mountebanks.' Margaret paused to tap the side of her nose, raising her eyebrows conspiratorially. 'We'll keep this between ourselves.' She thrust a heavy purse of coins into Alethea's hand. 'This should be more than enough, make sure you bring me back any change. Signora Pozzuto is staying in Long Acre so you haven't far to go.'

Seeing Alethea hesitate, Margaret pulled a veil off her dressing table and arranged it carefully over Alethea's head. As an afterthought she grabbed a nosegay that lay gathering dust. It was a little faded and had lost most of its fragrance.

'Take this too, just to be sure.'

Thus protected, Alethea went forth into the pestilential streets.

It was as though she'd been carried into a different city from the place she'd arrived in just two months previously. Then she'd been overwhelmed by the crowds that surged through the capital shouting and jostling for space. How exciting it had been to witness the variety of it all, the colour and the noise. Now London was as quiet and sombre as a puritan's conventicle. No one cried out their wares. The ballad singers had been silenced. There were still a great deal of people, but they kept to the middle of the road, away from the houses on either side. They did not bustle and barge into each other as they used to do, but walked carefully, eyes downcast, avoiding any contact with their neighbours.

At least it was easy to find Signora Pozzuto's house, for it seemed her reputation had already spread. A number of desperate-looking people were knocking at her door, demanding admittance.

'I've five children at home,' a woman pleaded with the impassive usher. 'Innocent babes depending on me for their lives.'

'My master's a brewer and the innocent citizens of our parish will die of thirst without his ale,' a scrawny boy shouted over her.

Alethea hung back for a moment, but the thought of returning empty-handed to Lady Calverton propelled her forward. Holding her posy up like a torch, she squeezed her way past the other customers and whispered to the usher that she had been sent by a wealthy and influential lady. He opened the door a fraction and thrust her into a dark hallway, pulling the door closed after her with a swift thud.

There were already several people waiting, each standing as far apart from the next as the space permitted. They observed one another uneasily, as though trying to detect any tell-tale signs of the plague. Looking out for flushed cheeks and glassy eyes, for boils or pustules hidden beneath lace collars or curling wigs. No one spoke, the atmosphere did not lend itself to conversation. The scents of posies and pomanders battled it out for dominance: lavender, marjoram and juniper barely masking the bodily odours that grew more pungent the longer they waited. Alethea stood in a corner, pressing her posy against her face and praying silently for protection against the pestilence.

How she longed to be back in Derbyshire, where the air was sweet and pure and she could roam as she pleased without fear for her life. The morning she left for London, she'd risen before dawn and walked the whole of the Measham estate, noting every spring flower just come into bloom; from the yellow saffron to the milk-white snowdrops her mother had called Candlemas Bells and her nurse, Death-Tokens. She'd watched the rising sun illuminate the sandstone walls of her home so they glowed a rosy-pink against the bare March landscape. There behind the east wall was the chamber where she had first come into the world and where, eleven years later, her mother had left it. Unlike most girls of her age, she had had no desire to enter London society, but would have stayed at Measham quite happily for the rest of her days.

It was two weeks since she had last written to her father explaining how the fever was raging in London and pleading with him to let her come home, but still she had not had any word back from him. It was her stepmother's doing no doubt. Frances was probably hoping Alethea would catch the sickness and die. Then, if her brother did not return from his banishment, that would leave the way open for Frances' children to inherit the Measham estate.

At last she was summoned into Lady Pozzuto's presence. The air in the room was thick with the perfume of roses and frankincense.

Although Alethea's head was aching, it came as a relief after the foetid odours of the hall where she'd been waiting for so long she'd counted the church bells ring twice.

Lifting her veil hardly improved her view. Heavy curtains had been drawn across the windows; a fire burning in the grate gave the only light. To the right of the fireplace a tiny woman perched on a great chair made of carved dark oak. Wooden leaves unfurled behind her head and branches sporting apples curled around the arm rests. Her face was covered with a black lace mantilla. Without speaking she beckoned Alethea over, pointing to a stool by her feet. Alethea sat awkwardly, her face level with Signora Pozzuto's knees.

'*Que bella, que bellisima*,' the Signora crooned, lifting Alethea's chin in her gloved hand. 'A handsome girl like you must be spared, eh? Unless God wishes you for one of his angels, mmm?'

Seeing Alethea's alarm she laughed, a high trilling laugh that seemed oddly out of tune with her surroundings. 'Do not be afraid. We will keep you safe and well. My plague water is famous throughout Europe, it has saved thousands. I myself have passed through numerous cities struck down by contagion and never suffered so much as a cough.'

'It's not for me, but for my mistress,' Alethea told her.

'Not for you? And who is your mistress?'

Alethea was not sure how to answer, since she'd been sworn to secrecy.

Signora Pozzuto seemed to notice her confusion and quickly interposed. 'She must be a fine lady to have a beautiful maid like you. And such a lovely dress, what fine silk. I think you come from a good family, no? You must purchase a little bottle for yourself. Is your life not worth saving also?'

'I haven't brought any money of my own,' Alethea explained, realising too late her oversight.

'But perhaps your mistress has given you enough for two.'

Pozzuto snapped her fingers and to Alethea's surprise a pair of legs stepped out from the shadows behind her. She saw at once they belonged to a young man: firm round calves tapered gracefully into slender ankles. He wore white stockings and his small feet were encased in high red-heeled shoes. Alethea looked up from her place on the stool expecting to see a gentleman as handsome as his legs promised. A huge curved beak hovered above her, like a giant leather crow come to peck her eyes out. She let out a cry of fear and nearly fell into the fire. The man swooped down and placing one arm about her waist swiftly pulled her upright. Alethea pushed him away, averting her face from his beast-like physiognomy.

'S'all right, miss.' His voice was muffled behind the mask. His beak smelt of mint and tobacco.

Signora Pozzuto let out another of her trilling laughs. 'Do not be afraid of Giacomo, my dear. He is my apprentice. He is a great scholar of natural philosophy, a master physician. One day, we are confident he will learn how to turn metal into gold.' She laughed again as though at some private joke. 'He likes to wear a physician's mask. He does not need to of course, he has my plague water, but we must humour him. At least I make him remove his leather coat. It is a shame to hide those lovely legs, no?'

Giacomo opened up a leather case and passed two small glass bottles to the Signora. She held them up so the deep red of their contents was illuminated by the fire.

'The herbs they come all the way from the East Indies and cannot be procured but at a great cost. The sun they need must be a burning sun.' And as if to illustrate her point she revolved the little bottles of ruby liquid before the flames. 'What is more, the process by which the vital juices are extracted is a sensitive one. My recipe I have to keep a closely guarded secret.' She pressed one hand to her bosom. 'I can tell you, my darling, there have been several attempts on my person by those who would force it from me.'

Leaning forward, she cupped Alethea's chin in her palm. 'But I will confide in you, my dear, for you have an honest face. This sweet liquid also contains the powder of several precious jewels. That is why it is my usual custom to sell one bottle of this life-saving elixir for two pounds. I must charge such a sum, which, truth be told, leaves nothing over for my own hard labour; not to mention the cost of transportation, lodgings and wages.' She counted her outgoings off on the fingers of her left hand. 'The whole process is hardly worth my efforts, but I am blessed with a loving heart that cries out to save those I can from this terrible disease.' She leant back for a moment as if to gather her strength, then continued wearily. 'I see a great destiny for you, my dear. Your life must be preserved. This is why I am going to give you a second bottle for only six shillings. Really, it is my gift to you.' Signora Pozzuto sighed heavily as though her loving heart were a great burden to her.

Alethea took the purse from beneath her cloak. It had not occurred to her to count the coins in it. She had no idea whether there would be enough to cover this large sum. And if there was, should she agree to two bottles? Six shillings in comparison with two pounds was little enough, she reasoned. Lady Calverton was unlikely to question her and as the Signora said, surely her life was worth something? She would be no use to the Calvertons if she caught the plague, worse she might infect the household. She felt she deserved a dose of Pozzuto's physic every bit as much as Margaret Calverton, who remained safely indoors.

Alethea tried to count the coins within the purse, but they fell together and in the semi-darkness she could not be sure how many there were. With great unease, as the Signora and her apprentice were watching her with lynx-like eyes, Alethea poured the coins into her lap. They made a little pile that glittered against the dark blue of her skirt. She counted them twice, moving them from one knee to the other. Each time they came exactly to the sum of two pounds and six shillings. It was a strange coincidence, but how could she then dispute with Signora Pozzuto over the cost?

'It seems I have just enough,' she said, looking up at the lady.

'Divine providence,' Signora Pozzuto said complacently. 'Giacomo will relieve you of the monies. You should drink your dose right away, then you can return the bottle to me.'

Giacomo scooped the coins up out of Alethea's lap with great alacrity, replacing them with the bottles of plague water. Alethea stowed one bottle carefully in her purse and lifted the other to her lips.

It tasted of rose-water, saffron and claret wine and though it had been sweetened with sugar it left a bitter aftertaste. She could not detect any other exotic flavours. No doubt they were too subtle for her palate.

As she was leaving the house it struck Alethea that she had not bought any plague water for Jane or Lord Calverton. Would Lady Margaret share her bottle, slipping a few drops into her husband's wine? Surely Margaret would want to protect her daughter? Alethea felt guilty now that she had drunk a whole bottle without sparing a thought for Jane, whose nature was as sweet as her mother's was sour.

It was a relief to be out in the street again and away from the oppressive atmosphere of the house. As she walked, Alethea marvelled at what good English Signora Pozzuto spoke, and with such a clear accent. Alethea's father sometimes entertained Italian gentlemen, but none had mastered English so well as the Signora. She must be a lady of good breeding. Alethea wondered if she ever got to travel, would she learn to speak like a native so quickly? Her brother William was a great linguist, he could read and write Latin and Italian.

She had been tempted to ask the Signora whether she had encountered a William Hawthorne on her travels, but feared it was too foolish a question to put to her. The Signora said she travelled widely, but there must be many English men touring the Continent, indeed Jane Calverton's betrothed was one of them.

Alethea was sure her brother must be in Rome; he had always wanted to visit Italy. He might have gone to the Pope to seek absolution from his crime. Perhaps he had been sent on a retreat or was performing some other penance that prevented him from writing.

William had been hurried out of the country so quickly Alethea had not even had a chance to say goodbye. There was something shameful about the duel he had fought, some matter not considered fit for her ears. His absence was a sore in her side, it nagged at her constantly. Her only consolation was that he had been the victor and though he was banished from England he was at least still alive.

She was so lost in thought that instead of walking to the end of Long Acre she wandered off down a side street and, without quite knowing how, found herself in an enclosed yard. The smell of privies broke in on her reverie, alerting her to her mistake.

The yard was made up of wooden sheds and outbuildings that backed on to the grander houses behind them. Piles of refuse had been left uncleared. Mangy looking dogs sniffed around the stinking heaps. Withered children sat listlessly in the doorways of what appeared to be their homes, too sickly for work or play. Alethea had not suspected such a world existed so close to the wide streets and smart brick houses of Covent Garden Piazza. She'd seen some degree of rural poverty before, but had never been exposed to misery such as this.

A small crowd stood gazing upwards, mouths agape. The spring sky was pretty enough, blue at last and only lightly flecked with cloud, but Alethea could see nothing to cause their wonder. It must be something miraculous, she reasoned, to induce the people to overcome their fear of infection and gather so closely together. Emboldened by curiosity and the protective properties of the plague water she'd just drunk, she approached the assembly.

An old woman was pointing to a strip of cloud. 'See there,' she cried, 'see the angel's trumpet ready to sound.'

'Yes, yes I see it,' a woman in the crowd called out eagerly.

'I can see horses,' shouted a boy. 'There, rearing up on their hind legs, ready to charge.'

'Look at the angel's hair streaming out behind it in a great mane,' the old woman continued, as if not to be out done.

'Oh, it is beautiful, look at its heavenly face,' someone cried.

'But what does it portend?' a deep voice demanded.

Alethea stood close to the old woman, but try as she might to find some divine form, all she could see were a series of shapeless white clouds.

'I cannot make it out,' she said in frustration, not realising she'd spoken out loud.

'There, child, see the angel flying through the heavens clothed in a cloud, and on his face a rainbow.' The old woman traced shapes with a bony finger over the nebulous forms in the sky.

Alethea frowned, wanting to see what the others could see, but unable to do so. She shook her head impatiently, wanting to clear her eyes of their impediments. She did not mean to cause offence but the old woman looked suddenly enraged.

'Toss your head, you trumped up young madam. Scorn and scoff all you like, but if you have not the seal of God you will suffer such torments as you long for death.' The old woman prodded Alethea in the chest with a blackened fingernail.

The crowd began to murmur, an angry rumbling directed at Alethea.

'Doubting Thomas!'

'Mother of harlots. Abomination of the earth!' The old woman was shouting now, her eyes deranged, yellow spittle flying from her mouth as she gesticulated at Alethea.

Voices leapt up from the crowd like flames, catching and spreading.

'She's an unbeliever!'

'A whore!'

'It's the likes of her that have brought these plagues upon us.'

Alethea backed away in terror. Sweat poured down her back, soaking into her shift. She suddenly and urgently needed to piss. She stared into the crowd; surely there was some good soul here who would recall these people to their right minds. Faces had appeared at windows as people looked out of the overhanging buildings to see what the commotion was about.

'I'm a God-fearing Christian,' Alethea cried, her voice emerging shrill and hoarse from her dry throat.

'She takes the Lord's name in vain,' the crone shrieked. 'She is Beelzebub.'

No one spoke out in Alethea's defence. The faces at the windows looked on impassively, like spectators at a hanging. The crowd advanced towards her, faces contorted with hatred. She remembered with horror her mother's tales about the London rioters; depraved citizens who had ripped the late King from his throne and caused his martyrdom. They would think nothing of beating a girl like her to death.

A stone thudded against her skirts and she saw a little boy, no more than five years old, raise his fist and throw another. It struck her hard on the shin.

This assault stirred Alethea to anger. She was not going to meet her end here at the hands of this rabble. She must live up to the name of her father who had fought so valiantly against fanatics like these. She must be brave like William and defend her life. Looking about for an exit, she spied a narrow alleyway to her right. She did not think they would want to follow her down such a confined space, but she would have to convince them she was contaminated.

She tried to picture the crowd, not as a violent pack of humans, but as the gaggle of geese they kept at home. The geese terrified her little sisters, but let her herd them about. She must master her voice and all her skills at playacting to perform a part that would tame her oppressors into submission.

'Keep away if you don't want to catch the plague,' she screamed, raising her arms and flapping them at the advancing crowd. They paused, looking at her doubtfully. 'I am diseased. All my family are killed.' She rolled her eyes and gnashed her teeth until, she hoped, she looked more demented than the old woman. 'I have no fear of you, for I am come like the King of Terrors to bring you to your deaths.'

Alethea continued to flap her arms as she sidled towards the alley. *'Ex toto corde pænitet me ómnium meórum peccatórum.'* She chanted an Act of Contrition, trusting the crowd would not understand, but that the popish words would sound suitably sinister to them. This served the double purpose of deterring her tormentors and gaining God's pardon for her deception of them.

The crowd looked fearful and started to retreat. Mothers picked up their children.

'She is a witch!' the old woman cried.

The alley was just behind Alethea. *'Homo fuge!'* she shrieked as she backed towards it.

The crowd were now some feet away. Seizing her advantage, Alethea turned and ran as fast as she could. The alley was dark and damp, her leather-soled shoes skidded in foul-smelling puddles and she nearly tripped over her skirts. She hoisted them up, leaping along with strides as broad as her long legs could take. A rat scuttled into the shadows. A cramp burnt into her side and her lungs were burning. If the alley turned out to be a dead end she did not know what she would do. She could not return the way she'd come, the rabble would set fire to her.

An archway of daylight opened up ahead. Racing towards it, she prayed the mob had not got round some other way and were not lying in wait for her there.

She emerged out onto a main thoroughfare. There were shops with gaily painted signs and broad windows. People hurried past, oblivious to her predicament. She looked carefully around her, but could see no sign of the furious crowd. At last she slowed her pace enough to get a sense of her whereabouts. To her great relief she realised she was back on Long Acre.

✦ Chapter Two ✦

'There's nothing left over?' Margaret gave Alethea a sharp look as she handed back her purse.

Alethea faithfully recounted what Signora Pozzuto had told her about the rare and precious ingredients.

Eventually Margaret nodded. 'Such a powerful prophylactic will hardly come cheap.'

'How now, ladies.' Lord Calverton strode into the bedchamber. 'What's all this bargaining about?'

'Why nothing, my dear.' Margaret slipped the plague water into her sleeve as she smiled up at her husband.

One only had to look at the Calvertons to see they were not a love match. He was tall and handsome, his brown hair curling so luxuriantly he had no need of a periwig. She was thirteen years his senior and had a plain face with an habitually anxious expression, as though she had just lost something precious.

Calverton smiled at Alethea. 'Your uncle has come to supper. He's had business in town and brings good news, I believe.'

'Hasten to dress yourself, Alethea, so that you can go downstairs and entertain him.'

Alethea did not need any encouragement from Lady Margaret. Back in her room she washed her face and hands, grateful that for once the water had not been strewn with herbs. Jane was always picking bits of lavender out of her hair. Then, throwing her best lace kerchief over her shoulders and tucking it into her bodice, she ran down the first flight of stairs, almost tripping over her skirts in her desire to catch Uncle Percy on his own. She began to lift the folds of silk, then remembered where she was and let them drop. She must not antagonise her uncle, he was sure to have a message for her from home.

She was pulled up short at the half-pace by his loud voice reverberating up from the hall. She looked down to see a shiny pink pate leaning in towards Jane's golden curls as though seeking out a wig to cover itself. Alethea was aghast. Why was her uncle not wearing a wig? What would the Calvertons think? Uncle Percy could hardly cover his head with his hat in their presence, he would not want to be mistaken for a mad puritan. How could her uncle flaunt his baldness? Had he no shame?

If he brought good news of William she would forgive him, or if he had come to take her back to Measham Hall. Although she disliked her uncle and did not relish the prospect of travelling with him, it was something she would willingly endure to be home again.

Jane looked at her with relief as she descended the final stair.

'Alethea, you are looking well, considering.' Percy grasped her hands between his sweaty palms.

'Thank you, Uncle Percy.' Alethea curtseyed.

'I hear you have been out delivering a letter for Lady Margaret.' He lowered his voice and brought his moist lips close to her ear. She could feel his breath blow against her cheek. 'I would never allow a young maid in my care to venture the streets of London alone. I am glad to say Mary is safely established with the Poor Clares at Rouen.'

'And is my cousin happy there?' Alethea stepped away from him, almost colliding with Lord Calverton in the process.

'Happy? What has happiness to do with it?' Percy expostulated. 'Mary has devoted her life to God, she knows to expect her happiness in the life to come.' Percy turned to Lord Calverton. 'One hundred and ten pounds it cost me to establish her with the nuns. But it is a price I am willing to pay, sir, for the furtherance of my religion and the good name of my daughter.'

Alethea's heart sank even lower. Why did her uncle have to trumpet his religious allegiances so?

'I hear you have good news, Uncle,' she said quickly.

'You might learn a little humility yourself, Mistress Impatiency.' Percy eyed her with annoyance. 'It is not your place to question your elders.'

'Why don't we go in to supper?' Lord Calverton smiled genially at Percy. 'Once you have eaten I am sure you'll be ready to deliver your message.'

But Uncle Percy continued to broadcast their religion at the supper table. Having downed several glasses of claret in quick succession, he turned to Lord Calverton with, what seemed to Alethea, uncalled for intimacy.

He patted Calverton's arm saying, 'I know you were a great general in the late wars, sir, none braver, and you stuck your neck out to employ Catholics like my brother Nicholas, so you know there are no subjects more loyal, more faithful to His Majesty than the English Catholics.' Percy wiped the mutton fat from his mouth onto his sleeve before continuing. 'For it is a fact, sir, that those who seek to bring down popery are the same scurvy rogues who brought down the monarchy.' He held out his glass for the servant to refill. 'And if there should be any English Catholics who conspire against the king, hang 'em, that's what I say, hang, draw and quarter 'em. But you will find the executioner's work is short, sir, for there will not be many Catholics found guilty of such crimes.'

Alethea wrung her hands under the table. Why had her father not come instead to see his friend and petition the King on William's behalf? Her father always said a person's religion was between himself and his own conscience, being nobody else's business. Uncle Percy, on the other hand, was on a personal crusade to promote the cause of English Catholics. But for all his high talk, everyone knew he had kept a low profile during the wars and quickly made his peace with the winning side. Alethea wondered that Percy had the gall to speak to Lord Calverton so when he had not risked his bald head taking up arms for the King.

'I hear you are in London on some legal business,' Calverton said.

'Bringing a suit against my neighbour, sir. He keeps encroaching on my land. As if I haven't paid twice over for it as it is. Two-thirds of my estates were taken from me under Cromwell, sir, two-thirds I had to buy back and now this mouse's arse-worm wants to take more from me. He will not get it, of that I can assure you.' Uncle Percy's thumbs sank into the cold quail in his hands, shattering its ribcage. He looked down at it with surprise, dropping the bones onto his plate. 'I hope His Majesty will see fit to recompense my brother, Nicholas, for all his sacrifices,' he continued more softly. 'He hasn't received a penny in compensation for all his lands that were seized. And his house ransacked by Parliament troops; all the tapestries gone and the paintings, one a portrait of our late father.' Percy drained another glass of wine.

Alethea looked across the table at Jane. To her relief Jane smiled mischievously at her. Lady Margaret, however, looked as though she had just swallowed a piece of rancid offal.

'I have raised this issue with His Majesty on several occasions, as your brother knows. The King promised to look into it, but with the war against the Dutch, resources are scant and the King has more pressing concerns.'

There was an edge of impatience to Lord Calverton's voice, but Uncle Percy was not listening.

'Even a younger brother can't help but be attached to the house he grew up in. Measham Hall was built by my grandfather, you know, and though it is unlikely it will ever come to me...' Percy looked suddenly at Alethea. 'Well of course we hope it won't, don't we, Alethea?'

'I must hope Measham Hall goes to William, Uncle. But I pray my father will live for many more years before that day,' she responded cautiously, aware that her stepmother was not the only one with eyes on the family estate.

'Of course, of course, we all wish for that, God preserve him. And that brings me to my news.'

Alethea sighed with relief.

'The King has forgiven William for his, ah, youthful indiscretion. The death penalty has been lifted. He is free to return home.'

Alethea clapped her hands with delight. 'Oh Uncle, – that is great news indeed.'

'Now it's just a case of locating the young skipjack.' Percy looked around for the servant, who dutifully stepped forward with another bottle.

'Nicholas has still not had word from him?' Calverton asked.

'Last heard from William eight months ago, a letter from Paris. I hope William has reformed his ways by now and not entered into any more duels. They fight nasty on the Continent, William may not be so lucky next time round.' Percy licked his lips. 'This barley cream is delicious.' He nodded at Lady Margaret. Thick daubs of yellow cream clung to the bristles on his chin. 'My commendations to the cook.'

Margaret sniffed. 'We must all hope William Hawthorne has changed his ways and does not bring any more scandal to his family.'

Percy looked affronted. 'Base insults were delivered to him; all slander with no foundation in fact.'

Alethea scowled at her uncle in frustration. No one would tell her anything. All she heard were angry murmurings behind closed doors; conversations that were broken off when she entered the room.

Lord Calverton surveyed the table, smiling pacifically at his disgruntled guests. 'I am sure William has learnt his lesson,' he said with finality.

'And the Fanshawes, they won't seek after William, to avenge their son?' Alethea could not help asking. She had spent many nights lying awake, imagining assassins hired by the Fanshawes hunting William down.

'Lord Fanshawe died of an ague two weeks ago. Why else do you think William was pardoned? Fanshawe had the ear of the King. William would never have been safe on English soil while Fanshawe was alive. Fortunately for us there are only females left in that family now and who listens to women, ay?' Percy laughed, turning to Calverton in expectation of his accompaniment.

17

'I find it is always wise to pay heed to the fairer sex,' Lord Calverton responded.

Lady Margaret smiled at her husband, placing her hand over his. It was well known she had brought him a fortune on their marriage. According to Margaret it was all thanks to her cleverness that fortune had not been lost under Cromwell's tyranny. Even during the 1650s Margaret had been able to travel freely between England and the Continent while Lord Calverton was forced to remain abroad under pain of death. In those days, as she often explained to Jane and Alethea, it had been an advantage to be female. She was able to oversee all their business interests. She had a network of trusted contacts and relatives she used to take over the leases to their land and properties, so they were not confiscated by Parliament and given to strangers. The Calvertons never had to borrow money when they lived overseas, which was quite a feat, considering the straights they were in. Alethea had the feeling this was said for her benefit. She was uncomfortably aware of the huge debts her own father had accrued during this time.

Calverton was fond of saying, only half-jokingly, that he would have starved had it not been for his wife and that he would never forget his great debt to her. But now it seemed all his time was taken up with the King's business and affairs of state. He had taken back the breaches, that was clear. Alethea knew that for all her past glories, as far as the world was concerned, Margaret was just an old wife beyond childbearing, who had failed to give Calverton an heir.

At last, having finished all the cold meats on the table, Uncle Percy took his leave. Alethea accompanied him to the front door, expecting a message from her father.

'I almost forgot,' Percy said, just as she had given up hope. 'Your father would be cross if I didn't give you this.' He reached into his pocket, but instead of a letter he drew out his purse. He dropped five shillings into her hand. 'As if Nicholas has anything to spare, especially with another child on the way.'

'My stepmother is breeding again?'

'Did I not say? You must pray for a little brother. Apparently the signs are good, not that I pay any heed to midwives' tales. That's why your father couldn't come to London himself. He fears bringing sickness into the house. He lacks faith, Alethea, but then I have St. Sebastian to protect me.' Uncle Percy smiled and pulled out the locket he wore beneath his shirt. 'The image of St. Sebastian. Touch it, Alethea, it will keep you safe.'

Alethea put her fingertips to it, but Percy grasped her hand and folded it about the pendant where it nestled against his chest. They bowed their heads as he whispered a prayer. Alethea hoped none of the servants were spying on them, they would make an odd sight. At last her uncle let go of her hand.

'I have suggested to your father that he sends you to the Poor Clares. He'll find them cheaper than most other convents. He doesn't think you have a vocation, but how can he know when he keeps you in an environment like this? As it is he talks of marrying you to some relative of his wife's. A Protestant gentleman.' Percy raised his eyebrows. 'For all that, he sends you his love and blessings, but cannot allow you home while your stepmother is breeding. I hope she delivers him a son this time. He lets that woman hold too much sway over him, she might at least repay him for his trouble.'

On that last point at least Alethea could agree.

'My stepmother is with child,' Alethea told Jane as she climbed into bed beside her. 'Mind you, Frances always thinks she's breeding, I think it's just so she can be cosseted. She makes such a fuss every time, pulling sickly faces, complaining of wind and pointing out her great belly, which is never so big as she thinks it is.' Alethea blew out the candle. 'Then she must drink Hippocras, but she always complains that the wine is too sour or the spices too pungent, and she calls for wafers and jellies in the middle of the night, putting the whole household to work. I am never allowed new clothes, but she must have new childbed-linen and swaddling clothes for each imagined child. She never cares so much for them once they are born as she does when she is carrying them.'

'How many has she been delivered of?' Jane asked.

Alethea wondered then if Lady Margaret had lost many children. 'Four I think,' she said more softly. 'But only Betty and Lucy lived. There was a boy that lasted two weeks and another born before its time. Uncle Percy says I must pray she is successfully delivered of a son this time.'

'I'm glad your uncle is not my father,' Jane said. Adding with a shudder and a giggle, 'Nor my husband neither.'

Alethea thought of her stepmother's Cornish cousin; he'd lost his first two wives and had half a dozen children in want of a mother. Frances had said he would look kindly on her and not ask too great a dowry. And of course, if she married him the dowry would be kept in the family. Finances were always Frances' first concern.

'I'd rather die of the plague than be married off to some old widower,' she told Jane. 'And Uncle Percy is a hateful man. I'm ashamed to own him as family.' It was all too easy to speak her mind in the darkness of the bedchamber with the curtains drawn about the bed.

'Do all English Catholics feel so strongly they are wronged?'

'I don't think so. It's not something my father speaks of, at least not to me. My mother was very devout. My nurse said it broke her heart, when my father took Cromwell's oath to get our house back.'

'Wasn't she happy, to have your house returned?' Jane turned on her side, propping her head against her elbow.

'I just remember her crying because everything was broken and dirty. Soldiers had been garrisoned there and they'd made a mess of everything. I was only six and hated to see my mother cry.'

Alethea pulled one of the pillows out from beneath her back, shaking it to even out the down stuffing. But instead of putting it back behind her, she held it closely against her chest.

'William was so happy to have our old home back again, he ran through every room shouting, "We are the masters of Measham Hall". I trotted after him, sharing his jubilation, even though I was too little to remember the house as it had been.' She stared up at the canopy above her head. She could just make out the gold thread work glittering in the moonlight. 'I feared Father for he was a stranger to me. That was the first time I recall seeing him, when he came to fetch us from my grandparents' house.'

'I suppose I was lucky Mother couldn't bear to be parted from my father. After the defeat she insisted on following him overseas. I was born in Paris, you know,' Jane said proudly. 'I can't tell you the number of places I've lived in, trailing about Europe after the Court. Bruges was my favourite, we lived there when I was eight. That is why I speak such good French, and a little Dutch.' Jane squeezed Alethea's hand. 'And that's why I'm not afraid of Catholics. I've lived among them most of my life. I am not like these ignorant English girls who think you're all the devil's spawn.'

'I thank thee,' Alethea said. The words sounded more sardonic than she had intended. They lay in silence for a moment.

'You must be overjoyed William has been pardoned.'

'I am of course, but I wish he'd write. I cannot understand what prevents him.' Alethea pressed the pillow between her hands. 'Maybe he has written, but the messenger was untrustworthy.'

'Perhaps he is consumed by a new passion.' Jane sat up. 'The ladies in Paris know just how to beguile a man. Or do you think he remains faithful to Christina? Can he have heard that her family have broken off their engagement?'

Jane had decided that William's duel had been fought over the Lady Christina, though neither William nor anyone else had ever declared this.

'Word might have reached him.'

Alethea was weary of Jane's fascination with her brother and his 'adventures', as Jane called them. Jane was betrothed, it was not seemly for her to take so much interest in other men. No doubt she had acquired bad habits at Court.

'What must it feel like to know a man has been killed on your behalf?' Jane stretched out in the bed, pulling the bedclothes down with her feet.

Alethea yanked them back up again. She felt cold despite the time of year. 'I hope William is not ill.'

William tended to melancholia and had always suffered from poor health. She used to sit on his bed and sing to him, in return he would read her the poems and essays he wrote whilst confined to his chamber. They both had strong, melodic voices; hers good for singing, his for oration. William was skilled at rhetoric and she knew he would argue her part. He would be able to persuade their father not to marry her to Frances' cousin.

'He has probably joined some foreign army and is away fighting somewhere. He will return to you all of a sudden, a gallant commander full of heroics. Or perhaps he has discovered some new land, so far away a letter will take months to reach you. Then he will return rich as Croesus with a country named after him, the William Islands.'

Alethea could not help but laugh at this latest of Jane's flights of fancy. 'Do you remember my brother at all, Jane?'

'Why yes, he is your copy, or you are his. I used to think you were twins.'

'We are not so alike.' Alethea could not understand why everyone insisted she resembled her brother. She found it very trying. It was true their eyes were similar, though William's often appeared darker and larger in his pale, slender face.

Jane shrugged. 'He was a comely gentleman, always very civil to me.'

'William was more a scholar than a soldier. I can't see him leading troops into battle, or embarking on great voyages. He's too slight, too delicate.'

William was an agile swordsman and an elegant dancer. It would have been nimbleness rather than strength that had ensured his victory in the duel. Alethea saw her brother so vividly before her and was so painfully conscious of his vulnerabilities, tears came unexpectedly into her eyes.

'You should prepare yourself,' Jane said gently. 'We none of us can know when death might reach out his hand for us.'

'I know William is living. I would feel it if he had died, I would feel it in my heart.'

⇥ Chapter Three ⇤

'**L**adies, you read your parts so well I do believe you have been rehearsing in our absence.' Sir George Hunt smiled ingratiatingly.

'What else is there to do?' Jane rolled her green eyes. 'Mother won't allow us to go to the theatre for fear of infection, or to Hyde Park because of the soldiers stationed there. We must find some means of amusing ourselves.'

'You're too young to remember the last outbreak of plague,' Lady Margaret called out from the corner of the room; where she sat watching the assembled company and pretended to sew.

Sir George's friend, Mr Darnley, bowed in her direction. 'And yet the playhouses are still packed.'

Margaret shook her head. 'My husband tells me it's only a matter of days before all the theatres are shut down. It is lunacy to keep them open.'

'If I may say, Lady Jane, you make a far superior Celia to that actress we saw perform the role, but of course she had none of your nobility, nor your charm neither,' Sir George persisted.

'Are you comparing my daughter to an actress?' Margaret looked ready to spring out of her chair.

'Why no, Lady Calverton, I would not dream of such a thing. It is just that *As You Like It* was the last play we had the pleasure of seeing together.'

Mr Darnley turned to Alethea. 'You read the part of Rosalind very well, Miss Hawthorne.'

'Thank you, Mr Darnley,' she replied politely, though she did not like his arch tone.

'Or perhaps I should say, Ganymede.' Mr Darnley tittered.

'You had better be careful, Miss Hawthorne,' Sir George said. 'Mr Darnley knows a fine Ganymede when he sees one. Your performance will have him sighing for you.'

Mr Darnley and Sir George both laughed. Alethea suspected they were mocking her. She knew she was not pretty. That was why, Frances said, Alethea's best hopes of marriage were to an old widower. But Signora Pozzuto had called her beautiful. Perhaps they had different ideas of beauty in Italy, or perhaps she was just being kind.

'There are so many pretty fellows in London it wouldn't be difficult for a woman to pass as a man.' Alethea looked pointedly at Darnley's petticoat breeches, which flapped like skirts about his knees and were trimmed off in several layers of multi-coloured ribbons. They might be fashionable, but to her they looked ridiculous. Darnley simpered and uncrossed his legs.

'A hit, a palpable hit.' Sir George laughed again and slapped Darnley on the chest. 'Darnley has a weakness for a lady in breeches, don't you, Darnley?'

Jane looked anxiously across at her mother. 'Why don't we have some music?' she said. 'Alethea sings beautifully.'

'Why then you must sing for us, Miss Hawthorne,' Sir George declared.

'My throat is rather dry after reading, I'd rather not.'

'We will call for some tea to refresh you,' Jane insisted. 'And then perhaps Sir George will accompany you. I hear you are a fine viol player, Sir George. My father also plays the viol, you may use his.'

Jane rushed across the room to where her father's bass viol stood and grasped it by the neck. It was a large instrument and Sir George hurried to her aid. Lady Margaret looked alarmed. Alethea knew what Jane was up to and felt ashamed. Jane was trying to make a match between herself and George Hunt. What the silly goose had not noticed was that Sir George had eyes only for her. That Jane was already betrothed did not deter a gallant like Sir George. Alethea had already heard about his exploits from an old gossip she'd been stuck next to at a dinner party. According to this woman, George Hunt had a list of conquests, from maids to marchionesses, half of whom he had infected with the French Disease. Indeed, said this lady, he even went so far as to boast about the number of women he had debauched. Alethea was receiving quite an education in London, though perhaps not the sort her father had had in mind. Even without this helpful information she knew she would not have been attracted to Hunt. He may have been a handsome, well-dressed fellow with a fortune to his name, but she thought him dull company. If she had wanted to discuss hounds and horses, she could have stayed in the country. And she was not impressed by how much he could drink or the fortunes he had won and lost at cards.

'You must forgive me, Miss Hawthorne, if I am a little wan, I have been the recipient of bad news,' Mr Darnley confided in her as they sipped their tea.

'I'm sorry to hear that, Mr Darnley.'

'My tailor's been carried off by the sickness.' Mr Darnley pressed an orange-scented handkerchief to his nose and inhaled deeply. 'They told me it was the spotted fever.' He lowered his voice. 'But you know plague deaths are being passed off as other illnesses, just so as not to alarm us.'

'God rest his soul,' Alethea said. 'Had he dependents?'

'Goodness, how should I know? More importantly how am I to find his replacement? No one cuts cloth as well as he did. Look at this coat, Miss Hawthorne, see how well it fits me.' Darnley stretched out his arms and twisted his torso to demonstrate the neat cut of his silk jacket.

'It's very fine,' she agreed.

Darnley was not satisfied, however. 'Look, Miss Hawthorne, see this gold embroidery, see how elegant the stitching is?'

'Exquisite.' Alethea stifled a yawn.

To her annoyance Darnley placed one foot on the corner of her chair. He turned it from side to side, inviting her admiration. She gathered up her skirts intending to push his foot away when she noticed he wore red-heeled shoes, just like Signora Pozzuto's apprentice.

'Your shoes,' she said. 'Is that an Italian fashion?'

'Italian? Goodness no, they are *a la mode de France*, my dear. But we have made the style our own with the green lining and the yellow ribbons.' Darnley caressed the leather upper of his shoe like a merchant advertising his finest wares. 'See the forked toe, how it overhangs the sole?'

'Indeed.' Alethea wondered why London gentlemen were so preoccupied with their footwear.

Sir George did not play so well as Jane had suggested and Alethea struggled to sing along to his uneven accompaniment. He'd insisted on a saucy ballad, much to her discomfort, but Alethea was determined not to let Hunt or Darnley get the better of her and sang the rude lines as clearly as if they had been the words to a hymn. She was singing 'oh to get a taste of her oysters' when she looked up to see Lord Calverton standing in the doorway, watching them and smiling. She faltered for a moment, but he nodded at her encouragingly.

'It's true what they say, music banishes sorrows and fears,' he said when they had finished.

The assembled company begged him to play a tune. He agreed so long as Alethea sang with him. He was a far more accomplished musician than George Hunt. His bow moved across the strings with a deft assurance, drawing a rich and sonorous melody from the same instrument that had just been whining unhappily. Alethea's spirits lifted with the music as voice and strings merged in harmony. As they played and sang together she forgot her homesickness and her anxiety for her brother. If only it were not for the plague casting its shadow over them all, she thought she could even be happy with the Calvertons.

As Alethea was retiring to bed, she encountered Lord Calverton on the stairs.

'And how is our nightingale?' He stood on the step above her and bent to brush the hair back from her face.

'Why I am well, sir,' she answered, pleased by his attention.

'I hope my little *rossignol* has not been caught in love's trap.'

'Oh no, sir.' Alethea blushed.

'Good, I thought you too wise a maid to be seduced by gallants like Sir George. He and his friend may be pleasant enough company for these times, but I would not want to see you consort with him too closely. I promised your father I would care for you as my own daughter and that I intend to do.'

'I have no esteem for Sir George or Mr Darnley.'

'Good girl.'

Lord Calverton's face seemed to have acquired extra wrinkles in the space of one day. The lines drew his expression down into uncharacteristic solemnity. There were dark pouches under his eyes. Alethea felt emboldened enough to ask him if something else was troubling him.

'My boatman collapsed on the way home this evening.' Calverton turned and stared down at the hall below. 'He was rowing slower and slower. I said, "What's the matter, man?" and he just slumped forward in the boat. I had to grab the oars before he lost them.' Calverton rubbed a hand across his brow. 'I rowed us ashore and then arranged for a pest coach to take him away. That's why I was so late back.'

Alethea stared at Lord Calverton in dismay. Was he not afraid that he might succumb to the disease? She thought of the boatman watching the black coach coming toward him like a coffin on wheels. If she could not die at home, in the comfort of her own bed, she would rather die out in the open, with a fresh breeze to cool her skin and birdsong to comfort her.

'Where are they taken?'

'We've set up encampments outside the city. Up until now it's been children mostly, children and women. They are weaker, I suppose.'

Calverton turned back to Alethea and patted her hand. 'Still, we cannot dwell on such matters. Say nothing to my wife or to Jane, I don't want to frighten them. A country maid like you is made of stronger stuff, eh, Alethea? You are not afraid of a minor thing like death.'

'I am always ready to meet my maker.' She lifted her chest, even as her heart was contracting within it.

Calverton looked at her thoughtfully. 'If you wish, I can arrange for you to attend a Catholic Mass at the Queen's chapel. I often have business at St. James Palace and could easily escort you there. Your father knows that I respect your religion.'

'Thank you.' She plucked at a loose thread on her sleeve. 'But I can wait until I return home.'

Lord Calverton smiled and lowered his voice. 'Perhaps you are like me, Alethea, not greatly troubled by religion.'

'Is that you, Henry?' Lady Margaret was leaning over the banisters looking down on them.

'Coming, my sweet,' Calverton called back. Turning to Alethea he put a finger to his lips and gave her a wink.

Alethea did not like being set apart by her religion, but neither did she wish to renounce her faith. Not because she was particularly devout, but because she associated it with her mother. Agnes had been a gentle, patient woman whose love for her children came second only to her love of God. Her religion was the mainstay of her life; it enabled her to endure the deaths of five of her children, separation from their father while he was at war and the physical pain of her final illness, with a composure that inspired admiration in all who knew her. Her belief in the Old Religion was unswerving, for her it was the only path to salvation. Anything else was a perversion of the truth. She would never take communion in the Church of England despite the fines this incurred, not to mention the social exclusion. Alethea's mother had little concern for human society, her mind was set firmly on the next world. Perhaps this was why their father had chosen a Protestant for his second wife. Though he shared his first wife's religion he did not match her in spiritual devotion. He had not expected his Protestant wife to be even less obedient than his Catholic one.

William and Alethea had grown up on their mother's stories of the courageous English men and women who died protecting the faith so that it might be passed on to them. The blessed priests who risked their lives to feed the English who were starving for the bread of life. William would ask again and again to hear the tale of Edmund Arrowsmith whose martyrdom their mother had witnessed herself when she was only ten years old.

Arrowsmith, she told them, was a Jesuit priest who had administered to her own family in Lancashire. He was a great favourite with local Catholics, being both wise and devoted. Warned by a magistrate that the soldiers were coming for him he made his escape on horseback across fields and through muddy back lanes. But at Brindle Moss his horse took fright and refused to jump a ditch. As he tried to urge his horse on the soldiers caught up with him, captured him and took him prisoner to Lancaster Castle. The tiny statue of Our Lady which Arrowsmith always carried with him was later retrieved from the ditch by a farmer.

On the 28th August 1628 Agnes and her family had watched as Arrowsmith was tied to a wooden hurdle and dragged through the town. They followed him up to the moor, praying all the while to give him the strength to endure his final torments. Though his body was nothing more than skin and bones, his calm and cheerful countenance amazed all who beheld him and everyone said 'Here is a man who embraces death free from fear'. His last words before he was hanged were *'bone jesu'* and despite his racked body he uttered them so clearly and so loudly they rang out across the moor so that all the crowd assembled there could hear them, 'Good Jesus'.

Agnes' father covered her eyes with his hand as the martyr's living body was cut down from the noose and disembowelled. But she parted his fingers to see the saint's head cut from his shoulders just like that of John the Baptist. And as the final acts of butchery were performed, she saw a golden halo enclose his face. Despite the savagery he had endured, his expression was one of peace and she knew his soul had flown straight into our Lord's bosom.

Afterwards his head was displayed on a pike above the castle and everyone passing by stopped to marvel at it. For the head, instead of decaying, became lovelier with each day that passed. Despite the hot August weather and its having been parboiled, the skin was clear and fresh and the cheeks a rosy red. The head looked with such a kindly expression down on the people passing below that it seemed he would like to speak to them and bless them all. Carts and horses all piled into each other as their riders stared up at the head of Edmund Arrowsmith and no one could pass by without remarking on the innocence and holiness of this blessed Father, who was content to lose his head in defence of his Mother, the holy Catholic Church of Christ.

Their mother's own face became radiant as she told them this story. Her eyes shone as if filled with a heavenly light. She held their hands loosely in her lap as she spoke, her gaze far off, away from her children and fixed on the miracle she had witnessed.

Arrowsmith's severed hand had been retrieved by their own cousin and was kept to that day in a silver casket. It had been used to cure the sick on countless occasions. Her mother had promised to take them to see it. William had been excited by this, he longed to touch the relic for himself, but Alethea was tormented at night by visions of the severed hand, yellow and waxy, pushing open the lid of its box and crawling towards her. She tried to picture Arrowsmith's face, peaceful and benign, blessing the people; but she could not exclude from her vision the gory stump of his neck skewered on its pole, the bones dripping jelly like a fat slice of raw oxtail. She feared there was something very wrong about her, that instead of being inspired by the saint's example like her mother and brother, she saw only the horror of it. A martyr reduced to a piece of meat.

'Don't be afraid,' her mother would soothe her after her night terrors. 'God is showing you a glimpse of Hell so that you, knowing what awaits those who sin, will be able to avoid it.' She had placed by

Alethea's bed her own miniature statue of the Virgin Mary. 'Look at Our Lady instead, remember she is always listening to your prayers, there to offer you comfort and salvation.'

Alethea prayed to the Virgin often after her mother died. The little statue fitted neatly into the palm of her hand, the stone smooth and cool against her skin. When she held it she felt her mother was near.

It struck her now that in the past few years she had neglected her devotions. The statue lay at the bottom of her chest, beneath the bed. She had been afraid to take it out in case Jane thought her superstitious. But the pestilence was only getting worse, who else should she turn to but God to preserve her life? She imagined her mother watching her from heaven, filled with sorrow at her daughter's lack of piety, fearing for her soul. She would take Lord Calverton up on his offer and attend Mass at the Queen's chapel.

So inspired, Alethea waited for a time when she might approach Lord Calverton alone. The opportunity came a few days later as he worked one afternoon in his study. She waited until his secretary had left before knocking on his door. Following his call to enter, she found him bent over several pamphlets that lay scattered across his desk. He gathered them up as she approached, shaking his long curls in irritation.

'If only the printing press had never been invented. When we relied on scribes working by hand we could be sure only writing of quality was circulated, now any dross gets gobbled up by the people. They think because they know how to read they can tell good work from bad. There are too many grammar schools educating people who would be better kept in ignorance.'

'Shouldn't the schools teach them to be discerning in their reading?' Alethea looked down at the pamphlets, trying to see what was printed on them.

Calverton laughed bitterly. 'If only. No, all such schooling does is make men restless. Men who would once have been content to plough the land and bring food to our tables are driven mad by controversy, like this cant.' He waved the sheaf of papers in the air. 'I would burn this seditious trash. It disgusts me even to have it in the house, but I need to preserve it in order to trace the authors.'

Alethea had never seen Henry Calverton so heated before.

He glanced up at her and said quickly, 'Forgive me, my dear, I didn't mean to frighten you.'

'You didn't,' she assured him. She was used to her own father's short temper. She was also curious about the pamphlets. 'What's so bad, that's written there?'

'The lunatic ravings of foolmongers who call themselves prophets and preachers. It's the sort of thing that caused the late wars. Garbage designed to stir up hatred and dissent.'

Calverton, his dark eyebrows drawn together, was staring intently at his bookshelves as if addressing the handsomely bound volumes arranged there. Alethea spotted Charles I's memoir, written as he awaited his execution, *Eikon Basilike*. It was one of the few books her father owned. No royalist household could be without a copy.

'It's all very well for philosophers to have their little controversies, but they should only be allowed to write them down in Latin, then we could keep the minds of simple English men and women free from contamination.' Calverton jabbed a finger at the papers on his desk. 'Any writing that threatens the Church or State should be burnt by the hangman and the authors executed.'

He regarded Alethea as if just recalling her presence, his voice calm and affable again. 'It's the only way to ensure peace is maintained in our beautiful land.'

'London is not so beautiful,' she observed, looking out of the window at the dirty streets and huddled, blackened houses below.

Calverton smiled at her bold reply. 'London is a monster. A great, vicious beast that needs strong men to control it; but once tamed it is also a magnificent creature, the best and the worst of us all.'

'I've heard London called the head of England, but never thought much of it, till I came here.'

'Most young ladies are desperate to get to London.' Calverton stuffed the pamphlets carelessly into a drawer and surveyed her curiously.

Alethea frowned. 'I like the country better.'

'You take after your father, he was never fond of cities.' Calverton rearranged the quills and ink bottles on his desk. 'Nicholas has become something of a reclusive, misanthropical fellow, has he not?'

She turned back to the window. 'He's not much given to company.'

She did not want to be disloyal to her father or smirch his reputation, yet what Calverton said was true. Her father was not an easy man to approach, he preferred his horses and his dogs to human society.

'We were good friends once.' Calverton came over to the window to stand beside her. 'Your father was the bravest man on the battlefield. There is no one I'd rather campaign with. He taught me a great deal, you know, being older and more experienced. But he couldn't accept defeat. The slaughter of our men, it was a terrible thing.' Calverton paused. Alethea could not make out his expression, but she thought she detected a catch in his voice. 'Over four thousand men we lost at Marston Moor. Your father went round the field afterwards identifying the dead where they lay, stripped naked by those pillaging vultures. He wept at the numbers.'

Alethea's fingertips had turned white from gripping the window ledge. She shook out her hands. She was proud to hear Calverton's praise of her father, she had never questioned his courage, but to picture him weeping shocked her deeply.

'Of course, one's honour is important to every gentleman, but for your father, honour was everything.' Calverton rested one hand on her shoulder. 'He believed he lost his honour that day.'

'My mother used to say it was the murder of the King that led Father into melancholy.' Alethea spoke cautiously, glad of the chance to talk openly with someone who knew and loved her father. 'She said he wouldn't be happy again until the monarchy was restored in England.' She sighed. 'I wish Mother had lived to see it too.'

She did not add that Charles II's return to power five years previously had done little to alleviate her father's black moods.

'Your mother was a pattern of virtue.' Calverton squeezed her shoulder before lifting his hand away.

Remembering the reason for her visit, she asked him about attending Mass.

'Certainly, I have business at St. James tomorrow morning, I can take you then. Make sure you're up early, my carriage will leave at eight.' Calverton gave her one of his usual, easy smiles.

As soon as Alethea walked into the parlour, Lady Margaret asked, without looking up from the letter she was writing, 'What did you want with my husband?'

Alethea stopped in surprise.

'His secretary told me you were hovering about outside his door.' Margaret looked sharply at Alethea, as if in warning. 'There is nothing you can do in my house without my knowing of it.'

'I just wanted to ask Lord Calverton if he'd received any word from my father, about William.'

Alethea had not meant to lie, but she knew Margaret disapproved of her and did not want to antagonise her further. 'How can you trust a Catholic?' she'd once heard Margaret ask Calverton, 'they will always put their allegiance to the Pope before their allegiance to England.'

✦ Chapter Four ✦

The morning came so bright with promise it was hard to believe anything was amiss with the world. That was until Alethea stepped into the street and saw a brazier filled with seacoals burning at the corner of the road.

'My wife will be pleased to see they are correcting the air,' Lord Calverton noted. 'And the street has been cleaned.' He nodded approvingly at the brown cobbles swept clear of refuse.

'Does Lady Margaret know that you are taking me to Mass?' Alethea spoke quietly in case her voice carried into the house where Jane and Margaret still lay sleeping.

'My wife is less tolerant than I am. She believes that papists en masse are dedicated to the destruction of Protestantism and the reconversion of England.' He smiled conspiratorially at Alethea as he handed her up into the carriage. 'She's afraid the monks will try to take back our lands in Nottinghamshire. The house was once a monastery, you know.'

He stretched out his legs and settled himself beside her, resting one arm along the back of her seat. She could smell the Cyprus powder on his hair, a rich mixture of civet, musk and sandalwood.

'Let me give you some advice. While it is always preferable to tell the truth, it's not always practical. There are occasions when, for the benefit of all, one must bend one's words to suit the ear of the hearer. Have you heard of Machiavelli?'

She shook her head.

'He's frowned upon by those who like to base their judgements on second-hand opinions instead of discovering a thing for themselves, but his writings contain a great deal of wisdom. For example, appearance is all; in religion especially. Most men view you as you seem to be, very few come to perceive and understand what you really are.'

Alethea shifted uncomfortably in her seat. 'So you are saying it is right to dissemble?'

'Only when necessary to advance one's cause, and that cause must be an honourable one. In this case the cause is peace and harmony and what could be more worthy than that?'

'So, what should I say if Lady Margaret asks me where I've been?'

Calverton pulled on his chin. 'We will tell her I brought you to St. James to meet Sir Meynell. He's an old friend of your father's and has an eligible son, I believe. Now I come to think of it I ought to arrange a meeting anyhow.'

He laughed and squeezed her shoulder, mightily pleased with his own ingenuity. Alethea was equally delighted. Sir Meynell's son might be her deliverance from the Cornish match.

Calverton had ordered a sedan chair to carry Alethea home after Mass. She hated being cooped up in such a small, dark space, being knocked about with every slow step the carriers took. She was used to riding and walking for miles at a time back home and could not understand why anyone capable of walking would opt for a chair. Unable to bear it any longer, despite Calverton's strict instructions to the contrary, she persuaded the carriers to set her down a few streets before they reached Calverton House.

She tumbled out onto the cobblestones, stretching her cramped limbs with relief. On the broad expanse of St. Martin's Lane, the sun could be seen clearly above the houses. She turned her face in its direction like a sunflower seeking out the light. How delightful it was to feel sunbeams warm her cheeks, as though God were reaching out his hand to caress her face. Having attended Mass she felt a restored sense of peace, her soul had been cleansed.

She closed her eyes and imagined herself in the garden of Measham Hall. She could almost believe the fumes of the street fire were smoke from a garden bonfire. Somewhere nearby a robin was singing. She half-expected when she opened her eyes to see rolling hills and the woods beyond. Instead, over on the east side of St. Martin's Lane, a watchman caught her eye. He stood in the doorway of a house, his wooden staff planted firmly in front of him. He was watching her for want of anything better to entertain him.

Alethea crossed the road to get a closer look. She knew the house; it was where the painter Mr Wilmot and his family lived. He had been painting Jane's portrait when Alethea first arrived in London. A fine picture it was too.

A large red cross had been painted across the middle of the Wilmots' door. She could see how hastily the paint had been slapped on, it had dribbled down to the front step in a trail of scarlet beads. A notice pinned beneath it read: 'Lord have Mercy upon us'.

Inside the house a woman was screaming. It was a terrible cry, like the howl of an animal caught in a trap, but whether it was from pain or fear or grief she could not tell. The watchman stared straight ahead and did not move. The rest of the street was silent. The windows remained closed, the doors shut. No one came running to help, to send for the apothecary or the parson. Not one curious head peeped out. For once, everyone was minding their own business.

She approached the watchman cautiously and asked who had been taken ill. The man seemed glad of someone to talk to.

'Can't say for sure. The house was examined yesterday and the searcher reported a member of the family as having symptoms of the distemper. I was sent down here by the constable to make sure they're all shut up within and nobody leaves.' He yawned, opening his mouth wide and arching his back in an exaggerated fashion. 'I was supposed to be relieved hours ago, but no one has come yet. I've not had so much as a cup of ale since yesterday suppertime.' He rubbed his stubbly grey chin and shifted his weight, leaning onto the staff. 'None of them have come to the door neither. When folk do it's either because they need the dead-cart or want provisions.'

'Hasn't a physician or apothecary called?' Alethea stared up at the windows.

'It was the apothecary what informed the authorities. He left them medicine, much good it'll do them. Could do with a drink myself though.' He smiled hopefully at her.

'But that poor woman inside,' Alethea said desperately, for the screaming had not abated. 'Something must be done to help her.'

'They're in God's hands now.' The watchman sighed. 'I expect they'll be calling for the dead-cart soon. That sort of carry on usually signals the end for somebody.'

Jane's portrait hung in the long gallery. Alethea went straight to it on returning to the house, the woman's screams still ringing in her ears. She could do nothing for the Wilmots, but at least she could pay homage to the artist's work.

It was a good likeness, though Jane's skin was not quite so smooth and creamy as Wilmot had painted it, he had caught something of her humour. Jane looked out of the picture with an amused, inquisitive expression, as if she were toying with the viewer from beneath her lowered eyelids. Her plump lips and cheeks were an apricot colour that matched the rich satin of her dress. Her high round breasts were white as fresh milk. Delicate curls framed her face and a bunch of golden ribbons rested lightly in her hair. Her soft arm curled around the spaniel in her lap. Jane had insisted on having the dog included, it had not been a willing sitter and had managed to increase the cost of the portrait with the extra time required to paint it. Wilmot had got the dog especially well, though, Alethea thought. Mitte looked as if she were ready to leap over Jane's arm and out of the picture.

Had Wilmot painted his own portrait and family? She could not remember exactly how many children he had, about five she supposed. How odd if all that were left of him were images of other people; people he hardly knew or cared for. And this dog, with its shining eyes and panting tongue, straining to be free.

She could not bring herself to tell Jane what she had seen and did not like to admit to the Calvertons that she had been out walking the streets again. Lord Calverton must have seen the Wilmots' house she was sure, but he did not mention it to his family.

After the long cold winter, it was turning out to be the hottest June anyone could remember. The servants complained about being made to stoke up the fires when they were already suffocating from the heat of the sun. All the talk was about the pestilence and how it would feed off this uncommon warmth. Alethea overheard the maids muttering about judgements from God on the vices of the Court and the corruption of the country.

Every evening she expected Lord Calverton to announce their departure, or at least if he were staying, to send the rest of the household up to their estates in Nottinghamshire. But he seemed to consider it safe for them to remain in London. He was unusual in this estimation. Alethea and Jane watched from their window as wagons piled with household goods rumbled out of the city, followed by men and women on foot, their belongings tied to their backs, driving their children before them like flocks of geese.

The sun was setting and Alethea opened the bedroom window a crack. A young woman was stumbling down the road, bent over the box she carried, she sobbed inconsolably. Alethea wondered who or what the lass had been forced to leave behind. Or was it fear of what lay before that made her weep so?

It was only as she passed directly beneath the window that Alethea saw it was not a box, but a little coffin the woman was cradling in her arms. She must have been the only member of her family left to bury her child. Or else she had been forced out alone at night because funerals were no longer permitted during daylight hours and no one was supposed to attend them either.

'God be with you,' Alethea called to her. 'I'll say a prayer for your child.'

The woman was too lost in grief to hear her and Jane quickly pulled Alethea inside and shut the window.

A few days later, as Alethea was passing his study, Calverton called her in and placed a book in her hands: *Nicholas Machiavel's Prince, Translated out of Italian into English; By E. D.* She opened the cover and saw 'Henry Calverton, his booke' written in looping letters on the first page.

'Take it,' he said. 'I have no son to give it to and Jane is not interested in such things. You might find it useful. You can always return it to me if it doesn't appeal.'

'Thank you, sir, that's very kind.' Alethea sneezed. She was always taken with fits of sneezing in the early summer. 'It is just a little summer catarrh, that's all,' she said as Calverton gave her his handkerchief.

He smiled. 'Don't worry, I'm not as anxious as my wife, I don't believe everyone around me is contaminated with the distemper.'

Remembering Margaret's warning about disturbing her husband, Alethea curtseyed and left his study as quickly as she could. Once back in her bedroom, she dropped the book and handkerchief onto her pillow, while she looked around for the playing cards she had come upstairs to collect. Finding them, she ran back downstairs to join Jane in the parlour for a game of Ombre.

'Did you see my mother? She was looking for you.' Jane shuffled the cards with practised dexterity.

Alethea picked up her hand. 'I haven't seen her all morning. Did she say what she wanted?'

Jane merely shook her head.

Alethea had a competitive streak and was soon engrossed in winning their card game, forgetting all about Margaret and the book she had left on her bed.

The next Sunday, Lady Margaret ordered Jane and Alethea into her chamber to pray. They knelt in silence for so long Alethea's legs began to ache. She could feel the sweat running down her spine and beneath her arms. Even the creases behind her knees were growing wet. She tried to focus on her prayers, fighting the urge to cough as the pungent fumes purifying the air filled her lungs.

At last Margaret began to speak.

'If any here have sins lodged in their hearts they must confess them up, so that their sins do not draw down punishment upon us all,' she declared. 'We must have no blight, no shame in this household, for those that practice lewd and provocative behaviour will find themselves struck down by the Lord. Fair flesh will soon burst open with the poison that contaminates it. Disease cares nothing for youth or prettiness.' She looked sternly at Alethea as she spoke. 'Roses on cheeks will soon turn to pustules, bright eyes will dim and plump breasts will wither like grapes on a blighted vine.'

'Mother,' Jane interposed, 'these are strong words.'

Margaret's voice softened momentarily. 'They may alarm you, my precious child, for you are innocent. But there are others who may not have been brought up to fear God and respect the sanctimony of marriage. Who may have been encouraged in vain and licentious ways.'

'There are none such here, I can vouchsafe that.' Jane stood up, reaching for her mother's hands, her voice placatory.

But Margaret only shook her head. 'Alas, my girl, you cannot. None of us can be sure of what others may be. Those we think closest to our heart may beguile and deceive.'

Margaret's shoulders were shining with sweat. She pressed a handkerchief to her neck. It was one of Lord Calverton's. Alethea recognised his initials sewn into the corner with scarlet thread. It reminded her of something, but her brain was too full of smoke and heat to recollect what.

When Margaret finally released them, Jane and Alethea quietly returned to their chamber. Without speaking they moved about the room, straightening neatly ordered cushions, tweaking the bed curtains and rearranging the silver flasks, bottles and pots that stood on the toilet table. Neither of them was inclined to sit.

'Will you unlace me?' Jane asked. 'I've got into such a sweat I must powder my underarms.' She stood holding out her arms while Alethea undid her stays. 'I don't know what's come over my mother. She never used to be so zealous.'

Alethea picked up the jar of sweat-powder. They had ground the rock alum up themselves one afternoon, mixing the resultant dust with starch and perfuming it with rose petals. It had been a cheerful time. The two of them employed side by side, testing out their assorted flowers and herbs to see which fragrance they liked the best. Now the scent of roses made Alethea think of summers spent at home, playing with her sisters in the garden.

'I don't think it's healthy to stay in London. I wish we could remove to the country, then perhaps Lady Margaret would not feel so anxious.'

'It is ridiculous that we stay.' Jane brushed the white powder onto her skin. 'Father says the Court will move to Oxford soon. Only he must be in London to oversee affairs of state, but that doesn't mean the whole household must remain with him. It's Mother's doing, she is so stubborn, she cannot bear to be parted from him.'

'She loves him passionately,' Alethea noted, tying Jane back into her bodice.

'It's because she is older than he is. I think that makes her uneasy about her position. She does not trust him enough, that's why she won't leave him in London. Father married her for practical reasons, but she married him for love.'

'And what of your marriage?' Alethea asked Jane, for she never spoke of it.

'What of it?' Jane answered flippantly, scooping some wax and almond oil balm out of a cup and rubbing it into her lips.

'Aren't you impatient to be married and have your own household?'

'I suppose I will enjoy ordering my own household as I please and not having to answer to my parents, especially if mother grows more pious and extreme.' Jane studied her shadowy reflection in the looking glass, a slight frown creasing her forehead.

'But you'll still have to answer to your husband.'

Jane pushed her hair back. 'Do you think my hair grows too low on my forehead? My friend Anne takes hers off with mastic.'

'Your hair is beautiful. Look at me, my eyebrows are like bushes, but I don't care.' Alethea pulled a monstrous face at Jane who laughed.

'But you make such a good Ganymede, *ma chère*.' Jane stroked Alethea's arm in imitation of Darnley. Alethea chuckled and Jane looked delighted. 'You don't laugh enough, *ma puce*. Not like me, I can never stop.'

'Do you like your betrothed?' Alethea persisted, absent-mindedly rubbing Spanish paper onto her hand and turning it red.

Jane took the paper from her and patted it onto her cheeks. 'It's a year since I last saw him. He has extended his tour of the Continent; I suppose he wants to enjoy his freedom before being tied down by a wife.'

'Your father is so wise, he'd only choose the sort of gentleman who will make you happy.'

Turning away from her, Jane sat down on the bed. 'Our marriage was agreed when we were both children; how could my father know what sort of man Roland Sellwood will prove himself to be?'

Alethea began tracing pictures on the sooty windowpanes. Everyone and everything in the house was coated in oily smoke particles from the resin Lady Margaret insisted on burning.

'Will you stay with me, when I am married?'

Alethea was taken aback by Jane's question and by the anxiety in her voice when she asked it. Jane always seemed so care-free, Alethea had assumed she was looking forward to being a wife.

'I thought you were trying to marry me off to Sir George Hunt.' She drew a hat with a feather in the dust.

'Oh, I am sorry for that. Mother chided me after and said George Hunt was not the sort of man we should have calling on us. She said he's already betrothed to some poor girl up in Scotland. Hopefully news of his exploits hasn't reached her there. I didn't know the extent of his debauchery till Mother told me. I'd never have put you in his way if I had.' Jane leant against the bedpost, wrapping her arms around it. 'I only wished you to marry him because he is a friend of Roland's and their estates are close by.'

'I don't believe Sir George has any interest in me, Jane.'

'Well, I am sure with greater exposure he would have grown to love you, as anyone must who knows you well. But you haven't answered my question.' Jane looked at Alethea with a gravity Alethea had not witnessed in her before.

Perhaps Jane's serious humour was just a result of her mother's fiery preaching, yet Alethea was moved by her kind words and by the vulnerability suddenly revealed in her friend.

'Until Father finds me a husband I can accept, and goodness knows when that will be, for I'll be twenty next year and he still hasn't located a suitable candidate, then I'll gladly stay with you for as long as you wish me to.'

Jane leapt up from the bed and threw her arms around her. 'Thank you,' she cried. 'That is such a comfort.'

Alethea returned Jane's embrace, patting her back as she used to do with her sisters, for though Jane was sixteen she was often more like a child than a woman.

They curled up on the bed together and Alethea sang to her in the same way she used to sing to Betty and Lucy at home.

The Frogge would a wooing ride,
humble dum humble dum
Sword and buckler by his side,
tweedle, tweedle twino.'

Jane laughed just like the little girls used to. 'The Marriage of the Frog and the Mouse' was Betty's favourite song. She saw no tragedy in the fact that Miss Mouse got eaten by Gib the cat, while Frogge was dragged off to the millpond by Dickie Drake. Betty saw only the humour in the mismatched couple and their wedding supper of three beans in a pound of butter.

She missed her sisters and hoped they would not forget her. Betty was her pet, a sweet-natured girl who followed her about like a little dog. Lucy was more wilful, no doubt she had felt the rod a few times since Alethea had been gone. But Lucy was clever; Alethea had been teaching her to read. William had taught her chess and though she was only six years old she had mastered the movements of the pieces and could play a reasonable game. If only she would learn how to keep her peace with her mother.

'Can my little sisters come to visit after you are married?' Alethea asked.

Jane squeezed her hand. 'Of course they can, and your brother too. What a merry company we'll make.'

Alethea thought Jane's tone rather forced. 'Your husband won't object?'

'Why should he? Doesn't a husband want whatever pleases his wife?'

'Exactly. And how will your husband be able to refuse you anything?'

'I've heard rumours he has a hot temper,' Jane said quietly.

'Well if he has I am sure you'll be able to cool it,' Alethea replied firmly.

She wanted to dismiss Jane's fears, but later she wished she had paid them more heed. She should have enquired further about the rumours, there must have been some grounds to them for Jane to take them so seriously.

⇥ Chapter Five ⇤

'Alethea, I have great news for you.'

To Alethea's surprise Lady Margaret sat down on the bench beside her. Alethea laid down the book she had been attempting to read, the translation of Machiavelli's *Prince* Lord Calverton had lent her. Her reading had already been distracted by Jane's lapdog, Mitte.

Since the mayor had ordered all London's dogs and cats be put to death in an attempt to halt the spread of the pestilence, Mitte had been kept within the walls of the house and gardens. The spaniel was as impatient as Alethea for further exercise and they had been playing with a ball around the walks of the parterre while Jane rested upstairs. Now it pawed at Alethea's skirts.

Margaret pushed it away with her foot. 'Your brother William is at Deptford and has sent for you to join him.'

Alethea leapt to her feet, hardly able to comprehend Margaret's words in her excitement. 'Does William know he's been pardoned?'

'Perhaps not, that may be why he is so secretive. You can be the first to bring him the good news.' Margaret gave her an uncharacteristically warm smile. 'His messenger waits outside to take you to him.'

Alethea rushed towards the house, Mitte jumping and barking at her heels. She had waited for this moment for so long she could not bear to lose a second.

'Don't wake Jane,' Margaret called, also rising to her feet. 'My physician says sleep is the best means of preventing sickness.' She caught Alethea's arm.

Alethea turned anxiously towards the garden gate, worried the messenger might leave without her. 'Perhaps I should leave by the side door. If my brother's afraid for his life, he won't want to tarry. I must catch him before he goes.'

'You're hopping about like a pilgrim on hot coals.' Margaret laughed. 'Well, I shall not keep you. I'll tell Jane where you are when she wakes. She'll be almost as delighted as you are.' She drew a gold coin from her pocket. 'Take this guinea, keep it safe.'

'But, Lady Margaret, I cannot take so much.' Alethea stared at the coin in her hand, amazed by Margaret's sudden generosity.

'See it as a loan.' Margaret shrugged. 'Your brother may be in need of funds. He can return it to me later.'

Alethea grabbed her cloak, stuffing the discarded book into her petticoat pocket along with the coin. Margaret led her towards the bolted side gate.

A man was leaning against the wall outside, his black, wide-brimmed hat pulled down low over his face. He gave Alethea a quick glance before nodding at Margaret, lightly touching the brim of his hat with two fingers.

'Godspeed.' Margaret barely waited for Alethea's reply before retreating back into the garden, pulling the gate swiftly closed behind her.

Alethea was glad she was not so confined by fear of contagion. Lady Calverton had become both prisoner and jailer in her own home.

The man walked so fast, even long-legged Alethea had almost to run to keep up with him. She followed him blindly down narrow cobbled alleyways, until the streets opened up to reveal the rolling grey waters of the Thames. Alethea felt her lips curl involuntarily into a smile. She was on her way at last, to William and to home.

Still ignoring her, the man summoned a boat. 'Deptford,' he told the waterman in a heavy accent.

Alethea asked his name, but he shook his head. She tried what little French she had on him, but he only looked at her blankly. He must come from some remote country. Perhaps he was a Moor, for his skin was golden-brown and his hair pure black. Maybe Jane was right and William had travelled to exotic lands, bringing this fellow back with him.

How slowly the waterman seemed to row. Alethea felt like grabbing one of his oars to help him along. She gripped the side of the boat, willing it to speed on in time with her racing heart. William was back in England and soon she would be with him. She pictured his joyful expression when she told him of his pardon. How he would sweep her up into his arms and dance around the room with her. Then they would travel home together. William would never leave her in London with the plague claiming more lives every day, no matter what Father said.

At last their boat moved beyond the crowded stretch of barges and wherries where the air was thick with the cursing of watermen. The sun scattered gold on the silver water and with each mile that took them further from the diseased city Alethea's spirits lifted higher.

She had not travelled so far along the Thames before. Beyond the busy wharves green fields spread out from the shores. She could see farms and hamlets where she imagined life carrying on as it always had done, unaffected by the plague.

They came alongside a great ship anchored in the centre of the river. Alethea could see children waving from the decks. The waterman noticed her waving back at them.

'They're Quakers. Been rounded up by Lord Calverton's troops and imprisoned there. Or *quarantined* as they like to call it.'

'Lord Calverton?'

'Oh yes, Calverton's known for being fierce in his pursuit of dissenters. He likes to ride out at night hunting them down. Newgate's full of poor bastards he's arrested; he doesn't spare them the rack neither.' The waterman spat into the river. 'Say his name in certain quarters and folk'll look at you like you've conjured up the devil hisself.'

'Lord Calverton is an honourable man,' Alethea retorted. 'He'd only arrest fanatics who threaten the peace of our kingdom.'

'His is a big net that catches a lot of little fishes. Maybe he catches some bad'uns in there too, maybe he doesn't. But there's a lot of innocent men, women and children dying in Newgate as didn't ought to be there.'

'If they have nothing to hide then they've nothing to fear.'

Alethea's heart was pumping even faster now, she could feel her cheeks burning red with indignation. She looked at the messenger, but he had pulled his hat down over his eyes again and appeared to be sleeping.

The waterman shrugged. 'Who can tell? The plague carries them off before they ever get to trial.'

Alethea said nothing for the rest of the journey. That waterman was an ignorant fellow. Lord Calverton would not torture the innocent or see them languishing in prison if they had done no wrong. He had marked several passages in the book he had given her and one of these explained that a ruler must not mind the infamy of cruelty if he was to hold his subjects united and faithful. Too much pity in a leader, Machiavelli wrote, led to public disorder, murder and rapine, which hurt everyone, whereas executions hurt only the condemned. Lord Calverton had a bad reputation among bad men. She knew him for what he truly was: a peacemaker, protecting England against the chaos and brutality of civil war.

The messenger's cloak had fallen open and she was surprised to see that he was armed like an old-fashioned gentleman. His left hand rested on a parrying dagger, a matching rapier hung on his right. None of the men she knew bothered with daggers. Perhaps on the Continent it was still the custom to wear both. He could hardly be a fencing master and he was certainly not a gentleman.

When at last they arrived at Deptford Bridge, he paid the waterman and helped Alethea on shore, lifting her up by the elbow. Then he set off again, leaving her to follow. She did not have to walk for long, after a few minutes he stopped outside the doors of The Swan Inn.

When she caught up with him, he opened the door for her with a slight bow, still keeping his face averted.

It was dark inside and smelt of stale beer, sweat and pipe smoke. Apart from one old man sitting in a corner by the fireplace, it was empty. Alethea was surprised her brother would bring her to a place like this.

When the innkeeper appeared, wiping his hands on a stained and greasy apron, the messenger gave him Alethea's name.

'Oh yes,' said the innkeeper, 'I'll show you to your room, shall I?'

'Is my brother here?' Alethea asked, relieved at least that she was expected.

'Upstairs,' said the messenger with a jerk of his head.

She had no choice but to follow the two men up the creaking backstairs to a small, uninhabited room.

'Where's William?'

'You wait here,' said the messenger, revealing a sudden facility with the English language.

'Waiting for your *brother* are you?' the innkeeper said with a wink. 'Well I'll send him up when he arrives. The bill's already been paid so we won't ask questions.'

'When he arrives? Isn't he here already?'

'She's impatient.' The innkeeper gave the messenger a lewd grin before waddling out. Alethea could hear his heavy tread clacking down the wooden stairs.

The messenger pushed the door closed. She did not like the way he stood watching her, his hands concealed beneath his cloak.

'Are you going to fetch my brother?' Her voice sounded feebly girlish.

She tried to adopt Lady Margaret's haughty manner, standing tall and staring hard at him, but all she could see was the top of his hat. There was an air of menace about him and he struck her as the sort of man to double-cross her brother. What was to stop him from inflicting harm on her?

She looked around the room for another way out. Despite being taller than the messenger, she knew the strength of his arm from the way he had propelled her from the boat. He could stop her from opening the door if he wished to.

A casement window looked out on to a yard below. It was too high to jump from, but at least she could call for help. She fiddled with the latch, pretending to be in need of air. The window was stuck. One of the panes was cracked and she could see the glass was thin, she could smash through it if she had to. A stable boy was carrying a bale of hay over to the stables. Would he come to her aid if she cried out?

Warm breath made the hairs on the back of her neck quiver. The messenger had crept up behind her. He was standing so close she could smell the spicy apple scent of his pomade. She tried to scream but her voice caught in her throat. His hand darted out from beneath his cloak, his arm brushing across her breast. She leapt back, almost tumbling onto the bed before grabbing on to one of the bedposts and righting herself.

He jerked the window latch open with a quick twist of his wrist. A gust of wind blew in, bringing with it the reassuringly familiar smell of horse manure. Somewhere out of sight a woman was laughing.

'Wait here.' The messenger nodded. 'He come.' To her great relief he turned, slipping away as quietly as the landlord had been noisy.

She sank onto a wooden stool beside the window and watched the yard, desperately hoping to see William ride in. But she was too impatient to be still for long and soon took to pacing up and down. What on earth had happened to her brother?

A church bell struck six. She must have been there for an hour at the least. She could not bear it any longer, she would seek out the messenger and demand to know where her brother was.

The inn downstairs was now full of men who stared at Alethea with insolent curiosity. She kept her head up and avoided their eyes. She could not see William's messenger, but the innkeeper stood behind the bar serving pints of ale. He smirked at Alethea.

'Where is the man who arrived with me?' Alethea demanded, swallowing down her discomfort.

'Left soon after he brought you here.' The innkeeper gave her a pitying look. 'Brother not arrived then? I'm sure I can find another gentleman for you.'

She resolutely ignored his insinuations. 'Did he leave any instructions?'

'Who? The black-haired man never said a word.'

Alethea felt as though her stomach were caving in. None of this made any sense.

'You said my room had been paid for, who arranged that?'

'Same chap as brought you here. He paid for your room this morning, said you'd be staying for one night. Do you want a drink? Glass of sack perhaps?'

'Didn't he book two rooms?'

'No, just the one.'

'And he said nothing else, about my brother William Hawthorne who is supposed to be meeting me here?'

The innkeeper shook his head and turned to serve another customer.

Alethea asked for some bread, cheese and wine to be sent up to her room, then hastened back to the safety of her chamber. She could only think that William, believing his life to be forfeit on English soil, was taking every precaution not to be apprehended. The fact he had paid for one night at the inn made her feel a little easier. Soon she was sure she would hear his knock on her chamber door. Soon she would behold his beloved face once more. William would appear with horses, ready to make their escape.

She was woken at dawn by the sound of a cock crowing. She stared about her in confusion at the unfamiliar surroundings. She had no recollection of falling asleep, but supposed exhaustion must have overtaken her at last. She had lain awake for hours listening to the carousing below. What could have delayed her brother so?

He must have sent his messenger ahead on a different ship. But why send such an incommunicative fellow and why had he not given him a letter?

She poured water into the washbasin and splashed her face in an attempt to wash away her tiredness and annoyance. What should she do if William did not arrive today? She prayed nothing ill had befallen him. If it had, his messenger would surely return to tell her. He would not just leave her here.

Alethea waited at the inn all morning, growing increasingly anxious and restless. She forced herself to eat a little dinner to keep her strength up, deciding to return to the Calvertons before nightfall. Perhaps there had been some misunderstanding and he had gone to Calverton House. Why he had booked her a room at The Swan Inn she could not understand. She resolved to speak to Lord Calverton; with his connections he could find out where William was. She could not bear to spend another night at the inn, listening to drunkards shouting and being subjected to the innkeeper's pointed remarks. He clearly thought she had been jilted by her lover. She paid him what she owed for the food, provoking some curious comments about how she came to have nothing smaller than a guinea, and found her way back to the quayside.

The sun shone again on the water, but now it only hurt her tired eyes. She had difficulty finding a waterman; only one stopped and he was surprised she wanted to be carried into London. She had to promise him twice his usual fare to take her.

The great ship moored in the river looked dark and menacing. No children waved to them from the silent decks. As they neared the city, Alethea spotted a bundle of clothes floating in the water. Black skirts spread out on the surface like an ink strain, swelling and subsiding with the waves. Why would anyone be so profligate as to throw their old clothes into the Thames?

The boatman cursed and steered swiftly away, but not before Alethea saw that the clothes had not been cast off. They enveloped the body of a woman. She was drifting face down, her hair moving in the water like weeds. Alethea screamed at the boatman to stop and rescue the poor creature. He told her harshly that it was no use, the woman was beyond the help of men. Why should he risk hauling a diseased body onto his boat? What good would that do any of them?

Squeezing her eyes shut, her hands clenched tightly in her lap, Alethea did as her mother had taught her, reciting the *Pater Noster* and then whispering a Hail Mary under her breath. The waterman said nothing, his mouth set in a grim line, but he crossed himself when she had finished.

She begged God in her heart to let William be at the Calvertons. She did not think she could stand it if he was not.

Once back on shore, she ran all the way to Calverton House, pausing only when she reached the doorstep to catch her breath and shake out her damp and muddy skirts. What a relief it would be to fall into Jane's arms, and how Jane would gasp as she related her adventures.

The front door was locked shut. She raised the great knocker, then lowered it with a gentle tap. Too gentle; she waited impatiently but no one came. She knocked again, more loudly this time, and hoped they would not think her presumptuous. One of Lady Margaret's scoldings would reduce her to tears.

She listened at the door expecting to hear the dog's excited barking, but all was silent. She counted to ten and then knocked again. Still no movement from within. Looking up she noticed all the shutters were closed over the windows. She stretched up to rap on the lower shutters, but they were too high for her to make much noise.

'Hello,' she shouted at the closed door. 'It's Alethea, please let me in.'

Dispensing with caution she brought the knocker down against the door as hard as she could. Again and again she smashed it against its iron mount, but still no one came.

At the neighbours' house an upper casement opened just enough for the maidservant to peer out. 'Who's there?' she called.

'It's Miss Hawthorne from the Calvertons'. I've just returned home, but no one will open the door.'

'They've gone. Didn't they tell you?'

'What do you mean, they've gone?' Alethea's legs felt so weak she thought she would sink to the ground.

'They left first light this morning, the Calvertons in their carriage followed by a coach full of servants.'

'But some of the servants must have stayed behind.'

'No, no, they all went.' The maid shook her head. 'Couldn't get away fast enough. I suppose they'll send someone back to pack up the house.'

'Didn't they leave some message for me? A note, a parcel?'

'Not with us they didn't,' the voice said resolutely.

'Can I speak with your mistress?' Alethea asked.

'She can hear you well enough. She won't come to the window.'

'But where am I to go?' Alethea found herself whimpering like a child.

'I can't help you, miss. I'm sorry, but I'm under strict orders not to open the door on any account. The way the Calvertons left, looked to us like they was getting away before they was shut in. Maybe somebody was taken sick.' She began to pull the window closed.

'I don't have the plague. I'm healthy,' Alethea shouted. 'I can show you, I have no tokens on me.' In her desperation she threw off her cloak and began to loosen her bodice.

'Stop that,' the maid called back. 'It'll do you no good. Whether you've signs or no I can't let you in. You'll have to make your own way, we can do nothing for you here.'

She went from the window. Alethea stood in the street, frozen in disbelief. A few moments later a little bundle landed at her feet. A handkerchief wrapped around a hunk of bread and a hard-boiled egg, its shell cracked from the fall. She heard the window pulled shut above her.

Soon I will wake, she thought. Soon I will wake and Jane will be lying beside me and the day will begin as it always does. Soon I will wake because this can only be a dream.

She stared down the silent street. Wildflowers bloomed at the side of the road. Tufts of grass had pushed their way up between the cobblestones. See, she told herself, grass does not grow on city streets; I am dreaming and soon I will wake.

Sitting on the Calvertons' doorstep, Alethea chewed on the piece of bread. She remembered her mother's instructions when she accompanied her to market as a small child. 'If we become separated stay where you are and I will find you. Don't go searching for me for then we will only miss each other.' She would wait here until either

her brother or the servant, who was surely on his way, came to fetch her. The Calvertons would not desert her. Something terrible must have happened for them to leave so suddenly. She hoped the maid was wrong, that none of the household had been struck down with the distemper. Lady Margaret would be sure to take fright at the prospect of being shut in, but could not Lord Calverton prevent such a thing? Alethea had not heard of any of the gentry being locked into their houses.

She looked up at the barred windows. If only she could find some way in. If she could climb the wall and get into the garden, but it was too high and too sheer. Then it struck her that William might have come to the house and found it empty. She should have waited longer in Deptford. What if he was at the inn now? Should she return? Questions chased each other around her mind until she felt she might scream.

She must not give way to despair she told herself. Who would the Calvertons send? The groom perhaps, or the stable boy with a horse. He would have to take care; horses were becoming rare in the city and were much sought after. Having done her best to reassure herself, Alethea applied herself to prayer with more passion and intent than she had ever done before. She prayed for the Calvertons, for William, for all the inhabitants of London and finally for her own deliverance.

A pink dawn stretched itself over the pestilential city like a silk cloth thrown over a rotting carcass. It was early, but that did not account for the lack of smoke. Since the taverns had been shut the brewers had closed. The lime burners, the butchers, the soap boilers and the chandlers, there was not a business left unaffected by the contagion. Even from her cosseted position in the Calverton household Alethea had heard people complain about the dearness of fuel. This quiet, clear sky signalled the absence of human activity. London was a city left to the dead and the dying.

She stood and shook out her cramped limbs. She had waited long enough. If she could not find a coach, she would walk home to Derbyshire. She reckoned she could do it in five days, a week at the most. Measham Hall was where William was most likely to be. He would never expect her to linger in a place like Deptford and if he did not find her in London he would know she had gone home.

She walked stiffly towards Oxford Street knowing only that she must travel north. She hoped to find somewhere she might buy a little breakfast; her mouth was dry and her stomach ached.

Up ahead a man was singing. A rare sound these days. His song was not joyful, but tuneless and bawdy. He weaved his way unsteadily back and forth across the street. His coat flapped open and his boots were worn down. He was evidently drunk. Alethea slowed her pace to avoid him, but he moved so slowly she could not help but overtake him.

'Morning, my pretty maid,' he shouted as she passed. 'And where d'you think you're going?'

Alethea walked faster, averting her gaze. She could smell him from across the street: beer and urine and something else, sickly sweet and foetid, like stagnant water or rotting meat.

'Think you're too good for me, do you?'

His tone was angry now and Alethea wondered whether she should hazard a smile to appease him. He quickened his step so that he was walking beside her. The stench coming off him made the bile rise in her throat. She glanced sidelong at him, catching sight of his eyes, bulbous and bloodshot, fixed on her with maniacal intensity.

'I'll have a kiss from you before I die.' He leered at her, licking lips that were wet with spots of yellow saliva. Alethea tried to run, but he caught her sleeve. 'I'll not go down to hell alone; I'll take a comely wench with me.'

She saw now the black pustule on his neck and the mottled red flesh spreading from it. She tore her arm away, leaving her lace cuff in the man's hand, and began to run.

'Why should you not have the plague as well as me?' he cried.

She ran as fast as she could, but she was exhausted from lack of sleep, while he was spurred on by his frenzy. She could hear him panting behind her, feel his hot breath against her neck.

Realising she could not out run him, she decided her only chance was to surprise him. Thinking that in his diseased state her strength would outstrip his, she spun round and pushed the man in the chest as hard as she could, hoping to send him flying. But his body was solid and weighty and his drunken legs stood firm. They were facing each other now and before Alethea could back away his arms shot out. This time his bony fingers clamped tight around her wrists.

She kicked him in the shin as hard as she could. Destabilised, he began to fall backwards, pulling her down towards him as he fell. Alethea could see the greasy spots on his coat and the dark stains beneath his arms. His putrefied face was coming closer; soon she would feel his diseased lips fasten on hers, his foul breath in her mouth.

Then just as suddenly she felt hands around her waist, hoisting her upwards.

'Let go of her, you filthy mutt!' A voice shouted as she was wrenched free and set back on her feet.

An arm about her shoulders propelled Alethea forwards and she found herself running once more down the street, this time in the close embrace of a young man.

→ Chapter Six ←

'We've lost him,' the man said, looking over his shoulder as he stopped to catch his breath. 'Crazed with the distemper like a poor mad dog.' The young man shook his head sorrowfully.

'Oh, sir,' Alethea panted. 'You've saved my life.'

'Jack Fleet, at your service.' The young man held out his hand with a look of some amusement.

'Alethea Hawthorne, at yours,' she replied, managing a slight curtsy.

'So where are you off to so early in the morning?' he asked.

'I'm trying to get home, to Derbyshire.'

'Derbyshire? That's a long way for a young lady on foot. Where are your companions?'

'I have none. I was sent on an errand yesterday and when I returned I found the house shut up and the family gone. I cannot understand it. There must have been some misunderstanding for them to leave without me.' Being forced to explain her predicament made Alethea's eyes fill with tears.

'Did they not provide you with funds at least, for your journey?'

'My Lady was generous.' Alethea felt in her pocket. 'Alas now I have lost that too!' she cried, discovering the money had gone.

Mr Fleet winked at her and with a smile drew some coin out of his breast pocket. 'Put it there for safekeeping. It fell out when he grabbed you.'

'But how…?'

'Come on, I know an alehouse that's escaped the closures and you look like you need a drink.'

For the second time in as many days, Alethea found herself following a strange man down a dark alleyway. Mr Fleet led her down a flight of steps to a courtyard, where the smallest tavern she had ever seen stood crookedly, squashed between two narrow houses. If it were not for the Dog and Duck sign she would have taken it for another house. Mr Fleet rapped on the closed door.

'If a duck wants water the river is here,' he shouted.

The door opened slowly.

'Still alive are we, Mr Fleet?' A gaunt, sallow-skinned man peered out, blinking at the sunlight.

'Thriving, Mr Hubbard, thriving,' Jack Fleet responded cheerfully. 'But this young lady is sorely in need of some refreshment.'

'I can see that, Mr Fleet,' said the innkeeper, looking at Alethea. 'Glass of small beer, mistress? While I see what we've got in the kitchen.'

'Yes, thank you,' she nodded.

'And a bowl of water and vinegar if you please, Mr Hubbard, the lady needs to bathe her wrists.'

Alethea looked at her arms, each one had a bracelet of livid purple bruises and still bore the red imprints of the madman's fingers. She was grateful to Mr Fleet for being so thoughtful and plunged her hands into the basin of tepid, grey water Mr Hubbard set down on the bar, eager to cool her burning skin.

Mr Fleet beckoned Alethea over to a rickety little table set in a narrow alcove. He too was small; a good few inches shorter than she was, with a slight frame and sandy curls. He reminded Alethea of the tales her nurse used to tell, of elf kings and fairy princes. That was until he smiled at her, revealing gums only half filled with the stumps of broken yellow teeth.

'Can we dispense with formalities? Given the times I think we might be so familiar as to use first names,' Mr Fleet suggested, as they tucked into their meal.

Since he had saved her life Alethea did not feel she could refuse him such an intimacy. There was something familiar about him, but she could not place what it was.

'Are we acquainted?' she asked, mopping up the gravy with a piece of bread. Boiled pigeon had never tasted so good, nor beer so sweet.

'That's a bit unlikely, don't you think?' Jack leant back in his chair as he lit a pipe.

'Do you have a trade?' she asked, thinking she might have been served by him when out visiting shops with Jane.

'I was apprenticed to an apothecary, but alas they died.'

'Was it of the distemper?' she asked with some alarm.

'It was, but you see this fume keeps me safe.' He raised his pipe. 'There's nothing better against plague than tobacco. Do you want to try?' He offered Alethea his pipe.

She took it and sucked in, but the smoke burnt her lungs and made her cough.

Jack laughed and handed her a tin. 'Chew a few leaves instead, not quite as powerful against infected air, but nearly as good.'

The leaves tasted even worse than the pipe smoke. He laughed again at Alethea's expression and ordered more beer. She gulped it down thirstily.

'What will you do now that your master is dead?' she asked.

'I'm going home to Highgate, my dad's got an inn there. I'll have to play the prodigal son and hope he takes me back.'

'Did you part on bad terms?'

'You could say that. He wasn't happy with my chosen profession.' Jack knocked the ash out of his pipe and refilled it.

'But an apothecary is a respectable trade. The only one that's flourishing in these times too.'

'That's grave-diggers. Apothecaries are dropping like flies.' Jack smiled indulgently. 'My dad wanted me to follow him and take on the inn.'

'Didn't you like working in an inn?' Alethea wondered why he seemed to find her so amusing.

'What a lot of questions you ask, Alethea. The most pressing question, though, is what we are going to do with you?'

'With me? Might I accompany you as far as Highgate? That's north, isn't it?'

She thought her chances of reaching her destination would be much better with Jack, who was evidently far more experienced than she was at navigating London's streets.

He drew on his pipe and surveyed her thoughtfully. 'Well, leaving you to your own devices would be as cruel as throwing a kitten into a bear pit.'

'I'm not completely helpless,' Alethea said with some indignation.

'And neither is a kitten, but still it wouldn't last long. I've no objection to your company. My dad might even let you stay at the inn for a few days.'

'That would be most welcome. I can write to my father from there and he will send someone for me,' she said.

'So you're not without family?'

'Oh no, my father is a gentleman. He will settle any debts I incur. You can tell your father that I am not entirely without means,' she assured him. 'Besides, I've enough money to keep me for some days.'

'In that case perhaps you'd be kind enough to settle the bill, I find myself a little short.' He leant forward, patting his coat pockets.

Jack was a considerate and engaging companion. He distracted Alethea from the boarded-up houses and the diseased beggars crouching by the roadside, by regaling her with exotic tales from his past life as an apothecary's assistant. Soon she was quite caught up in the case of Sir Fairlove the hypochondriac, whose treatments became successively stranger.

'He was always reading up on the latest cures, not to mention the latest diseases. One time he insisted on the apothecary bathing his feet in cat's milk. She wasn't too happy about that.'

'Cat's milk must be tricky to collect.'

'Oh the cat's milk came from the local dairy. But Sir Fairlove's feet, they were something to behold. My assistant will do it for you, Signora Pozzuto told him, he specialises in feet. But no, it was to be her soft hands or none at all. I think Sir Fairlove liked to watch her, crouching at his feet as it were. Tiny as a fairy she was, but she did have a beautiful bosom, poor Olivia.'

'Signora Pozzuto did you say?'

Jack looked startled. 'Did I? I don't think so, you must've misheard me.'

'It was,' Alethea said, 'Pozzuto. I bought her plague water. Stop a moment.'

She placed one hand on his arm and he paused. She stepped back and surveyed him, his light frame and his shapely calves, ending in red-heeled shoes.

'You were her assistant, Jack – Giacomo!'

'Mistress Hawthorne, I fear you have grown fatigued. Would you like to sit down and rest awhile?' Jack looked at her with concern.

'You wore a mask, but I know you by your legs,' she said triumphantly.

'You do?' He twisted his body to look down at his legs. 'They are rather fine, ain't they? My lady always kept me in silk hose. Show off your assets, Jack, she'd say, keep them looking at your legs not your face.' He shook his head. 'Never one to mince her words, but a fine judge of character, none better.'

'So, when you said you worked for an apothecary, you meant you worked for Signora Pozzuto. But why didn't you say so in the first place?'

'Lady apothecaries are not much known of in England and I was afraid you would think the less of me,' he explained.

'It's true I didn't know there could be such things as female apothecaries.'

'Signora Pozzuto was indeed a great and learned lady apothecary, respected throughout Italy. We Englishmen are low fools who don't appreciate the female mind.' Jack gestured with his arm as if to encompass the nation, but found himself waving only at an empty street. 'In Italy they take girls from the age of three and train 'em up in the art of physic.'

'That's very young,' Alethea said doubtfully.

'They have special convents dedicated to the healing arts. Parents bring their girl children to the apothecary nuns. If the stars are aligned right at birth they know their daughters will grow up with a natural skill at chemistry, so they dedicate them to Asclepius, god of healing. Been doing it since antiquity. They devote their lives to healing the sick and discovering new recipes to cure diseases. That is why our blessed Lady Pozzuto crossed the seas to bring her plague water to the London populace.'

'How wonderful,' Alethea said, imagining a life spent in herb gardens and laboratories. She was surprised nuns would acknowledge a pagan god, but in Italy no doubt they liked to honour their Classical past. 'I would happily enter a convent such as that. And yet,' it occurred to her, 'Lady Pozzuto was not preserved by her own medicine.'

'Alas yes, well no.' Jack scratched his head. 'Turned out her plague water wasn't strong enough to counteract the number of different diseases she encountered. The week she died she had cured a baby of colic, an old man of a bloody flux – that was nasty – and a young boy bitten by a mad dog. This combination proved fatal, overcoming even the strongest of potions.' Jack looked downcast.

'She must have been a most courageous and learned lady,' Alethea exclaimed. 'I'm sure you miss her sorely.'

Jack nodded and fell silent for the first time.

By now they had reached the outskirts of Islington. They stopped and rested for a while beneath a beech tree.

Jack pulled a paper out of his knapsack. 'This is a certificate of health. They won't let us into the parish without it. You must say you're my sister, Anne Fleet. I happen to have a spare certificate under that name.' He shook his head before she could question him on this. 'It's a long story.' He rolled his eyes as if to indicate how long. 'You're leaving London like every other sane person, to avoid the contagion. You do not know anyone and have not been in contact with anyone who has had it,' he explained emphatically.

Alethea felt uneasy, she'd had enough of subterfuge.

'Will they believe me?'

'Of course they'll believe you, why wouldn't they?' Jack smiled at her. 'You've been working for the Calvertons and now you're returning home to your father, only he lives in Highgate, and your name's a little different.'

'So it's only partly a falsehood.'

'That's right, it's always best to stick as close to the truth as possible,' he said with satisfaction.

'It's a sin to lie.'

'Of course it is. Only when your life depends on it, then it's not a sin.' Jack got out his tobacco and stuck his pipe in his mouth.

'Don't you trust Signora Pozzuto's plague water?' Alethea asked.

'What?' he said, struggling to light his pipe.

'You said tobacco fumes were the best prevention against the plague, but what about Pozzuto's plague water?'

'I always say, two cures are better than one. You can never be too careful.'

'I drank Pozzuto's water, will I be safe?'

Jack looked Alethea straight in the eyes. 'I will ensure it,' he promised her.

When they came to the green at Islington they found their way blocked by a cordon of armed men. A constable stood in front of the line, surveying the road before him.

'Papers?' he demanded as Jack and Alethea approached.

'Of course.' Jack smiled, handing over the certificates.

Alethea concentrated on keeping her expression as bland and innocent as possible. The constable studied the papers for so long she began to wonder if he could actually read. She was uncomfortably aware of his guards standing silently behind him, staring hard at her and Jack's bodies, as if they might see right inside them to find any diseased parts out.

'Names?' the constable asked.

'Jack and Anne Fleet, travelling to our father's inn, The Red Hart, Highgate.'

'I didn't ask you where you was going, did I?'

'No, sir, you did not.'

The constable nodded and resumed his scrutiny of the certificates. 'Occupation?' he asked.

'Blacksmith,' Jack answered promptly.

Alethea glanced at him with surprise, then quickly resumed her wide-eyed gazing at the heavens.

'And you?' The constable jabbed a red finger in her direction.

'Serving-maid,' she and Jack answered together.

'She can speak for herself, I see,' the constable said. 'Did anyone in the household where you was working display at any time any sort of fever, phlegm, stinking sweats, hickhops, retching, vomiting, looseness or bloody flux of the bowels, drooping, swooning or deliriums?' He paused long enough to allow himself to draw breath and Alethea to answer in the negative and then continued. 'Have you seen on their bodies or on your own body any boils, pustules, abscesses, swellings or other such superfluous out-growings, blots or stains?'

Alethea shook her head vigorously. The constable proceeded to ask Jack the same set of questions. When Jack had answered the constable returned to staring at the papers as if waiting for them to speak to him and confirm or deny their owners' statements.

At last he grunted, handed back the certificates and nodded to his men to let them pass. The men shifted unwillingly to one side and Jack and Alethea walked through.

It was a while before either of them spoke again, but as they walked along the Upper Street Jack whistled merrily to himself as though he had not a care in the world. His whistling lifted Alethea's spirits and made her less afraid.

'Why did you say you were a blacksmith?' she asked.

'You heard the constable's questions. Do you think he would've let me through if he knew I'd been working with sick people?'

This explanation seemed reasonable enough. It was certainly an occasion when Lord Calverton would have considered honesty impractical.

'We should reach my father's inn within the hour,' Jack said.

Despite everything, Alethea felt more cheerful now than she had in many days. The sun was shining on the open fields and she anticipated a night spent at a comfortable inn. She was sure her father would waste no time in sending someone to fetch her home. He was bound to have heard from William by now, who would either be at home or on his way.

Soon, she would be back at Measham Hall with all its old comforts and beloved familiarity. She pictured her little sisters running to the gates in their excitement to see her again. They would throw their arms around her neck and kiss her cheeks. And when her father heard how she had been abandoned by the Calvertons he would be overjoyed to see her alive and well. Frances, she hoped, might be confined to bed and they would not have to endure much of her bad temper.

Jack was whistling 'the brave jolly gypsy' and Alethea sang along to his accompaniment.

'My but you've a fine voice.' Jack looked at her with admiration.

She smiled back at him. 'So I've been told.'

At the bottom of the Holloway Road, Alethea looked up to see a group of figures ranged against the horizon. A fire was burning behind them, the smoke spiralling up into the summer sky. Perhaps the plague was not so bad up here and people were not afraid to gather together. Maybe there'd be market stalls selling bread or fish or some such, where they could replenish their supplies. She was beginning to grow hungry again.

But as they got closer she could see from the outlined profiles that there were no women among them. Nor were the men milling about in a sociable or business-like fashion. They stood still, legs set wide apart, muskets resting on their shoulders.

Jack continued to whistle, though Alethea had stopped singing some way back. She saw a tall man to the right of the group carried a longbow. His narrowed eyes were trained on her. His gaze did not waver as she and Jack approached and he pulled an arrow from the quiver at his side, locking it against the bow string.

Alethea grabbed Jack's arm. 'Let's go back, we're not wanted here.'

'Don't be afraid.' Jack patted her hand. 'I'll parley with them.'

He sauntered towards the men, his gait easy and assured, as though he were approaching a group of old friends instead of an armed militia.

The archer kept his sights on Alethea while the other men raised their guns to point them at Jack. A couple of them lifted the burning match cords that hung between their fingers and blew on them in readiness to fire.

'We come in peace.' Jack waved the certificate of health in the air. 'We've not met with the plague. We were cleared by the constable back there.'

'Keep away,' one of the men shouted. 'If you come any nearer we'll shoot.'

Alethea could hear the desperation in his voice. She saw how the men's clothes hung off their gaunt frames, ragged and dirty.

'Jack!' she called anxiously, as she spotted one of the men putting his match to the open pan of his gun.

'We're healthy travellers making our way home. We need to take this road,' Jack persisted.

A bullet went flying past his left ear, splitting the bark of a tree behind him. Jack ducked.

'My family are in Highgate, will you let us pass?' he tried again, this time from a crouching position.

'No one comes any closer. You'll have to go elsewhere,' another of the men shouted.

Jack backed away from them to where Alethea was hunkered down at the side of the road.

'Let's go, Jack.' She pulled on his arm with shaking hands.

'Not too friendly are they?' He rubbed his ear. 'We'll try another way, across country.'

They turned and walked back the way they had come, casting uneasy looks back over their shoulders. The men watched them leave, their guns trained on them all the while. The last time Alethea looked back she saw the archer lower his bow, but not his gaze. She could not be sure, but she thought he nodded at her.

'Do you know another way?' She asked nervously.

'We can make a detour, it shouldn't be too hard.'

Two hours later they still seemed no closer to their destination. They had traced their way across fields and rutted muddy paths, been chased off by dogs and shouted at by villagers. No one would allow them entrance.

'It's as if we're at war,' Alethea said. 'Only we are the enemies and the rest of the country is against us.'

'Look, there is a barn over there.' Jack pointed to a group of ash trees which partially screened a wooden building.

'There may be people there. They won't want us any nearer.' Alethea was so fearful by now she dreaded the sight of another human being.

'Let's try it and see. We need somewhere to shelter for the night.'

Jack went forwards cautiously while Alethea loitered behind. She hardly dared to breathe as he entered the barn. She waited for the sound of shots being fired or angry voices shouting, but there was only the wind in the trees and the birds singing, oblivious to human misery.

At last, to Alethea's great relief, Jack reappeared in the doorway, smiling and beckoning her in.

'It's empty,' he called. 'And there's plenty of straw for a comfortable bed.'

The barn smelt of hay and old wood. Alethea spun round, arms outstretched in the cavernous space, motes of dust and chaff dancing in the air around her.

'It's a palace,' she declared.

Jack laughed. 'Well I wouldn't go that far, but it'll do all right.'

A shallow river flowed beside the barn; they drank from this and ate the stale bread Jack carried in his bag.

'Oh for a flagon of beer or wine.' Jack sighed.

'Or a piece of meat pie.' Alethea's mouth watered as she imagined biting through crisp brown pastry into soft spiced meat.

Exhausted, they retired soon after, making nests for themselves in the hay, a few feet apart. Alethea wondered what her father would think of her sleeping like a vagabond, beside a man he would hardly consider trustworthy. But she felt completely at ease with Jack and would rather have him as her bedfellow than the likes of George Hunt.

Lying on the prickly straw, the droning of a fly near her ear, she tried to ignore the rumbling of her belly. This was not the bed she had been looking forward to. She hoped tomorrow they would reach Highgate in safety. They seemed to have come a long way without getting any closer to Jack's home. At least she had a companion, she told herself. Without Jack she might have been wandering the streets of London still.

Alethea was woken by the sound of voices. She could just make out Jack's form, sitting upright a little way from her. He turned and put one finger to his lips. The voices were growing louder, men and women's, joined by the crying of a child. Jack stood up.

'Who goes there?' he shouted in a voice so deep and threatening Alethea could scarcely believe it issued from his slight frame.

'Alas,' a woman's voice murmured. 'There are people here already.'

'Don't go near them,' another female voice could be heard whispering loudly outside the barn. 'They may carry the pestilence.'

'We are a band of weary travellers seeking shelter. If ye carry the plague we'll pass on without troubling ye, but will remember you in our prayers.' A man's voice this time, calm and clear, called in through the doorway.

Jack looked at Alethea, seeking her approval. She nodded.

'We don't have the plague,' he said. 'But how can we be sure you're not infected?'

'Thanks be to God we have all been preserved thus far.' The melodious voice came again. 'We have fled from the parish of Whitechapel and our good Lord has brought us here to your door. May we rest here awhile good people? There are women and children among us.'

'He sounds like a preacher,' Jack noted.

'We cannot turn them away,' Alethea whispered. 'Besides it's not our barn.'

'Nor theirs neither,' Jack muttered. 'And you do assure us that you're all sound folk?' he called out.

'Ye have nothing to fear from us. We hope likewise that we have nothing to fear from you,' the voice replied.

Jack and Alethea rose and went to the doorway of the barn. Two men and three women, one carrying an infant, stood outside. Behind them a young boy held the rope of a horse laden with goods. They looked healthy enough, but it was too dark to see if their bodies were marked with plague tokens.

'Are there only two of you?' the first man asked.

'That's right,' Jack said.

'Well,' said the man. 'The barn is large and can accommodate us all with ease. Our party can lie at one end and ye at the other.'

Jack held one arm open to usher them in. He and Alethea moved back from the door while they passed. The women stared at them, their faces in the moonlight were strained with anxiety. The group went to the back of the barn where they settled the children. The man who had spoken smiled at Alethea and Jack, touched his broad-brimmed hat and bowed, as though they were meeting in a church on an ordinary Sunday.

'Samuel Byrd is my name. We are but a small band of weary pilgrims fleeing a common enemy, I believe. What part of the city have ye come from?'

'St. Dunstans in the West,' Jack answered brusquely.

'And is it bad there?' the man asked.

'Bad enough,' Jack replied.

'Well, I will leave thee to thy repose. Ye have been most kind and charitable.' The man had a soft, North Country accent, Yorkshire perhaps.

'Goodnight,' Alethea said awkwardly, conscious of Jack's rudeness.

'Goodnight. God bless ye both.' The man bowed again and joined his comrades at the far end of the barn.

❧ Chapter Seven ❧

Waking in the morning to the sweet smell of unadulterated woodsmoke, Alethea thought for a moment she was back at Measham Hall. Only the itching of her face soon reminded her she was lying in a pile of straw. She rolled onto her side and pushed herself up stiffly, shaking out her skirts and her aching limbs.

Outside, a red-headed woman was stirring the contents of a large pot over a neatly laid fire. She looked up and smiled kindly at Alethea.

'Good morning, sister. Would you like some porridge?'

'That's very kind, thank you.'

Alethea sat on the grass beside the boy, who was minding the baby. He looked at her suspiciously. The rest of the group were down by the river either washing or fishing, she could not quite see what they were up to. She asked the boy his name.

'Seth,' he said reluctantly, then, after a pause added that the baby was Robin.

Alethea told them her name and the woman said she was called Lizzie. Having overcome the previous night's wariness Lizzie proved a talkative companion. Seth, her son, was eight years old. The younger of the two men was her husband, Jeremiah Tyler, a carpenter by trade. The mother of the baby was her sister Ellen, whose husband was a cowardly devil who had deserted his wife and child, fleeing from the city to save his own skin.

'Why didn't he take them with him?' Alethea asked.

'He was in too much of a hurry and saw that it would go easier for him to travel unburdened by those he had a duty to.' Lizzie shook her head, frowning.

The third woman was Barbara Greaves, a member of their small congregation who had taught in the parish Petty School.

'She has great learning for a woman,' Lizzie noted with a mixture of awe and disapproval.

'And Mister Byrd,' Alethea asked, 'what is he?'

'Why Samuel Byrd is a prophet of the Lord,' Lizzie said, as though it were the most obvious thing in the world. She was about to continue when they were interrupted by the rest of the company returning from the riverbank.

'Good morning, mistress...?' Mr Byrd smiled.

'Hawthorne.' Alethea stood up, holding her bowl and spoon awkwardly in one hand.

'We have been giving thanks for our deliverance. How blessed we are to find ourselves here with all we need on this beautiful summer's morning.'

Looking about her, Alethea saw that he was right. It was a beautiful morning. The river and its banks of golden kingcups and yellow flags glittered in the sunshine. Birds sang from the green boughs whose shade they enjoyed as they ate their breakfast.

Observing her companions, she was struck by their evident good health. Their eyes were clear and bright, their skin smooth and rosy. Their movements were steady and assured and they ate in a leisurely fashion, seeming in no hurry to be gone. They treated Alethea with the greatest civility, sharing their food and addressing her with gentleness and respect. There were no raised voices, no petulance, even among the children. Little Robin was passed from one to another, dandled on knees and covered in kisses, while Seth was allowed to join in the conversation, his contributions treated with the same seriousness as those of the adults.

How different it was to her own family where children were not allowed to speak unless addressed and they all lived in fear of her stepmother Frances' sharp tongue and quick hand. Alethea's father was an equally intimidating presence; his children respected his authority, courted his approval and avoided his anger. Meals with the Calvertons were formal and restrained, even Jane maintained a quiet, deferential manner before her parents. Despite the peculiar circumstances, this breakfast was the most tranquil Alethea had ever experienced.

'There thee go.' Mr Byrd passed Robin into Alethea's arms.

It was a pleasure to hold the warm roundness of an infant body again. Alethea had always enjoyed playing nursemaid to her sisters and missed having a baby to pet. She sang to Robin now just as she used to do for them. Initially alarmed by her strangeness, the baby began to smile and curled his fingers around a lock of her hair.

'What a gift thou art blessed with,' Mr Byrd said.

'She sings like an angel,' exclaimed Lizzie.

Alethea smiled. 'It is just a nursery rhyme.'

Jack emerged from the barn covered in wisps of straw. 'Well this is a fine camp,' he said, smiling at the company and brushing himself down.

He raised an eyebrow at Alethea and she became conscious of how comfortable she was, sitting in the middle of this group, cradling a baby on her lap. Introductions were passed around again and Jack was handed a bowl of porridge. The company had assumed that Jack and Alethea were man and wife. Alethea hastily explained this was not the case.

'We're heading for Epping Forest,' Mr Byrd said. 'I've heard some former friends of mine have set up a camp there. I'm sure they will offer a warm welcome to us all.'

'We're on our way to Highgate,' Jack said firmly.

'Highgate.' Jeremiah Tyler shook his head. 'Highgate's closed off entirely. We met some folk on the road yesterday who'd been turned back from Highgate.'

'Well we can but try.' Jack patted his pockets.

'But Jack,' Alethea said. 'We've already tried, and if every road is closed off…'

'I'll explain that I've family there. Why, I'll most likely know those who're protecting it.' Jack lit his pipe from the fire.

'The folk we met were also from Highgate, but still they were not allowed through,' Mr Byrd said gently.

Jack drew on his pipe, looking unhappy. Ellen was collecting the dishes. Alethea, tired of sitting still, got up to assist her and they took the plates down to the stream to wash them. Ellen knelt on the riverbank dipping the bowls into the water to clean. Alethea, unused to such work, admired the grace and simplicity with which she moved. Ellen was a pretty young woman. She wore her fair hair tied loosely back so that it fell over her shoulders, unlike the other two women who kept theirs secured tightly under linen caps. Alethea noted that all three women covered their breasts with linen collars in the puritan style.

'It must be difficult,' Alethea said. 'Travelling like this with an infant.'

'I'm just so thankful to be out of London and in such godly company.' Ellen placed the last wooden bowl on top of the neat stack on the ground beside her. 'I was sore afraid before.' She hesitated before continuing, 'To find myself alone in the midst of the contagion, that was terrible, but Brother Samuel has led us out and I know we can trust our lives in his hands.' Resting her hands on her knees, she arched her back, lifting her face to the sun.

'You've a great deal of faith in Mr Byrd,' Alethea said.

'He is God's instrument. He'll lead us all to glory.'

Alethea was somewhat disconcerted by this, but was saved from replying by Seth who came running down to join them.

'Look, look.' He held a paper boat aloft. 'See what Samuel has made for me.'

'He's very familiar!' Alethea turned to Ellen, shocked by Seth's use of Mr Byrd's Christian name.

'Mr Byrd – Samuel – likes us all to use our Christian names,' Ellen explained. 'He does not believe in rank. He says we are all equal before the Lord, brothers and sisters in his love.'

'Are you Quakers?'

'We belong to no particular sect. We're true Christians who follow Samuel as our guide.' Ellen clasped her hands against her heart. 'You should hear him preach, Miss Hawthorne – Alethea, if I may – then you'd understand what a great man he is.' She looked at Alethea with an expression of pure joy, her eyes bright and her cheeks flushed. 'There are some as call us Believers, because of the strength of our convictions.'

'Believers in what?' Jack had crept up behind them.

Ellen looked up at him. 'Believers in the love of Christ that will redeem us all. A love that knows no impediments, no differences; that does not need bishops or churches to reveal itself.'

Jack nodded thoughtfully, but said nothing.

'Jack,' Alethea asked. 'May I speak with you a moment?'

They walked some way down river.

'I think we should travel with these people to Epping Forest. There's safety in numbers and they seem better prepared for the road than we. From what Mr Tyler and Mr Byrd said it seems getting to Highgate is an impossibility.'

'Well you have free agency, Miss Hawthorne, you can go with them if you wish.'

'Jack, do not be so cold. Our acquaintance may be short, but after all we've endured together I should not like us to part ways.'

'They're a bunch of hot gospellers. Do you really want to throw your lot in with a band of prick ears?' Jack's voice was low but urgent.

'I agree Ellen's words were somewhat extreme, but have you noted how kind and gentle they are? They're not Quakers.'

Jack laughed. 'Oh, well that's all right then.'

'These are not violent people, Jack. They won't do us any harm and if we are secure in our own faith they cannot lead us astray.'

Jack kicked a stone into the river.

'We don't have to stay with them,' Alethea coaxed. 'We can travel with them as far as it suits us and if we find we don't like them, they won't stop us from leaving.'

'Very well.' Jack shrugged. 'It's true they're better equipped than us. We may as well stick together for the time being.'

'Are you very anxious to return to your family?' Alethea felt guilty now.

He sighed. 'To be honest, I'm not entirely sure what sort of reception I'll meet with anyway. Dad and me, we didn't part on good terms and if the way's blocked off...'

'This plague cannot last forever. Once it has passed we'll be able to get home,' Alethea said, as much to reassure herself as him.

'Yes,' Jack agreed. 'It's at its worst now because of the summer heat. By winter it will have burnt itself out, if only for lack of people left alive to feed it.'

Alethea shuddered at this and crossed herself.

Jack looked at her appraisingly. 'Are you a papist?'

She nodded.

'Well bless me, here I am in a right old stew of papists and sectaries. Seems I'm the only citizen upholding the Church of England here.'

Seth's paper boat sailed towards them and then got caught by a branch lying across the water. It looked as though it had been made from an old pamphlet or sermon. Alethea could make out some of the words on the side: '*If this be not true we are undone for ever*'. The river tugged at the little boat, until its message blurred and it was pulled beneath the surface.

Alethea was charmed by the delight with which their new companions met their request to join them. Dropping the belongings they were packing up, they welcomed Jack and Alethea as if they were relatives, not strangers encountered under hostile circumstances.

'We open our hearts to the traveller.' Samuel turned from the horse he was loading, holding its neck loosely in his right arm, while he lifted his left palm to the heavens.

The horse turned his head to one side and observed them solemnly, as if evaluating their godliness.

'Better hold on tight to your rosary,' Jack whispered in Alethea's ear. She swatted him away with her hand.

'I have to warn ye, however,' continued Samuel, adjusting the wanty rope around the horse's belly. 'While Caleb here is a great blessing, carrying more than we could ourselves, he also constrains us to keep to roads. We cannot go across country as ye might do on foot, for we'll not spoil the land by breaking down gates or going over enclosed fields. Not unless we're forced to it.'

Jack and Alethea looked at each other.

'We'll throw in our lot with you and keep to the roads also,' Jack agreed.

Ellen and Lizzie smiled and clapped their hands while Seth danced with elation. Only Barbara remained aloof. A thin woman dressed in dark-grey worsted, her only adornment was the chain around her narrow waist from which hung a leather purse. She carried herself very upright and spoke with a dignity that suggested she was accustomed to a degree of deference.

Now she looked down at Jack's shoes. 'You wouldn't get far across country in those heels anyhow.'

Jack laughed at this. 'No indeed, mistress, they were made for city streets not muddy fields.'

'You can walk alongside of me,' Seth told Alethea, having lost all his initial wariness. 'I've a pipe and can play tunes to help us along when we get tired.'

So they set off, with Samuel and Barbara leading at the front, Alethea, Jack and Seth following in the rear.

The day grew hot and Alethea's linen shift stuck to her back with sweat. She wished there were some water she could bathe in. The roads were little better than rutted dirt tracks. Her thin leather shoes, which were not much more suited to walking than Jack's, were wearing out. The white heels were caked in mud, the tattered velvet roses hung on by a thread. After a few hours the balls of her feet were becoming so painful she had difficulty putting one foot in front of the other.

'Thou art struggling, sister.' Samuel fell back beside her. 'Ride on Caleb a while.'

Alethea looked at the poor horse already over laden with goods, and refused.

'I can take one of the horse's bags; by the look of thee, thou art lighter and Caleb will be glad of the exchange.'

'Oh no, Samuel, I don't want to burden you.' Alethea had become accustomed to hearing his Christian name and it no longer felt strange to use it.

'Thou art no burden, come.'

Samuel stopped the horse and unbuckled one of his bags. The horse snorted and bent to eat some grass, glad of the respite. Then, to Alethea's surprise, Samuel picked her up and lifted her onto the horse's back. She grabbed its mane. She was not used to riding without a saddle or stirrups.

'Don't worry.' Samuel laughed, mistaking her surprise for fear. 'Caleb is a placid fellow, he'll not throw thee. Here, I'll take the rope and lead him.'

'What about Robin, shouldn't I take him too?' She could see Jeremiah carrying the baby.

'He'll be all right for a bit. Make sure thou art comfortable first.'

Soon she was so at ease on Caleb's back she was able to look around at the land they were travelling through. Beyond the dense green walls of planted hedgerows, she could see enclosed fields of corn and barley. The stalks stood tall, while their ears bent under the weight of their tightly packed golden seeds. The land was more cultivated than Derbyshire. There were more houses and cottages too. It was productive land, she could see that, but she missed the steep crags and rolling hills, the brooks and rivers of her native county. She held up one hand to shield her eyes from the glare of the sun.

'Here, take my hat.' Samuel swept his hat from his head and held it up to her. 'We cannot have thee falling ill with the sun stroke.'

'What about you?' she asked, holding the hat in one hand. She had not seen it leave his head before now.

'I am a seasoned traveller, a little sun will not bother me.'

As he spoke, the breeze blew Samuel's hair back off his face to reveal a red 'B' burnt into the flesh of his forehead. Alethea was so unnerved she dropped his hat. He caught it with one graceful swoop of his arm.

'Forgive me – I should have warned thee. I forget that it is there.'

'Does it hurt?' she asked foolishly, stumbling for words.

'No. Of course it was painful when I was branded, but I kept my mind on our Redeemer and His sufferings on the Cross to save mankind. When I compared the humiliation of the stocks with the taunting of our Saviour at Calvary; the branding of a single letter onto my forehead with the crown of thorns pressed into His flesh and the vinegar and gall given Him to drink, why then my pain melted away as to nothing.'

Alethea nodded. At Samuel's words her family's wooden crucifix had appeared in her mind. Christ's contorted body nailed to the cross, his wounds bright red against the whiteness of his skin, his eyes dark and sorrowful. She saw her mother's eyes, fixed on the cross as she fought the last spasms that wracked her body.

After walking on for a while in silence, she could not resist asking Samuel why he had been punished so.

'They called me a blasphemer for preaching the gospel, nothing more.'

'But it is not a crime to preach the gospel.'

'Except there be those that do not want the truth told; that do not want the people set free, but instead to keep them in bondage, slaves to false doctrine.'

'What is the false doctrine?' Alethea asked uneasily.

Samuel pointed to a church steeple rising above the trees on the horizon.

'Look at the churches filled with gold and silver paid for by the poor with their last pennies. Think on those ministers of the cloth, ministers of damask and velvet more like, their fat bellies filled at the expense of the common people. The clergy claim their place in heaven while

80

demanding their heaven in this world too. And who do they expect to pay for their earthly paradise? The common people, who are told to be content with poverty. Mayn't we have a comfortable livelihood on the earth and heaven hereafter too? Is that so much to ask?'

'It does not seem too much,' Alethea answered cautiously, for indeed his request seemed reasonable.

'I'll not trouble thine ears with all my speeches just yet.'

He smiled at her and she was struck by the beauty of his smile. His whole face became radiant, as if touched by grace. When he smiled he looked like a young man, yet the hair at his temples was flecked with silver. She found it impossible to judge his age. His eyes were deep blue and fringed with lashes so long and curling they cast shadows on his cheeks. The branded mark on his forehead had pulled the skin of his brow taut, so no furrows appeared there. He had thick brown hair which he wore without affectation or adornment. It hung to his shoulders, neither long enough for a cavalier nor short enough for a puritan zealot.

'Art thou ready to have Robin up with thee now?' Samuel asked.

'Oh yes, of course.' Alethea looked guiltily at Jeremiah, who was plodding stoically on with the baby in his arms.

As they rode on, she thought of Lord Calverton and wondered whether it was true that he rounded up people like these and imprisoned them in Newgate. It was clear they had no respect for the Church or its clergy. Samuel had not said anything against the King or Parliament, but then, as he had pointed out, she had not heard all his speeches yet. She hoped he would not put her loyalty to the test; it would be hard not to speak out if he attacked the institutions her father had risked his life and lost his fortune for.

Part II
Epping Forest

✦ Chapter Eight ✦

The great forest of Epping appeared before Alethea as a sanctuary from the hot summer's sun. Clouds of densely packed green foliage massed together on the horizon, signalling, she hoped, an end to their travails. A sandy track curled invitingly between broad trunks of oaks and elms. The silvery grey bark of hornbeams shimmered in the semi-darkness. Birds could be heard singing from the branches while the leaves danced in attendance. Between the trees, arching fronds of bracken unfurled in wild abandon. Here was woodland open to all, with no locked gates or armed guards to keep them out.

Inside all was green, cool and calm. The air was fragrant with the scent of meadowsweet and ground elder. A stream flowed clear over brown stones. They ran to the bright waters, quenching their thirst and splashing their faces. Alethea peeled off her stockings and bathed her swollen feet, gasping at the coldness of the water. Seth laughed and joined her, splashing back and forth across the shallows.

'Here is a fountain in the wilderness to refresh our withered spirits,' Barbara said, filling her cupped hands with water and pouring it over her neck.

Alethea noted that Barbara had gone so far as to remove her puritan collar revealing a smooth white bosom that made her look younger than she had first appeared.

'The Lord thy God bringeth thee into a good land, a land of brooks of water, of fountains and depths that spring out of valleys and hills,' Samuel declared. 'A land of wheat and barley and vines and fig trees. Thou shalt not lack any thing in it, then thou shalt bless the Lord thy God for the good land which he hath given thee.'

'Amen,' everyone except Jack and Alethea responded with fervour.

'Don't see much sign of fig trees, or vines,' Jack whispered to Alethea with an exaggerated look around him.

'Don't you know your Bible?' she whispered back.

'Enough to get by, though it seems I'm destined to learn a lot more of it.' He sighed and rolled his eyes.

Progress into the forest was slow as the horse had to navigate his way over fallen branches and under low hanging boughs. The women lifted their skirts, doing their best to avoid the stinging nettles or being caught in the tangle of brambles that covered the forest floor.

They had got some way in when they spied figures moving among the trees. It was difficult at first to distinguish them or to see how many they might be. They stopped, instinctively wary, and Samuel held a finger up to his lips. The figures were collecting firewood. They too stopped and straightened when they noticed the newcomers.

'I was told I might find my old friend, Thomas Gray, here,' Samuel called to them.

'Where have you come from?'

A man stood, legs wide, an axe in one hand. His tone was neither friendly nor threatening, but it was clear they should keep their distance.

'From various parts, but we are all sound and carry no diseases. My name is Samuel Byrd.'

'Samuel Byrd! Please wait there till I fetch Thomas.'

The man hurried off, leaving a group of youngsters gathered in a huddle, watching them warily.

A short while later a large man with a thick black beard came striding towards them through the trees. He held up his arms and roared, 'Samuel Byrd, what a blessed day is this!'

A great smile spread across Samuel's face. 'We are a small party of healthy folk, come to join thee if we may.'

'Tush, fellow, we'd be honoured to have you.'

Thomas threw his arms around Samuel and almost lifted him into the air. Samuel returned the embrace, laughing, all the sombreness of the preacher replaced with an enthusiastic affection.

They were led to a clearing in the forest where the trees had been coppiced to allow the sunlight in. Alethea was astonished to see a primitive village of wooden huts thatched with straw. A pig was roasting on a spit. Children played on the grass nearby while their parents sat on low stools around the fire. They rose to meet the newcomers with excited curiosity.

All the adults knew Samuel, welcoming him with a marked deference. Most of them also knew Barbara, Jeremiah and Lizzie, greeting them as old friends. Alethea understood that they had been close when they were young, but had not seen each other for some years. Ellen, Lizzie's sister, was much younger and the women gathered around her, exclaiming over the woman she had become, kissing her baby and reminiscing about the sweet child they remembered her as.

'Ye are better equipped here than I could have imagined,' Samuel said, looking about him.

'We've met with great generosity,' Thomas explained. 'At first the local people were against us, but we've convinced them we are good, God-fearing folk untroubled by the distemper.'

'How did you manage that?' Jack voiced the question that had been on Alethea's lips.

Thomas chuckled. 'I also reminded them that London is the market that buys all their produce, so they wouldn't want to make the people of London their enemies.'

Jack grinned and nodded; this was a strategy he could understand.

Thomas conducted them around the encampment with evident pride.

'We've built some makeshift huts as you can see. The local squire, hearing of our plight, was good enough to provide straw for our roofs. Not a day passes but we receive some act of benevolence from that gentleman or the local people. That porker you see roasting there was a donation. They've given us chairs and tables, pots, blankets, all manner of things.'

'It seems as though we have reached the land of Canaan.' Samuel pressed his palms together against his chest.

'Indeed, Sam, here is the free commonwealth we used to dream of.' Thomas grasped Samuel's shoulder. 'It is rough and ready but we live as equals, slaves to no man.'

Stools were brought out of the huts for them to sit on. Alethea sank onto hers, relieved not to have to sit on the ground for the first time in days. She could have cried with relief to be among friendly, welcoming faces. It had been a long and arduous journey and she had experienced so many strange encounters it felt like weeks, rather than days, since she had left London.

Thomas' wife, Martha, cut them slices of meat from the roasting pig, while her husband passed out cups of ale from a barrel. Martha's eyes, under their dark brows, were bright and sharp, but there was a hardness too in her steady gaze that made Alethea a little wary. Still, she could not fault Martha's kindness. Noticing Alethea's tattered shoes and bleeding feet she gave her a pair of her eldest son's old boots.

'Tom's grown so fast he hardly wore those before needing a new pair. They look about the right size. Lucky you've got big feet for a wench and his are even bigger,' she said gruffly when Alethea thanked her.

Once they had been fed and rested, the newcomers set to work building their accommodation. It was agreed Alethea would share a hut with Barbara, Ellen and baby Robin. The Tyler family would have their own shelter. Samuel was taken to stay with his old friend Thomas, whose wooden house was the largest of all the campers' dwellings. Jack insisted on building himself a one-man tent.

They were shown how to build frames out of branches and then cover them with boughs of greenery and finally with fallen leaves which would keep out the rain. The other residents of the wood pitched in cheerfully, sawing and hammering. The children ran back and forth with armfuls of dried brown leaves.

Within a few days they had made decent enough cabins that would keep out the cold and wet. Alethea felt a satisfaction in her handiwork she had never experienced before. She enjoyed this shared physical labour. She was quick to learn practical skills and the people here enjoyed passing on their expertise. They expected the women to work just as hard as the men, making no allowances for feminine delicacy. Despite scratched and callused hands and aching limbs, Alethea slept as contentedly on her bed of leaves and straw as a dog that curls up before the fire after a day spent hunting.

'Those will do you,' Martha told her husband, holding up a pair of breeches she had just finished mending.

'I shall look quite the gentleman in those,' Thomas said appreciatively, looking up from the rabbit he was skinning. 'Sam, do you remember when we had only one pair of breeches between us?'

'It was a wonder we got any fighting done,' Samuel said. He and Seth had just returned to the campfire with arms full of sticks.

'You had to share a pair of breeches?' Seth asked wonderingly, looking from Samuel to Thomas.

'Sam could have fitted into one leg of your breeches, Tom,' Martha chuckled. Her husband was a giant of a man, over six feet tall and broad as an oak.

'One of us had to stay abed for decency's sake while the other went on duty. We couldn't fight naked.' Thomas laughed heartily and shook his head. 'That was until we got some fine trousers off a papist dog at Naseby.'

The knife Alethea was sharpening slid from her grasp, cutting into her finger so that the blood welled up in crimson beads. Jack, who had been attempting to shape a wooden bowl under Jeremiah's instruction, was instantly by her side, pulling out a handkerchief to bind her hand with.

'Are you all right, lamb?' Martha looked concerned. 'Daniel, run to my hut and fetch the leather bag I keep there,' she called to her youngest son. 'I've cobwebs collected for wounds.'

'It's just a scratch.' Alethea regretted drawing so much attention.

'At least you know you've given that knife a good sharpening,' Jack said, covering for her.

Samuel looked over at her, before turning back to stoke the fire. 'Our army had to march for days without food or sleep, dressed in tatters, no shoes or stockings for our feet. It was only to survive that we took clothes from those as didn't need them anymore. Both sides did it.'

'That's right.' Thomas skewered the rabbit onto a wooden spit. 'War only seems sweet to them that know it not.'

He nodded his head sagely in Seth's direction as if to warn the boy. Seth frowned and went back to shaping a stick into a sword.

'The truth is, the enemy behaved themselves with as much valour and steadfastness as ever man saw allied to a bad cause.' Samuel stretched and rubbed his back.

Alethea stared into the flames. She suspected Samuel was speaking for her benefit and feared he had guessed where her family allegiances lay.

'Only we were fighting against popery and tyranny so we had God behind us,' Thomas added. He raised his arms and sang. '"Let God arise, let his enemies be scattered." Remember that one, Sam? There's nothing like the sound of an army singing psalms.'

Samuel closed his eyes. '"He that is our God is the God of salvation."'

'Amen,' Martha said fervently, as Daniel arrived back with her bag.

Alethea woke as the sun was rising. She crept out of her hut as quietly as she could, not wanting to wake her companions. The air was already warm. She would steal the opportunity while everyone else slept to go down to the river to wash.

At the edge of the encampment a stag stood bathed in the first milky light of the morning, his antlers silhouetted against the trees. Alethea remained where she was, squatting on the ground like a frog, trying not to move. The stag raised his head and regarded her with one eye. She looked up at him, hardly daring to breathe, hoping no one else would stir and break the spell. The stag inclined his chin as if nodding at her and then turned slowly and ambled away into the forest.

Alethea wondered if the creature had been sent to her as a sign not to renege on her loyalties; to keep her brother and Measham Hall always in her heart. Epping was just an interlude. Soon she must continue her journey home.

The beauty of the woods banished all anxieties from her heart. Moss-covered branches curled upwards through layers of greenery. The air smelt rich and peaty. Birds called to one another as if in celebration of the dawn. How much better it was to be here than in the narrow stinking streets of London.

She slid down the riverbank to a place where the water gathered into a clear, still pool. Samuel was sitting on a large smooth rock, quite motionless, a fishing rod held loosely in one hand. He smiled, seemingly unperturbed by her sudden arrival and wished her a good morning as though he had been expecting her. She apologised for disturbing him, conscious of her dishevelled and noisy appearance, and pushed herself upright against a tree trunk. He waved her apologies away, beckoning her to sit with him.

'I've a spare rod if thou wants to try thy hand at fishing. Thou may have better luck than me, I've not had a bite yet.'

He showed her how to bait her hook and cast her line. They sat for a while in companionable silence watching the gnats and dragonflies skimming over the green water.

Samuel had been accepted immediately by the community as their religious leader and Alethea felt honoured to share in this task with him. He had an intensity of purpose so forceful all other considerations were burnt away by it. When he fixed his eyes on a person he made them feel as though they were the only being in the world he wished to converse with, that their opinions and concerns were of the most pressing importance to him. So each person felt blessed by his attention and basked in the warmth of his enthusiasm.

'Thomas is a great friend of yours,' Alethea ventured at last.

'You'll not find a truer or a braver man in England. Sometimes his zeal causes him to speak harshly, but he would lay down his life for any child, woman or deserving man that needed it.'

Alethea was prevented from responding to this by a sudden tug on her line. 'I've got a fish!' she cried with excitement.

Pulling in her thread she landed a small trout. It thrashed on the rock beside her, its scales bright gold in the sunlight. Samuel knocked it on the head with a stone and placed it carefully in the basket beside him.

'Well done,' he said. 'A few more of those and we'll feed the camp.'

Alethea, who usually found it so hard to be still, was content to pass the morning fishing. She hardly noticed the hours slipping by as Samuel explained to her how he had come to fight for Parliament in Cromwell's new model of an army.

'I was only a lad of fifteen when I joined up. I never wanted to fight my fellow countrymen. My family were farmers, freeholders from West Riding. My father spent his life building up our flock; we had the finest Lincoln Longwools as any you might see in England. We were living a comfortable life on the proceeds of their wool when the wars broke out. Father supported the Yorkshire treaty of neutrality. He always thought peace better than war. But of course, the King had no time for such treaties.

'There was a garrison of the King's men a few miles north of us. They thought it their right to plunder the neighbourhood, torching the houses of those who refused to pay what they liked to call "their assessments".

'It was the twelfth night of April in the year of our Lord 1643 when I was sat up watching the sheep. We had already lost several, stolen by soldiers. We kept the ewes in the field above the farm while they were lambing and I was to blow on my horn if I saw anyone approach. But I was weary for it was not my first night of watching and the young, well, when sleep takes them they cannot fight it.

'I was woken by the dogs' barking. Looking down I saw the yard before our house thronged with soldiers on horseback. The moon was full and I could spy them clearly. They swayed on their mounts as if drunk. Many carried flagons they passed between them. I could hear them jeering and blaspheming. How I cursed myself for sleeping through their approach.

'Father stood in the doorway arguing with the soldiers. He began to shout and wave his axe, which was the only weapon he owned. I heard the blast of a gun being fired and saw my father fall to the ground. He was dragged into the house by his heels. I could hear my mother screaming, but it was as though I'd been bewitched for I could not move my feet to go to their aid.

'Soon the soldiers reappeared from our house carrying the family plate and the chest from my parents' bedroom. I guessed they'd left my mother alive for they secured the door with a pitchfork so she could not escape. Then they set fire to the thatch.

'It did not take long for our home to burn. I stood on the hillside looking down. I was armed only with a stick and outnumbered twenty to one. Perhaps I should have run down to the house and joined my lot with my parents, but I stayed with our flock. That was until the soldiers turned their sights on the sheep. Then I scrambled up the brae and threw myself down among the furze to hide like the coward that I was, while the soldiers slaughtered our sheep. Some they left bleeding in the grass, the rest they carried away, our dogs barking uselessly at their heels.

'I gave over our land to my cousins to graze and went by foot to Bradford where I joined the parliamentary army under Sir Thomas Fairfax. From there we were forced to retreat, first to Leeds and then to Hull. But defeat only made us stronger. God gave us courage and led us to victory, first at Marston Moor and later at Naseby.

'It was on the battlefield of Marston that I learnt to respect the cavalier soldier. Outnumbered and surrounded, they died fighting. Falling under the swords of their enemies rather than give ground.

Well they were Yorkshiremen, so I should not have been surprised by that. The Lancashire lads, they threw down their arms soon enough and came to join us, but a Yorkshireman, he won't give in.'

Alethea just stopped herself from telling Samuel that her father had also fought at Marston Moor. 'Didn't you hate the cavaliers for murdering your parents?' she asked instead.

'Good and bad was done on both sides.' He pulled another worm from a moss-lined bag and fixed it onto his hook. 'At first I was fighting only for vengeance. Tom taught me to know better. Tom joined up out of principle; he was fighting for a better England.'

They lapsed once more into silence, catching three more fish as the morning progressed.

As Samuel put the last one into his basket he said, 'We wanted to build a New Jerusalem. An England where every man would get to vote and have the right to live free from persecution and the burden of poverty.'

'But that did not come to pass.' Alethea twitched her rod impatiently.

He sighed. 'We were so close, Alethea. So close to having a true republic of equals, but we let it be taken from us.'

⇝ Chapter Nine ⇜

Jack often found occasion to be alone with Alethea and they would walk in the woods together. No one commented on this. Women and girls were not chaperoned and relationships between the sexes were as free and easy as between brothers and sisters.

'You're very quiet, Al,' Jack said as they walked out one morning, tasked with gathering elderflowers, wood sorrel and any other edibles they might find. 'Why don't you join in the conversations like the other women here do?'

'I don't know what to say. I grew up believing their sort of people were all depraved, yet now I live amongst them and they seem more civilised than many of my former companions.'

Jack laughed. 'They're that all right, a bit too civil. You wouldn't ask one of this lot to a playhouse would you?'

Alethea laughed too at the thought of it, for their companions were a sober, serious group. 'I would like to ask them, though, how exactly they think uneducated, unlettered men could be entrusted with a vote. Surely anarchy would follow.'

'Just because a man can't read and hasn't been to university or the inns of court, doesn't make him a fool.' Jack slashed at a bramble hanging across their path.

'I wasn't suggesting that, but men must be trained up to understand the workings of state. Without strong leadership everything falls apart.'

'And do you think the gallants the King promotes understand the needs of the common man? What do they know of the people who serve them? Of the hardships they endure?'

'You sound just like Samuel.'

'I'm no Samuel.' Jack dropped a bunch of elderflowers into her basket. 'I'm a sceptic if you like, I don't think it matters who's in power. Life's a game of chance.' He blew a fly off his hand. 'It's all down to how you play the cards you're dealt.'

'And what if you can't see the cards in your hand?'

'Why that just makes it more exciting.' Jack grinned. 'Don't forget, if you're playing blind so is everyone else.'

Alethea thought of Lady Margaret who always seemed to know exactly what cards were in her hand. Alethea now suspected she had been outmanoeuvred in a game she was not aware of playing.

'Machiavelli says Fortune is a mistress who must be forced into obedience,' she said, remembering another passage of the book where Calverton had drawn a pointing finger in the margin. 'She favours young men who are bold with her.'

'You're no Machiavel are you, My Lady?' Jack raised his eyebrows in mock horror. 'His followers are always the villains in tragedies.'

'Lord Calverton says Machiavelli is misunderstood.'

She bent down to a ruby-red cluster of wild strawberries sitting like jewels in the long grass, popping one into her mouth before depositing the rest in her basket.

'I'm afraid to admit to the others here that my father fought for the King, and if they knew I'm a papist, well, I think they'd all hate me.'

'You didn't fight against them. Besides, men who wouldn't have thought twice about slitting each other's throats during the wars now go hunting together and live as neighbours.' He smiled thoughtfully at her. 'Still, I'd keep quiet about your religion and don't let them know whose household you were living in. They hate Lord Calverton worse than the devil.'

Because he believed that life was a game to be played, Jack drew the children of the camp to him like a magnet. They adored this adult version of themselves; this diminutive man who kept them entranced with his fantastical stories and his card tricks. As she returned from collecting firewood one afternoon, Alethea heard Barbara scolding him. Jack was squatting on the ground surrounded by his usual retinue. They were looking up at Barbara with anxious faces, while their leader smiled nonchalantly.

'Rest easy, Mistress Barbara, it's an instructive game that teaches the children how to count their money.'

'How to lose it more like,' Barbara retorted.

'You don't think I'd stoop so low as to gamble with children,' Jack said with exaggerated indignation.

'He gives us back our coins after,' Seth explained.

'He can weigh coins with his hand,' Daniel said.

'Show Barbara how you do it, Jack,' eight-year-old Philippa insisted.

'Close your eyes, Jack.' Seth took the purse Jack was holding and the children huddled together, counting out a number of coins in whispers and then pouring them into the bag.

'Tell us how much exactly,' they cried, dropping the bag into Jack's palm.

Jack threw the bag into the air. 'Four pennies and a farthing.'

'He's right! He always gets it right,' Seth said excitedly, showing Barbara the contents of the purse. Barbara shook her head disapprovingly.

'Let me have a go.' Alethea joined the group as a thought occurred to her. 'It's easy enough to guess with the same few pennies. I'll test him with some coin of my own.'

She went to her hut where she kept the change she had left from the guinea Margaret had given her and putting several coins in her pocket returned to where the children were waiting.

'So tell me, Master Jack, how much do I carry?' She raised her arms, inviting him to search her.

Jack never could resist a challenge. He brushed her skirts with his hands as if tidying them. 'Two pound, six shilling.'

The children looked at Alethea expectantly.

'Oh yes.' She nodded. 'He's right again.'

She gave Jack a hard stare. Jack's cheeks flushed red.

'You're teaching these children to be pickpockets,' Barbara said, scandalised.

On any other occasion Alethea would have defended Jack, but now she was too angry.

'You and your Signora Pozzuto, you knew how much money I carried even before I did. What did you have, some sign to tell her, so she knew what to charge me for her plague water? Was she even an apothecary? Was she even Italian?' Alethea's voice rose with each new realisation.

Soon most of the camp had gathered round to see what the commotion was about.

'Is there some trouble here?' Thomas asked, striding over to join them.

Silence fell on the group.

'I must apologise.' Jack held up his hands. 'I forgot myself and my responsibilities. I meant only to teach the children games that are instructive and useful, but Sister Barbara, as always, is quite right.' Jack bowed to Barbara. 'These are not suitable games for Christian children. In future I will be more careful.'

Thomas looked at Alethea. 'Did you have something you wanted to say?'

'No,' she said. 'I'm sorry for raising my voice and frightening the children.'

For the youngest had begun to cry. Everyone looked at Barbara. Barbara looked appraisingly at Jack, who in turn looked sheepishly back at her.

She nodded. 'Very well, but I shall be keeping an eye on you, Master Jack.'

Alethea learnt from Barbara that Samuel was a widower. His wife and children had all been taken by the plague while he was away preaching in the Northern counties. Barbara had been one of his followers; she had even preached herself on occasion, when the Lord called her to. Alethea marvelled at Samuel's equanimity. To have suffered such loss, but never show a moment of self-pity or bitterness.

'He who trusts in our Saviour has no need to mourn,' Barbara told her. 'For on the day of reckoning the deserving shall be reunited and death shall be no more.'

This made Alethea think of her mother, even though she knew Barbara did not count Catholics among the deserving. She wished she did not have to be on her guard all the time, fearful lest she say the wrong thing. She respected these people and wanted to be accepted by them, but it was wearying, having to hold herself constantly in check.

Samuel offered an understanding of the Bible she had never considered before. He spoke of Jesus as a dear friend who suffered with the common people, championing the poor and the outcast. Instead of dwelling on the punishments that awaited those who sinned, Samuel spoke only of God's compassion. His was a merciful God who embraced his children for all their weaknesses and failings, seeking to heal and restore, not to condemn. This almost made her feel able to confide in Samuel, but she knew he would seek to convert her and feared his disappointment even more than she feared the hostility of their companions.

Nonetheless, inspired by this doctrine Alethea approached Jack, determined to pardon him for his trickery. Jack, however, was not as contrite as she had expected. He insisted that he and Olivia Pozzuto, real name Mrs Potts, had provided a valuable service to those who sought it.

'Olivia knew as much about healing as any apothecary or doctor of physic in London,' he claimed. 'What good do all your fancy physicians do? Apart from lining their own pockets handsomely. Have any of them cured a person of the plague, or anything else for that matter?'

Alethea searched her memory for an example of a person she knew who had been cured by medicine, but could think of none for sure. Certainly there were those of her acquaintance who had recovered from illness after being treated by a physician, but there were equal numbers who had not. Of those who had survived who was to say they would not have got better anyway?

'You still swindled me out of two pounds and six shillings I bet you didn't charge all your customers that amount.'

'We charged them what they could afford and they went away a lot happier than they were previously. You said you'd been sent by a wealthy lady and you got a bottle for yourself out of the bargain.'

'So your Mrs Potts, she really had discovered a protective against the plague?'

'She created a medicine that made the blood strong enough to fight against the air's infection. You drank it; you might not be standing here now if you hadn't.'

'So why the deceit? Why pretend she was Italian?' Alethea was not to be mollified that easily.

'People like to feel they're getting something special. They're more convinced by exotic arts than home-grown ones. And that's the most important thing Olivia taught me; nothing is more powerful than belief. If you believe you can be kept well, if you believe you will be cured, why that's the best medicine there is.'

'But it isn't true,' Alethea insisted. 'Belief cannot turn something false into something true.'

'Can't it?' Jack said.

⇸ Chapter Ten ⇷

The days in the forest fell into a rhythm. Alethea worked with the other women gathering firewood, mushrooms and berries, collecting rabbits from traps, scrubbing out dishes and preparing meals. In her past life she would never have considered undertaking such menial labour, but while she was not fond of cleaning or sewing, she enjoyed the foraging.

She had always loved to be outdoors. When her father was in a good humour he used to call her his 'wild romping girl'. Frances on the other hand accused her of being a wanton tom-boy. Here at last Alethea found she could indulge her active nature, often wandering far off into the forest so that she walked many miles a day. Then by evening she was exhausted enough to sit through the long meetings the campers liked to hold.

'All this discussing and voting,' Jack complained to her in private. 'Sometimes I wish we had just one leader who could make a quick decision.'

Alethea sympathised with Jack's view, but in principle she had come to admire this system as being by far the fairest. Even the women here were allowed a vote and were listened to with respect by all assembled. The women of the camp did not have to resort to the subtle manipulations used by ladies to gain what they wanted. They could be forthright in their opinions and were never called shrewish or accused of being scolds, for they spoke just as men did.

She and Jack had become so embedded in the life of the forest community, they no longer spoke about leaving. Neither were in any hurry to confront the violence and hostility of the world beyond the woods. They knew they could not stay indefinitely, but were comfortable for now and saw no reason to return to the road until the danger of the plague had abated.

'We're lucky to be here in fine weather,' Joan observed as the women carried the camp's dirty laundry down to the river.

No one in the camp had more than one change of clothes. Since this great outbreak of the plague, the buying and selling of second-hand clothes had been outlawed. Instead they made their own clothes with cloth they bought in Epping Town. Alethea had never worn such roughly made garments. Although her wool sleeves itched, she enjoyed not having to mind the mud and dirt or worry about tearing her silk dresses.

Living in the forest they had not gone to such lengths as soaking the laundry in lye, relying instead on the river water and their own strength. Martha and Lizzie had already located a suitable spot where the water ran fast but shallow and there were smooth rocks for scrubbing on.

Alethea watched the other women carefully, noting how they rubbed and pounded their washing in the cold water. She had not expected her wet clothes to weigh so much and lifted them with difficulty. Her back and arms were soon aching and her hands were pink and raw.

'Watch your fine lace collar!' Ellen cried, snatching Alethea's collar up before it was carried away on the current. 'It'd be a shame to lose such a pretty thing.' She held it up, caressing the dainty material between her fingers before hanging it carefully from a branch. 'Me and Lizzie, we grew up in a draper's shop. We sold some beautiful cloth – French linen, Italian silks, even Indian muslin.'

She looked around to make sure the other women were not listening, and seeing they were busy chatting to each other, turned back to Alethea. 'I've been to Hyde Park a few times, to see the lords and ladies. Such an array of colours! God forgive me, but I liked to look at them in their gowns the colour of daffodils and their coats as blue as forget-me-nots. It was like the coming of Spring.' She smiled apologetically. 'Father had to take a stick to me a few times for wrapping myself up in red cambric or putting ribbons in my hair. Lizzie is lucky, she's never been cursed with vanity.'

'Would you like it?' Alethea gestured to the collar. 'It would set off your lovely long neck.'

Ellen blushed and pushed her fair hair back over her shoulders. 'I couldn't. What would the others think?'

Alethea stared down at the sarcenet petticoats she was standing on. It was easy to see how much finer they were than any of the other women's garments.

'We can share our clothes if you wish.'

Ellen laughed. 'I don't know why you'd want to wear my clothes. Maybe I could try on your gown some day and you could teach me how to dance.' She looked at Alethea with all the eagerness of a young child. 'Have you ever been to a ball?'

'Only to a few country dances where I had my feet stamped on by old men. I never liked them much.'

Because of her height, Alethea had not been a popular dancing partner. No man wanted a woman towering over him, especially not a clumsy, discomfited one.

'Here, Sister Martha, here's a green ribbon for you.' Lizzie pulled a reed up out of the bank and threw it at Martha.

The damp leaf stuck to her skirts. Martha pulled it off and draped it over her breast. 'We were proud to wear the green ribbons once. Do you remember, Liz? Those were some times, weren't they?'

'She means the Leveller's colours, not ribbons for ornament,' Ellen told Alethea.

Lizzie grinned back at Martha, her cheeks bright red with exertion. 'That they were. Do you remember back in '49 when we only just escaped being sent to the House of Correction? I've never run so fast in my life as when we were chased down Whitehall by soldiers.'

'Oh, and the soldiers treated us roughly.' Joan, who had been quiet until then, spoke up for the first time. 'The sergeant-at-arms told us to go home and meddle with our housewifery.'

'He'd be happy to see us now, washing our linen in the river,' said Martha, laughing.

'That was the least provoking.' Joan slapped a shift against a stone. 'The newsletters called us a bunch of Oyster wives. I'd never even been to Billingsgate.'

'Don't forget the troops of Amazons looking to ravish the poor members of Parliament,' added Lizzie, wiggling her hips.

'As if we'd want to. We've men of our own to satisfy us.' Joan wrung out the shift and smacked Lizzie with the rolled garment.

Lizzie shrieked and gave a raucous cackle.

'Mistresses, really, remember we have a young lady present,' Barbara cut in, nodding over at Alethea.

Alethea did not like to be set apart in this way, especially since it was Barbara who recoiled at crude talk.

'I'm sure Alethea's heard worse,' Lizzie said.

'Yes, and I know a whole repertoire of bawdy songs,' she boasted.

'Well we certainly don't want to hear those,' Barbara said quickly. 'If the villagers overheard us they'd soon change their minds about letting us stay here.'

'Alethea sings like an angel, even a naughty song would sound like a psalm if she sang it,' said Ellen.

Alethea was touched by her camaraderie. She instinctively warmed to Ellen, who was the closest to her in age and temperament. Although she admired the other women, she could see how Ellen's nature was squashed by them. Why should Ellen not delight in fine clothes and the pleasures of life, surely these were also gifts bestowed by God?

She must watch her tongue though, she had been in danger of giving away whose household she had been living in. Her new-found friends would soon turn to enemies if they thought she was in allegiance with the man who hunted them down.

Alethea's favourite place to rest when she was off roaming by herself was a mossy bank beneath an old oak tree. Its roots curved to form a seat and she could lean against its broad trunk. It was far enough away from the camp that no one ever disturbed her. She liked to sit here and practise her singing.

Sometimes in the evening Alethea was asked to sing to the camp. Dorcas and John both had fine voices and they had taught her some of the psalms they had set to music. They would sing together or singly as the spirit took them. Alethea rarely sang the ballads or ditties she had learnt as a young girl for fear they would seem silly and frivolous. And she avoided anything that might smack of popery. But, alone in the woods, she could sing whatever took her fancy without fear of causing offence.

One afternoon, late in July, she sat singing '*In quel gelato core*'. It was a favourite of William's, a nonsense song, each line came from the index of a book of Italian songs. William liked her to sing it to visitors who would remark, sometimes wiping a tear from their eyes, on how very moving it was, so full of poesie, so full of pathos; when in fact the words put together meant nothing. She was singing '*O sempre, e quando / Tu di salvarmi / Certo e scorno*' when she was startled by Samuel's voice.

'I wondered what sort of bird call that could be,' he said. 'Dost thou mind if I join thee?'

'Not at all.' Alethea wrapped her skirts around her legs to make room on the ground beside her.

She was a little flustered to be caught out by Samuel singing a song composed in mockery. At the same time, she was pleased he should favour her with his company.

'Thou art the very picture of harmony. A soul at one with the creating spirit,' he said. 'Art thou as happy here as thou seems?'

'I love the forest. It's as if these great trees were standing sentinel, keeping us safe from the world outside. And the light falls so gently through the leaves it seems to soften everyone's moods, for there's no real discord here nor can I imagine that there ever will be.'

Samuel smiled. 'Nothing in this world is eternal, sister. All things must pass.'

'When the plague is over, do you think everyone will return to their old ways of life?' Alethea was disappointed, for she was beginning to believe they could live this way forever.

'Possibly,' Samuel said. 'This is a little paradise, but my experience is that such harmony among men rarely lasts.'

'Do you not believe then, like Thomas, that a new commonwealth can be built in England?'

'Not in England, no. We tried and failed to do that. Look how the people welcomed back their oppressor.'

'Do you mean the King?' She stared down at the little posy of red campion lying crushed in her palm.

'Aye. Does that offend thee?'

She let the flowers fall from her hand. 'At first I was disturbed by the way you all talked, about the monarchy and revolutions and such like, but now I understand it better.'

They sat side by side observing the world around them. Neither of them spoke, it did not seem necessary. Samuel had a way about him that allowed for silence and yet in that silence Alethea felt as though they were communicating something profound and wonderful. She lost all notion of time; they might have sat for minutes or for hours, she could not tell.

At last she felt an overwhelming urge to confess to him. 'My father fought on the royalist side. He's very loyal to the Stuarts and I was brought up to be so too.'

He smiled gently. 'There's no shame in that. Many honourable men fought and died for the King. Misguided men in my opinion, but I respect them for their bravery. Does Jesus not teach us to love our enemies?'

She turned towards him, her heart beating rapidly. Here was her chance to unburden herself. 'I hope you'll not hate me when I tell you that we're Catholics too.'

He took one of her hands in his. 'I could never hate thee; nor would I hate any Christian for their religion, nor a Mahometan neither. Thou art an innocent yet to be shown the light of reason. I hope thou wilt open thy mind to the Lord as he speaks through me, his humble servant. That is all I ask of thee.'

No man had ever held Alethea's hand for so long, yet she felt quite at ease as Samuel retained hers between his two palms. He had long fine fingers that wove themselves between hers. The skin of his hands felt smooth and cool. The blackened nails, the scratches and abrasions could not diminish their refinement.

'Wilt thou pray with me, sister?' Samuel asked.

'Gladly.' She bowed her head and opened her heart to the light within.

❖ Chapter Eleven ❖

They had been living in the forest for a month or more when Jack took Alethea to one side and asked her if she would accompany him into Epping on market day.

'Just the two of us, for I've not had much of your company lately.'

She felt concerned for him. Jack was not as at home in the encampment as she was. He missed the amusements of the taverns – dice, cards and drunkenness. He could not see any pleasure in discussing scripture or new ways of communal living. He got on well with everyone, he had that sort of temperament, he liked and was liked in return. But Alethea knew the city was his natural environment and that as soon as it was safe he would return there. When that would be, no one could tell for certain. News reached them that the distemper was raging worse than ever; bodies were piling up in the streets with no one left to bury them. People refused to be quarantined, breaking out of their houses with no one there to stop them.

The campers had acquired a cart, which Jack and Alethea drove into town, pulled by the old horse Caleb. Alethea enjoyed being able to look out from this vantage point to the green and gold land beyond the hedgerows. Strips of barley and wheat glistened and rustled as a light breeze stirred them. The wind brought welcome relief from the heat of the sun which burnt bright and hot in the blue sky. Although she loved the forest, she was pleased to be out on an excursion. She had not visited the town for a long while and found the prospect of streets and stalls exciting.

They had not travelled far when Jack turned to her, the reins loose in his hands. 'Seems like you've lost that rosary,' he said.

'What?' she asked.

'They've made a convert of you, just like I warned you they would.'

'My eyes have been opened, Jack, if that's what you mean.'

'Opened or dazzled?'

Alethea twisted in her seat, turning towards Jack eagerly. 'You know the established clergy were some of the first to flee the plague, deserting their flocks just as they were most afflicted. I've come to understand that priests and bishops are not conduits, but obstructions to the word of God. Look at how much scripture is ignored by those who believe their wealth is theirs by divine right. Maybe it's true that the plague came as a judgement on the Stuart court for its debauchery.'

'Are you going to ask your family to give up their lands then?'

'I've been praying every night that I might be able to convert my brother. William was always more devout than me, I'm sure if I could just persuade him to listen to Samuel with an open heart, he too would be enlightened.'

Alethea had begun to question all her prior assumptions and even the wisdom of her parents. How could any one family lay claim to that which was created by God to give sustenance to all? Her treatment at the hands of the Calvertons only strengthened her new philosophy. She saw that she had been disposable to them. All their high words of fidelity and honour were as sounding brass, or a tinkling cymbal, for they had no knowledge of love.

Jack frowned, squinting against the glare of the sun despite his hat. 'Don't you think it blasphemous the way they all hang on Samuel's every word? They worship him as though he were Jesus Christ reborn. And now you seem to have joined in their adoration. I thought you had more sense.'

'You're the one who's being blasphemous. You've clearly understood nothing, nothing of his faith.' Alethea could feel her cheeks burning red with anger.

But Jack merely shook his head and said quietly, 'I understand a lot more of his type than you do.'

'His type? He is not of a type.'

'He's an Enthusiast and a seducer, can you not see that? For all his holiness he exerts an unhealthy sway over women. See how you all flock to him, lapping up his every word.'

'How despicable to suggest such a thing. Do you think men like Thomas Gray would love and respect Samuel if he were really as base as you suggest?' Alethea could hardly believe her ears. How could Jack be so disloyal?

'These men have no more sense than their wives. They're all gulls as far as I can see.'

'Well your vision is clearly limited, perhaps it's tainted by your past connections. I doubt Signora Pozzuto or Mrs Potts, or whatever her name was, was a woman of honour.'

'Olivia had her own sort of honour and you've no right to sit in judgement on her, but that's how it is with those that think they've got religion. They believe they're more precious to God and know his mind better than anyone else.'

They spent the rest of the journey in silence, too angry to converse further. The day seemed to have grown colder and the countryside duller. Alethea pulled her shawl tightly round her shoulders and stared grimly out with her back turned on her companion. She wished she could get him to see Samuel as a minister of the Lord, an honourable man who would help him to salvation, but she was too hurt and cross to find the right words.

Once in Epping Town they agreed to fulfil their errands separately. Jack was going to sell some of the wooden utensils the men had made – bowls, spoons and birch brooms.

'Do you want to meet at The White Lion for some dinner, or don't you frequent such places now?' he asked.

'There's no need to be so churlish. I'll happily take dinner at the Lion.'

Alethea entered The White Lion at midday feeling immensely proud of herself. She had managed to sell some small linen goods worked by herself and the other women. She had made fewer items than the others, but believed she'd got a good price for their goods and her friends would be pleased.

She found Jack sitting in a dark corner hunched over a tankard of ale. He looked so forlorn that all her affection for him returned in a great rush. The sight of an injured creature always stirred her compassion and Jack was looking particularly small and wounded.

'Why, Jack Horner, what're you doing in the corner? Waiting for your Christmas pie?'

He looked up at her with surprise, then smiled reluctantly. 'The Stump pie does look good as it happens. You can see they've been generous with the sugar on top.'

The thought of crisp brown layers of pie crust sharpened her appetite. Having no oven, the campers lived on porridge, soups and stews. She looked around at the other tables hoping there were some other pies or tarts on offer besides Stump pie. Their cook at home had once told her that cheap establishments used sugar and cloves to mask the taste of bad meat. There was nothing worse than rancid mutton mixed with eggs and currants. She did not like to mention this to Jack, however, in case he thought she was sneering at his choice of hostelry.

'I'm sorry if I spoke out of turn, it's only that I wish to protect you from harm. You do understand that, don't you?' Jack stared up at her earnestly.

She sat down opposite him, reaching out a hand towards his. 'I haven't become some sort of puritan fanatic. It just makes me sad to hear you misjudge Samuel so. The devil must be stopping your ears when Samuel preaches, for you are not hearing his words truly.'

'The devil was one of God's angels once. Are you so sure you can tell the difference between the two?'

'I can read the Bible, Jack, and I know that Sam speaks honestly from it, without perversion.'

Jack sighed. 'Well, let's not argue. I've had enough of lectures, and controversy will only give us indigestion. Let's enjoy our dinner, shall we?'

She happily assented to this and the rest of the meal passed agreeably, Alethea tucking into a venison pasty, Jack enjoying his Stump pie. They chatted about their fellow campers as they ate. Robin was a shared favourite, being a sweet angelic child whose face, with his apple cheeks and golden curls, matched his temperament. He had a special love for Jack and would beam with delight whenever he appeared.

Jack unwrapped a bundle from his bag and showed Alethea the gingerbread tablets he had bought for the children. 'The alphabet is baked into each one. Won't that be a tasty way for them to learn their ABCs?'

He was a kind-hearted fellow, she was glad they were friends again.

The following night Alethea dreamt that she and Samuel had become lovers. It began with an innocent hug, such as parents give their children, but soon they were caressing and exchanging passionate kisses. It was a shocking dream for she had never entertained such ideas before and yet in this other world, their relationship was as ordinary and acceptable as buying a loaf of bread. Differences in age, experience and rank meant nothing.

The dream had a different quality to any other she had had before and she was convinced it had come to her as a premonition. Excited by this knowledge, her life felt charged with significance. Her body hummed with coursing spirits that drove all thoughts of devils and temptation from her mind.

Her apprehension of Samuel changed. She no longer viewed him disinterestedly, as a minister and a leader, an elder of the community. Now when she looked at him she imagined standing beside him as his wife, his chosen one. And in the dark of the night, when she lay between waking and sleeping, she could almost feel his graceful fingers tickling her skin, his shapely lips pressed against hers. How she burned.

⇥ Chapter Twelve ⇤

In August the group agreed to build a hall that would accommodate them all if necessary. A place where they could gather in the evenings to eat and talk, and that would shelter them during the days when the weather was bad. They built an earthen wall at one end with a chimney in it and a hearth to cook on. It was not the most effective of chimneys and often the hall filled with smoke so that they were forced to open the door for ventilation, but it was warm and snug. The building conferred a sense of permanence on the camp and Alethea began to think she could live out her days with these people. They were content here and had all that they needed, why should anything change? She thought less and less of her family in Derbyshire, it was as if they belonged to a world she no longer inhabited.

'I thought I might discover thee here.'

Alethea looked up with a start to find Samuel smiling down at her. She had been so deep in thought she had not heard him approach, or perhaps it was that he trod so lightly he had made no sound to disturb her.

The other campers were all busy working on the new hall and Alethea had slipped off under the pretence of collecting firewood, to spend a few hours on her own. She reassured herself that she was not being selfish or lazy, for her motives were good ones. She needed to spend some time in silent communion with God and there were too many distractions in the camp. Even though they prayed together daily, it was not the same as seeking out God alone. She needed to still her mind, to allow some quietness in to quench the lustful spirits that heated her blood.

Of course, there was the possibility that Samuel might happen upon her under this oak as he had done before. He had been applying daub to the east wall of the new building as she walked past and there was no reason for him to break off what he was doing and follow her here, unless God directed him to do so. Which it appeared He had done, for there was Samuel standing with one hand resting lightly on the trunk of the oak. His brown clothes blended with the colours of the forest and though the fabric was coarse it hung gracefully from his broad shoulders. He appeared suddenly to Alethea like a creature of the woods, a Puck or a Pan rather than a Christian preacher. His figure was tall and slender as an ash, but his arms were strong as the branches of an oak. His dark blue eyes shone like rain-washed slate.

'I was just contemplating the courage of the disciples in giving up everything to follow Jesus.' Alethea was gabbling, but she wanted to secure his attention, to prevent him from leaving.

In this she succeeded for he sat down on the ground beside her. 'I see great courage in thee, Alethea, for hast thou not already given up the false doctrines taught thee as a child?'

'I suppose I have. But I fear that if we return to our old lives, why then it'll be hard for me not to return to my old ways of thinking and believing.' She concentrated on pinching the fabric of her skirt into pleats, avoiding Samuel's eyes.

He placed his hand over hers, where it lay in her lap. 'There is no need to return to thy old life, Alethea.'

'What would I do otherwise?'

'Throw thy lot in with ours. It's not an easy life I grant, but it is a good life. One that will reward thee on earth and hereafter.'

'I'm not sure I am worthy,' she said, looking up.

And then it seemed they moved towards each other in unison, for she could not have said who acted first, but their lips were pressed together and his tongue was nudging against hers and his mouth tasted sweet as honeycomb. She felt her body opening to him like a flower unfurling for a bee and in that moment she would have done anything he desired of her. But Samuel pulled away, raising his hands to his head.

'Alethea, forgive me, please forgive this lapse.'

'There's nothing to forgive.'

'It was wrong to kiss thee. I should have been stronger. I should have withstood the weakness of the flesh.' Samuel was on his feet now, brushing the leaves from his breeches and looking anxiously about him.

'You mustn't blame yourself,' Alethea said with dismay. 'I foresaw this very thing in a dream and it seemed right and good. But perhaps it was just a sign of my own frailty.'

Samuel leant towards her and taking her hands in his, he pulled her to her feet. 'It may be that God intends us to join together and sent a dream to prepare thee. I feel a strong spiritual kinship with thee, but we must pray and ask God for guidance.' He studied her face with a gravity that troubled her.

'I will, Samuel.'

'It would be a terrible thing for our desires to bring discord to the camp. I know its harmony is precious to thee, Alethea, and for that reason we must act with temperance and discretion until we are sure of God's will.'

'I would never willingly do anything to disrupt our community; every member of it is dear to me as a family member.'

'I know it and I commend thee for it.' Samuel smiled his beautiful smile. 'So we must not allude to what just passed between us, not to anyone.'

'I understand.' Alethea gripped his hands, unable to relinquish them.

'Thou must watch thy tongue. Be on thy guard at night when ye talk with Ellen and Barbara, as I know women like to do, for that is how petty jealousies arise. Likewise with Jack, he is a close companion is he not?'

'Not so close as that,' she said hastily. 'I need no other confidant than you, and God.'

'Thou art truly wise beyond thy years.' He disentangled his hands from hers. 'Now,' he said briskly, looking around him once more. 'Remain here and I will return to the camp.'

Alethea watched him as he moved off swiftly through the trees with the precision and grace of a hunting dog. Once he was out of sight she tried to pray, but however hard she tried to discipline her thoughts she could not shut Samuel out. She knew the strength of her love was no proof of its virtue; that she had to be on her guard in case it was the devil leading her astray. And yet, she could not extinguish the bubble of elation that rose within her. Out of all the women in the camp he desired her.

Alethea was careful to conduct herself as naturally as possible around Samuel. She could not detect any outward change in his manner towards her. In front of the others this was a relief, but afterwards she found herself tormented by doubts and desires. She picked over his every word and gesture, trying to glean some additional meaning from them.

Was he still drawn to her or had God directed him away? Did he see her only as a temptation to be avoided, a weak woman driven by common lust? She could not bear to be viewed in such a light and yet lust came to her in the night, depriving her of sleep, teasing her with images: Samuel's body as naked as Christ's on the crucifix, his arms pulling her to him, his hands on her breasts, his lips on her mouth, his legs pushing against her legs. Her body ached for experiences her mind had no knowledge of. She stuck pins into her feet in an attempt to purge herself of her desire. If only she had access to a trusted physician who might open a vein and bleed her until all noxious passions left her body. She thought of searching for leeches to apply to herself, but could not bring herself to do it.

Since sleep eluded her, Alethea stayed up late one night playing chess with Jack after everyone else had retired to bed. She even accepted a few sips from Jack's secret flask of brandy, hoping this might sedate her, though generally she followed the rest of their companions in eschewing strong drink.

'I'm glad to see you've distanced yourself from St. Samuel,' Jack said as he studied the board.

'What do you mean by that?' Alethea demanded, squeezing the pawn in her hand so tightly it marked her skin.

'Easy, easy, My Lady.' Jack held up his hands in mock defence. 'It's just that you don't seem to hang on his every word the way you did a while ago.'

'I don't agree that I ever did.' She placed her pawn carefully on the board, hoping Jack would not notice her red palm.

He took the pawn immediately with his bishop. 'You need to respect the bishops, see.' He held the pawn up triumphantly.

'Honestly, Jack.' She sighed. 'You like it here don't you? You seem to agree with this manner of conducting our lives.'

'I've great respect for this company. I can see that they're good, honest folk who care deeply about the fate of their fellow man. To tell you the truth, I've never known such considerate, true Christians before.'

Alethea smiled back at him with delight.

'With one exception.' Jack held up a finger. 'There's a level of ambition and vanity in Samuel that contradicts this saintliness of his. He doesn't like to be crossed. It rarely happens because you all think he can do no wrong, but he likes to reign over us all just as much as any king on his throne, only his means are more sly.'

'You're mistaken. You told me once that your father was unhappy with you because you wouldn't follow his example. Do you think perhaps you do not like any man to have authority over you? Maybe that's why you found an apprenticeship with a lady, you find it easier to work under a woman.'

To her surprise Jack laughed. 'Well of course, I'm always happy to labour beneath a comely woman, my services are at your disposal.' Since she failed to respond to his attempted witticism, Jack changed his approach. 'I see you've given this some serious thought. You're correct in one aspect, I enjoy the company of women more than that of other men. I find women to be more good-natured in general. It's also true that I do not accept Samuel's authority for I don't believe he has the ear of God, however much he might like to think he does. I fear he will disappoint you, Alethea.'

Jack looked at her so sorrowfully she reached out instinctively for his hand. He stroked hers tenderly in return. He began to paddle his fingers in her palm. She wanted to pull her hand away, but feared a sudden movement would convey her repulsion too strongly. If only her wit were quicker she might come up with some humorous retort that would make him see the folly of his actions. The sort of jest Jack himself might make. But Jack's mood was serious.

'Could you, could you ever think of the likes of me as a suitor?'

'Jack, no, do not consider me in that light,' Alethea said with alarm. 'You are my dearest friend and like a brother to me.' She paused, not knowing what else she could add that would restore their friendship to its old footing.

Jack patted her hand and let it go. 'Of course. Forget I mentioned it.'

He took another slug of brandy and returned his attention to the chessboard.

Every day Alethea slipped off into the woods, returning to her chosen oak. Its canopy of leaves provided shelter from rain and sun alike. She told herself she was retreating to this spot in order to pray, but in fact she was hoping Samuel would join her there again.

It was ten days before he answered her wish. She knew as soon as she saw his jubilant smile that God had spoken to him and that he had received the answer they both wanted to hear.

They embraced with an irresistible hunger, covering each other's faces with passionate kisses. Pushing back her neckerchief, Samuel pressed his mouth to her exposed breasts, running his tongue over her nipples. She gasped at the unexpected pleasure. Her body felt like a lit match cord, the flame racing up her arms and legs to converge at the centre.

His hands were under her skirts, caressing her thighs and her belly. His nimble fingers moved lightly between her legs. She froze for a moment with the surprise of it, that she could feel such delight in those parts.

'Alethea,' he whispered in her ear, 'wouldst thou have me stop?'

'Not for the world,' she answered him.

The next time they met beneath the oak Alethea gave herself to Samuel, just as she had foreseen that she would, and it felt natural and right. For why would God arrange things in this way and make bodies feel such joy if they were not meant to make sport with them? The instrument maker did not craft a lute to remain unplucked. And besides, it would not be long before they were wed.

They met several times after this, slipping away from the camp whenever they could. It was easy enough for Samuel to explain that he needed solitude. The others assumed he was communing with God. It was more difficult for Alethea to extract herself; she became skilled at dodging the children who wanted to follow her. Since her rejection of him, Jack had stopped seeking her out. They still chatted amicably together at mealtimes and played chess together sometimes in the evenings, but he no longer tried to catch her in private and this made it easier for her to meet up with Samuel.

In public, Samuel and Alethea were careful to act with discretion. At first the secrecy of their relations made them all the more thrilling to her. She carried her clandestine love like a stolen jewel hidden in her bosom. It pressed heavily against her heart, but every time she felt its cold weight against her breast she shivered with the sweet agony of it. How exquisite, how precious it was, and how exceptional the possessing of it made her.

As her love for Samuel grew, however, she found it increasingly difficult to maintain her distance. She was not ashamed, but proud of their union and she wanted Samuel to acknowledge her before their community. She was also aware that the longer their relationship continued the more hurt their friends would be by its concealment. She thought acceptance would come more readily with an earlier disclosure.

'Shouldn't we marry now?' she asked Samuel as they lay together.

They had found an even more secluded spot in the forest, where they had cleared a bed for themselves, hidden by brambles.

'I consider us to be man and wife already,' Samuel said, caressing her hair. 'I believe God smiles on our union and that is all the sacrament we need. Were Adam and Eve wed in a church?'

'Then should we announce our union?'

'The time is not yet right. As soon as it is, I promise thee I will pronounce our bond.'

'Is it because of your wife that died?'

Samuel pushed himself up onto his elbows. 'So thou hast heard about Rebecca, what hast thou been told?'

'Only that you had a wife and children who perished in the plague. You must grieve for them.'

'Their loss was a terrible affliction; one that thou hast helped me to bear.'

She lay staring at the smooth grey bark of a hornbeam whose leaves fluttered just above her head. 'I'm glad I've been able to comfort you. Perhaps one day I'll give you more children.' The idea of bearing his child excited her even more than it terrified her. To carry his child would be proof that God approved of her as his helpmeet.

'Perhaps,' he said, tracing the outline of her nose and lips with his finger.

'You had seven?' She pushed on.

'Altogether, yes, it was God's pleasure to take three in their infancy, before they were many weeks old.' He sat up, bending his legs and resting his arms on his knees.

Alethea was afraid she had offended him, but he continued. 'Another, our little girl Mercy, we lost to the smallpox when she was but two years old. She was her mother's favourite and Rebecca was sorely afflicted by her loss. She could not resign herself to God's will and would not be comforted by the knowledge that Mercy was with her Lord Jesus.'

'It's hard to bear the loss of one who is dear to you,' Alethea said, thinking of her mother.

'God does not give us any cross too heavy to bear, remember that. Rebecca allowed her heart to become hardened, she doted too much on one child and then shut out all love when that child was taken from her.'

'Your love included?' Alethea could not resist asking.

'We were somewhat estranged. She could not understand my calling.' Samuel rubbed his temples. He looked tired suddenly.

'She didn't like you going away to preach?' Alethea felt guilty for taxing him in this way, but had a compulsion to discover as much as possible about his previous life.

'She did not, but only for practical reasons. She wanted me to stay in London and work in the haberdashers' trade. I am not a man of trade.' He looked ruefully at Alethea, then turned his gaze upwards towards the green canopy of leaves. 'I'd not seen my family for many months when I received news that our son Mark had died of the distemper. I hurried straight home despite the danger of arrest. For many of our congregation had been rounded up and imprisoned. But I was too late. They were all gone and no notice even of where they'd been buried. Perhaps that was Rebecca's final punishment of me.' He sighed. 'Still, she's at peace now, reunited with her little ones.'

Alethea and Samuel always returned separately from their trysts in the wood. Sometimes they met before the sun had risen, while everyone else was asleep. Samuel would give a low whistle and she would count to a hundred before slipping out to join him.

Early one morning as Alethea made her way back to the camp, she saw Jack emerging from a small tent. It was one of many that were appearing, springing up like mushrooms in damp grass, as more people fleeing the plague sought refuge in the forest. Jack was lacing up his breeches. A woman's laugh, gritty and low, floated out of the tent. A harsh sound amid the morning birdsong.

'Stay awhile, Jack, 'tis early yet, no one will miss you.'

'I promised Jem I'd help him with a table he's making.' Jack stretched and smiled.

Caught in a shaft of light that dropped between the trees, he blinked in sleepy satisfaction. Alethea knew she should creep away before he saw her, but she was rooted to the spot by her surprise.

A woman's bare arm, round and white, stretched out of the tent opening and tried to grab Jack's ankle. He hopped nimbly away.

'You won't catch me so easily, Kate.' He laughed.

'Come back tonight then,' the rough voice called.

'I'll see what I can do.' Jack turned and looked directly at Alethea. He stumbled and almost tripped over a fallen branch. 'Morning,' he called. 'You're up bright and early.'

'I couldn't sleep,' she called back.

He nodded and strolled towards her, his composure restored. 'I've been visiting a friend,' he said as casually as if he had met her on a city street one afternoon.

Alethea brushed down her skirts, conscious suddenly of the leaves and moss she had just been lying on. 'Who is she?' she asked, tipping her chin towards the tent.

'Made her way here a few days ago. She was working in a tavern near Romford, but all the public houses have been closed there as well now. She came here for want of anywhere else to go.'

'And you've been helping her to settle in.' Alethea pulled a twig out of her hair and hoped Jack had not noticed it.

'Well, someone had to. The poor wench hadn't a clue how to make herself any sort of dwelling.' Jack straightened his jacket.

'Are you sure she's healthy?' Alethea whispered.

'I've given her a thorough examination and not found a trace of disease anywhere.'

Alethea could not help laughing at Jack's shamelessness.

'And who's that creeping through the forest?' Jack looked northwards to where Samuel could be seen quite clearly, striding between the trees.

'Is it Thomas?' she asked stupidly.

'If Thomas has shaved off his beard and shrunk in the rain; or perhaps some naughty wood sprite has turned him into his friend Samuel,' Jack said scornfully. 'It seems I'm not the only one who has risen early for a morning visit.' He gave Alethea a sharp look.

'The forest is open to all.' She shrugged and tried to look unconcerned.

'Aren't you going to introduce me?' Kate was crawling out of her tent in a rather ungainly fashion, her breasts spilling out of her loosely tied bodice.

'Mistress Wright, Mistress Hawthorne.' Jack bowed with mock gentility.

'Pleased to meet you I'm sure.' Kate Wright bobbed a curtsey.

'Likewise.' Alethea lifted her skirts, feeling somewhat ridiculous at the formality.

Kate was pretty enough, she supposed, especially from the left. Her right cheek was disfigured by an ugly scar, as though she had been in a fight and someone had taken a knife to her face. She must be a low-bred sort of woman, still Alethea was grateful to her for the diversion.

'Would you like to come back to the camp with us?' she felt compelled to ask.

To her relief, Kate declined the offer. 'No disrespect, but Jack says you're all fierce puritans.'

'Some being more pure than others,' Jack said pointedly.

'I take it you are referring to yourself,' Alethea said quickly.

'I don't pretend to be any better than I am.'

'Except when you're selling false physic.'

'At least I've never peddled false prayers.'

Kate looked from Jack to Alethea with a perplexed expression. 'I've never had much of a head for the niceties of religion. I'm off down the river for some water.'

Jack and Alethea tramped back to the camp in silence. Just before they arrived, Jack turned to her, his forehead creased with anxiety.

'Don't forget who you are, Alethea. Don't throw away your honour for a dream. You can't stay sleeping here forever, you've a family to return to.' He shook his head, his voice urgent. 'Once you're undone you cannot be made innocent again.'

'I'm more awake than I have ever been. This is my family and my life, I need no other.' She gestured to the clearing before them.

The children and their mothers were already up and awake. Daniel had let out the chickens and they pecked in the dust around his feet. Martha sat in the sunshine, combing out her daughter's flaxen hair. Ellen stood in the doorway of the hall, holding Robin up to greet them. He kicked his legs in excitement at the sight of Jack and Alethea.

'Look what I've made.' Seth came running towards them waving a wooden pipe in the air.

Alethea took the pipe and blew into it, releasing a bright peeping note. 'I have all the wealth and happiness I need right here, see, my cup overflows with joy.'

Robin clapped his hands and struggled in his mother's arms, wanting to fly to the objects of his adoration.

Here were people who loved her truly, who had taken her in and accepted her, when her own father had refused to allow her home. There was no place for her at Measham Hall, Frances had made sure of that. She'd rather live here like a primitive with her true love, than be married off to a man who wanted her only as a nursemaid to his children.

✦ Chapter Thirteen ✦

Samuel's preaching had become well known in the local area and people from as far away as Waltham Abbey on one side and Brent-Wood on the other began to come to the forest on Sundays to listen to him. They would stand beneath the trees in clusters, keeping their distance from those unknown to them for fear of contamination.

Jeremiah built a platform with a cover over it for Samuel to stand on. His congregation grew each week, come rain or shine. Some of those who came to hear him had also been displaced by the plague and settled in the forest, building their own tents and huts at a small remove from the original camp. Alethea tried to be glad that Samuel was able to inspire so many, but she feared the impact these increased numbers would have on their way of life. Samuel warned her that they must exercise greater caution. Surely, said Alethea, this meant they should live together openly. But still Samuel insisted he had not yet received the sign from God telling him the people were ready for him to acknowledge her as his wife.

At least he had moved out of Thomas and Martha's dwelling to a hut that stood a little way off from the rest of the encampment. He explained that he found the noise of children distracting to his daily meditations. Everyone assumed infant laughter and cries were also too painful a reminder of his own recent losses. Alethea hoped his move might have been undertaken with an eye to this becoming their matrimonial home.

They no longer risked meeting in the woods. Instead Alethea would wait until she was sure the rest of the camp were asleep and then steal to Samuel's hut, relying on the moon or the stars to light her way. Some nights she had to feel her way in the darkness, slipping one foot slowly before the other to avoid tripping over something and raising the alarm. Then there were nights when quietness never descended and she lay for hours listening to the snapping of branches or the rustling of leaves, trying to distinguish the animal from the human. That was when it was not a child wailing, or men sitting up late talking. Other times she would fall asleep only to wake to the terrible disappointment of sunlight and her friends' low voices, knowing she must wait another whole day before she might lie in her lover's arms again. But the joy she felt when she reached the refuge of Samuel's bed and his embrace and his body belonging to her alone for a precious few hours made the waiting and the subterfuge worthwhile.

She longed to lie beside Samuel all night, feeding him with kisses. How wonderful it would be to wake in the morning to his face beside hers. To watch him sleeping, his long lashes curling beneath his closed eyes, his lips gently parted as the breath passed between them soft and slow. His body warm and yielding to her caresses.

She found it even harder now to restrain herself from placing a hand on his arm or leaning against his shoulder when he sat close to her. There were times when Samuel looked at her with alarm and she realised she had spoken to him with too easy a familiarity. Their physical intimacy had given her a sense of ownership over him. A sense of ownership Samuel, free man as he was, could not consent to.

'Are there any further matters for discussion?' Thomas looked around the table. Alethea prayed not, it had been an especially long meeting and she ached for her bed. Her eyelids were so heavy now she struggled to keep them open. To her dismay, Joan raised her hand. Thomas nodded at her.

'Some of us have encountered a certain woman living close by.' Joan exchanged glances with Dorcas before continuing. 'Just south of our camp, towards the river.'

'A filthy woman, we overheard her taking payment from a local man for her services,' Dorcas said.

'We were blackberrying,' Joan explained.

'How do you know what he was paying her for?' Jack asked.

'She bears the whore's mark,' Dorcas said conclusively.

'A scar across her cheek? That's not proof of wrongdoing.' Jack looked over at Samuel as if to prove his point. Samuel put his fingers instinctively to the B burnt onto his forehead.

'You are very eager to plead her case, Jack,' Barbara noted wryly.

'We must run her out,' Joan cut in. 'We cannot live amongst whores.'

'Whoa.' Jack raised his hands. 'What harm has she done you?'

Alethea was wide awake now. She thought of Kate Wright, her prettiness marred by her slashed cheek, and how she had laughed and called to Jack to stay. She was sure Jack had not paid for her pleasures for the girl seemed genuinely fond of him.

'Her bawdiness will bring us all into disrepute.' Martha's sharp eyes glittered. 'Our detractors have been quick enough in the past to accuse us of loose behaviour. If people think she's one of our number they'll turn against us.'

Lizzie, Joan and Dorcas all nodded and murmured in agreement.

'That's true enough.' John tapped the table thoughtfully. 'We might ask her to move on. After all we have children here, we don't want them contaminated with her foulness.'

Ellen was looking around at the other women with an anxious frown. Alethea caught her eye and smiled at her. She knew Ellen was tolerant by nature, but always looked to her sister and Martha for guidance.

'Or we could, as true Christians, provide a good example and exhort her to change her ways,' Barbara said. 'Maybe she is forced to sell herself for want of any other means of sustenance.'

Ellen and Alethea looked at Barbara with a mixture of admiration and relief.

'The way she was talking to that man it was clear no sense of shame would ever hold back her nasty desires. She'll be on our doorsteps next, plying her trade.' Joan leant forward, her face flushed.

Thomas smiled at her. 'You need have no fears on that score, sister. We're all honest men here and know how to withstand the temptations of the devil.'

Alethea looked down at her lap. She felt sick with discomfort.

'Unless she's the devil's concubine.' Dorcas gasped. 'She may be a witch for all we know. She'll bring the plague down upon us if we don't act against her.'

There were mumblings of alarm from around the table.

Lizzie turned to her husband with excitement. 'I saw a great bird fly over the camp last full moon, do you remember, Jem? I pointed it out to you.'

'That's right, you did,' Jeremiah agreed, rubbing his face in consternation.

'I recall that night.' Dorcas clasped her hands together. 'I heard a mighty flapping as I lay in bed.'

'I knew she was evil. As soon as she came close I felt a prickling all over, like needles being stuck into my flesh. Didn't I say to you, Dorcas, "I've been stung by nettles". But when we looked we could see no nettles anywhere.' Joan turned triumphantly to her friend who nodded emphatically.

'Enough!' The table shook as Samuel brought his fists down against the wood. He stood, glaring up and down the table at every person there until all sat still and silent. 'If you want to find the devil look into your own hearts, not into the faces of fallen women.' Samuel shook his head sadly. 'How quick ye all are to lift thy stones in readiness to throw them. Well judge not lest ye be judged. Where would we be now if the people of Epping had accused us of witchcraft?' As he surveyed the company they shifted uneasily in their seats, like grass ruffled by the wind. 'Who here is so proud they believe they own this forest? Who has staked his claim on this land that he might say who trespasses and who has leave to stay?'

'Amen,' Thomas said softly.

Samuel studied his friend for a moment. The group waited in apprehension for what he would say next, but when it came it was not what anyone had expected.

'There is no one I hold in higher regard than this man here.' Samuel patted Thomas' shoulder. 'When I first joined Cromwell's army all I wanted was to kill cavaliers, as many as I could, in retribution for the murder of my parents, God rest them. Thomas taught me that we were fighting for the common man; that he might live free from persecution, free from poverty. That he might be assured a roof over his head and enough food for his table.'

The campers nodded in relief, they thought they knew where Samuel was heading.

'But while our cause was right and true, our behaviour was not always worthy of Christian men.' Samuel paused, pointing upwards as if to heaven. 'It was our own acts of cruelty that opened my eyes to the Lord our Saviour. For what is a comfortable home, an unburdened life, a full table, if it has been bought with the blood of innocents?'

Some of the women snorted at this, while the men looked uneasy.

Samuel continued unperturbed. 'I know there be many here who believed everything they read in the newsletters during the late wars. The pamphlets recording the battle of Naseby especially.' He looked pointedly at Joan and Dorcas. 'Perhaps some of ye thought it was work well done when ye read that we had dispatched over a hundred cavalier whores and cut the faces of many more. Ye might have read that they were the wives of Irish rebels, armed with daggers and come to slit the throats of English babies at the breast. Indeed, some claimed them as witches, though they had no sorcery to help them fly, but fell like helpless children before our swords.'

'Easy, Sam, easy.' Thomas laid a restraining hand on Samuel's arm.

But Samuel only spoke louder, his voice gathering momentum as he continued. 'I did not see a single long knife in the hands of those women, whether they were Irish or no. Some were crones too old to be whores and any knives they had were used for cutting food, not throats. They were camp followers, the same as we had. But our blood was up and truth be told we didn't care who or what they were; our swords were like scythes in our hands and they just so much barley to be mown.'

The faces around the table turned away from Samuel, to study the floor, or their hands, or some crumbs left on the table. Alethea could not believe the man she loved capable of such brutality.

'Well,' said Thomas. 'War brings out the worst, as well as the best in men. These things are better not dwelt on.'

'But Samuel's lesson is an important one,' Barbara insisted. 'We must not act out of fear or anger. We must make sure we have evidence before we seek to punish.'

Samuel threw up his hands in disgust. 'Ye judge after the flesh, I judge no man.' He turned and strode out of the hall.

There was an uncomfortable silence, followed by muttering as the campers turned to one another, exclaiming over their unexpected sermon.

'Samuel might have regrets,' said Gilbert, who had also fought at Naseby. 'But I've nothing to feel sorry for and neither have you, Thomas. Those women at Naseby, running after the king's army, were Irish devils who'd slit your throat as soon as look at you.'

'It was all so long ago now.' Thomas shrugged apologetically. 'It doesn't do to keep raking over the past.'

Alethea ground her teeth in exasperation. Thomas liked nothing better than to recall past triumphs. Most of his time was spent dwelling in the past.

'Samuel is a man of God, so he feels these things more keenly than most,' Martha observed.

Thomas nodded, pulling on his beard. 'We were so young then. Sam took it very hard.'

Alethea understood now why Samuel was so forgiving of his enemy and what he had meant by evil deeds done on both sides.

'Samuel is a man of peace, as befits a spiritual. He seeks to fulfil God's commandments,' Barbara declared.

Everyone was eager to assent to this. Samuel was held in such high respect no one wanted to appear critical of him. But, Alethea realised, it was also a convenient way of distancing themselves from his example. As a preacher he should be more forgiving of sins and less tolerant of normal human concerns, such as the need to protect one's territory from outsiders.

'It is getting late, time to retire.' Thomas pushed himself up from the table.

Martha stood too, clearly relieved to call an end to the night's proceedings.

'But we haven't agreed what to do about the Jezebel.' Dorcas' cheeks were red with indignation.

'We can't vote without a full assembly,' Barbara pointed out.

'It isn't our fault if some people absent themselves,' Joan said grumpily.

'I'm with Samuel on this one,' Jack declared as he got up from the table. 'Forbearance, my friends, is that not what we're all about?'

Alethea caught up with Jack as he was heading into the woods. 'It was your friend, Kate, Joan and Dorcas saw, wasn't it?' she whispered to him.

'Well there can't be many women around here with a scarred cheek.'

'And it was Samuel who stood up for her.' Alethea hoped Jack might have been won over by Samuel's defence of his lover.

'Yes, that was some speech.' Jack shook his head and whistled. 'Didn't please everyone though. Those old scoldsters won't be satisfied until they've seen the back of her.' He nodded over at Dorcas and Joan who were walking back to their huts arm in arm, heads bent towards each other. 'I'm going to warn Kate she'd better pitch her tent further off.'

Seeing that the others had disappeared into their huts, Jack held his lantern up. The light swayed in his hand and the path bobbed before him. He nodded at Alethea before making his way gingerly through the trees. She watched his departing figure. The delicate way he lifted his feet, stepping silently over puddles and fallen branches, reminded her of a cat out on the prowl.

Somewhere above her an owl called. Its hollow hoot was echoed in the distance with a trembling 'tu-whoo'. The first owl called again, more insistent this time. The night air was sharp and clear and the sky was sprinkled with stars. She inhaled the damp earthy smell of the forest. One by one candles were blown out until the campsite lay in darkness. A tear ran down her cheek. She had not expected to encounter such ugliness here.

The glow of a taper leaked out from the cracks in the walls of Samuel's hut, pooling beneath his door. Alethea felt a surge of excitement at the prospect of being alone with him.

'Samuel,' she whispered, tapping gently on his door. There was a murmuring within.

Pushing the door open, she was dismayed to see he was not alone. Barbara sat perched on the end of his bed, hands folded demurely in her lap. She gave Alethea a questioning look, as though Alethea were a child who had interrupted an adult conversation. Samuel smiled wearily at her, but offered no explanation for Barbara's presence.

'I, I just came to see if you are all right,' she said.

'That is very courteous of thee.' He ran one hand through his brown hair, pushing it back off his forehead. 'Perhaps I was a little heated earlier, but I had to put a stop to such dangerous talk. I don't want to see our company, blind with prejudice, stoop to violent acts of intolerance.'

Alethea was confounded by the distant formality with which he addressed her.

'There's not a person here who doesn't love and respect you, Samuel.' Barbara gazed earnestly into his eyes. 'Don't become downhearted; we are all your followers in Christ. Careful guidance will keep your flock on the right path.'

Samuel merely raised his eyebrows.

'Come, Alethea.' Barbara rose up from the bed, taking her candle from the floor by her feet.

The roof was too low for her to stand fully and Alethea was forced to back away from the door as Barbara moved out of the hut. 'It is time we both retired.' Linking her spare arm through Alethea's, she led her firmly away.

'Samuel is quick to see enemies where there are none.' Barbara spoke quietly as they made their way back to their own hut, careful not to trip in the dark. 'He fears dissent, and of course he is right to, for we have seen good people divided over minor quarrels. It is my task to cheer him, to keep his spirits strong.'

Though she knew it was selfish, Alethea could not help wishing Samuel relied only on her for encouragement. Barbara and Samuel's friendship pre-dated her knowledge of them and she had no right to question it. Still, she could not help but feel frustrated and excluded. Samuel was all the world to her, yet it seemed she was just one of many to him.

'I hope the talk tonight did not frighten you,' Barbara said kindly. 'So long as we hold God in our hearts we have nothing to fear, from whores or witches.'

'I am not afraid of such creatures as those,' Alethea said scornfully. Then, regretting her tone, added, 'It's the lack of charity that upsets me.'

Barbara squeezed her arm. 'I am proud of you, Alethea. By our thankfulness we can remind our friends of the loving kindness of the Lord and draw them back into His ways. Their hearts will be filled with mercy once again, I am sure of it.'

'Did you know about the slaughter of those women at Naseby?' Alethea kicked a stone out of the way.

'I heard of it at the time and Samuel has spoken of it to me. He did not strike a woman himself, he was hardly more than a boy. But he could do nothing to prevent the violence perpetrated that day and carries a terrible burden of guilt for it.'

'He's never talked about it before, at least not to me.'

'Why would he?'

Alethea shrugged. She wished Samuel had more confidence in her. She had learnt more of his history from Barbara than she had from his own lips. So much of his life was a mystery to her.

For the next few days the campers treated each other with an especial degree of consideration and deference. It was as though everyone felt they should be on their best behaviour. There were no more conversations about the past; instead the children became their focus, with many humorous anecdotes about their faults and foibles being recounted.

Jack asked Barbara to tell the rest of the group that the woman they had been so concerned about had moved away. The mood lightened after this and Alethea believed that harmony had been restored.

On a quiet afternoon when she had their hut to herself, Alethea pulled the book Lord Calverton had given her out of her straw mattress. She brushed the dusty stalks from the cover before letting it fall open. To her relief the pages were still intact and clear of mildew. The ink had not faded on Henry Calverton's bold signature.

She felt more strongly than ever that she could not risk it being found by any of her forest comrades. The likes of Joan and Dorcas would be sure to turn on her. The best thing would be to burn it, but that would be hard to do without anyone seeing. Besides, when she held the volume in her palms she thought of her brother and his love of learning. How horrified he would be at the idea of casting a book into the flames. She could tear out the page with Calverton's signature, but again it seemed too valuable a piece of evidence to destroy. Who knew, but it might save their lives if Calverton ever did send his soldiers after them. She thrust the book back into the middle of her bedding.

She thought differently now of her brother's duel. She wondered if he regretted taking another man's life. A man who had once been his dear friend. Was William as changed by his experiences as she was by hers? She hoped he was safely back at Measham Hall.

She prayed for all her family, even for Frances that she might be delivered safely of a healthy baby boy. She would send word to them as soon as she was able, but she had no means of conveying a message to them now. This conveniently allowed her to delay composing that message. For she did not know what to tell them or how to explain her new life and beliefs.

'You are very fond of Samuel, aren't you, Alethea?' Barbara said.

She and Alethea were alone together, tidying the hall.

'As we all are.' Alethea's heart beat hard in her chest. Despite everything Samuel had said to her, she thought Barbara might be the right person to confide in.

Barbara had a short temper and expected others to live by her own high standards, but she was also a trustworthy friend who always put the welfare of others before her own. Alethea knew that if she asked Barbara to keep her confession secret she would and that if Barbara thought she and Samuel should marry publicly she would say so. She hoped Barbara might push Samuel into an open avowal. There was also a part of her that wanted to prove to Barbara that she was a mature and important woman who had earnt the love of their spiritual leader. Seeing how close Barbara and Samuel were made Alethea want to assert her own position. Often she felt Barbara dismissed her too easily.

'But for you, I think Samuel has become a proxy father,' Barbara continued. 'I imagine your own father to be affectionate and indulgent of you.'

'Why do you say that?' Alethea dropped the wooden bowl she was carrying and it clattered onto the floor.

Barbara continued calmly, picking up the bowl and placing it on the table. 'The way that you deport yourself with Samuel suggests it.'

'Deport myself?'

'Don't be upset, I just wanted to offer a few words of caution, that is all. Samuel has an important mission, one he must not be distracted from. He must love all his flock equally, singling none out for particular consideration.'

'I understand that,' Alethea said. 'I'm not a child.'

'No, but you have led a privileged life up till now. One that may have led you to expect grace and favour.'

Alethea was so distressed by Barbara's words she could think of nothing to say in reply. She realised she could not expect any sympathy from her regarding her relations with Samuel. She busied herself sweeping the floor so that Barbara would not see her consternation.

'Do not retreat into pride, but consider my words carefully,' Barbara told her.

'Don't I work as hard as anyone else here? Have you ever seen me shirk my duties or expect anyone to wait upon me?' Alethea thumped the broom on the floorboards.

Joan, Lizzie and Dorcas walked into the hall carrying firewood. They moved about the hearth, stoking the fire and stirring the rabbit stew that bubbled over it. Dorcas laid the table for dinner, while Lizzie cut slices of bread. None of them noticed as Alethea withdrew from the hall.

How could Barbara suggest she viewed Samuel as she would her own father? The two men were so different, it was a ridiculous assertion. Alethea knew of several marriages where the disparity in ages was far greater than hers with Samuel. If she had gone along with her stepmother's plans she would be engaged now to some old widower. For all she knew her parents still planned to marry her to him; that was reason enough to remain in Epping. But what would a spinster like Barbara understand of love?

'Are you all right, Alethea?' Ellen was walking towards the hall, carrying Robin on one hip.

She tried to swallow down her anger, afraid of giving herself away. 'I've just been reprimanded by Barbara,' she admitted.

Scoldings from Barbara were not unusual, Ellen had felt the lash of her tongue often enough and Alethea felt confident she would take her part.

Ellen laughed. 'Don't mind her, she's often waspish.'

'Barbara seems to think I am too forward with Samuel.' Alethea needed to test out another's reaction, to see if anyone else had noted her behaviour.

'Does she now?' Ellen raised her eyebrows. 'Well, Barbara has always seen Samuel as her own personal property. She's very protective of him.' Ellen lowered her voice. 'I think Barbara had hopes when Samuel became a widower, that he might take her for his wife.'

'Is that so?'

'Some said she was too hot in her promotion of Samuel, that she was heard to call him the only begotten Son of God. They were even accused of having improper relations,' Ellen whispered. 'But those were just slurs cast by enemies who wished to blacken Samuel's name and our religion,' she added quickly.

A nauseating clamminess spread through Alethea's belly. 'When? Who said such things?'

'When they were travelling together, you know, when he was preaching in the North. It was hard for poor Rebecca to hear such slander.'

Robin, growing bored of the conversation, began to struggle in his mother's arms and tug on her hair.

'It isn't true of course,' Ellen said anxiously. 'Samuel is above such lewdness.' Robin was kicking her now. 'Stop it, Robin.' She slapped his leg. 'He's hungry. Will you come in for dinner?'

'No, I'm not feeling so well. I think I'll lie down and rest for a while.'

'You do look a little pale. I'll save you some stew for later.' Ellen smiled reassuringly at Alethea and hurried off with her impatient son.

'I have brought thee something to eat.' Samuel stepped into Alethea's hut, bending over because of the low roof. 'May I?' he gestured to her bed.

'Of course,' she said, pushing herself up into a sitting position.

Samuel sat beside her, leaving the bowl on a stool. 'Ellen said thou weren't feeling well.'

He placed his palm against her forehead. Lifting her thick hair, he examined her neck. How exquisite it was to feel his cool hands against her flesh. The rest of the world vanished when she was in his presence.

She reached out to put her arms around his neck, but Samuel held them firmly down.

'There's no sign of a fever,' he said.

'It's in my stomach,' she said. 'And my heart.' She leant forward to kiss him, but Samuel dodged her mouth.

'These are difficult times. We all have burdens to bear. I am needed now as a man of God; thou sees how our flock increases daily. Be patient, Alethea, now is not the time for us to love one another in that way. God will show us when the time is right.'

'What do you mean?' She was overcome with dread that her lover was abandoning her.

'Come, thou art wise enough to understand. It would be selfish of us to indulge each other when there are more pressing demands.'

She was dismayed by Samuel's impatient tone. 'I am selfish,' she wept. 'I can't help it. It's torture to see you every day and have to keep my distance.'

Samuel released her arms, placing his palms down on either side of her. 'Think of this as the period of Lent, when we fast and set our minds on the suffering of our Saviour. Thee and I must fast now from each other, but remember how much sweeter that tastes which we have denied ourselves.'

'So it is only a provisional abstinence?'

'We have been blessed with the physical knowledge of each other, now thou must concentrate on the spiritual.'

When she considered Joan and Dorcas' attitudes to the unfortunate Kate Wright she had to agree. Who among their friends would understand the nature of their relationship? Many, she feared, would not be able to see beyond the carnal. They would condemn as sin what she saw as blessed.

'Barbara would not be happy to see you here,' she could not resist telling him. Samuel looked at her so sternly she found herself adding. 'Ellen said there were rumours, cast by your enemies, regarding your relations with Barbara.' As soon as the words were out she regretted them.

'There are no depths too low for my enemies to plunge to; no calumny so heinous they'll not resort to it.' His cheeks flushed red against the pallor of his skin. 'Thou must understand that if thou art to remain with us. It is not an easy path. Thou must have great strength and great faith to endure all that will be required of thee.' His eyes blazed so brightly Alethea felt herself wither under his gaze. 'Thou cannot prove susceptible to rumour. Remember the Lord hates a false witness that speaks lies and sows discord among his brethren.'

Alethea clutched at her blankets. 'Ellen didn't mean any harm. She only mentioned it because I was upset, because Barbara had chided me for being too fond of you.'

'Well,' he said. 'Maybe Barbara was right to chide thee. But it is me she should chide first and foremost. I have encouraged thee, when I should have shown greater self-restraint.'

This was not what Alethea wanted to hear. 'Do you regret what has passed between us?' she asked.

'It was a pure union, not a corrupt one, I am convinced of that, but it may have been better to wait until we could proclaim our vows before our friends. We must hold our tongues and our hearts in abeyance now, until the time is right for us to live honestly and openly.'

'And when do you think that might be?'

Samuel pressed his fingers to his temples. 'I cannot know everything, Alethea. Please don't test me so. People think it comes naturally to me, to be a leader of men, but it is a heavy cross to bear and sometimes I feel as though I will sink beneath it. It requires all my strength to inspire and support so many on their spiritual journeys. Thou promised me once thou wouldst be my helpmeet. I need thee to fulfil that promise, not to make ever more demands upon me.'

Alethea was distressed to see how tired and frail he suddenly appeared. 'Samuel, forgive me, I've been self-regarding and thoughtless. How can I undermine your mission here when I see how vital it is? I will do better from now on. I will be your staff and not your rod.'

To her relief he smiled at these words. His hand hovered over her arm. It hardly touched her and yet she could feel such warmth generating from his palm she thought it might burn her.

'Can thou be'est my Mary Magdalene? So I ask thee now to "touch me not" but to go instead to our brethren and spread our message.'

Her heart swelled with pride at his words and she assured him of her devotion as well as her restraint.

Alethea was to be tested further in the coming days as life grew more challenging for all of them. Now she could not roam in the woods without tripping over yet another makeshift dwelling. Birdsong was submerged by human voices, coarse and dissonant, as the newcomers called to one another, shouting and laughing. The barking of their dogs was less alarming than the hacking coughs that rose up suddenly from beds of leaves.

She tried to be a good Christian and honour her neighbours, but there were so many of them now. And it was hard to feel charitable towards people who disburdened themselves where they pleased without taking the trouble to bury their stinking ordure. Or who left their scraps on the forest floor with no thought of the rats this might draw in. When Sir Alcott sent them another pig to roast they found a crowd of people waiting for a slice. They could hardly refuse them, but there was not enough to go around.

'St. Samuel not able to feed the five thousand?' Jack whispered in Alethea's ear.

She elbowed him in the ribs and tried to ignore the rumbling of her belly.

Sometimes she fantasied that she and Samuel would leave the camp together, just the two of them. Free from past associations, they could live openly as a married couple. But as much as she longed for this outcome, she knew these dreams were the product of a wicked selfishness. She could not steal God's minister from the very people who had nurtured them both. It was just that she craved his presence. The loss of his physical love was a constant ache within her so that sometimes she wished she had never known it, to be denied it now.

Alethea was not the only one who thought of leaving; as the death toll round them grew, many others in the encampment discussed moving to new ground. Some planned to travel to the West Country having heard that it was safe there. All were sorry to have to quit a place that had become so dear and had been so hospitable, but they felt increasingly that it was becoming too dangerous to remain.

Only Samuel spoke strongly against their removal. Despite the plague he continued to attract a large crowd every Sunday. He did not want to abandon these new disciples who, he said, had not yet grown sure enough in their faith to be left untended.

Early one September morning, Alethea was woken by the shouts of a woman. She forced her eyes open to see Ellen and Barbara out of their beds, pulling shawls around their shoulders.

'What is it?' she asked, still half-asleep.

Barbara held up one hand and the three of them listened intently. The calls were getting louder and were as savage and demanding as the cawing of a rook.

Robin woke with a sharp cry, distressed to find himself alone in the bed that he shared with his mother. Ellen gathered him up in her arms, rocking him over her shoulder and the three of them made their way single file out of the hut and into the half-light of an overcast dawn.

'Samuel, Samuel Byrd, are you here?' The words rang across the encampment, loud and urgent.

A scrawny woman strode towards them, her feet enclosed in a pair of battered men's boots. Her head was bare and her long hair hung in matted locks so filthy it was hard to tell what colour it was. Her gaunt, sun-burnt cheeks made her blue eyes blaze all the more brightly as she stared savagely about her, her head jutting forwards on her skinny neck. Alethea thought she must be one of Samuel's congregation looking for help or else driven mad by the distemper. Then she felt Barbara's fingers gripping her shoulder.

'Becky, it's Becky,' Barbara whispered, her voice filled with fear and wonder.

'Who?' Alethea asked.

'It is your wife, Samuel. Show yourself for pity's sake,' the woman cried.

✦ Chapter Fourteen ✦

'**B**lessing and honour and glory and power be unto him that sitteth upon the throne and unto the lamb for ever and ever, amen,' Rebecca intoned, before raising the bowl of soup to her lips. Before she had drunk any of it, she set it down again. 'This humble and penitent sinner raises up her thanks to the Lord for saving her children from everlasting death.'

For a moment Alethea expected a procession of Samuel's children to troop in and complete the family reunion, until she recollected what Rebecca meant by 'everlasting death'.

'I see them, Samuel,' Rebecca continued, gazing up at the air above her. 'I see them now in their white raiments, golden trumpets at their lips, stars encircling their curling locks, their eyes bright with joy. God has wiped away all their tears and they shall never know pain nor hardship anymore.'

Her words were met with a collective 'amen', spoken in hushed but ardent tones. For who could not be moved by her vision? Samuel, Alethea noted, was as white as if he had in fact seen a ghost and his eyes were as wide as a trapped rabbit's.

Alethea had not seen their reunion. She had returned inside, too sick with shock and too afraid of her own passions to join the others as they rushed out to witness this miracle, Rebecca Byrd come back from the dead. So she did not see Samuel's face when he encountered his wife again and did not know whether he had greeted her with joy or doubt.

Rebecca turned to Samuel and pushing the hair back from his face, traced a grimy finger over his scar. 'And they shall see his face, and his name shall be in their foreheads,' she muttered, half to herself.

She and Samuel sat quite still, staring into each other's eyes, while the rest of the company looked on in silence. Suddenly Rebecca pressed her blackened palms to Samuel's cheeks and pulled his head towards her as though she might kiss him. For a horrible moment Alethea thought she would have to watch as their lips met, but Samuel placed his hands over Rebecca's and pulled them down gently into her lap.

'I was told thou had perished, Becky, along with the children.'

'I told my neighbour, I shall go to my grave with my babes, let me be buried with them and if Samuel comes tell him we are all dead of the plague.' She shook her matted locks and leant forward in her seat. 'But death did not come and I was filled with bitterness. Distracted in myself I knew not where to turn. Then God spoke to me in a dream, he told me we must be reconciled lest Satan tempt you with incontinency.' She caressed Samuel's hands, turning them over and pressing her fingers into his palms. 'I travelled the country over searching you out, until the Lord took pity on me and sent me a messenger. He said he'd heard of a preacher by the name of Byrd over this way. The nearer I got to Epping the more folk had heard of you and our old comrades here, living in the forest.'

Alethea looked round at their 'old comrades' to see faces rapt with wonder. I am the stranger here, she thought grimly, the interloper at the feast. Only Barbara sat studying her hands as though they were a more pressing concern than the sudden arrival of Samuel's wife. Barbara looked as distressed as Alethea felt. Her hair, always neatly pinned back, had come loose, messy strands stuck to her forehead with sweat. Her apron too was uncharacteristically dirty.

Jack caught Alethea's eye, he raised his eyebrows and gave her an enquiring look. She frowned and turned away.

Trusting that the others were too busy exchanging news to miss her, Alethea walked out into the forest. As she made her way through the huts and dwellings that clustered around their enclosure she heard someone coughing. She was tempted to seek them out deliberately in the hope they had the plague and would contaminate her. She knew she was only compounding her sins by giving way to despair, yet she had never felt so desperate. She was trapped and could see no way out of her predicament except through death.

'Alethea, hold on.' She turned to find Jack hurrying after her. She had no desire for company, but had not the heart to turn him away.

'Are you all right?' he asked.

'Why wouldn't I be?'

'Don't you want to join in the celebrations? We haven't had much to be thankful for of late.'

'I thought I should leave them to it, they're all old friends and have much to talk about.'

She found tears rising in her throat and clogging her voice. They began to leak from her eyes, but she was afraid wiping them away would only draw attention to them. She averted her face from Jack and they walked on in silence until they found themselves alone.

'Are you in love with him, is that what distresses you?'

'In love with who?'

'With Samuel, who else?' Jack said as though it pained him to have to repeat the name.

'You've lived among disreputable folk and seem never to judge them. You've consorted with actresses and women of ill repute, but you don't seem to think any the less of them for their lasciviousness...' Alethea trailed off.

'What, are you suggesting Rebecca Byrd is a trull?' Jack said with much surprise and some amusement.

'No, no, nothing of the kind,' Alethea replied aghast. 'No, it is not *she* who has behaved dishonourably.'

'Ah,' Jack said, 'but her husband has.'

'Not he, he could never be dishonourable.'

'Who then?' Jack eyed Alethea sharply.

She wrung her hands and swallowed down her tears. 'We gave way to passion. We thought our union a beautiful, blessed thing. But now I find I am compromised. I think I might be with child.' She had not meant to confide in Jack, especially not before informing Samuel, but she must tell someone.

'You think?' Jack said. 'When did you last have your courses?'

'I should have bled at least three weeks ago and my terms have always been regular, but there has been nothing. At first I thought it might be the greensickness, but I've had some nausea too, the same as my stepmother whenever she is with child.'

'How could you be such a fool as to let him seduce you?' Jack looked quite sick.

'I cannot explain it right. It was not a seduction. We were going to announce it, we thought of ourselves as already wed in the eyes of the Lord.'

'So that's what he told you. Only now his wife has come like Lazarus back from the dead. I'll wager that was one miracle he didn't long for.'

'I know you think the worst of him. I wish I could make you see otherwise. Only now I'm quite lost and don't know where to turn.'

'You aren't lost. Didn't I promise you when we first set out on our journey that I'd keep you safe? Well maybe I failed to protect you from this rake in puritan's clothing, though I did my best to warn you, you wouldn't heed me...'

'Jack,' Alethea interrupted.

'No, hear me out,' he continued. 'I don't go back on my pledges. I'll marry you and claim the child as my own; if you don't still consider me beneath you that is.'

Alethea was touched by Jack's loyalty, but nettled that he thought her so proud. 'You know I no longer hold with distinctions based on rank. I could not marry you because I do not feel for you as a woman must toward her husband.'

'And yet you could feel that way for him.'

'I cannot help it. Believe me, if I could change my heart I would.'

'You still love him then?'

'I must.' Alethea wept.

'Some day you'll see him for what he is. But anyway, whether you do or not, he already has a wife who lays claim to him.'

'I thought God intended for us to be together.'

'God had nothing to do with it. I'm offering you a way out, Alethea, but if you think me too loathsome to contemplate, well then you must shift for yourself.'

Ignoring his last comment, she grabbed his arm. 'You won't tell anyone will you, Jack?'

'You needn't worry on that score, I know how to keep a secret. Though yours isn't one that'll keep itself for long.'

This was something she knew only too well.

The hall was hardly alive with rejoicing when they returned. In fact, the atmosphere was surprisingly subdued. Samuel looked strained and anxious. The others talked quietly as they prepared an evening meal. Rebecca sat in the corner rocking back and forth in her chair and muttering to herself.

'The poor woman is half distracted,' Ellen whispered to Alethea. 'She has suffered so much it's softened her mind.'

Alethea looked over at Samuel's wife. How could she ever allow her to know that she carried Samuel's child when all hers had been taken from her? Rebecca was too pitiable and wild a figure for Alethea to be jealous of her, even so she could not bear to think of Samuel sharing her bed.

'Have you seen Barbara?' Ellen asked, her voice low.

'No,' Alethea said and wondered whether Barbara was also hiding somewhere, nursing her disappointment at Rebecca's arrival.

'I've looked for her in our hut but she isn't there and her cloak and blankets are gone,' Ellen said.

By nightfall Barbara had still not returned. In the general excitement nobody else noticed her absence. Ellen and Alethea decided not to speak of it yet; they did not want the others to think Barbara had gone off in a fit of pique. By daybreak, however, when she was still missing, they became alarmed and spoke with Thomas and Martha. It was agreed they should search the forest for her.

'Barbara ought to know there are more ties than one to bind her here.' Martha shook her head.

Thomas gave her a warning look and she said no more.

'Let's keep this between ourselves for now,' he said. 'There's no need to upset the whole camp.'

Alethea had some difficulty disengaging herself from the children, who wanted her to join in their games, but once free she set off eastwards as Thomas had directed. She was grateful for an excuse to get away from the camp and relieved he had sent her in the opposite direction to her former love nest.

The spiders had been hard at work decorating the woods. Everywhere she looked cobwebs were stretched between twigs and hung over shrubs, their filaments beaded with dew like necklaces set out for display. Or like pretty nets waiting for their quarry. They clung to her face and arms when she blundered through them and she had to keep stopping to pull the sticky threads from her skin and clothes.

She desperately needed to speak with Samuel, but he was occupied with his wife. He had taken Rebecca back to his hut the previous night and why would he not? They were married after all. When he returned to the hall for a jug of water to wash Rebecca, Martha offered to tend to her, but he insisted on caring for Becky himself.

Alethea stood beside him as he heated a pot of water, thinking he would make some sign to her, but he had stared into the fire as though she was not there. She had followed him out, watching as he made his way back to his hut, carrying the jug as though it might leap from his arms and scald him.

'Shall I light the way for you?' she had called to him.

But he had just shaken his head without even turning round. She had lain awake all night hoping to hear his tapping on the wall of her hut, but no sound came.

What would the rest of the camp think of her when they discovered her condition and how would she explain it? She had heard of women who had had babies in secret and then farmed them out for adoption with no one the wiser. But they were women of means; women with allies to hide them and the connections to place their child in a good family. What could Alethea do to cover her shame?

The day was growing warmer as the sun rose. Acorns crunched beneath her feet. A light wind blew and leaves dropped like yellow coins, paving the forest floor in gold. Alethea wished she could remain suspended forever within this honeyed world. Perhaps that is what Barbara felt. Perhaps she had lain down somewhere on a crimson bed of beech leaves; perhaps Alethea would find her slumbering still.

As she walked, a disturbing idea came to her. She recalled the *Book of Genesis* where Rachel and Leah gave their maids to their husband Jacob to bear children for them, and Hagar the maid of Sarai and Abram who bore a son for her barren mistress. What if God intended Alethea's child with Samuel be given to Rebecca to replace the children she had lost? It seemed only right and just. But Alethea was no servant girl to bear children for her mistress. Or was she too full of sinful pride, a pride she must now overcome?

Samuel had told her she would never be given a cross too great to bear, yet how was she to recognise the cross that was hers? And what of those who sank beneath the weight of their sufferings? Alethea thought of the stoicism with which her mother had endured her final illness, certain always of God's love and the paradise that awaited her. How ashamed Mother would be of her. What should she do to redeem herself?

She wished she had her little statue of the Virgin Mary even if she did not believe in such things anymore. Just to feel the cold, smooth stone in the palm of her hand again. She wondered what the Calvertons had done with it.

'Barbara!' she called again and again. But only the harsh croaking of the ravens answered her.

The light was dying and Alethea returned to the camp weary and downcast. On the outskirts she met Martha, who had gone south, but had had no more luck in locating Barbara.

'Barbara always was an independent soul,' Martha said. 'Maybe she's decided to follow her own path.'

'But surely she would have said goodbye.'

'Hmm, Barbara can be wilful and Rebecca's return, well, that may have thrust her nose out of joint. They never did see eye to eye.'

Alethea was about to press her further but remembered Samuel's admonishment on the dangers of gossip, so said only that she would pray for Barbara.

Martha nodded. 'We all need prayers now,' she said.

Thomas was the next back, also alone. Alethea wondered that Ellen was so long. Dinner was on the table and the company all assembled in the hall. Robin, who had been in the care of the older children, began to cry for his mother.

'Where is Ellen?' asked Lizzie, looking around. 'And Barbara?'

The sound of Barbara's name stirred Rebecca from her place by the fire. She sat up with a start. 'That woman, Jezebel,' she shrieked. 'Who calleth herself a prophetess. She is but a fornicator, a seducer of men. Now she sees the true wife return she scurries off to hide her shame!' Rebecca glared around the room and then spat furiously into the fire.

An awful hush fell on the hall. The younger children hid themselves behind their mothers' skirts. Robin whimpered. Lizzie picked him up and held him closely in her arms.

If this is how she talks of Barbara, Alethea thought, what might she do to me if she finds out about my dealings with her husband?

'Stop, Becky, for pity's sake,' Samuel said. 'Barbara's never done thee any harm.'

Alethea was dismayed by the timorousness in Samuel's voice. She had never seen him afraid before.

He knelt down beside his wife, enclosing her hands in his. She leant against him moaning, 'Sam, Sam, why did you desert me?'

Robin was crying loudly now. Rebecca looked up at him with surprise.

'Who is that child?' she demanded. 'Is it yours, Samuel?'

'This is my sister Ellen's son,' Lizzie said. 'Ellen and Robert's little boy,' she added firmly. 'He is named after his father.'

As if in response to her name, Ellen appeared in the doorway. Alethea could tell from her face that she had found Barbara and knew before she said it what news she carried. Ellen went straight to the fire and held her hands over the flames as if to warm them, though Alethea suspected she was purifying them in the smoke.

'Take the little ones outside to play,' Martha instructed her son.

'But we haven't had our dinner yet,' Daniel complained.

'You can have it later,' she said, shooing them out.

Ellen sank down on a bench, receiving Robin into her lap.

'What is it, Nelly?' Lizzie sat down beside Ellen, putting an arm protectively around her shoulder.

Samuel tried to persuade Rebecca to return to their hut to rest, but she refused to move. The adults gathered at the table.

'Barbara said she would perform a quarantine if she thought she had the distemper,' Ellen said quietly. 'And that is what she did. I found her in an abandoned tent at the edge of the forest, towards North Weald. She was not long dead when I got there – her hand was still warm. But, oh Lizzie, she died alone.' Ellen turned to her sister, laying her head on her shoulder and the two wept together.

'Serves the harlot right,' Rebecca muttered.

'Hush, woman,' Thomas said.

Samuel looked pained; whether from his inability to control his own wife or for grief at the loss of a friend, Alethea could not tell.

'She was not alone, Ellen. Jesus was with her, to bring her comfort at the end and to welcome her into his kingdom.' Martha's voice was resolute, her tone almost reproving.

'That's right, she did a noble thing to protect her friends.' Thomas nodded vigorously, but his eyes shone with tears. After a pause he asked, 'Were you with her long, Ellen?'

'I touched her hand, that is all. Then I prayed outside the tent,' Ellen assured him. 'Nor did I breathe in whilst I was in the tent, but held my breath 'til I got out.'

'Can you be sure it was the plague, Ellen?' Jack asked her.

'I did not like to go too close. It could have been the sweating sickness or an ague, for her face and hair were damp as though she'd had a fever.'

'We cannot leave her there,' Lizzie said. 'We must bury her.'

'I'll do it. Who will help me?' Jack looked around.

The other men quickly offered their services. Alethea was surprised Samuel did not volunteer, but thought anxiety about his wife probably prevented him.

Samuel's behaviour troubled Alethea again that Sunday. She went as she always did to hear him preach to the people. She did not take up her usual position in front of the platform Jeremiah had built, but stood to one side instead, close to a hedgerow that bordered the meadow. The crowd assembled in small groups; friends and families gathered together, while couples and individuals stood apart, each marking out a little patch of ground considered far enough away from their neighbours to avoid contagion. Many carried medicating posies of wildflowers which gave the throng an oddly festive appearance. Despite their wariness they shouted cordial greetings, blessings and hopes of good health across to one another. They had come looking for salvation, not discord.

A quiet settled on the crowd as Samuel ascended the platform. Alethea was alarmed to see Rebecca following closely behind him. She waited for Jeremiah or Thomas to lead Rebecca away, but instead Samuel put his arm around his wife and brought her to the front of the stage. An expectant murmur rose from the crowd.

'Brethren, what a testimony it is to thy faith and endurance that ye have gathered here today. Many of ye I know have walked miles to congregate on this humble ground. Ye could have stayed in the seeming safety of thy homes, but instead ye have sought out the Lord, here under this open sky.' Samuel swept an arm up towards the heavens. 'By doing so ye prove thy faith is greater than any fear of sickness or diseases. Thy faith is greater than the threat of arrest and imprisonment. Thy faith is greater than the false doctrine imposed on ye by man-made laws.'

'Christ hath redeemed us from the curse of the law,' Rebecca shouted, and the crowd gave out a great cheer.

'We seek for signs, wonders and miracles to affirm our faith. Behold this woman, my wife, whom I believed dead. She has been returned to me.' The crowd cheered again.

'The Lord is my rock, my fortress, my deliverer,' Rebecca called.

'Amen,' rose from the crowd.

'I doubt there is one amongst us who has not tasted loss or known great sorrows. Many of ye will have buried one or more of thy children. Rebecca, my wife, buried all her children. She watched them sicken one by one. She nursed them, she prayed for them and she mourned them. But she did not allow self-love to consume her. She rejoiced that the angel of the Lord found our babes fit for Heaven, cutting short their earthly travails. For who can grieve to know their children have obtained eternal happiness?' Samuel held fast to his wife as he spoke.

The crowd murmured their praise. Alethea remembered him telling her Rebecca had doted too much on their daughter and had been unable to resign herself to her loss. It seemed God had bent her to his will by imposing more suffering.

'After burying our children, Rebecca set out in search of me, for in the confusion of the times we had been separated. She did not falter in her quest, for the Lord made her feet as strong as her will. Though she knew not whither I had gone, our Lord showed her the way.'

'Thou enlarged my path under me so my feet did not slip,' Rebecca proclaimed, her voice rising as she declared: 'For who is God, except the Lord? And who is a rock, except our God? God is my strength and power and He makes my way perfect.'

The crowd roared their approval.

Alethea understood then that her place was not beside Samuel. She was not destined to be his helpmeet for he had one already. She could hear from the conversations around her that with his wife beside him, Samuel was all the more convincing a prophet. The people took hope from Rebecca's reappearance and consolation from the fortitude with which the couple bore the loss of their children. Rebecca's forceful delivery carried well across the field and her interjections enhanced his sermon. Alethea would not have expected this from the woman she had been told about, or the one who appeared at their door. It seemed miraculous indeed, Samuel's healing of his wife in the past few days. Was this a sign? Was God asking Alethea to prove herself a true Christian and give her child over to them?

She thought Samuel would find some moment when they might speak in private, but whether he wished to or not, he did not manage it. She waited for him in their secret places, under the oak tree and behind the briars. She kept thinking she saw him moving towards her through the trees, but her eyes deceived her. It was never more than the sunlight flitting from the tree trunks, or deer, or men whose business was not with her.

She supposed he could not get away. Rebecca followed him like a shadow. She considered asking one of the children to deliver a note to him, but the risk of it falling into Rebecca's hands was too great. After her damning of Barbara, Alethea could not help but think of Rebecca as something akin to a witch.

Apart from Jack, everyone else seemed to view Rebecca as a being touched by God, a blessed fool. Alethea was repulsed by her. She searched her conscience, trying to ascertain whether her feelings were motivated by envy. But God's voice never spoke clearly to her as it seemed to for others. She could not bear to think of handing over her helpless infant into Rebecca's hands, even if it might be the means of healing her. If only she could talk to Samuel. He would know what to do for the best, but his eyes never met hers and she felt as though she had ceased to exist.

⇥ Chapter Fifteen ⇤

Two days after burying Barbara, Jack told them he was returning to London. With the temperature dropping and winter not far off he considered it safe enough to venture into the city again.

'I just wanted to say goodbye.' Alethea hovered at the entrance to Jack's tent.

Since turning down his proposal, relations between them had been strained. Now he was leaving in the morning and this was her first opportunity to speak to him alone; the children had been hanging off him all day, trying to persuade him to stay with them. He was packing up his knapsack with what few possessions he owned: his apothecary's case, a pipe Seth had made for him and a handkerchief embroidered by Ellen. A stout walking stick carved by Jeremiah lay against the doorway. A handy instrument for an unarmed man travelling alone.

Jack looked up at her and smiled sadly. He seemed to have aged before Alethea's eyes, his cheerful features dragged down under a weight of sorrow.

'Have you spoken to Samuel about your predicament?' he asked quietly.

Alethea shook her head. She looked down at his bag. 'Perhaps you have something that might cure my condition?'

'I carry nothing of that kind. Signora Pozzuto was always very strict on that matter. When such desperate remedies work they're likely to do their job too thoroughly and destroy the mother as well as the child.' Jack met her gaze for the first time in weeks, his eyes wary. 'I'm surprised you'd ask me such a thing.'

Alethea looked away. She had not expected Jack to have such scruples.

He moved to stand beside her. 'I do know of a midwife in London who runs a house where women can stay and be delivered. Then afterwards she takes care of the child for them.'

'Takes care, in what way?'

'For a fee she'll send it off to a nurse to be fostered. But it's not a place for you, Alethea. You'd be living amongst whores. I wouldn't like to think of it.'

Jack sounded so distressed, she felt compelled to reassure him. 'Don't worry about me. My father won't disown me. I was planning to return home and be delivered there.'

'We're waiting for you in the hall, Jack.' Thomas strode over, clapping Jack on the shoulder. 'Everyone's gathered there for a farewell drink and a bite to eat. Are you going to sing for us, Alethea? It's a long time since we've had any music. Perhaps a psalm in memory of Barbara?'

'Of course,' Alethea said. For it was better to sing than to cry.

By the time Alethea was up the next morning Jack had gone.

Since Samuel now appeared to deny her, she could see no other option but to throw herself on the mercy of her father and beg for his forgiveness. She toyed with the idea of telling him that, having been abandoned by the Calvertons, she had been raped by some ruffian on the road. That at least would excuse her of culpability. Even more than her father's disapproval, Alethea dreaded the disgust her brother must feel when he learnt of her fall. To lose his friendship and respect would be worst of all. She was afraid Father would send her to a convent. Perhaps a life enclosed in a convent was all she deserved. Some women thrived in the cloistered life, but they were women who enjoyed study and contemplation. Alethea was not such a woman. For her it would be a prison. Her only small consolation was that, given her condition, any plans of marrying her off to Frances' cousin would have to be abandoned. Even the Cornish widower could not be so desperate he would accept a fallen woman for his bride.

Rebecca's appearance and Barbara's funeral had delayed the departure of those families who intended to travel west. Now, as they began to make arrangements for their journey and to plan their route, Samuel announced that their numbers would be increased.

'Rebecca and I, after conferring for some time and seeking for the answer in the Good Book, have found our path lies with our friends in the West Country.'

He looked at the table as he spoke and though Alethea stared hard at him, he never lifted his eyes to meet hers.

'Well this is a change of heart, Sam,' Thomas said. 'What about your congregation?'

'Did the angel not preach to every nation and to all folk?' Samuel answered.

'We're delighted to have you join us,' Dorcas said to Rebecca.

The others quickly added their assent, though Rebecca hardly seemed to hear them. She jerked her head dismissing their overtures of friendship with a curt, 'God's will be done.'

Samuel's announcement resolved Alethea's deliberations. 'I must return home to my family,' she told them.

'You're always welcome with us,' Joan turned to her.

The others agreed, the children begging Alethea to join them. Only Samuel and his wife remained aloof.

'I'm most grateful, but my family must be grieving, not knowing what's become of me. I must go back to them.' She picked up little Ruth, hugging her close to hide her distress.

Then Samuel spoke to Alethea for the first time since Rebecca's arrival. That is, he addressed his words towards her, while directing his gaze just above her head. 'I am sure God is with thee in thy decision. Thy family will rejoice to see thee safe and well.' His tone was cold and conclusive.

If he had raised his fists against her, he could not have hurt Alethea more.

Despite feeling permanently tired, Alethea could not sleep. She lay staring into the blackness of the night, a blackness that filled her heart and her soul. She was nothing to Samuel therefore she was nothing. Nothing but a licentious wench who had been so proud as to think she understood the workings of men. One who had had the temerity to believe she had an insight into God's intentions. How her body had betrayed her. When she had thought herself free it had trapped her, with its lust and its female weaknesses. Now she longed to be nothing. For the blackness to obliterate her entirely, baby and all.

'Alethea,' Ellen whispered.

Alethea turned to face her. Barbara's empty bed lay between them like a reproach. There was another being whose life Alethea had misunderstood. She wished now that she had asked Barbara what Samuel had been to her. Had Barbara loved him as she had?

'What is it?'

'You must want a companion for your journey home.'

'I'll manage,' Alethea said, more bravely than she felt.

'I'm surprised Jack didn't wait to accompany you.'

'My father would not approve of Jack.'

'Would he approve of me, do you think?'

'Of you? Why, Ellen, he would think you the sweetest creature on earth, and little Robin too.'

Robin coughed and snuffled in his sleep.

'Can we come with you?'

Alethea was astonished by Ellen's request. She propped herself up on her elbows. 'I can't tell you how happy your words make me. I was dreading undertaking that long journey alone. But, don't you want to stay with your sister and Jeremiah?'

'They're going to travel west with the others. I think everyone will leave together now, though how long they'll stay together I don't know. It's not that I don't value their company. I shall be very sorry to part ways with my sister, of course. It's just, I long to know more of the world. I would so like to hear musicians play, to attend a playhouse, to dance.' Ellen spoke in a great rush as though once her tongue had been loosened she could not stop the flow of words. 'I love my Bible, I do, but sometimes I long for something else to read. And I know it's vanity, but I'd like to wear dresses like the ones fine ladies wear. To be surrounded by colour, like you described it, with all the hangings and carpets and flowers in your old home. I can't see any of those things if I stay with Lizzie and our old companions.'

'What about your husband, don't you want to find him?'

'That scoundrel? Goodness no, I'm better off without him.'

Alethea felt redeemed by Ellen's offer. Of all their comrades she could not think of anyone who was more likely to be sympathetic to her predicament. Ellen would be shocked of course and Alethea did not think she could bring herself to tell Ellen who the father of her child was, but Ellen was not so puritanical as some of the other members of their group. Besides, with any luck the exertions of the road might induce a miscarriage and then no one else need know of her shame.

Alethea thought Ellen must have fallen asleep, but then she asked suddenly, 'Won't you miss Jack or is he more fond of you than you of him?'

She stretched uncomfortably in her bed. 'He's fond in a different way. I cannot love him as he loves me. God knows I wish I could.'

'So that's why he went back to London. I couldn't think what would drive him to part with you.' Alethea did not know what to say to this. After a pause Ellen continued, 'Jack's not overly fond of Samuel, is he?' She sounded a little sad.

'No,' Alethea said. 'He's not.'

'Does Samuel seem different to you, since his wife found him?'

Alethea had to stop herself from laughing in bitterness. 'He's afraid of her, I think,' she managed.

'I always believed him to be fearless. What could he fear with God behind him?'

Alethea grimaced in the darkness. 'What shouldn't he fear? Remember "my thoughts are not your thoughts, neither are your ways my ways, saith the Lord".'

Part III
Measham

Part III

Measham

✦ Chapter Sixteen ✦

The journey to Derbyshire was slow and difficult. The grey October skies often filled with rain and the roads became clogged with mud. Fear of contamination had reduced the number of public coaches which meant delays and frequent changes, sometimes in towns that took Ellen and Alethea away from their desired route. Finding people to give them directions was not an easy task either, for everyone kept to themselves. Alethea had enough money left over from Lady Calverton's guinea to afford accommodation at inns that were as decent as the local town could supply, but some places would only allow them to sleep in their barns or outhouses. In the morning they were told to gather up the straw they had slept on and leave it outside to be burnt, so afraid were the locals that they might be carrying the plague.

Robin whined and grizzled. He had teeth coming through, but more than that he was distressed by the disappearance of his beloved companions. Alethea did her best to cheer him up by telling him about the beautiful house they were going to, and her little sisters, Lucy and Betty, who would make a pet of him and feed him sweetmeats. She told him he would have William's old hobby horse to ride and his greyhound Caesar to play with. If Caesar was not still living, she thought, a new dog was bound to have taken his place. Robin was too little to understand what she said, but he smiled at the words horse and dog. In truth her speech was designed to reassure Ellen and herself as much as him.

Alethea worried that her stepmother might make life difficult for them when they did eventually arrive. Frances would not look kindly on extra mouths to feed. She might even make them stay somewhere else for fear of the distemper. Alethea now hoped Frances had not had a boy child to consolidate her rule over all at Measham. She needed to convince her father to let Ellen be her companion and to keep Robin with her. She could not disappoint Ellen's expectations.

Every day Alethea promised herself that she would tell Ellen about her pregnancy, but each evening she found some excuse to postpone the disclosure. Meanwhile Samuel's baby lodged firmly in her belly, refusing to budge no matter how much they were jolted about on coach journeys over rough country roads.

On the fourth day they reached Northampton. As their coach drove in through the South Gate they saw the city walls were nothing more than rubble. The only other passenger, a resident of Northampton, explained that the King had ordered the walls and the castle torn down because of the town's former allegiance to Cromwell.

He was a corpulent, oily skinned man who panted slightly as he spoke. 'You ladies should get yourselves some fine shoes while you're here. We're famous for our shoemakers, you know. Dainty feet like yours should not be so roughly shod.' He grinned at Ellen. 'Perhaps, you might permit me to give you a tour of the city. We still have many fine buildings.' He rubbed his hands together and ran his tongue over a bulbous lower lip.

Alethea thanked him, but refused his kind offer, explaining that they needed to get the baby settled for the night.

'Don't you have friends or relations in Northampton?' he asked Ellen, who merely shook her head in reply.

They had stopped at an inn near the Sheep Market. Their companion helped them down out of the coach. The hand he offered Alethea was damp and soft to the touch, the fingernails clean and neatly pared. She realised then how long it was since she had been in genteel company. No wonder this fellow assumed he could be so familiar with them.

'Let me make enquiries of the innkeeper on your behalf,' he said and bustled off inside.

'He couldn't keep his eyes off my bubbies,' Ellen complained. 'If only Robin hadn't wanted feeding so often.'

Their fellow traveller quickly reappeared. 'It's fortunate for you I am here,' he told them. 'You would have been required to sleep in the stables had I not vouched for your good health.' Placing one hand on Ellen's elbow he steered them inside.

At the door to their room they bid their self-appointed saviour a firm farewell. But when they came downstairs for something to eat they found him ensconced in the bar, waiting for them.

'Doesn't *he* have any friends or relations?' Alethea muttered.

'Ladies, ladies, I have taken the liberty of ordering you some chicken pie and a jug of ale.' He spread out his arms, herding them towards a table. 'As a native of Northampton, I feel it is my duty to act as your host while you are here.' And before they could stop him he sat down beside them.

They passed a very disagreeable meal being quizzed by their benefactor, who went by the name of Montague, as to why they were travelling alone and where they were travelling to.

Finally, Alethea stood up. 'Thank you for your hospitality, Mr Montague, but we are tired after our journey and must go to bed.'

Montague chuckled. 'You go to bed by all means, my dear, and take the baby with you. Mrs Liddell and I can take a tour of the town. You needn't fear the cold.' He turned to Ellen placing one hand on her knee. 'I'll keep you warm.'

Ellen slapped his hand away. 'I'm a respectable widow, how dare you make so free with me?'

'A lusty widow more like. I saw you making eyes at me in the coach. Displaying those milky orbs just to tempt me with. And such a heavenly neck, it could drive a man mad.' Seizing Ellen round the shoulders Montague stuck his face into the curve of her shoulder.

With Robin sleeping in her lap, Ellen had only one hand free to push at her assailant with. Alethea leapt up in fury and grabbed Montague by the ears, pulling his head away from Ellen. In doing so she dislodged his wig which slipped forward over one eye. Montague shrieked in pain and lashed out at Alethea, who, standing behind him, had the advantage and was able to dodge his flailing hands whilst maintaining her grip on his ears. The baby woke in the tussle and began to whimper.

'Hey, I'll have no brawling here,' the innkeeper shouted.

Alethea pulled Montague to a standing position. Leaning over him, for she was a good head taller, she snarled in his ear, 'Get out of here, you old goat and don't come near us again or I'll have the constable on you. I am a woman of good family and my father will not look kindly on your insults.'

Montague pushed his wig back and rubbed his ears. 'Reputable ladies don't go gallivanting about the country unattended.'

Alethea shoved him in the back. 'Leave before you bring more trouble on yourself.'

Pulling on his coat, Montague turned to Ellen. 'I see you have quite the virago here as your protectress. I hope the minx has not enslaved you completely. You'd do well to find more pleasing company.' Thrusting his chin into the air he stamped off, his ears still glowing red.

'Lord, Alethea, I never knew you to be so fiery.' Ellen stared at Alethea with admiration as she tried to soothe her son.

'I wish I had a sword,' Alethea said, her heart drumming fast.

'What, would you be like one of those she-soldiers who follow their husbands into battle?'

'I could carry it off. Like the woman in the ballad.' Alethea sang: *'With musket on her shoulder, Her part she acted than, And everyone supposed, That she had been a man.'*

They both laughed. 'How much ale did that man feed us? He said it was only small beer, but it must've been stronger.' Ellen wiped her eyes. 'I think we're both a little giddy.'

'Vile creature.' Alethea shuddered. 'Are you all right?'

'I'm fine, thanks to you.' Ellen smiled at her.

Alethea surveyed the room. They were the only females in the place. She thought of the plaguey attacker Jack had rescued her from. 'Putting on men's apparel would make travelling a lot easier. We would be treated with more respect as men.'

'I don't think I'd make a convincing man,' Ellen said, lifting Robin onto her shoulder and rubbing his back. 'But you would. You could be my husband.'

'You're not the first to tell me I play a male part well.'

Alethea remembered Hunt and Darnley commending her performance of Ganymede. How foolish to have been insulted by fops like them. She hardly recognised the girl she had been then. What would they think of her at home? They would find her changed, no doubt. And there were more changes to come; changes she had yet to explain even to Ellen.

Alethea lay on her back, trying not to fidget in case she woke Ellen and Robin. She would be back at Measham Hall in only a couple more days now. Despite her worries, she ached to be home again. To wake in her own bed, with the green curtains and the gold embroidered birds. How often she had lain in bed on a summer's morning gazing at those birds and imagining that they were singing to her, just like her mother used to do.

She thought of all the times she had been woken by Betty and Lucy, impatient for her to play with them. Then she had let them climb into bed with her and the three of them would cuddle up together while she told them stories. She couldn't wait to lift her little sisters in her arms again, swinging them round until they shrieked with delight, their curls flying and their cheeks red as apples. They would always love her, no matter how she was disgraced. No matter what their parents told them.

When she thought of Samuel tears sprung up and stung her eyes. She was so hurt and bewildered by his treatment of her, she did not know what to make of it or how to judge him. Of course she could not expect him to forsake his wife, but he might at least have made some private farewell with her. She felt guilty for not telling him about the child they had conceived, and proud for not burdening him with the knowledge of it. Still, she would like to have witnessed his response; to know what he would have done. She was haunted by the fear that she would be punished for her transgressions by producing an idiot child or something horribly deformed. Her nurse had told her that base-born children were cursed with bad blood.

Sometimes she hoped to die in childbirth that she might be absolved of her sin. Then Ellen would get a message to Samuel and he would be overcome with grief and remorse for abandoning her so cruelly. He would realise how deeply he loved her and how foolish he had been to let her go. She would have to confide in Ellen first, though, in the next two days before they reached Measham, if she was going to claim she had been raped. What if Ellen refused to corroborate her story? What could she say then?

It was no good, she would never sleep. The church bell had only just struck midnight. She would go downstairs and ask for a glass of something strong that might make her drowsy.

Apart from the innkeeper the only person left downstairs was a young man who sat by the fire clasping a tankard of ale. He was staring into his cup despondently, but when he saw Alethea he looked up and smiled.

'Why, it is the brave Amazon.' He spoke warmly, without any trace of raillery.

He had a pimpled face and dark shadows under his eyes. His cheeks were clean-shaven, but his upper lip sported wisps of straw-coloured hair. He was clearly trying to cultivate a moustache with what little he had at his disposal. It was unfortunate the colour did not match his wig which was a rich brown.

'Why so downcast?' Alethea asked, sitting down on a nearby stool.

'My troubles are beyond your comprehension.' He sighed with an air of studied melancholy, leaning his head on his upturned palm.

'They cannot be so great as mine,' Alethea responded.

'What, don't tell me, you are a runaway lady jilted by her lover?'

Alethea flinched. 'I asked you first,' she said, primly rearranging her skirts about her knees.

The young man took a swig of ale and raised one eyebrow. 'I'll wager you five shillings my afflictions are more pressing.'

'I bet *you* five shillings I can guess the source of your afflictions.'

The young man blinked and wiped the sweat off his brow with a large handkerchief. 'Go on then.'

'You have lost your fortune gaming and now you must go cap in hand to your father to explain yourself.'

'Very good.' The man leant forward and offered her his hand. 'I bet you ten shillings you can't guess how much I have lost at gaming, to the nearest pound, you don't have to be exact.'

Alethea shook her head.

'Come on,' he stood up. 'What would you like to drink? A little Canary perhaps?'

Alethea tiptoed into their bedchamber with a lighted taper in one hand. She set it down beside the bed. Ellen opened her eyes and let out a cry of alarm. Alethea placed a restraining hand over her mouth and another against her shoulder. Ellen struggled furiously, but Alethea, being upright and able to lean all her weight against her friend, had the advantage.

'I mean you no harm,' Alethea said in a low voice. 'If you promise not to scream I will let you go.'

Ellen nodded, her eyes round with fear. 'We've no jewels and little money,' she said as soon as Alethea released her. 'Pity my poor innocent babe that lies beside me and leave us unharmed.'

Alethea felt simultaneously exhilarated by this new-found power and sorry for causing Ellen such distress. Robin began to cry, pulling himself up by the bedspread he clutched at his mother.

'It is only me.' Alethea pulled off her wig and hat.

'You wicked strumpet, you scared me half to death. What are you playing at?'

'You took me for a man, didn't you?' Alethea spun round beside the bed.

'Well of course I did, you're dressed up as one. Have you lost your wits?' Ellen cradled Robin in her arms, comforting him until he quietened down. 'Where did you get those clothes anyway?'

'I won them off an undergraduate from Cambridge who's staying here,' Alethea said proudly.

Ellen rubbed her eyes. 'I must be sleeping still, for I am dreaming.'

'No, no, you're quite awake. He won some small sums off me and then I bet him his spare suit of clothes he could not tell where or how I'd spent the last three months. I allowed him three guesses.'

'Did you get a sword into the bargain?'

'No, alas, he'd already pawned that.'

'I was only joking when I said you could be my husband.'

'We have another two coach journeys to undertake and lodgings to secure. We'll be safer if people think I'm a man.' Alethea pinched Robin's chin. 'So my little man, how would you like me as a father?' He gazed at her uneasily, surprised by her low voice, his mouth beginning to quiver.

Ellen sighed. 'I hope this undergraduate of yours was healthy.' She picked up the wig, sniffing it cautiously.

'Profligacy is his only disease,' Alethea told her.

'Who knows what you might catch from those then.' Ellen pointed at Alethea's breeches in alarm.

'Cards and dice aren't catching, I think those are his only vices.' Alethea gave a short laugh.

'Well I hope you enjoy playing the man, I for one need some more sleep.' And placing Robin down in the middle of the bed, Ellen rolled over onto her side.

By the following evening they had got to the outskirts of Leicester. They stopped at an inn, just off the London Road in Stoneygate. The landlady, a small wiry woman with anxious eyes, looked them up and down.

'Are ya from London?' she asked.

'No, from Epping,' Alethea answered. They had grown accustomed to this question.

'Have ya business in Leicester?' the landlady continued. 'They only opened gates to travellers a couple of week ago. No one from London were allowed to stay here before September were over.'

'We're travelling home to Derbyshire,' Alethea explained.

'Well,' said the landlady. 'I've a nice big room upstairs at back y'can have. Ya might sit in parlour while it's aired; chamber 'asn't been used since the Spring.'

'I'm so tired I could sleep anywhere,' Ellen said, looking out at the rain and wind battering against the windows.

''Ark at it.' The landlady shook her head. 'It's fairly puthering down. All right then, I'll show ya the way. Sarah, fetch some clean linen will ya,' she called to a serving girl.

Once the fire had been lit and the bed made up, their room was not so bad. It was as spacious as the landlady had suggested, with a chest for their belongings and two chairs. The canopy over the bed was a little dusty and the air somewhat damp, but compared to some of the places they had recently slept in it was quite palatial.

Alethea strode up and down with barely contained delight. 'They took me for a man! Did you see? They didn't so much as change their countenances when I spoke to them.'

'They were too busy looking for signs of ill health to worry about the rest of your appearance.' Ellen sat down by the fire to nurse Robin. 'Maybe they think all men from the south are effeminate.' She looked up at Alethea. 'You need to watch how you stand and lower your voice or you'll give yourself away.'

'Jack once said that disguise is all in the costume, wear it right and people won't see beyond it. They will see you as they think you ought to be, not as you really are. Perhaps they think I'm a university man; a

171

delicate and scholarly youth who spends his days shut up in his study surrounded by dusty old books.'

'I don't think they gave you that much thought. I'd say having me and Robin with you did as much to aid your disguise. They see you have a wife and babe and believe you must be a man.'

'Maybe.' Alethea went to the window. 'I reckon it is but one day's ride to Measham Hall from here.' She was filled with nervous excitement at being so close to home. If it hadn't been growing dark she would have commandeered a horse and set off at once, ahead of Ellen and Robin. 'I hope William is there.'

'Perhaps you could send word to your father, to let him know that we are near.'

'Of course.' Alethea danced back and forwards. 'Then he'll send the carriage for us. I hope he won't be aggrieved that I stayed away so long, but there was no way I could have come sooner with so much of the country closed off.'

Ellen smiled. 'You'll have to put your bodice and skirts back on to go home in.'

But Alethea was already dashing off downstairs. 'I'll ask the landlady about sending a messenger,' she called back.

The landlady was gossiping with the serving girl. They fell silent when Alethea entered the room, putting down the tankards they were polishing. 'Everything all right, sir?'

'Yes, fine, thank you,' Alethea said gruffly, slowing her walk down to a wide-gaited stride. 'I was wondering if there might be someone, a stable boy perhaps, who might take a message for me.'

'A message?' The landlady looked doubtful. 'How far?'

'Have you heard of Measham Hall? The Hawthornes of Measham?'

'Measham Hall.' The landlady paused as though the name were familiar to her and then turned to Sarah. 'Is it Measham Hall that's all shut up?'

The girl shrugged. 'I never heard of it.'

'Stop a minute.' The landlady went over to the cellar door. 'Davey,' she called.

A minute later a man appeared carrying a barrel of beer. He set it down with a grunt.

'Gisit 'ere,' she said, taking it from him and rolling it behind the bar. He mopped his brow with his handkerchief while his wife poured him a cup of ale. 'You've 'ad dealings with steward, 'aven't ya? Over Measham way?' she asked him.

'Oh ah,' he said. 'Mister Crewe, that's right. He's staying in Leicester now. I knows his cousin Andrew, he's a brewer, you know.'

Alethea had jumped at the name of their steward, Crewe. 'And Measham Hall?'

'Ah, that were a terrible business, you know.' Davey sat down on a stool and took a long slow drink.

'D'ya want owt?' The landlady asked Alethea.

She shook her head. 'What terrible business?' Her breath had caught in her chest and she had to force herself to breathe.

Davey set his tankard down. 'Whole family carried off by pestilence. Not often it takes gentry that way, usually it's the poorer folk as gets taken. They say it were Sir Nicholas Hawthorne brought it into the house, you know. He'd been down to London to fetch his daughter back – a wayward girl, she run off from the family she were staying with.'

'Nay, she didn't run away, she were taken by distemper,' his wife corrected him. 'It were 'er clothes, as were sent home, that brought in the pestilence. Andrew's wife Hetty told us.'

She nodded at Alethea, but she could hardly follow what they were saying; they must have been talking of some other family, some other Hawthornes, or else they had got the name wrong.

'And how could Hetty know that?' the landlord said incredulously.

'Andrew heard it from Mister Crewe; it were a trunk for the Hawthornes sent on from Lord, oh who worrit now?'

'Calverton?' Alethea said, hoping they would contradict her. She felt as though she was drowning under the torrent of their words.

'Aye, that's right, Lord Calverton. How did ya know that?' The landlady looked at Alethea with surprise. 'Ar'ya all right, sir? Ya look frit ta death yaself.'

Alethea had sunk down onto a stool. She swallowed the rising nausea that threatened to engulf her. 'I am acquainted with the Hawthornes,' she managed hoarsely. 'Are you quite sure they all fell sick?'

'All dead, but the eldest son,' Davey answered. 'The house is shut up and waits his return from overseas, but when that might be no one knows. The steward still keeps an eye on the place, makes sure it don't fall derelict, you know, but there's no servants there to maintain it.'

'They're all too frit to stay there. They say it's haunted.'

'Tush, woman, don't talk daft, it's lack of money, not ghosts, as keeps them away. Why would they work for free with no surety the son will ever come back to pay them their wages?'

Wishing the pair a curt good evening, Alethea made her way up to her room with difficulty, groping for the stair rail like a blind woman. All gone? It could not be true. That foolish couple must have made some mistake; they were wrong about her fate, they must be wrong about the rest as well. William was overseas they said. What did that mean? Perhaps he had never made it back to England at all.

She had assumed her family were beyond the plague's grasp, but it seemed it had travelled all over in search of victims. It must have spared some of them. Samuel's wife had survived when he thought her taken. Then she remembered Lord Calverton telling her that children were the most vulnerable to the disease. Let her little sisters have been spared, she begged God, leave them on this earth a while longer.

As soon as she closed the chamber door behind her Alethea collapsed onto the floor. She bit down on her sleeve to stop herself from screaming; drawing her knees into her chest as great heaving cries tore through her body. She slapped the floorboards with one hand, banging her forehead on the ground. It was not true, it could not be true. Had her family perished while she was off playing the whore with a band of malcontents?

Setting a startled Robin down on the floor, Ellen crouched over her, stroking her hair and begging her to explain this transformation. She had left the room in such high spirits, to return so distraught. Alethea explained as well as she could, her mind half-frantic with despair.

When she was calm enough, Ellen told her she would go and talk to the landlord herself. Perhaps, they both hoped, the story had been exaggerated, or erroneously told. Alethea lay on the bed, too astounded to move, waiting for Ellen to return.

Ellen might have been gone for hours or only for minutes, when she reappeared carrying a tray with a glass and two bottles on it. 'Sarah is minding Robin for me.' She set the tray down on a chair beside the bed. 'I have a bottle of very fine cordial water here for you, and another of wine. We must mix the two together to revive your spirits.' She set about pouring the drinks carefully into the glass and mixing them with a spoon.

Alethea watched her dully. She could not bear to question Ellen and the longer she delayed, the more she feared her answer.

'I want you to drink this before we talk.' Ellen sat down on the bed beside her, speaking to Alethea as though she was a young child.

Alethea took a sip of the sickly brown liquid. It smelt of nutmegs, cloves and old wine.

'Shall we say the Lord's Prayer together?' Ellen asked.

Alethea could hardly speak for weeping, but she clung to those familiar words like a drowning man to a raft.

'Your parents and their little girls, they are free of all suffering and sorrow now.'

'But I promised Lucy I would bring her a cap with feathers, and Betty a toy-baby back from London. They must have been waiting for me and I never so much as wrote to tell them I hadn't forgotten them.'

'They knew you loved them.' Ellen stroked Alethea's cheek. 'Why, they may be smiling down on you now as we speak, exhorting you to be strong in the face of these trials. To seek comfort in our beloved Lord Jesus, who is with us in all our sufferings. Keep him close now, Alethea, let him be your shield of faith, for the Devil is always nearby when we're at our weakest.'

Alethea looked away from Ellen's earnest gaze. 'I never shall see Father's face again, nor make him proud of me. Perhaps it is better this way, for I only come home to bring disgrace to his door.'

'What do you mean, lamb?'

'I have already fallen in sin.' Alethea stared down at her belly. 'I am got with child.'

Ellen was silent for a moment. She poured herself a glass of wine and swallowed two large mouthfuls before replying. 'I should have noticed. How far gone are you?'

'Not more than a couple of months.'

'Was it Jack? Is he the father?'

So many thoughts swirled around Alethea's head she could not locate the best answer.

Ellen gripped her hand. 'Whoever he is he must marry you. Your father's not here now to disapprove of the match and a loving husband can be better than a wealthy one.' Ellen had clearly decided that Jack must be the father.

'Please don't press me on this. There is no chance of marriage. I must hide this baby from the world, no one must know of it.' Alethea could hear her voice rising unsteadily; it sounded alien to her.

Ellen patted her shoulder. 'All right, darling, all right, we'll speak no more of it for now.'

When at last she slept, Alethea dreamt she was chasing her little sisters across the lawns at Measham Hall. Betty still wore leading strings, they trailed on the ground behind her. Lucy had her best blue satin on, she had gathered her skirts up in her fists, her red stockinged legs speeding her away. However fast Alethea ran they were always ahead of her, looking over their shoulders and laughing. She willed her legs to move faster, propelling herself forward with her arms. She could almost touch Lucy's back, almost reach out and tug Betty's hair. Her heart ached and the breath burnt her lungs. She bent over, gasping for air. When she looked up, they had gone.

'Here is some bread and butter for you and nice plain biscuit-cakes with caraway seeds.'

Alethea opened her eyes to see Ellen hovering over her with a plate in one hand and a cup of ale in the other.

'You must drink something at least,' Ellen urged.

She was surprised to feel hungry. Perhaps it was the baby in her belly that needed feeding, but she ate all the bread and drank down the ale. 'What time is it?' she asked, looking out of the window. The shutters were open and the autumn sun shone brightly between banks of cloud.

'It's after midday,' Ellen said, running to retrieve Robin who was crawling towards the fireplace. She sat him on her knee and fed him crumbs of cake to placate him.

'We must go to Measham Hall, to see if it is true, about my family,' Alethea said.

'I did question them thoroughly. I don't believe they are mistaken. They know your steward, a man named Crewe?'

Alethea nodded.

'The thing is...' Ellen patted Robin's back as he coughed on a bit of cake. 'They, Mr and Mrs Clarke, took note of your distress and of how you knew the Hawthornes and the Calvertons, and what with you being dressed as a man and all, they've come to the conclusion that you are the missing heir.' When Alethea stared at her blankly Ellen continued. 'They think that you are your brother, William.'

'Didn't you correct them?'

'How could I?' Ellen said uncomfortably. 'They believe Alethea is dead. How could I tell them that you're not a man, but a dead girl come back to life? They would think us both mad.'

Alethea rolled out of bed placing her feet on the floor. She pressed her toes against the wooden boards. Her feet, white and waxy, seemed a long way from her body. They looked as though they belonged to someone else. She was beginning to think that she was indeed dead and that this was purgatory. What should she do to prove herself worthy of heaven? To gain entrance to where her sisters and her parents must surely be? She half-expected her stepmother to appear before her, for if she was in purgatory Frances must be also. Or would she be in the other place? Where did Protestant souls go? Frances was not entirely wicked, but she was not virtuous either.

'William must come home soon,' she said, as much to convince herself as Ellen.

'If he was going to return surely he would have done so by now,' Ellen said quietly.

'Crewe will remember me. Though he was always Frances' man, never had much liking for me or William.' Alethea leant on the windowsill. She felt overcome with a terrible weariness. 'I'm surprised Uncle Percy hasn't moved into Measham Hall. He has always had his eyes on the house and this is just the excuse he needs to take over Measham in William's absence.'

She remembered Uncle Percy's lectures on the importance of chastity. Maidenhead, the most valuable jewel a woman possessed, one that must be guarded with her life. A ruined woman was a blight on the family name, contaminating all in her sphere with her filthiness. Once a woman had parted with her virtue only death could rid her of her shame.

'Your uncle would not turn you out,' Ellen said.

'You don't know my Uncle Percy, he will be only too eager to dispatch me to a convent to join my cousin Mary. In fact, when he discovers my condition he will probably send me to the Carmelites so that I can be hidden away from the world entirely.'

Ellen looked over at the wig and hat she had placed on top of Alethea's folded clothes. 'What if you play along with being William? Just until your brother comes back? He'd be glad wouldn't he, if you looked after the place for him, stopped your uncle getting his hands on it?'

Alethea did not know whether to laugh or cry. It was a lunatic proposition. And yet. Even if Crewe vouched for her, she would be at the mercy of her uncle. Measham Hall was settled on the next male Hawthorne to preserve the family name. As Alethea she had no claim to it, but as William she could live there quite safely. Uncle Percy would cast Ellen and Robin out on the mercy of the parish, but as William, she could honour her promise to Ellen and shelter them both.

Drops of rain began to chase each other across the panes of glass. 'But I don't know how to run a household and I've no money to pay the servants,' she said.

'You can leave that to the steward, that's what they're there for isn't it, to bring in the money?' Ellen placed Robin in the middle of the bed and tickled his belly. 'You told me people always commented on how alike you and William are; "peas in a pod" you said.'

'But that was when we were both children.'

'And how long has William been away? People will remember him as a boy, not a man.' Ellen sighed. 'If only Jack was here. He'd think this was a great plan, and he'd know just how to pull it off.'

Alethea nodded in agreement. The words of the ballad she had sung only a couple of days ago echoed round her head.

> She found by several passages,
> Herself to be with child,
>
> . . .
>
> Yet secretly she kept it,
> As long as ever she could,
> Till such time a Commander,
> Her belly did behold.
> What is the reason, Tom, quoth he,
> That you are grown so fat.
> 'Tis strong beer and tobacco, sir,
> Which is the cause of that.

Afraid of encountering Crewe in broad daylight where he would be sure to see through her disguise, Alethea persuaded Ellen to go in place of William as his servant, saying he was suffering from a fever he had contracted in Italy. Fear of infection should put Crewe off requesting a meeting, but if he did insist, Alethea could close the shutters and partially conceal herself beneath the bedclothes.

She coached Ellen as well as she could for her encounter with Crewe, giving her as thorough a description of William's character and life as she could think of. Still she was sick with anxiety as she waited for Ellen to return. She prayed Crewe would find Ellen convincing and that he would not have any prior intelligence from William that would expose their fraud. Most of all she prayed the landlord had been mistaken, that she had not become an orphan.

Robin soon grew weary of Alethea's distracted mood and cried for his mother. It struck her that they would have to practice their forgery on Robin too or else he might give them away. She nearly despaired then that they could ever carry off such an audacious scheme. At any moment Alethea expected the parish constable to come knocking at the door, but at last she heard Ellen's swift steps outside their room.

Ellen flung open the door with a triumphant look on her face. 'He believed me,' she said with amazement. 'He eyed me up and down like a saucy knave, but he believed my whole tale.' Ellen was clearly exhilarated by her adventure.

'And my father, my sisters, did he confirm…?'

Ellen's face fell. 'I'm so sorry.' She wrung her hands. 'It's true, they have all departed this world, God rest their souls.'

Alethea nodded and wiped away her tears. Too much was at stake for her to give herself up to grief. She had to become a man of action, a man who could take over and manage her father's estate.

'When can we move into Measham Hall?' she asked.

'Crewe said he'll let us know when the house is ready to receive us. It was well fumigated with sulphur before being shut up, but has fallen into disrepair and may take a while to prepare for you.'

'But we do not mind if the house is a mess,' Alethea said impatiently. 'God's wounds, imagine if he knew we'd been living in a forest.'

'He was very firm on the matter and I did not like to push him.'

'And what of my uncle, did Crewe mention him?'

'He said your uncle is preoccupied with some dispute with his neighbours. It seems no one wants to enter the house. Though Crewe appeared glad enough to go back to his position at Measham.'

'You cannot sit like that,' Ellen spoke sharply. 'You must spread out your legs, take up more room. That's it.' She nodded as Alethea adjusted her position. 'Now, place one hand on your thigh, good. Don't fiddle with your neck like that, you must scratch yourself openly, with big movements. It's one thing to play at being a man in front of strangers, it's another with people that know you.'

A week had passed and still Crewe had not sent for them. Alethea, Ellen and Robin were all growing tetchy. She swaggered about the chamber, trying to imagine herself as her brother.

'Keep your coat unbuttoned.' Ellen watched her, arms akimbo. 'Otherwise it draws attention to your waist. You'll have to wear gloves too, your hands are too dainty for a man. Come over here.' She beckoned impatiently.

Alethea stood still while Ellen stuck another pin into her jacket. The undergraduate was a skinny youth, even so his jacket hung unconvincingly large on Alethea; Ellen was going to have to take it in at the shoulders.

'I still think I should wear my upper bodies. How will I keep my back straight without support?' Alethea looked wistfully at the whaleboned bodice discarded on the floor. 'I'm like a tortoise without his shell, all soft and exposed.'

'Have you ever seen a man in a pair of stays?' Ellen tutted. 'It's just as well your breasts are small. We need only bind them with linen.' She moved Alethea round as she adjusted her clothing. 'We'll keep the breeches and jacket loose enough to hide your belly as it grows.'

'What will I do about the child?' Alethea said, holding out her arms. She could not imagine herself as a mother; could not really believe she was going to produce an actual, living child. It seemed too improbable, too miraculous a thing.

'I've been thinking about that. If we're successful in this venture, well, then you can pass your baby off as mine.'

'Would you do that for me, Ellen? Claim my child as yours?'

'Didn't Samuel always say we should think of children as the offspring of the whole community, not just one family? And you've been like a second mother to Robin.' Ellen smiled bravely. 'I don't intend to be reconciled with my husband or to find another, so who's to question how I got this child, or be offended by it?'

Alethea grasped her friend's hands. 'And I will never part ways with you, but always support you. Measham shall be your home as much as it is mine.'

'We can't be sure Measham will be home to either of us yet,' Ellen reminded her.

At last Ellen was satisfied. 'You'll pass as a youth who has lost weight due to sickness so his clothes no longer fit him. We can dust your face with Cyprus powder to make you look pale.'

'You must cut off my hair too, so the wig sits properly.'

'Are you sure? You have such pretty hair.' Ellen looked at her sadly. 'We could just curl it in the style of a man's.'

'A periwig will complete the picture.' Alethea did not add that this extra layer of disguise would also increase her confidence in playing her part. 'We can sell my hair to a wig maker and get something back for it,' she said more cheerfully than she felt.

When it came to it Alethea was glad to be rid of her hair. She had thought of cutting it as an act of penance for her transgressions, but it felt more like a liberation than a punishment. Samuel had been fond of her hair and liked to coil it round his hands as they lay together. She told herself she would cut him out of her mind with as much ease as the thick brown locks fell from her head. Now he will not know me, she thought. I will create myself anew and forget the simple girl I used to be.

✦ Chapter Seventeen ✦

The ancient coach creaked and heaved like a boat on choppy waters. They sat in silence, Ellen clasping Robin tightly in her lap, afraid they would end up in a ditch. The interior of the hired carriage smelt of sweat and stale hair powder. Alethea swallowed down the nausea rising in her throat and pushed up the blind to look out through the window. She watched eagerly for the sight of something familiar. If she could make it through the first few hours without giving herself away, maybe she would be able to carry off the whole lunatic enterprise. She just needed to establish her claim on the house; to be received as its master. And then who would dare question her? Who would admit to being so soft they mistook a sister for her brother? Not a proud man like Crewe, that was for sure.

The plodding horses lugged the coach around a bend in the road and there was the chestnut tree that stood on the hill behind her home, reaching its naked branches up into the darkening sky like a suppliant in pagan times. With another jolting turn she could make out the walls of Measham Hall, as square and solid as they had ever been. Her heart began to race and her mouth grew dry. She felt like a moth fluttering about a flame; no matter the increasing heat, the light dazzled, drawing her in, throwing all other paths into obscurity, so there was only this, to be home once more.

'You can manage this.' Ellen turned and grasped her hand. 'You are William Hawthorne and this is your birthright.'

Alethea nodded. She had saved some of her hair to use as a moustache, gluing a few strands to her upper lip with mastic. It itched horribly, but she did not dare scratch it.

'Act like you own the place. Remember, big gestures, feet wide. Boldness is all.'

'And to think, you've never even been to the theatre.' Alethea managed a sickly smile.

'But one of these days, Master Hawthorne, you are going to take me.'

'That's right, I will.' Alethea clenched her fists, her nails digging into her damp palms. She pulled on her leather gloves. 'I am the master of Measham Hall,' she intoned, remembering William when they had first returned to this house thirteen years before, marching through the rooms, his cloak thrown back over his shoulders, waving his wooden sword in the air. Laying claim to every broken pane of glass, to every smashed tile and scratched wooden panel.

Crewe must have heard the coach and horses on the drive; he was standing on the front step holding a lantern. Alethea had deliberately timed their journey so they would arrive as the light was fading. She could hear the driver climbing down from his box. The coach tilted and groaned. The horses snorted, shaking their harnesses. The driver pulled open her door. She could see the cook and her father's footman standing behind Crewe, lighted tapers in their hands. She thought she might faint.

'Help us out then.' Ellen shoved her in the ribs.

Alethea climbed down, then offered a hand up to Ellen, grateful for the distraction. She tried lifting Robin from Ellen's arms.

'Don't overtask yourself, sir,' Ellen said loudly. 'Remember your physician advised bed rest.'

'Welcome home, Sir William.' Crewe came forward and gave a low bow.

He was not as wizened as Alethea had remembered, but even the glow of the lantern failed to bring any warmth to his pallid skin. His hooded eyes carefully avoided Alethea's. Crewe had always known his place, that at least was to her advantage.

'Can I offer you some assistance, sir?' He held out his arm.

Alethea waved him on imperiously. Speaking from low in her chest, keeping her voice as gruff as she could manage, she told him to 'Lead the way.' She wanted Crewe to walk ahead of her, but instead he stood close by her side holding up his lantern to guide her in. From beneath his lowered lids, she could feel him watching her. She pulled her hat down over her brow.

As they reached the steps, a tall, lean-fleshed dog pushed his way between the servants' legs. With two bounds he was at Alethea's feet. 'Caesar!' She knelt down and stroked his soft ears, as overjoyed to see him as he was her. Noting the white hairs on his muzzle and the stiffness in his back legs, she pressed her nose to his and he licked away the tear that slid from her eye. Ellen gave her foot a surreptitious kick. Recollecting herself Alethea rubbed the old dog roughly in the way her brother used to do. He trembled and pressed himself against her side with slavish devotion.

'A dog does not forget his master,' Ellen declared.

'No indeed, Mistress Liddell' Crewe agreed. 'I have cared for Caesar myself in your absence, sir. He can still chase a stag or a hare, though he is not as fast as he used to be.'

'Master Hawthorne's not well enough to go hunting,' Ellen said quickly.

Alethea rose and nodded at the servants who parted before her, their heads respectfully bowed. She wanted to express her gratitude to them for their loyalty but was afraid her voice would break.

'You will remember Mr Palmes the footman and Adam Tickell the cook,' Crewe was saying behind her. 'The serving boy here is Miles; one of the gardeners has also promised his services, sir. I will await your instructions before hiring any more.'

She swallowed hard and pushed back her shoulders, stepping into the doorway. She was almost over the threshold. Planting her feet firmly apart, she looked about her. 'I am indebted to you all for your service to my family. I have dreamt of your pies, Mr Tickell, even the French cannot make puff pastry to rival yours. And their footmen of course are not a match for Mr Palmes.'

The men laughed and murmured their thanks. Alethea stepped into the hallway, the great staircase rising up before her. How many times had she trailed her hand against the wooden posts, feeling for the reassuring comfort of the smooth round balusters against her palm? How many times had she sat on the stairs tracing the outline of the flowers carved into the brackets, while waiting for her brother or her mother?

The wainscot that lined the walls was so familiar she felt as though she had stepped back into her own past. She half-expected her father to come marching out to greet her, the little girls trotting at his heels, giggling and chattering. But the old house was silent and still.

Here to her left was the court cupboard she had once thought so stately and grand, now it looked worn and old-fashioned. She could feel the coldness of the flagstones seeping through her boot soles. The rush matting must have been burnt and no one had thought to replace it. The air was thick with the greasy smell of tallow candles. Clearly her return did not merit beeswax. How was she to raise the money for such things? How would she pay the servants' wages? The care of Measham Hall rested on her alone now. This new burden weighed so heavily on her already frayed nerves she thought they might snap. It was only having to play the part of a man that kept her upright.

'May I offer my condolences, sir, for the loss of your family?' Crewe was at her elbow again.

'Have you a bedchamber ready for me?' she asked.

'I have two rooms prepared, your old room and your father's. I was not sure which you would prefer.'

Alethea paused; her father's room was of course the best in the house. Facing south it overlooked the gardens to the rear. It was not a room she had entered much, but she remembered it always being full of sunlight.

'Now I am master of the house, I suppose I should inhabit the master's chamber,' she said, making for the stairs. 'And Mrs Liddell, you have a room for her?'

'Of course, sir. I thought perhaps the small chamber adjacent to your own.'

Crewe did suspect then, as Alethea had thought he would, that Ellen was William's mistress. She had made the correct choice too, for he had clearly assumed she would want her father's old room. A fire was burning in the hearth and the chamber smelt sweetly of rose-water and cloves. Alethea was glad to see that the hangings over the bed and the tapestries on the walls had not been quietly sold off. Perhaps Crewe was more trustworthy than she had given him credit for.

'Sir,' Crewe murmured close to Alethea's ear. 'There is a certain gentleman I thought you might be eager to converse with.' He lowered his voice still further. 'A gentleman of the cloth, sir.'

Of course, Crewe was intimate with the family's religion, he would assume William wanted to see a priest. No doubt he thought William had much to confess. Alethea had noticed him looking quizzically at Robin, who sat perched on his mother's hip.

'That can wait, Crewe,' Alethea said brusquely.

'Mr Hawthorne is fatigued by his journey, I'll prepare him for bed,' Ellen said.

Crewe looked around the room as though missing something. 'Where is that boy? Has he not brought up the master's trunk?' he said with annoyance.

'All my belongings were lost at sea,' Alethea said. 'We have only Mrs Liddell's bag.'

'I am sorry to hear that, sir.' Crewe sounded sorry indeed. Perhaps he had been hoping William had a chest full of gold for him. 'Will you be wanting any supper, sir?'

'Please send some up, Mrs Liddell and I will dine in my chamber.' Alethea stood with her back to him, warming her hands before the fire.

'Well, I hardly know you myself,' Ellen said as soon as Crewe had left the room. 'I feel as though I should bow my head and curtsy to you.'

'They would suspect me if I didn't act the master.' Alethea turned to her. 'But I hope you'll never forget my love and friendship for you.'

'Not so long as you remember it.' Ellen gazed about her. 'Only it's strange to enter this world that's so different from what I'm used to.'

She paused. 'We've lived so long as equals, perhaps it's better if I think of you as William Hawthorne, my master. Then I won't forget myself.'

'There's no need for that when we're alone,' Alethea said, saddened by her words.

Ellen stroked the carved poster of the bed and its velvet curtains. 'I've never seen a bed so grand as this, nor a room so beautiful. Come, Robin, let's see where we are sleeping.' Alethea was relieved to see her looking cheerful again.

When Ellen had gone Alethea went into her father's closet. She had never been permitted inside this, his private chamber, before. She felt a mixture of curiosity and apprehension. She was trespassing on forbidden ground, only it was hers now, for the time being at least.

It was a small room panelled with green painted wood. Beneath the narrow window stood a table covered by a rich red turkey carpet. It was colder in here, the corner fireplace had not been lit. She set her candlestick on the table. There were few books: a Bible, a Book of Hours she recognised as her mother's, and the obligatory copy of *Eikon Basilike*, all bound in leather and stamped with the demi lion of the Hawthorne family, along with a small pile of almanacs. Her father was not much given to reading. She would place her book of Machiavelli here and one day she would get it bound in matching leather and stamped with their crest. Her first addition to her father's modest library.

A wooden press stood to one side of the table, a small key in the lock. Perhaps in here she might find some clue as to William's whereabouts. It was lined with shelves, all neatly arranged with bottles of ink, quills, sealing wax, ribbons and parchment. No letters, though, no personal papers at all. She wondered whether Crewe had removed them. And then she saw the little statue of the Virgin Mary her mother had given her. She picked it up off the shelf and it lay in the palm of her hand, fitting perfectly just as it had always done. Had it been one of a pair? She did not think so. Her mother had only ever referred to that one, given to her by her grandmother. How then had it come to be here? Her father must have taken it from her trunk. Had he placed it here in memory of her, or of her mother? Or simply to pray to? She hoped he might have felt some attachment to it on her account.

Alethea had been brought up to revere her father; to look up to him with gratitude and obedience, never to question his decisions. He in return had always shown concern for her welfare. She knew that sometimes her behaviour amused him and sometimes it exasperated him. Whatever Barbara might have thought, Alethea was not his favourite child. She was important as a representative of the Hawthorne family and he probably loved her because she was his, but beyond that she was not of great interest to him.

Unlike his youngest daughters he had seen little of Alethea when she was small, spending the first five years of her life exiled in France. After his return, when he was not out hunting or overseeing the estate, he would often shut himself up in this closet. He was given to fits of black choler, brooding and sullen he would turn on anyone who dared approach him.

After his initial rejoicing at the restoration of the King, Nicholas Hawthorne had become bitterly disappointed. His loyalty and sufferings seemed to have gone unnoticed, while men who had fought against the King were promoted in the new parliament. Nicholas could not reconcile himself to the depredations that had been made on his land and home. The acres he had lost and could not recover.

Despite this there were times, especially when he had had a good day's hunting, when he could smile on his family, when he would call on Alethea to sing to him and her sisters to dance. On days like that Alethea had felt that all was right with the world; the spheres were in their correct places and order was restored.

She wished she could discuss the estate with her father now, learn of his plans for it and obtain his advice. Although he had never valued her as he did his son, or cherished her as he did his little girls, of all his children Alethea was the one who most resembled him. She made a vow in the memory of her father that she would do everything in her power to make Measham Hall as great as it had been before he went to war. To turn it back into the home of his memories. The place he had spent her childhood longing for.

Chapter Eighteen

Alethea passed the next few days confined mostly to her bedchamber with the curtains closed against the daylight. Palmes delivered her meals to her there and Crewe came up to discuss the estate with her. She spoke as little as possible and did not permit either of them to come too close. A pair of spectacles hung from ribbons around Crewe's neck, but to her relief he was never so ill-mannered as to scrutinise her through them.

As she grew more confident at playing her brother, she ventured out of her chamber more frequently. She hated to be cooped up in near-permanent darkness. The house was quiet and sombre with half the rooms shut up and most of the inhabitants gone. Roaming through them, Alethea felt she was the only ghost haunting Measham.

Unlike William's room, which was exactly as she remembered it, her old bedroom lay shrouded in dust. All the hangings had been taken down and her possessions removed. She was afraid Frances might have sold or destroyed them, but Crewe told her they had been placed in a chest in the attic, perhaps by her father, he could not recall. Crewe assumed William wanted them as mementoes of his sister and Alethea did in a strange way need these reminders of her former self.

She went through all her old trinkets with a mixture of amusement and disdain. The books and scraps of writing brought her the most comfort. The fans, ribbons and pendants that had been her treasure as a girl struck her now as vain fripperies, though Ellen exclaimed over them with delight for she had never owned such things. Alethea gave them all to her, along with a half-finished piece of needlework which Ellen received with less enthusiasm.

Uncovering her lute and sheets of music filled Alethea with joy, until she recollected that she could not play it within the hearing of the servants because William had never cared for the instrument. Nor, she realised, could she sing, for though she could lower her speaking voice she could not sing as a man. In her current state of mourning Alethea did not think this mattered. She did not believe she would ever want to sing again.

William had loved to dance and although Alethea felt little inclination for dancing, she promised Ellen that once her finances were more secure she would hire musicians to play for them and a dancing teacher for Ellen. Ellen's elation made Alethea glad she had suggested it. She could not expect Ellen to share her grief and wanted her friend to be happy at Measham. Besides, she could only be William with Ellen's assistance.

'Was there another chest, one sent from the Calvertons?' Alethea asked Crewe as indifferently as she could manage.

'There was, sir, but Lady Frances ordered it burnt on arrival for fear of contamination.' Crewe remained bent over the papers on his desk, one hand holding his spectacles in place.

And yet her father had managed to remove the Madonna statue. 'But they got sick anyway,' she said.

'God rest their souls.' Crewe looked up and his spectacles slid off his nose, dangling from one ear by a greasy ribbon. He squinted at Alethea. 'I suspect it was your stepmother's nurse who brought the disease into the house. She came to help with Lady Frances's lying-in, but soon became ill, followed by my mistress and the baby, then the little girls and finally your father. I believe he was carried away by grief at so much loss.'

'Not of the plague?'

'No, his illness was different. The physician said his heart stopped.' Crewe was silent for a moment, then continued pointedly. 'I was with your father at the end. He sent all the servants away to safeguard their health, but I refused to leave him. I was able to fetch a priest, so he received absolution.'

'Your loyalty is commendable, Crewe, I'm sure you were a comfort to him.' Alethea could not afford to dwell on thoughts of her father's death.

She was about to turn away when it occurred to her to ask about the baby. She had been so dazed by bereavement she had never enquired about it.

'It was a boy, sir, named Charles.'

'After the King?'

'I believe so, sir.'

Alethea shook her head. 'What a strange act of Providence. The son they had prayed so long for was the instrument of their demise, if indeed it was his nurse that introduced the plague.'

'The designs of the Almighty are beyond the comprehension of man.' Crewe turned back to his book-keeping.

'Indeed, Crewe, that they are.'

'Crewe showed real devotion to my father,' Alethea told Ellen that evening as they sat in her chamber eating their supper.

'If you believe him,' Ellen said. 'There are no witnesses to his story.' Ellen, who was usually inclined to think the best of everyone, had taken against Crewe.

'I thought it was Frances whom Crewe was loyal to,' Alethea continued, not really listening. 'But Father would have chosen his steward. And Crewe is Catholic, I'd forgotten that.' She speared a hard-boiled egg with her knife and several capers along with a slice of preserved orange slid off it onto her lap.

Ellen looked at her disapprovingly. 'You don't have to eat like a peasant just because you're being a man.' She took a dainty bite out of a Shrewsbury cake. 'It can't have been easy for your stepmother, coming into this household as a young woman.'

Ellen shook her head at the tapestry that covered the wall opposite. It had belonged to Alethea's grandparents. There was the Virgin Mary seated on a throne and surrounded by angels, a crown on her head and the infant Jesus at her breast. Alethea supposed Ellen thought it idolatrous.

'Why not?' She spooned a little of the foam off the top of the sack posset Tickell insisted on making for her. The thick yellow concoction of eggs, cream and wine turned her stomach, but she did not want to disappoint him.

'I'll finish that for you, I need to grow plumper.' Ellen patted her belly. 'I don't suppose you or William were too happy to have Frances as your mother, were you?'

'I suppose not.' Alethea had not considered this before.

Frances was twenty-one when she married their father. She had come into a stranger's house with only her maid for a friend. Their own mother had died less than a year before and both had been dismayed by their father's hasty remarriage. There had been scant acknowledgement of charity or duty on either side, let alone familial affection. Frances had arrived determined to shape the household to her will, with no patience or sympathy for her recently bereaved stepchildren.

Despite this there had been times when they had enjoyed each other's company. Frances liked to play at cards and encouraged Alethea's singing and music lessons. She brought a lightness and vivacity to their gloomy house. Sometimes, when Father was out, Frances would read romances with Alethea. Frances liked to dress her up, to curl her hair and hang jewels about her neck. But just as quickly her mood could sour and she would dismiss the bewildered girl from her company. Perhaps she was bored and lonely.

Now Alethea had taken over the house much as her stepmother had done eight years prior. Only, for the time being at least, Alethea had the house to herself, to order it as she wished, with no husband to obey or unruly children to navigate. It was a daunting and exhilarating prospect.

Alethea stretched out her legs in front of the fire, admiring her calves in their silk stockings. As a girl she was always tripping over her skirts, longing to run about in breeches like her brother, and now she could. She did not know how she would ever tolerate wearing heavy dresses again. She was even enjoying doing without a bodice, being able to breathe more deeply and eat more without giving herself indigestion.

She was discovering that she liked being a man. Living with her friends in Epping Forest had aided her adoption of masculine traits; she had become used to being treated as an equal, having her opinions listened to respectfully and being free to come and go as she pleased. She was grateful to Barbara most of all, for she had shown her how to exert authority over others, even if she had only practised this on children. Now she found that overseeing and managing a household, small though hers was, came naturally to her.

The servants were too well trained to look their master in the face, even short-sighted Crewe avoided such disrespect, directing his gaze slightly to the left whenever they conversed. She had been afraid her voice might give her away, but no one seemed surprised by it, assuming perhaps that William had affected some foreign intonation and that his travels had softened, rather than hardened him.

William had liked to ride, so Alethea asked Crewe about his old horse, a fine Barbary stallion named Sans Pareil. Crewe told her that, alas, the horse had been sold by his former mistress. Frances saw no reason to stable such an expensive animal when William had taken up residence abroad.

Alethea was both relieved and frustrated. The horse was temperamental, letting only her brother ride him, but she had decided to risk being thrown. She could explain a fall by her long absence – the horse was no longer used to her, and with any luck a tumble from a horse might induce a miscarriage.

'Your sister's old mare is stabled over at Measham Grange. A steady horse not likely to startle, your little sisters liked to ride her. You might find her suitable during your convalescence, just until we can acquire a better mount for you.'

'Bella Donna?' Alethea said with surprise. 'Why didn't you tell me she was still here?'

'You did not ask, sir.'

Crewe's thin lips drew upwards into the semblance of a smile and for a moment Alethea thought he had found her out. She shook her head, that could not be. Crewe would be the first to tell her uncle if he suspected anything untoward.

The gardens, though overgrown and losing their summer leaves, were still glorious. The birds had got the pick of the berries, but the trees in the orchard were laden with apples, pears and plums. They needed picking and storing before the winds and frosts destroyed them. Alethea noted that the vegetables in the kitchen garden, while doing battle with the usurping weeds, were still plentiful enough to feed the household. Stocky leeks and the feathery plumes of carrots and parsnips were clearly visible above the ground. Fat round cabbages were being slowly consumed by grubs.

The hedges of lavender and rosemary had lost their neat profiles but still filled the air with their scent as she brushed past them. Alethea remembered all the times she had chased her little sisters around them, playing hide and seek in the bushes. Lucy never could stay hidden long, peeking out and giving herself away. Betty did not hide at all. Standing stock-still she would close her eyes, thinking that if she could not see others then they could not see her. Alethea could almost hear their excited shrieks and high-pitched laughter following her down the gravel paths. For a moment she thought she glimpsed a flash of skirt disappearing behind a wall and expected to feel Betty crashing into her legs in her pursuit of Lucy, but it was only Caesar chasing a rabbit in vain. The animal disappeared into its burrow with a flash of white tail.

'Whole place is overrun with rabbits and all my tools is rusty. Can't do anything without a decent scythe.' An old man stomped up beside her.

Alethea had known Elliot the gardener since she was a child, when he had cleared a bed for her to grow flowers in. She thought he at least might recognise her, but like the others he did not look past the clothes or the title. She listened patiently to him while he grumbled about the condition of his tools, promising to buy him a new scythe. She also agreed that he would need at least one under gardener to help him, hoping what they gained in produce would compensate for the cost.

As Alethea surveyed the rest of the land, however, she was dismayed to see the depredations that had been made. Little was left of what had once been a large flock of sheep and she could not see any cattle grazing in the fields.

She had been looking forward to showing Ellen the woods she remembered so fondly, but when they reached them they found them ravaged, half the trees had been felled, leaving ugly patches of brown earth in their wake.

'Can this all be Frances' doing? Why didn't my father stop her?'

'Maybe it was Crewe,' Ellen said. 'He looked put out when you insisted on touring the estate without him. I can't see why your stepmother would want to sell the livestock. The timber, yes, she could make a quick profit from that, but cows must be valuable assets what with all the milk and butter and that. Not that I know much about farming.'

Over where Measham Grange lay, in the dip between two hills, Alethea thought she could make out smoke rising from the chimneys of the farmhouse. 'I know someone who does know all about farming though,' she said.

She hoped John Thornly was still there. He and his wife had always been kind to her, giving her fresh milk and slices of cake whenever she and William turned up on their doorstep, muddy and dishevelled after one of their adventures. Alethea did not admit it, but she was eager to see her old horse again.

Thornly looked delighted to see them, ushering Alethea into his parlour for a glass of ale and a piece of his wife's almond cake. Ellen and Robin were left in the kitchen with Mrs Thornly, which they did not mind as she treated them to all the best of her baking.

'Bless my eyes to look upon you again, Sir William. Crewe told me you was too ill to leave your chamber. I feared the worst and thought it was all over for us at Measham Grange.'

Thornly was only too glad to list at great length the livestock he had been forced to part with and who had forced him into it. Ellen had been correct in her supposition. According to Thornly, though he hated to speak ill of the dead, it was Lady Hawthorne who had begun the selling off of the timber. She was always meddling in business that did not concern her. She had persuaded the late master to raise the rents of the tenants on the land, evicting those who could not pay and ordering Crewe to find new ones who would. Crewe had his own game going on too, cutting deals with some of the tenants to lower their rents in exchange for certain favours.

'He's got his own farm now, up in North Derbyshire, bought with bribes from the tenants,' Thornly said. 'You should go up and see it some time, maybe you'll recognise some of the livestock. You might even find that fine stallion of yours in his stables.'

While it was only to be expected that Crewe would make sure he was financially secure, Alethea had not anticipated this level of wrongdoing from him. She was not ready to dismiss him from her service, he had an understanding of the estate and how to run it that she lacked, but she was determined that once she'd learnt how to be master of Measham she would find herself a steward she could trust.

Bella Donna whinnied when Alethea entered the stables and she could not help throwing her arms around the old mare's neck. The horse rubbed her muzzle against Alethea's cheek, nibbling at her wig. Her grey coat had got lighter so that she was almost white now. Alethea patted the horse's rough flank and hoped no one could see the tears in her eyes.

'We've taken good care of her for you,' Thornly said.

Alethea lifted Robin from his mother's arms. 'Shall we take a ride?' Robin bounced up and down with excitement.

'Oh no,' said Ellen. 'I don't think that is a good idea.' She gave Alethea a meaningful look.

'She's as steady as an ox this one, isn't she, Mr Thornly?' Alethea winked at him.

'None steadier,' Thornly agreed.

Alethea rode around the farmyard holding Robin in front of her while Ellen watched them anxiously.

'Don't worry,' Mr Thornly reassured Ellen. 'There's no better rider in the county than Sir William. Looks like he'll train your son up to be a fine rider too.'

Alethea smiled down at them, pleased she had carried off the part of a father so well, for it was clear Thornly assumed Robin was her bastard child.

'What were you thinking of, getting up on a horse in your condition?' Ellen demanded as they walked back from the farm.

'Don't fuss, Ellen, it was perfectly safe. Do you think I would take a risk with Robin?' Alethea did not mention the risk she would happily take with the child lodged in her womb. 'We'll have to tread carefully with Crewe,' she continued, wanting to change the subject. 'I'll tell him I want to see all the account books and the rent rolls. I only hope I can make some sense of them.' She slashed at a bramble with her stick. 'If only William was here, he'd know how to manage this better than I.'

'You'll manage,' Ellen said confidently. 'Besides, I like accounts. I used to keep them for my father. He never had a son that survived so he trained me up in his drapery business. I was so good at accounting he let me do it all. Poor Lizzie never had a head for numbers.'

'Well you might have to teach me.' Though Alethea was not sure that being able to keep accounts for a shop would be the same as tallying up all the figures for an estate like Measham.

'You will make the rents fair, won't you?' Ellen turned toward Alethea, staring intensely up at her. Ellen's hazel eyes, picking up the greenness around them, looked lighter here than they had in Epping. Her finely arched eyebrows were pulled together with uncharacteristic severity. 'Turning people off their land, it goes against all we've ever stood for.'

'Of course I'll make them fair.' Alethea gave a short indignant laugh, surprised by her friend's misgivings. 'We can visit the tenants ourselves and make sure all is well with them.'

Ellen passed Robin to Alethea as she climbed over a stile. 'You mustn't take on too much, especially as it gets nearer to your time. You'll need to plan for your lying-in. We'll have to find a trustworthy midwife, one that won't blab, if such a thing is possible.'

'Can't you be my midwife?' Alethea had pushed all thoughts of giving birth out of her mind as a prospect too terrifying to contemplate.

'I don't have enough experience. I wouldn't know what to do if something went amiss. God willing all will go well, but we must be prepared. I can't deliver your baby on my own.'

Ellen's face was strained with anxiety and it occurred to Alethea that she had been worrying enough for the pair of them.

'We are agreed, we'll pretend it's you who is pregnant, that it's your child?'

Ellen nodded grimly. 'Perhaps you'll have to make an honest woman of me. You wouldn't be the first gentleman to marry his maid.'

'There was an earl in the next county who married his maid, but he was cut off by his family for it.' Alethea put her hand up to Ellen's face and tucked a stray lock of hair behind her ear. 'Ellen, if it was in my power I would marry you and leave everything I own to you. Whatever happens I'll make sure you are well recompensed for your friendship to me.'

'Friendship doesn't want payment. We like living here, don't we, Robin?' Ellen took Robin back into her arms, holding him up to survey the countryside. 'It's so healthful compared to London, and brighter and more open than Epping Forest.' She lowered the child onto her hip. 'I can handle the gossip of the servants. I only worry what your brother will make of it all when he finds out.'

'If we can improve the estate and keep it safe for him, he'll have nothing to object to,' Alethea said stoutly.

'What do you think Jack would make of all this, eh? He'd think it a fine game.' Ellen's voice dropped off and she glanced at Alethea apologetically. She was still convinced Jack must be the baby's father.

Alethea hated keeping secrets from her, and since Ellen was to be the child's mother it seemed only fair she should know who its father was.

'It is Samuel,' she blurted out.

'What is?' Ellen asked.

'The father. Samuel is the father.'

Ellen staggered and nearly fell. Robin cried out in alarm.

'Let's sit beneath this tree for a moment.' Alethea helped her over to the large chestnut tree whose boughs she used to play under.

Sinking to the ground, Ellen sat leaning against the trunk, her face rigid. Robin crawled about, collecting fallen nuts which he placed in his mother's lap.

'I'm sorry, Ellen.'

Alethea began to weep. She had tried to shut Samuel out of her thoughts, but he would come unbidden. Sometimes when she remembered his slate-blue eyes she felt such a thirst for him, and when her body recalled his lithe hands caressing her skin, her flesh burnt for him. She longed for him to feel the growing weight of her breasts and belly in his palms and reckon her worth to him.

But as the heaviness inside her grew so too did the anger. She could not have been so precious to him if he could cast her off so easily. Even this burden she carried added little to her value, for his wife was not beyond childbearing and might still replace their lost children with another legitimate one.

Ellen looked away, down the grassy slope to the house below. 'When I first started attending Samuel's meetings I thought he was God's chosen witness, a man as like to an angel as I would ever meet.

Then he was called away, he and his closest followers, such as Barbara, to preach up North. I thought he'd abandoned us because we weren't worthy of his message, but I was wrong. He returned to lead us out of London to safety, despite the danger to his own life. He is a good man, a holy man. Oh why did you succumb? Why didn't you remind him of his duties and point him to the path of righteousness?'

'I was weak. I was weak and foolish and proud too, thinking myself so special that God had chosen me to be Samuel's helpmeet, that our union was a spiritual one. If either of us had known his wife was alive we would never have lain together.'

Ellen said nothing for a while. Her brow furrowed, she sat pulling up tufts of grass. 'Does he know that you are with child?'

Alethea shook her head.

'Rebecca would've torn you to pieces if she'd found out.'

'Do you think, because this child was conceived in sin, it will be monstrous?' Alethea voiced at last what she had been trying not to dwell on, but feared most, that she would be punished through her offspring.

Ellen smiled warmly at her then. 'Remember our blessed Saviour's answer to his Disciples when they saw the blind man. They asked him who sinned, the parent or the child, that he was born blind? Our Saviour replied, neither he nor his parents, but that the Judgements of God might be made manifest in him. These things are causes of nature, not God's vengeance, for our God is a kind and loving God.'

'Mama.' Robin dropped a chestnut, still in its spiny green shell, into Alethea's lap.

'That is Mama,' she told him, pointing at Ellen. 'I am William.'

Heaving himself up against her shoulder, Robin pushed his palm against Alethea's cheek, attempting clumsily to wipe away her tears. 'Dada.'

Alethea kissed his plump cheeks. 'Oh, Robin, I don't know if it is a good or a bad thing if you call me that.'

'We'll have to be careful, Al—' Ellen corrected herself, 'William, we must watch how we address each other. As for the true parentage of that one.' She nodded at Alethea's belly. 'Maybe it will be for the best if it never knows.'

Alethea got to her feet. She had done with weeping, she would shed no more tears. Since her body had proved a weak vessel it would have no more mastery over her. She would take on the mind of a man, an honourable, noble man. She would carry this child and then she would give it away. It was Ellen's baby, not hers. Once she had rid her body of it she would forget she had ever been a woman, or known such soft sentiments as women feel.

If Crewe was alarmed by Alethea's request for the account books and tenants' rolls he did not show it. His face remained as impassive as ever as he laid them out before her. Crewe made Alethea think of a statue come to life. His skin was grey and lined as if of marble and she imagined that it would be just as cold and slightly damp to the touch. Even his wig smelt faintly of mildew beneath its powder of lavender and marjoram. She was not surprised he had survived the pestilence. He scarcely seemed human.

'A great deal of livestock has been sold off,' she noted.

'The burden of taxation on your late father forced him into selling some of the land and much of the sheep and cattle. Times have been difficult with low prices for grain. Sacrifices had to be made, he did what was necessary.' Crewe paused before adding drily, 'Though I am aware Thornly takes a different view.'

'What of our tenants? I should like to visit them.'

'As you wish. I will have a horse saddled and ready for you whenever you require it. We have cleaned out the stables as you requested and brought back some of the horses from the Grange.' Crewe gave a low bow.

When Alethea got to the stables the next day she found Crewe ready and waiting to accompany her. She was not pleased to see him, but at least he could introduce her to the cottagers. In his presence they would recognise only her status and see her as her brother, not as herself.

'Now that you are recovered, sir, I thought you might wish to attend Mass,' Crewe said once they had ridden out beyond the courtyard. 'Father Hainault is no longer with us, but I know of a priest who would come to the house.'

'I am no longer of that faith, Crewe, it is all hypocrisy and superstition.' Alethea would not have been so blunt, but Crewe had caught her off guard. She had not expected such directness from him.

'Your father would be sorry to hear that, sir.'

'My father is not here, Crewe, and it is not your place to question my religion.'

No more was said on the matter.

'What of the tenants?' Ellen asked Alethea when she returned.

'I met with all seven families, they seem well provided for and contented enough, though with Crewe there they could hardly say otherwise.' Alethea lay on the bed, utterly exhausted. All she wished for was sleep. How easy it would be to leave everything to Crewe's management, but then she might find herself with nothing and now she had a household to provide for, not to mention principles to observe.

'You must go out again without him,' Ellen said. 'We could go together in the coach.'

'That old thing, it's rusting in the stables, it would fall apart before it made a mile.' Alethea closed her eyes. 'Crewe wants me to build more cottages. He says tenants are more profitable than livestock.'

'But you don't want to make a profit out of poor folk.' Ellen got onto the bed beside her. 'The earth was made to be a common storehouse, not a private treasury for the benefit of a few.'

'What would you have me do? This house needs money to maintain it. We cannot live on vegetables alone.'

Ellen sighed. 'My allegiance has always been with the oppressed people. Now I find myself on the other side of the gate, I'm at my ease and yet full of discomfort.' She fidgeted with the bedclothes, as if to illustrate her point. 'Couldn't we send word to the others? To Lizzie and to Thomas? They could come and live with us here.'

'I have thought of it, but Measham belongs to William. I couldn't go inviting our friends here without his consent.'

Alethea had indeed thought about whether she ought to send for their old comrades and offer them accommodation on her land, but had concluded that it would make her life far too complicated. They would think her a hypocrite, deceiving and dissembling and living the life of a gentleman. How would she ever persuade them to go along with her masquerade? Besides, they would not respect the traditions she had grown up with or appreciate the house and gardens in the way she did. More than this she also discovered in herself an unwillingness to make her childhood home over to communal living. She enjoyed being in charge here and liked the way things were organised, she did not want to have to put every decision to the vote. It would raise a great deal of suspicion among their neighbours to have a band of dissenters taking up residence. And what if Samuel and Rebecca followed their friends here? Samuel had been so much under the sway of his wife, if she insisted how could he stop her?

'It was just a fancy I was taken with. I miss their company that is all.' Ellen sounded wistful.

'You said you were happy here.'

'I don't mean to sound ungrateful. Only I've always had my sister near me. And it is a little lonely, having always to pretend that I am something I am not.'

'You're free to leave, Ellen. I don't want to hold you here against your will.' *How can she complain about pretence*, Alethea thought bitterly. *She hasn't had to change her sex.*

'And you'll manage your pregnancy alone, will you?' Ellen jumped up from the bed. 'I'll leave you to consider the uncharitable nature of your words. Perhaps some time spent in quiet reflection would not go amiss.'

'You sound just like Barbara,' Alethea said. But Ellen had already closed the door behind her.

After sleeping away the afternoon, Alethea came downstairs to find Ellen bent over the account books.

'Forgive me, Ellen, I didn't mean to sound ungrateful. I am thankful to you, truly I am.'

To her great relief, Ellen turned and smiled at her. 'Don't fret, we're both out of sorts. I have found something though.' Ellen looked pleased with herself, as Alethea took a seat beside her. 'See here are the monthly totals for the amounts collected in rents.' Ellen pointed to a page of the rent rolls. 'Now here,' and she pulled the heavy account book towards them, 'are the monthly outgoings. And here is the total left for last month.' She thumbed through several pages. 'A shortfall might be understandable if you could see where the money had gone, but there are gaps for the past few months between what's been coming in and what's been going out. A few hundred pounds a month are unaccounted for.'

'Even when my father was alive?' Alethea asked.

'It seems so.'

'Can I be of assistance, sir?' Crewe had entered the room silently behind them.

'Just puzzling over the accounts, Crewe.' Alethea wondered how much he had heard. Crewe seemed always to be everywhere at once, it was difficult to elude him.

'They are complicated and take some time to master. Certainly they are beyond female understanding.' Crewe inclined his head towards Ellen with a slight smirk.

'It's not beyond female understanding to see where the sums don't add up,' she retorted.

'If you can reckon correctly you will find the sums add up as they should.' Crewe turned from Ellen to Alethea. 'I would be happy to go through them with you, sir, at your convenience, but I came to give you this letter.'

Alethea's heart leapt in her chest and she took the letter eagerly, thinking it might at last be news from her brother. To her dismay she recognised the Calverton crest standing proud on the red wax seal. The Calvertons were staying at their Nottinghamshire residence and requested her company for dinner the next day.

'Thank you, Crewe, that will be all,' she said.

'The Calvertons' boy is waiting in the kitchen for your reply,' Crewe said.

'Tell him I am indisposed. I have no desire for company. This morning's ride tired me out and I fear a return of my sickness.'

'I'm sorry to hear that, sir. I will tell the boy. Let me remove these for you. If you are not well they will only tire you further.' Crewe began to gather up the books and papers from the table.

Alethea stopped him. 'That's all right, I'll take them up to my closet and look over them again there,' she said firmly.

'As you wish, sir.' Crewe bowed slightly, without any apparent concern. 'Your son is in the kitchens, Mrs Liddell, perhaps you should collect him,' he told Ellen.

'Miles was minding him for me.'

'Miles has other work to do. He is not a nursemaid.'

She rolled her eyes at Alethea, but followed Crewe out of the room in search of Robin.

Alethea's thoughts were racing so fast she felt as though her brain would combust. After their desertion of her the Calvertons had the gall to ingratiate themselves with her brother, sending their condolences and wishing to pay their respects. The Lady Jane Sellwood was with them, they wrote. So Jane was married now. Alethea remembered how Jane had feared her future husband's temper and how she had promised to stay with her. Perhaps fears of the plague had pushed them to hasten the wedding. She would like to see her, to know if she was happily settled. She wished she could write to her at least and tell her she was still alive, but she could not risk the letter falling into Margaret's hands. Alethea was no longer so trusting as she had once been. Who was to say Jane would not betray her, especially since her loyalties must be with her husband now.

She would not see them. Indeed she could not see them; they would be sure to perceive her disguise for they would not be blinded by deference. Alethea imagined Henry Calverton seizing her hand and looking straight into her face. Jane had always been interested in

William. No doubt she would play the coquette with Alethea now, hoping to make William love her. Yet how amusing it would be to parade Ellen before them as William's mistress, a humble draper's daughter from Whitechapel. How insulted Lady Margaret would be.

Alethea was almost tempted to pay them a visit, taking Ellen and Robin with her, just to have some paltry revenge on them. She did want to find out why the Calvertons had fled London so suddenly and how they would justify leaving her behind – and to quiz Margaret on the fool's errand she'd sent her on. She decided she would feel safer inviting them to Measham Hall where she was at least on her own territory and could maintain some control over events.

She now believed Margaret had invented the story about William in order to get her out of the house before persuading the rest of the family to leave London without her. There was nothing she could think of to warrant such treatment, but Margaret's behaviour had become increasingly strange. It was possible she had conceived an irrational hatred of Alethea, born out of her jealous nature. It seemed clear that William had not returned to England since his banishment.

When William returns, Alethea told herself, *then I will right the wrongs Margaret has done me.* But she was beginning to fear William would never return; that he had died abroad and she would be consigned to play out the rest of her life as her brother.

✦ Chapter Nineteen ✦

Remembering her visit to Signora Pozzuto, Alethea had the shutters closed over so the Calvertons would see her only in candlelight. Ellen refused to meet them, being too afraid of speaking out of turn and giving the game away. Alethea was secretly relieved; she thought Margaret might leave rather than share a meal with a woman as common as Ellen, a woman reputed to be William's mistress.

When the Calvertons were announced Alethea strode into the hall to meet them. Her increasing girth, rather than hampering her impersonation of a man, facilitated it, for it meant she spread out her legs when she sat and she moved with a broader stride. She shook Henry Calverton's hand vigorously, whilst averting her head. She bowed to the ladies with a show of ostentation. Crewe, as always, hovered in the shadows behind her.

'I must apologise for my voice,' she explained in a low growl. 'I have a bad throat.' She pulled her muffler up so that it partly covered her face.

The Calvertons stepped back a little. Henry was the same handsome fellow he had always been, but Margaret had aged. Despite her fine clothes, her face looked careworn. Jane stood behind her mother.

'Congratulations on your marriage, Lady Sellwood.' Alethea studied Jane's face.

Jane merely curtseyed in reply, tilting her head slightly to one side. Jane was so pale Alethea wondered if she had painted her face. If so, she had forgotten to rouge her cheeks, they were as white as the rest of her. Jane had lost weight too. She seemed diminished in both body and spirit.

'How long is it since you were wed?'

'One month.' Jane's voice was flat and despondent.

'I must offer my personal condolences on the loss of your relatives, Sir William,' Henry said. 'Alethea in particular. Such a dear sweet girl. As I told your late father, I was deeply grieved not to have been able to keep her from the clutches of that terrible disease.'

Alethea nodded. 'It was most unfortunate. Did anyone else in your household contract the pestilence?'

'Mercifully all were spared,' Margaret answered. 'Alethea had gone out visiting. I did advise her against it of course, but you know your sister was quite headstrong.'

Alethea wished she could challenge Margaret to a duel. How she would love to run the woman's stout body through with a sword, but she restrained herself to a verbal challenge. 'My sister was always an obedient, respectful girl.'

To Alethea's surprise, Jane began to cry. 'She was, sir, the truest friend anyone could wish for. I wanted to attend her burial at least, but it was too dangerous. Mother said the family were shut up in their house and all died, one by one.'

'She died at a friend's house?' Alethea asked.

'Very quickly after her arrival.' Margaret interposed. 'There was nothing we could do for her. We had to leave London as soon as we received word of her death. They were desperate times, with families being locked up in their houses if the plague was so much as suspected.' She looked Alethea directly in the eyes. 'You were abroad, I believe?'

'I was.' Alethea could feel her advantage slipping away and was wondering how to regain it when Palmes called them in to dinner.

The seating was arranged so that she sat at the head of the table while the Calvertons sat at the other end. If they found this odd, they did not comment on it. She had also made sure the candles were all placed far from her, so she sat in obscurity. She had invited Crewe to join them for dinner, seating him between herself and Margaret, partly as a barrier and partly to annoy the lady.

'I'm surprised you are not at Oxford with the Court, Lord Calverton,' Alethea said. To her gratification there was an uncomfortable pause while Henry and Margaret both glanced at their daughter.

Jane, who had been staring down at the untouched food on her plate, looked up at Alethea. 'It is my fault, Sir William. I absconded from my husband's house in Sussex and travelled to Nottinghamshire. My parents rushed up here to retrieve me. They intend to return me to Sussex tomorrow.'

Margaret laughed. 'Lady Sellwood does like to exaggerate. She has been unwell and thought to find me at our Nottingham house. Now she has recovered it is time for her to return to her husband. He is so enamoured of her he cannot bear to part with her for long, and of course a wife's place is beside her spouse, not her mother.' She laid a firm hand over Jane's.

'I'm glad to hear Lord Sellwood is so fond of you,' Alethea said.

Jane gave her an odd grimace, jerking her head in assent.

'You have some fine land here, Sir William.' Calverton gestured vaguely towards the covered window. 'I remember how dear to your father's heart Measham Hall was.'

'It has been somewhat neglected of late, but I intend to restore it to its former glory,' Alethea replied.

'If you require the services of an architect or a mason, I can recommend ours to you.' Margaret leant forward with sudden animation. 'We've had so many improvements made to our properties both up here and in London. We've had an indoor bathing house and a dining room put into Rufford Castle and I want to have the façade of Calverton House redone before we return to London. A row of Grecian columns to enhance its nobility.'

'Measham Hall is substantial enough for my needs. I don't intend to waste money on lavish expenditure, either by entertaining or building,' Alethea said, cutting her off short. 'Wasn't it Machiavelli who wrote that a wise man should not mind being called a miser. For a prince who squanders all his resources will become odious and be despised. And one of the powerfullest remedies a Prince can have against conspiracies, is, not to be hated nor despised.' Alethea watched Henry as she quoted from the book he had once given her, but he just smiled approvingly.

'Well I must say, Sir William, while you have avoided ostentation you have still managed to provide an ample supper.' He stretched across the table for another slice of beef. 'If this all comes from your own lands I can see you are doing very well indeed.'

Alethea did not correct him, though in truth the meat had been bought in especially.

'We'll have no Irish beef here, eh.' Henry raised his glass. 'Personally, I support banning the Irish cattle trade entirely. English agriculture is suffering enough. I hear many of the rural gentry complaining about the low rents they are forced to charge their tenants. I know mine are always whining and demanding repairs to their cottages, no matter how little they pay in rent.'

'I charge my tenants a fair rent; one they can afford and I can eke a living out of.' Alethea was relieved Ellen was not with them.

Crewe coughed and leant forward. He kept directing Palmes to refill the Calvertons' wine glasses while ignoring Alethea's. He was particularly obsequious towards Margaret, much to Alethea's irritation. At least he was unwittingly supplying a useful distraction and preventing the Calvertons from scrutinising her too closely.

'You are singularly unambitious, Sir William. Have you no desire to pursue a Court appointment? Or to enter politics in any way?' Margaret reached around Crewe in an attempt to catch Alethea's eye.

'My religion bars me from public office,' Alethea responded gruffly.

Margaret looked pained. 'Of course, you are not a member of the established Church.'

For once Crewe also looked directly at Alethea, his eyebrows raised enquiringly. Had she made a strategic mistake in allowing him to dine with them? Alethea tugged at her cravat, suddenly feeling uncomfortably hot, and wished she was wearing a simple low-cut bodice instead of all these masculine ruffles and bows. Think as William, she told herself.

'Nonetheless, you are very young to retire from society,' Henry observed. 'Since the distemper is abating I intend to return to London after Christmas. Hopefully the Court will be back by February. You are welcome to stay with us. I can easily get you a licence to travel and would be happy to introduce you at Court. Catholics, as you know, are tolerated there.' Henry lowered his voice. 'And your previous misdemeanour has been quite forgotten.'

'Has it?' Alethea asked with a start. Perhaps here was her chance to discover more about her brother.

'There's no need to hide away here. The Dutch wars and the plague have provided plenty of distractions from stale gossip. Besides, I see you have matured into a sober young man.'

'Indeed, I drink only in moderation.'

Henry smiled. 'Well it wasn't the drink I was referring to. Young men often conceive ill-judged amours and indeed, what love is higher than amity between brothers? Women for breeding and men for friendship, eh? Everything in its place.' Henry seemed to be offering some sort of warning, but Alethea did not fully understand his meaning.

'I know of several young ladies who would be only too happy to make your acquaintance,' Margaret interrupted with forced jollity. 'Don't you agree, Jane?'

Jane only shrugged and pushed bits of calves' head pie around her plate. Alethea regarded her sadly. That pie was the crowning glory of her table.

'I'm very grateful for your kind offer, Lord Calverton, but I have so much work to do here and I am really quite content in my country retirement.' Alethea wished she could quiz Henry on his hounding of dissenters, but she bit her tongue and turned to Jane instead. 'Will you keep a house in London, Lady Sellwood?'

'My husband has a house in London, but he considers the capital too full of temptations and insists I remain in Sussex.'

Jane's cheeks had gained some colour and Alethea hoped she might draw her out further, but Margaret interrupted. 'He's anxious for his bride's health.'

'Trade should pick up again now,' Henry observed simultaneously.

'I hope so. I've heard there is a great deal of discontent about the cost of the Dutch wars and the burden of taxation suffered to support them.' Alethea was momentarily grateful to Crewe, who took it upon himself to keep her up to date on the news from the Court and the country.

'People will always find something to grumble about,' Margaret said.

'Would you try a little syllabub, Lady Sellwood, or perhaps a sugar cake?' Alethea gestured to the dishes spread out on the table.

Jane ignored her invitation. 'Do you play an instrument, Sir William? Your sister was a very fine singer.'

'Alas no, I am not so musical as my sister was.'

'You look very like her.' Jane regarded Alethea mournfully, her eyes huge in her gaunt face.

'We were often mistaken for twins as children. I know my sister loved you dearly, Lady Sellwood,' Alethea could not resist adding.

'You received her letters?' Jane became suddenly animated. 'She was always so anxious for your well-being, not knowing your where-abouts or hearing any word from you.'

Alethea swallowed. She was on treacherous ground here. How to discover what Margaret knew without giving herself away? 'Her letters reached me too late, alas. I didn't know my sister had other friends in the city. Who were the people she was visiting when she died?'

'She told me they were relatives of yours. Perhaps she too had conceived a secret amour,' Margaret answered swiftly. 'Such a turbulent time, I don't recall their names exactly. The Frasers perhaps?'

She was clever. Alethea remembered her father mentioning some distant cousins of that name who lived in London.

'Have you acquired any French customs since your stay in that country, Sir William?' Margaret continued.

'Only the sauces you enjoyed on your meat, Lady Margaret, though some say my manners are Frenchified.'

'Life back in the English countryside will soon knock those out of you.' Henry smiled again.

Fortunately, the Calvertons could not stay late. They had a long ride ahead of them the next day and their driver was unhappy about having to navigate the roads back to Rufford Castle that evening. Alethea waved them off from a distance.

'They must have thought me an odd fellow.' She and Ellen sat side by side on Alethea's bed. 'But I think I got away with it. I don't believe they recognised me.'

'Why would they? Calverton and his daughter believe you perished. And even if Margaret recognised you, she can't give you away without revealing her own tricks.'

Alethea nodded. 'I suppose we stand at a stalemate then.'

'Do you really think she meant to have you killed?'

'She was taking a great risk otherwise, unless she thought me too stupid to find my way back from Deptford. I think that messenger was an assassin, but for some reason he changed his mind. Perhaps he never intended to go through with it.' Alethea took a sip of the milk and mint concoction Ellen insisted would soothe her indigestion.

'He might've thought the plague would do his work for him, or maybe he took pity on you. But why did she give you money if she was planning to do away with you?'

'Perhaps it was meant for the assassin to take, once he'd murdered me.'

'Margaret Calverton must be a heartless devil if that's the case.' Ellen sat up straight. 'Still, I hope she does help her daughter. From the glimpse I got of her, the girl looked a miserable wretch.'

'Jane used to be a lively spirited, cheerful maid, now she's shrunken in on herself.'

Ellen shook her head sadly, then brightened as an idea struck her. 'Maybe you could invite Jane here. Offer her a place of refuge.'

'And have her husband come thundering after her? I've enough to manage taking care of things as it is.'

'Would you leave her to suffer under the hands of a tyrant?'

'The Calvertons won't allow any harm to come to Jane. Whatever else their faults might be, they love their daughter.' Alethea hoped, as she said the words, that they were true.

❧ Chapter Twenty ❦

A lethea tried in everything to conduct herself as a man. To think as a man and to feel, as far as her body would allow, as a man. She prepared herself for childbirth, not like a woman, praying to God to keep herself and her baby safe from death and deformity, but as a soldier approaching the battlefield. If she should perish, she would do so nobly, without succumbing to womanish tears. She would bear the pains as an officer might the wounds of war, without screams or plaintive sobs, but with hard held breath and teeth set tight.

In the meantime, she focused all her energies on the estate. According to Crewe it was Thornly who had failed to take good care of his animals, cutting costs on feed so that half of them grew sick and died. Thornly's son was the better farmer, Crewe said. William should go around the father and deal with the son directly.

While she distrusted Crewe, Alethea could see the sense in what he said. Thornly was elderly and looked more to his fireside than his fields, whereas his son was keen to build up the Grange once more and took a lively interest in the welfare of his stock.

Thanks to her father's reputation and the security of the house and estates, Alethea was able to get credit from local merchants and traders. She built up a good working relationship with young Thornly.

Together they selected and bought more cattle and sheep, so that by the following spring Measham's fields would be full once more.

She also agreed with Crewe that there was room for a few more cottages and that the cost of building them would soon be repaid with the rents they would gain. She insisted, however, that she oversee the collection of the rents herself to ensure they were fair and the dwellings well built. This was something of an empty promise as it was becoming increasingly difficult for her to travel out on horseback.

As he did with all her commands, Crewe appeared to be in complete agreement. He only reminded her that her father had always offered a preferential rate to Catholic tenants. Alethea told him she would not discriminate on religious grounds.

She knew she was becoming perilously dependent on a man who could still prove to be her enemy, but there was no one else who understood the workings of the estate so well. Perhaps Crewe was creaming off profits to stock his own private dairy, but she could find no evidence of this and believed he held the upkeep and improvement of Measham first and foremost. Where was the money going?

One afternoon in early December, when Ellen was out visiting the Grange with Robin, Crewe asked to see Alethea in private. He carried several rolls of parchment under his arm. He spread one out on the table.

'Mrs Liddell raised some concerns I was not at liberty to answer.' He looped the ribbons of his eyeglasses around his ears. 'I think you will find these records explain any discrepancies in the accounts.' He put one hand up to his mouth as he cleared his throat with a dry rasping. 'It is a delicate matter, one your late father entrusted to me. I had to honour his wishes but did not like to disclose them to any not of our faith.'

Alethea was surprised by this sudden revelation. He knew her faith had lapsed. Was he trying to divide her from Ellen? Was it because he knew Ellen to be the better accountant?

Crewe coughed again. 'I hope you will not think it impertinent if I request a promise from you. Will you swear to keep what I am about to show you secret?' He pushed a Bible towards her.

Curious, Alethea took it in her right hand and swore.

He pointed to the sums recorded neatly in columns of iron dark ink. 'His Lordship had this regular bequest to the Jesuit College in St. Omer set up. You will have heard of your mother's cousin, Matthew, who is also your father's godson. He was taking orders there. It was in her memory he wished to uphold the support of this promising young priest.'

Alethea did not like to admit to not remembering Matthew in case William knew of him, so she just gave a curt nod.

'It was, as you can imagine, a delicate matter; one he thought better not to reveal to Lady Frances. I am certain, however, your father would want you to continue the payments.' Crewe ran a finger down the page. His nails were surprisingly long, yellow and ridged, as though they too were made of old parchment.

'Did he include these payments in his will?' Alethea asked.

'We would need to consult his will to establish that. I was one of the witnesses for it and do not recall such a bequest, but then Lady Frances did have him re-write his will several times.' Crewe paused. 'Until it was more to her, ah, liking.'

Alethea looked closely at him to see if he was being sardonic, or even humorous, but his expression was as veiled as ever.

Crewe's story was plausible. Her father was a devout man in his way and a charitable one. His first wife's family was not a subject Frances liked to discuss and she would certainly have tried to put a stop to any payments to them. While she endured Nicholas's religion, perhaps because it was the one thing he refused to give way on, Frances stuck to her Anglican allegiances and would have been hostile to giving away her inheritance to papists of any kind, most especially to Jesuits.

Alethea wished she had not sworn to keep the bequest secret. She did not like to keep such important information from Ellen, who could not understand why she kept Crewe on. She thought him practically the devil incarnate. Crewe evidently thought little better of Ellen; to him she was a whore, and worse, a fanatic republican whore. The antagonism between them was palpable.

Crewe surprised Alethea again one afternoon by placing a large book in front of her, *Sylva, or, A discourse of forest-trees, and the propagation of timber in His Majesties dominions* by John Evelyn, fellow of the Royal Society.

'Having noted your concern over the depletion of Measham's woodland, I took the liberty of obtaining a copy of this for you. It has been commended in several quarters.'

She turned the pages with increasing fascination. 'This is a marvellous work indeed, Crewe, one that will be invaluable in assisting my attempts to plant up our woods again.'

'I am glad it is to your liking, sir.' Crewe bowed stiffly.

After the success of this gift Crewe continued to supply Alethea with books, not only on plants and agriculture, but also on travel, history, and philosophy. He seemed bent on making sure his young master had a well-rounded education.

Christmas was approaching and although she did not feel much like celebrating, Alethea wanted to create for Ellen the sort of Christmas they had always kept at Measham Hall. Even during the 1650s when Christmas had been banned officially the Hawthornes had continued to hold their own festivities. Now she took the boy Miles out with her to gather greenery. They came back their arms laden with holly, ivy and bay. Alethea picked bunches of sharp-scented rosemary along with mistletoe from an old apple tree where it had always been encouraged to grow. They hung their green garlands all over the house, suspending a huge bouquet from the hall ceiling like a chandelier. Red and white berries glittered like jewels against the dark leaves and the house was filled with the scent of fresh herbs.

Ellen was delighted by the transformation. She entered enthusiastically into the spirit of the season, enhancing the decorations with ribbons of scarlet and emerald twisted into pretty bows. She listened with interest as Adam Tickell, the cook, explained in great detail the abbreviated version of the usual Hawthorne Christmas dinner he was planning. She spent hours in the kitchens cutting out elaborate ornaments in pastry and making marzipan decorations, Robin playing with lumps of dough beside her. Ellen's nimble fingers worked quickly with the ingredients, moulding them into miniature works of art, much to the admiration of all who saw them. It gave Alethea great pleasure to see Ellen chatting happily with Adam and Miles, her cheeks flushed from the heat of the kitchen fires, her hair dusted with flour. She and Robin had become cherished members of the household with everyone, except Crewe.

On Christmas Eve, ignoring the rain that had begun to fall, the whole household joined together to carry in a yule log. Tickell located the branch kept from the last year's log to light it with and they all stood together before the flames drinking spiced ale and eating Tickell's dainty mince pies which had been shaped by Ellen into holly leaves and fleur-de-lis. To surprise her, Tickell brought out a plate of little pies shaped into robins. All agreed Ellen's handiwork was the neatest they had ever seen and the pies the tastiest they had eaten.

Alethea thanked them all for returning to Measham and helping to restore it to some semblance of what it had once been.

'If only Mistress Alethea were with us now she might have graced us with a carol,' Palmes the footman said, rubbing his eyes.

She was touched by Palmes' remembrance of her, but did not want the little party to descend into melancholy. 'I know Alethea would have wanted to hear you wassailing, even in her absence,' she said. 'What say you, Tickell? You always had a good voice.'

Tickell began obligingly, '*Wassail, wassail all over the town, our toast it is white and our ale it is brown.*'

The rest joined in with more enthusiasm than harmony, while Alethea beat time with a wooden spoon and Robin clapped his hands and laughed.

They assembled together again for dinner next day. The long wooden table was entirely covered in dishes. There were plates of pickled oysters, neat's tongues and larded eels, white bread and preserved fruit. In pride of place was a kid goat, its belly stuffed with pudding, and a huge pie filled with turkey, goose, duck and pigeon, shaped into a giant crown. Ruby jellies and golden custards shimmered under candles garlanded with holly. Tickell sat Robin on his knee and fed him crumbs of plum pudding and spoonfuls of mutton broth. Even Crewe ate heartily, joining in the general merriment.

After dinner the servants staggered off into the village to see what sport was to be had there.

'Do you want to go, Ellen?' Alethea asked. 'There'll be dancing and revels of all sorts.'

But Ellen shook her head sleepily. 'I'm too full to go anywhere. That was the greatest feast I've ever eaten of.'

They settled themselves on either side of the fire, in the winter parlour.

'These have been joyful days. I always spent Christmas Day in prayer before. We weren't allowed to play games or dance. I used to find it a long old day as a child.' Ellen smiled contentedly.

She and Alethea stayed up long into the night exchanging stories from their lives and when they had exhausted those, stories from the lives of friends and relatives. They giggled and gossiped like a pair of young girls.

'We've run out of firewood,' Alethea noted, standing at last. 'Time for bed.' She stretched out her arms, feeling suddenly very weary.

'There's something I've been longing to tell you, only I was sworn to secrecy and could not break my oath.' Ellen spoke in a quiet, urgent rush.

Her words were interrupted by the return of the servants, who crashed about in the hall, their voices loud with drink. There was a knock on the parlour door and Crewe came in looking sombre. 'I am sorry to inform you, sir, but Miles has been taken unwell in the hall. We are just cleaning up after him now.'

Alethea laughed. 'Poor lad. Not to worry, it can happen to the best of us. Don't be too severe with him. Crewe, why don't you join us for a drink?' Alethea did not know why she had extended this invitation, but it was Christmas. To her relief Crewe declined.

'The hour is late and it is getting cold, perhaps it is time we all retired. You must consider your health, sir, you don't want to catch a chill.'

'Quite right as always, Crewe.' Alethea smiled. 'Can we leave you to put out the candles?'

'Of course, sir.' Crewe bowed as Alethea left the room followed by Ellen.

'It was good to have you back,' Ellen said softly, as they stood outside their chamber doors.

'What do you mean?'

Ellen hesitated. 'I don't like William so much as I like Alethea. I mean, when you are William you think like a gentleman, always preoccupied with business. Tonight you were a woman again and I could talk to you about anything.' Ellen held on to the door latch. 'I miss our friendship, how it used to be.'

As Ellen's door closed, Alethea felt loneliness plunge into her chest like a sword. The evening had felt joyful and intimate, now Ellen had shown it to be nothing more than a hollow sham. She wondered, with a stab of remorse, what it was Ellen had been about to tell her. She supposed Ellen was offended that she had invited Crewe to join them.

Alethea had not been aware of changing, of moving from one persona to another. Now Ellen was telling her she did not like who Alethea had become. But the truth was she liked being William. She liked it a lot more than she had ever liked being Alethea.

✦ Chapter Twenty-one ✦

Though she did not like to admit it, pregnancy was slowing Alethea down. Ellen had sewn padding into the shoulders and chest of a large jacket which gave Alethea a manly frame and helped to conceal her growing belly. Alethea pictured herself as Falstaff, adopted a swaggering gait and loudly praised the cook for feeding her so well. She ordered copious amounts of wine and ale to explain away her spreading girth. Drinks she poured into the flower beds beneath the dining-room window, for she could scarcely stomach them.

She had Ellen's favourite dishes sent up to her chamber, pretending they were for her own consumption. Pickled herrings with mustard, eels jellied with oranges and sugar, squares of gingerbread and almond cake; Ellen tucked in with relish, only concerned by Alethea's unhealthy preference for salads of red beets, boiled parsnips and minced cabbage.

Ellen had also strapped padding to her own stomach, increasing it gradually over the months so that it would appear as though she were the one breeding. The servants must have noticed, but they never dared refer to it. While they may have been disapproving, Ellen's pregnancy helped reinforce Alethea's masculine disguise, for everyone was convinced she had fathered this child. She enjoyed this misconception because it eliminated Samuel as the father, making her semi-divine.

While her days were spent masquerading as a man, Alethea's nights were disrupted by the turning of the child in her belly. 'What strange sort of hermaphrodite am I?' she asked herself as she looked down at her swollen stomach. The taut skin pressed outwards into odd humps and ridges as the infant within kicked and pushed against its confinement. Alethea could not envisage this child or its release. How the being that had transformed her belly into this great mound was to make its way out through that narrow gully between her legs was incomprehensible. Only the waiting and the discomfort made her forget her fear in the desire for ease. The pains of labour might be the curse of Eve, but Alethea would bear them with a masculine fortitude. She would expel this invader at last, then at least she could shed one layer of disguise. And if she lost the battle, Ellen would have to pretend that William had gone abroad again. Alethea could not kill off her brother and lose his inheritance. If William himself did not return, the estate would revert to her uncle.

She had written out a will claiming her child as Measham's legitimate heir and Ellen as its guardian, but could not be sure this would stand up in court. What would happen to them if she died? Crewe would not support their cause and Uncle Percy would be quick to challenge such a will. She locked a sum of money away in a chest and gave Ellen the key. She did not tell her how much was there, but it would be enough to keep them for a few years at least; enough for Ellen to find Lizzie and set up a business if she wished.

Alethea placed a long letter to William in the chest too. In it she tried to explain all that had happened to her since he had fled England. She hoped his own transgressions would soften him towards hers, that he would forgive her for her impersonation and understand her reasons. The letter begged him to look after Ellen, who had been so loyal and so true, and to provide for his niece or nephew should it survive.

Ellen calculated that Alethea should be delivered of her baby by mid-April, given the size of her belly and when she had lain with Samuel, insisting that in March the two of them should travel to

London where Alethea would have the baby in lodgings. Alethea hated the thought of being delivered in a strange place and did not want to undertake a journey. She wanted to be at home, surrounded by all that was familiar, to give birth in the house where she had been born, arguing they could smuggle a midwife in and swearing she would not cry out. Ellen told her she could swear all she liked, a body on the rack screams in spite of itself. The risk of discovery was too great, especially if Alethea were taken ill, or worse. Ellen could not pretend to lie-in for the expected month and administer to Alethea who would also, still disguised as William, need to take to her bed. And if Alethea were to die, how would Ellen explain her body?

After making some enquiries, Ellen found an old friend of hers, Margery, had spare rooms in Stepney they could rent. Alethea suspected the rooms' former inhabitants had died of the plague, but eventually acquiesced to Ellen's plans. Ellen wrote, explaining Alethea's condition to Margery, telling her discretion was needed as Alethea was from a good family, but had been abused by a gentleman. For an extra cost Margery agreed Alethea could have the child there, she would provide all the linen necessary.

Ellen also arranged for the midwife who had delivered Robin, a skilful and trustworthy Quaker woman, to tend to Alethea. They employed a girl from the village to take care of Robin while they were away. He had become quite the darling of the household and both Ellen and Alethea knew he would be well looked after in their absence.

The plague had gone from London and though they feared its return as the weather grew warmer, it seemed safe enough to undertake the journey. Crewe no doubt found it odd that William should be so contrary as to go against fashion and spend the winter in the country and travel to London in the spring, but Alethea told him she had private business to attend to in town. If he wondered what the business was he did not inquire and for once she was grateful for his reticence.

They set out for London at the end of March in the year 1666, just as the first buds of spring were beginning to appear. The roads were rutted and muddy from frost and rain and they were jolted about so much during the long coach journey Alethea was surprised she did not go into labour on the way.

At last they stopped at an inn where Alethea changed out of her male dress and into Ellen's loose gown. Ellen was delighted to cast off her cumbersome padding. Alethea had ordered a new dress and matching slippers made up for Ellen as a surprise gift. She had chosen green satin with a yellow underskirt and lace trimmed sleeves. Sea-green ribbons were sewn onto the yellow shoes and the shoulders of the dress.

'For our Leveller friends,' Alethea said, indicating the ribbons.

Ellen held the gown up before her. 'It's beautiful.' Her face flushed red with pleasure. 'Margery won't recognise me. I shall be quite the lady about town.'

Though Alethea was glad to be rid of her heavy jacket, she missed her breeches and the freedom of movement they allowed. She realised how used she had become to acting the man. It was odd to be a lady again; she felt both vulnerable and constrained. She had to keep reminding herself to lift up her skirts to avoid tripping over them or trailing them in the mud.

The coach driver was surprised to be told that one passenger had been substituted for another, but so long as they paid the fare he had no objections. Only a lady of quality would act with such an air of entitlement, issuing commands and taking up the space of two passengers as she spread herself out in the coach.

The fear that Samuel might have gone back to London with Rebecca gnawed at Alethea's mind. If they were to return, Stepney was the most likely place for them to settle in. She told herself they would not return to a place that held such sad memories and where he risked imprisonment for sedition. Jane Calverton should be back at the Sellwood estates in Sussex and she had no fear of encountering the Calvertons in Stepney.

The one person she really wanted to meet again was Jack. She thought of their last evening together and how sadly Jack had looked at her. She ought to have written to him at his father's inn, to make sure he was alive and well, if for no other reason. It was just too complicated and too risky to try to explain everything in writing. Crewe would wonder what she was up to, sending letters to a tavern in Highgate. Once she was delivered of the baby she would seek him out. Just the thought of being with Jack again lifted her spirits. She would visit him in her male disguise, that would turn the tables on him. She looked forward to seeing the expression on his face when she revealed herself.

It was a year since Alethea had arrived in London with the Calvertons, full of bright expectations. It felt as though she had endured a lifetime's worth of death and disappointment since then, but she reminded herself that she was not alone in this. Many had suffered greater losses. At least she was not destitute; in fact she was proud of her achievements in restoring Measham to a functioning estate, one that was now bringing in a profit. Ellen was in high spirits, eager to see old friends again and show off her freshly rounded figure in all its new finery. Alethea had not realised how much Ellen had been missing London.

Waking in the middle of the night, Alethea found her bedclothes wet. A sickly sweet smell rose up from the sheets. She hauled herself out of the bed and stumbled across the room squelching footprints across the floor. Ellen rose quickly from the pallet bed where she was sleeping.

'Is it time?' she asked.

'I don't know; only there is so much water.' Alethea clutched Ellen's arms in terror.

'That's a good sign,' Ellen reassured her. 'Better than the midwife having to break the waters for you.'

The sky outside grew light as the pains grew worse; rising and falling in great swells they knocked Alethea off her feet until she found herself kneeling on the floor, rocking back and forth and moaning quietly. She vomited into the chamber pot like a dog.

'That's the way, Mrs Swan, everything must come out,' Mrs Wright, the midwife said cheerfully.

It had amused Alethea to give a name linked somehow to Samuel Byrd's; now she wondered who the midwife was talking to.

'Give her some cinnamon water,' Mrs Wright told Ellen.

Ellen pressed a cup of spiced wine to Alethea's lips but the smell nauseated her. Perhaps death came like this for soldiers on the battlefield; all dreams of valour and glory gone, the spirit once again conquered by the flesh.

'Pray my sweet. Pray to the Almighty and look to the love of Jesus,' Ellen urged.

But Alethea could feel only nature at work here – fierce and inexorable, with no notion of religion or mercy. She felt as though her belly were being crushed by a great vice. The pain shot down her back and into her legs with such violence she could scarcely breathe. This was all there was and all there ever would be. She was staring into the abyss of hell, for where else could she be destined? A man could not be delivered of a child. A maid could not be loved by God when she had fallen in lechery.

Mrs Wright took Alethea in her arms, thumping her back with her fists as she rocked her back and forth, chanting in her ear, 'All shall be well, all shall be well.'

Alethea felt her breath returning with the rhythm of the midwife's voice. They rocked together back and forth and the hours stretched and contracted. Then Alethea was pulled under again, sucked down gasping for air. Her ears were filled with the roaring of her heart and the rushing of her blood. A pitiless current bore down on her, her body straining and heaving, every sinew pushing. She could hear Ellen and the midwife spurring her on, but their words were useless for she knew she could not survive this agony. Her limbs were being rent apart and she had no strength left. It was no good; she could not go on.

'It is a boy. A sound and lusty boy.' Mrs Wright held the blood-soaked body aloft. It writhed and wailed in her arms. She took it to a basin and washed it carefully, examining its limbs as Ellen looked on, as anxious as any parent.

The baby was rolled up in the cloths they had ready and laid in a cradle beside Alethea. When she was delivered of the afterbirth they rubbed her belly with oil and covered it with a hare's skin. She was so exhausted she hardly stirred when Ellen and Mrs Wright bound her up in clean linen.

Margery brought in a bowl of broth which Alethea drank greedily. It was over a day since she had last eaten and she could not remember when she had last taken such pleasure in food. She did not look into the cradle.

'Let her give the infant suck,' Mrs Wright instructed Ellen.

'Ellen is to nurse it,' Alethea said.

'Still, you should give him suck at first, mother's milk agrees better with a newborn than stranger's milk. And if you feed him yourself you will keep his affections and he will prove a dutiful son to you.'

'Ellen is not a stranger.'

Mrs Wright turned to Ellen. 'She'll love it better if she nurses the child herself,' Alethea heard her say quietly.

Ellen looked uneasily at Alethea. Ellen still had plenty of milk from nursing Robin and they had agreed she would feed the child, but she did not like to go against the midwife.

Sensing her uncertainty, Mrs Wright jumped in. 'Did not Sarah suckle Isaac? And what of Eve, our first mother, who else but she could feed her babes?'

'Ellen is the wet nurse. Ellen will feed it,' Alethea ordered in a voice that had become accustomed to command.

Mrs Wright looked put out, but Ellen put the baby to her breast and he began to feed at once, oblivious to whose womb he had exited.

'There's a vigorous and hearty lad,' Mrs Wright noted with satisfaction, looking to Alethea for some sign of maternal pride.

Alethea looked over at Ellen. She was smiling with delight at the baby in her arms. Wisps of dark hair lay plastered to the crown of his head. He paused in his feeding and turned his face in Alethea's direction, revealing round, rosy cheeks and oval eyes, the darkest of blues. Alethea observed him with detachment. He will do, she thought.

'Have you a name for him?' Mrs Wright asked.

'Nicholas,' Alethea said. She hoped her father would be glad to have his first grandson named after him, even if it was a bastard child.

They remained in Stepney for a month, waiting until Alethea was sufficiently recovered to make the journey home and resume her role as William. Ellen made up plasters of bean meal, vinegar and roses to dry up her milk, but Alethea's breasts became inflamed and she suffered great discomfort for some days. It was a relief when at last the milk was gone. She would not allow herself to feel any greater attachment to Nicholas than she did to Robin. She remembered how her father used to kiss her little sisters and dandle them on his knee, but she decided she would not indulge in this sort of behaviour too often, for she wanted the baby to look to Ellen and not herself for affection. A few days after his birth, she gave way to tears, but only once. Ellen said that was natural in all new mothers and Alethea soon regained her self-control.

After ten days had passed, Ellen allowed Alethea to come downstairs and sit with her and Margery in the parlour. Ellen was taken up with the baby. Margery sewed. Alethea felt bored and discontented. She wished there were something other than the Bible to read. Margery disapproved of card games and had no musical instruments to play.

Alethea sat staring out of the window at the street outside, straining to hear a ballad singer peddling his latest song. As far as she could make out he was singing, in a flat voice, about the eternal rise and fall of fortune. *It's a shame he can't follow the rise and fall of a tune*, she thought grimly.

'I clean forgot to tell you, Ellen.' Margery paused in her needlework. 'I had news of Brother Byrd, the preacher, yesterday.'

The baby gave an indignant squeak as Ellen involuntarily jerked his head from her breast. Alethea did not dare turn from the window. Her nails dug into the sill, leaving small crescents in the painted woodwork.

'Is that right?' Ellen said. Alethea was impressed by the level tone of her voice.

'He and his wife have been making quite a stir in the country-side. Do you remember Humility Dyer? She used to attend Brother Samuel's sermons with us. She travelled all the way to Oxfordshire just to hear them. Rebecca Byrd has the gift of prophesy they say.'

'She was a poor befuddled creature when we last saw her,' Ellen said.

'They say the Lord speaks through her now. She's correctly predicted all kinds of events. The Byrds can't come near London for fear of arrest else I'd go to hear them myself.'

Discouraged by the silence of her companions, Margery spoke no more on the matter. Later, Alethea overheard her asking Ellen if the young lady disapproved of dissenters.

'She's a haughty creature, considering she's been undone,' Margery said, loudly enough for her voice to carry up the stairs. 'I suppose she's paying you handsomely for your services, but as a Christian I won't enquire after pecuniary matters.'

One night, Alethea came downstairs to catch sight of a handsome young woman on the other side of Margery's parlour window. She wondered for a moment who it could be, before recognising the image as her own reflection. It startled her; she was not used to seeing herself as a woman, let alone as an attractive one.

Although she felt a great sense of relief to have survived childbirth and to be freed from the burden of pregnancy, a terrible despondency fell on her. She could not envisage any happy future for herself. Was this her punishment for fornication, that at twenty years of age she should never know a man's love again, never have a family that could be recognised?

It was almost two years since William had gone abroad and in all that time there had not been one letter or message from him. She was beginning to resign herself to her brother's death. For what other explanation could there be for his silence? Living out the rest of her life as William was a lonely prospect. She enjoyed the power and the independence, but that only made her less fit to be a wife. For even if William did return, how would she ever find a suitable husband, one that would overlook her spoilt state and allow her the freedom she had become accustomed to? She did not want to end up with a husband like Ellen's, or Jane's.

Another ballad singer could be heard in the street, singing more tunefully this time. Opening the window, she leant out. It was a drinking song; it made her smile and think of Jack.

> '*The miser with all his bags*
> *Is not so content in mind*
> *As honest good fellows in rags*
> *That are to each other kind*
> *Tush we have and shall have abundance*
> *Come fill us the other odd quart.*'

Her thoughts kept returning to Jack. She missed his company more than her former lover's. Samuel had sunk so low in her opinion she could hardly bear to think of him. She doubted Rebecca had been touched by God. That woman was no prophet, merely a useful conduit for Samuel. Who then was the greater mountebank? Jack at least had always been honourable towards her. All his kindnesses came back to her now; how seriously he had weighed her opinions, how concerned he always was for her well-being. She loved Ellen, but could not share a joke with her, not in the way she had done with Jack. She missed his sense of humour and his easy-going nature. She had been far too harsh in her judgement of him, she realised that now. Who was she to judge anyone, fraudster and fallen woman that she was? She should not have been so churlish when he offered to marry her. A sense of shame rose in her when she thought of it. When he had been generous and loving, she had responded with rudeness and arrogance. There was Jane, married to an earl and as miserable a woman as any you might find in England.

Now she had established her position at Measham and earned the respect of the servants, she was in a much stronger position to bring Jack into her household. He would be delighted to see Ellen and Robin again. She wondered what he would make of her son and hoped he would not hold the baby's father against him, but Jack was not like that. He was never one to bear grudges.

She could just see him now, admiring the house and gardens. Ellen liked to retire early to bed, but she and Jack could pass their evenings playing chess and drinking wine, just like old times. They could go out to taverns as two men together. How amusing Jack would find that. What a relief it would be to have another accomplice; a man to aid her in her deception. Eventually, she could even replace Crewe with Jack as her steward. That would make her life so much easier.

'Shall we look for Jack?' she said to Ellen the next morning.

'I was hoping you'd suggest that, but didn't like to ask,' Ellen said.

'His father's inn was called The Red Hart; there can't be many taverns in Highgate with that name.'

Alethea insisted on hiring a coach and visiting The Red Hart herself, despite Ellen's protestations that such an excursion would damage her health. She was forced to compromise, however, on dressing as a man.

'Margery will throw us out if she thinks I've been stepping out with a gentleman,' Ellen said. 'You'll never be able to leave the house and come back again without her or the neighbours seeing you. Especially when she's agreed to mind Nicholas for us. You could blow your whole disguise and for what? To play a trick on Jack?'

After some enquiries and an uncomfortable ride in a Hackney, with Ellen fretting about infectious air and Alethea's condition, and the driver swearing and complaining about passengers who did not know where they were going, they arrived at The Red Hart. The front had been newly painted and the tavern was clearly doing well. Inside it was busy with customers, talking and laughing over their ale. A rosy cheeked woman with a low-cut bodice was busy filling up their tankards from a pitcher. She chatted to the drinkers with an easy familiarity. Alethea and Ellen fought their way to the bar, looking around all the while for a sign of Jack. Alethea heard him before she saw him.

'I kid you not, my friend, I saw it with my own eyes.' Jack was perched on a high stool behind the bar, entertaining a large, well-dressed man.

Alethea felt a great swell of affection for her old friend, the sort of heartfelt emotion she had not experienced in many months. There he was, alive and well and looking like his old self again, animated and confident. For a moment she questioned her decision to bring him back to Measham. Could Jack be happy there? She quickly shoved all doubts out of her mind. Jack would love it at Measham; she would make sure of it.

'Hello, Jack,' she said, smiling at him.

Jack nearly toppled from his stool, but quickly regained his composure. 'Alethea, Ellen.' He looked from one to the other. 'Welcome to my establishment.'

'This is your place is it, Jack?' Ellen looked around in admiration.

'Since last February. My old dad died and left me the tavern. I'd been helping him out with it anyway and d'you know what, I appear to make a very good host.'

Ellen smiled. 'And why would that surprise us?'

'Now, what can I get you ladies? On the house, of course.'

Ellen took a pot of small beer while Alethea had a cup of Rhenish.

Jack looked at Alethea with concern. 'You got home all right then? Your father must've been glad to see you.' He raised his eyebrows enquiringly and she realised he was being careful about what he said in front of Ellen.

'My family died of the plague. All except William and we don't know where he is,' she said. 'I'm in charge of the estate now. With Ellen's help, of course.'

'I'm so sorry to hear that,' Jack said warmly. 'To lose them all in one go, what a terrible thing.' He looked quite stricken. 'But the two of you are running the place, that's quite something. So, we've all become persons of substance.' He smiled encouragingly at them both.

'Yes,' said Alethea, finishing her drink. It was a long time since she had enjoyed a glass of wine so much. Jack refilled her rummer. 'You must come and visit us. You'd be a very welcome guest, wouldn't he, Ellen?'

'Of course,' said Ellen. 'Robin would be overjoyed to see you.' She gave a sidelong look at Alethea, wondering whether she should mention Nicholas or not.

'How is the little lad?' Jack beamed at the mention of Robin.

'He's very well. He'll soon be walking and he has some words. We left him up at Measham.' Ellen swallowed. 'He has a little brother now, born three weeks ago.'

'Does he?' Jack stared at them in astonishment for a few moments, then nodded slowly. He was always quick to catch on. 'A little playmate,' he said, looking at Alethea.

'Called Nicholas,' Alethea said. 'After my father. Though Ellen is his mother.' She looked down at her empty cup.

Jack topped it up again. 'I must get you something to eat.'

'I'll just visit the privy,' Ellen said, clearly wanting to give them some time alone.

'Through that door and out the back,' Jack indicated. Turning back to Alethea, he spoke quietly. 'So, you were delivered all right then?'

She nodded.

'That's very good of Ellen, to take the babe on as her own.'

'Yes, it is. I treat her well in return, though, she wants for nothing.' The wine had gone to Alethea's head, her thoughts and her voice had lost their clarity. 'Will you come to Measham, Jack? It would mean a lot to me.' She put her hand out to touch his but it had disappeared behind the bar. She wobbled slightly on her stool.

'Steady there,' Jack said. 'Must get you some pie.' He surveyed the room, trying to catch the eye of the barmaid. 'The thing is, Alethea, I can't leave my tavern to go travelling up to Derbyshire.'

'Can't you leave someone else in charge? You never wanted to work as an innkeeper, Jack. I can offer you a much better life. I'm in charge at

Measham, you know, I can do what I like.' Alethea was forestalling the moment she told Jack about her change of identity. How impressed he would be! She was trying to formulate in her mind how best to tell him to create the greatest impact.

'Of course,' Jack said, 'I could never run this place without the help of my sweet Rose.' The pink-cheeked woman had set her pitcher down on the counter beside them.

'What's that? You talking about me?' she asked, leaning over the bar to pinch Jack's chin, rubbing his nose with her own.

Jack gave her a kiss. 'These are some of the folk I resided with in Epping Forest, my dear.' Jack gestured to Ellen, who had just returned from the privy, and Alethea who swayed on her seat. 'May I introduce my wife, Mrs Rose Fleet,' he said with evident pride.

Ellen put one hand against Alethea's back to prevent her from slipping off her stool.

Rose smiled warmly at them. 'Pleased to meet you, I'm sure.'

Her face, though not exactly pretty, was made attractive by her friendly expression and lively eyes. Rose's teeth were as crooked as Jack's were yellow, but her engaging smile rendered their uneven appearance endearing. Beyond her natural charm she boasted a fine bosom, shown off to advantage by the low cut of her bodice. It was not surprising she was popular with the customers, Alethea thought.

'Jack's told me all about his adventures in the woods. He was quite the Robin Hood, I believe. Are you the lady he rescued from bandits?' Rose turned to Alethea.

'From bandits?' Alethea chuckled. 'Well maybe one.'

Rose looked confused.

'My cup is empty.' Alethea waved it in the air.

'We're honoured to meet you, Mrs Fleet,' said Ellen quickly, patting Alethea's back.

'Rose was working here when I got back from Epping. I was laid up with a fierce ague by the time I got home, if it wasn't for her nursing me through it I doubt I'd have survived.' Jack put an arm around his wife who had moved behind the bar to stand beside him. She laughed and rested her head on his shoulder. It fitted snuggly for she was a full inch shorter than he.

'My honey-sop, it was your own knowledge of physic that saved you.' Rose looked up at Ellen and Alethea. 'Jack trained as an apothecary, you know. He's very learned. He only took this place on to please his dad. That's Jack all over, always putting the welfare of others before his own, but I'm sure I don't need to tell you that.'

'We are very grateful to you for helping to save our friend, nay our *hero's*, life,' Alethea told Rose. Even she was surprised by how slurred and bitter her words sounded.

Rose just shrugged. 'Have you tried our eel pie, ladies? It's the best there is north of the city. Let me fetch you some pie and ale.'

'I'm a lucky beggar.' Jack watched his wife hurrying off into the kitchen, then shook his head in wonder. 'I don't deserve her, but by God I'm glad I've got her.'

'A wife that's a hard worker is always an asset,' noted Ellen. 'We're very happy for you, Jack.'

'That was a quick courtship,' Alethea said grumpily.

'Five months is not so quick. We were in Epping for less than four.' He looked sharply at Alethea.

'I was a different person then,' Alethea said. 'A different person entirely.'

'Jack has done well for himself,' Ellen noted as they returned to Stepney. 'They're a right pair of love-mates aren't they?'

'They were certainly putting on a show of it. What did you think of his wife?'

'I think she's lovely. You can see she dotes on Jack and she's just the right sort to help him run a public house.' When Alethea did not respond Ellen continued, 'You aren't regretting turning him down are you? I can't see you waiting tables.'

'Of course not. And Jack would never have fitted in at Measham Hall neither. I am glad to see him married. I wish him much happiness.'

'Only you don't like his wife?'

'She seems a rough sort of woman,' Alethea said.

'That,' said Ellen, 'is William Hawthorne speaking.'

Alethea folded her arms and turned her face to the window.

'I hope Nicholas has been all right with Margery,' Ellen said. But Alethea did not respond.

→ Chapter Twenty-two ←

H alfway back to Derbyshire Alethea turned herself once again into a man. It came as a relief, to shed herself of all things feminine; to refuse to dwell on womanish melancholy. She was the guardian of Measham Hall and had duties to fulfil. All her efforts would go into making her estate as prosperous and happy a place as anyone could dream of. She would build a maze to the west of the house, there was ample space. The boys could play in it when they grew older. The lake too needed improving, the ground around it was no more than a bog. Their neighbour, Sir Peverell, had a beautiful lake and had made some impressive developments to his land. Alethea decided to approach him for advice on draining the land and stocking her own lake.

She would employ a dancing master for Ellen and hire musicians to play for them. She would also write to the Royal Society to enquire after some up and coming philosopher in need of patronage, someone who could make Measham Hall a place of enquiry and learning. Robin and Nicholas would be well educated. She also wanted to improve her own education. If she must live out her life without the comfort of a mate, she would make it a life of richness and variety, cultivating her mind as well as her land.

As they approached Measham Hall, Alethea felt her spirits lift. She looked out of the coach window at the familiar landscape with increasing enthusiasm. Here was home. She was as much a part of Measham as it was of her and she never wanted to live anywhere else. She was filled with pride as she looked out at the plump cattle grazing and the lambs playing in the fields; at the verdant parkland fringed with newly planted saplings. She could not underestimate the hand of spring in transforming the countryside around her, but she credited herself also for the improvements she saw everywhere – walls mended, hedgerows clipped, brambles cleared. Surely God had placed her here, in this position for a reason. She was the chosen guardian of this land and nothing else mattered so long as she followed her vocation.

'We have a new addition to our household,' Alethea told Crewe as he came out to greet her. 'Meet Master Nicholas.'

Ellen held up the baby that lay sleeping in her arms. 'Isn't he beautiful,' she said, raising her eyebrows, daring Crewe to disagree.

'Master Nicholas, indeed,' Crewe said. He looked a little paler than usual, but apart from that there was no discernible change to his countenance.

'When you have refreshed yourself, sir, you might like to come into the winter parlour. You have a visitor waiting for you.' Crewe spoke softly into Alethea's ear, leaning on the word 'visitor' with a significant emphasis.

All Alethea's bravado deserted her in an instant. What sort of visitor would Crewe have ensconced in the parlour? Why had he not told them to come back some other time? She hoped it was not Lord Calverton or a priest come to reclaim her soul.

'I am very weary, Crewe,' she said.

'I will send some claret up to your room; you can come down as soon as you are able.' Crewe's smooth delivery brooked no opposition.

Ellen was busy embracing an excited Robin. The nursemaid, Abigail, had taken Nicholas and was exclaiming over him with equal delight. Alethea went to her room, checked her appearance, knocked back a glass of wine and went down to the parlour.

Despite the mild spring evening a fire burnt in the grate. A chair was pulled up towards it and Alethea could just make out the back of a man's head. Caesar lay in front of the fire. He lifted his head, looking up at her lazily. His tail thumped against the hearthstone, but he did not leap up and run to her as he would usually do.

'Good evening,' Alethea said, with more confidence than she felt.

She pushed back her shoulders and stuck out her chin. I am the lord and master here, she told herself, I fear no one. She strode towards the fire, her boot heels rapping the wooden floorboards. The man did not rise from his seat, but as she drew level with him he looked up at her with a smile.

His large round eyes, brown and lustrous as polished chestnuts, looked straight into hers. 'Perhaps you should close the door,' he said quietly. Alethea turned back quickly and pulled the parlour door shut. 'What a fine gentleman you make, Thea,' he said with some amusement as she did so.

Alethea fell to her knees in front of her brother, throwing her arms around his legs, too overwhelmed to look up at him, unable to speak.

He patted her shoulder. 'May I remove your wig?' he asked.

'Of course,' she said, pulling it from her head to reveal her cropped hair. 'I have been longing for your return,' she told him. 'Holding your place only until you were ready to fill it again.'

'But why the impersonation, Thea?'

'I was afraid Uncle Percy would take over the estate in your absence. I had nothing to prove who I was.'

'Nor anything to prove that you were me neither, yet you seem to have managed that quite well.'

Although Alethea had practised her explanation to William many times in her mind, now she was in his presence her rehearsed speech deserted her. It was two years since she had last seen him, she did not know how he might have changed, or how he would react to her fall from grace.

Caesar shoved his nose against Alethea's cheek, excited to find her sharing the floor with him. She struggled awkwardly to her feet, then absent-mindedly grabbed a log from the wood pile and dropped it onto the fire. She paced the room as she told William about the Calvertons' disappearance and the false errand she had been sent on. William was horrified to hear how she had been left friendless in the city. He had not been in England before the last week and had certainly not sent any messenger to arrange a meeting at Deptford. Alethea explained that she had been befriended by kind people and lived with them in Epping Forest until she thought it safe to venture home.

'Won't you sit down?' William asked, gesturing to the chair opposite him.

She sank heavily onto the seat, staring intently at her brother's face. 'I have missed you so, William. I was afraid you had perished. Why did you not send word?'

William studied the flames in the grate. 'When I received the sad news about our family, I was too unwell to travel. I was filled with grief at so much loss, most especially when I thought you too had died. Sorrow hampered my recovery, otherwise I would have come sooner. I was overjoyed to learn that you were alive. I was also rather curious to hear of your antics and wanted to see how you played my part.'

'You knew?' Alethea said in astonishment. 'But how?'

'After Father died, Crewe became my intercessor, making sure I was provided for, notifying me of all events at home. He was most perplexed when a young woman appeared, claiming I was in the country and that she was acting on my behalf. A young woman who seemed to know a great deal about me. He sent word post-haste and I sent the messenger straight back to tell him I was still in France and had no knowledge of any Ellen Liddell. Crewe had wanted to go to the magistrates, but I advised caution. I thought we should wait and see what game this woman was playing.'

'So that is why he kept us waiting at the inn. But Ellen was only doing what I asked of her.'

William got up and poured them each a glass of wine from a jug that stood on the table. 'You must be hungry after your long journey, would you like some food?' He gestured to a plate on the table. 'I had Crewe leave out some salad of cold hen for you.'

Alethea shook her head. She was too shocked to be hungry, besides her stomach had not recovered from being rattled about in a coach for several hours. 'So, Crewe recognised me?' Did all the servants know, she wondered.

As if in response to her thoughts William said, 'Don't worry, Crewe is a most trustworthy fellow. He is the only one to guess your secret; indeed he has helped you to keep it.'

'Helped me? But why didn't he say anything? He never even told me he knew your whereabouts or that you were alive.'

'He was acting under my instructions,' William said.

'I thought Crewe was Frances' man; didn't she bring him here? He was always castigating us when we were children and I have good reason to distrust him now.'

'You won't remember this, but Crewe worked for Father before the wars and fought with him during them. He was exiled like Father, only returning after Father's remarriage. He has an absolute loyalty to our family. It was he who arranged my passage to France.' William picked a violet out of the salad and chewed on it slowly. 'Mrs Liddell is a puritan, I believe. And has a little boy.'

'Two boys. She has just been delivered of a second child, in London,' Alethea said awkwardly. She despised herself for lying to William but could not bring herself to tell him the truth.

'A second child? And who is the father?'

'Ellen's husband died of the plague, at least we think he did; he abandoned them in his desire to save himself. She is a good woman, William, a kind and true friend and as honest a Christian as any I have met.'

William nodded thoughtfully but said nothing.

'Where have you been? You must tell me everything. Did Crewe not inform you that you were pardoned by the King months ago?' Alethea leant forward eagerly in her seat, resting her forearms on her thighs.

'He did indeed.' William took a sip of wine. He had aged since she'd last seen him, now looking weary and pensive. 'As you know I went first to Paris. My time there I spent in as dissipated a way as ever I was accustomed to do, drinking, gambling and whoring. I received word

243

from Father that Lord Fanshawe had the ear of the King and would do all he could to prevent me from being pardoned. Father urged me not to fritter away my youth, but to make a good life for myself on the Continent if that was where I was destined to remain. At about this time I met a young Englishman who was studying philosophy at the Jesuit College in St. Omer. He was superior in intellect and wit to any of my companions in debauchery. To tell you the truth, I'd grown tired of drunkenness and gaming, I was thoroughly sick of the futility of it all. I travelled to St. Omer with my new friend and enrolled at the college, where I have been studying natural philosophy and humanities.'

'So the payments Crewe said were going to Father's godson were going to you. Why didn't he tell me? Do you know how fearful I've been for your welfare?'

'At first Father urged secrecy on me in case Fanshawe sought vengeance for the death of his son. After some months at the college, however, I realised why I had been directed there. I understood my vocation, Thea. This September I intend to make my vows and enter the Society of Jesus as an aspirant to the priesthood.'

Alethea stared at her brother. Her companion and guide through all the rough terrain of childhood. The only person imprinted with the same early joys and sorrows, the only one left who shared her history. Measham's heir, the eldest son, there to protect and shelter his siblings, was abandoning her to become a Jesuit priest.

'It has already been decided; I shall take up my training in Valladolid where I will study theology.'

'In Spain?'

'Yes, but my mission ultimately will be to return to England. The English are starving, Thea, starving for the food of life. I took away a young man's life and I will make amends for that by bringing the bread of life to those who are willing to receive it.'

'Father agreed to this?'

'When Frances provided him with a new heir he accepted my vocation. Of course, we hoped that little Charles would outlive us all, but that was not to be.'

'Exactly, so you must come back now. Your duty is here. Of all the orders why choose the Jesuits, the one most hated in England?'

William smiled indulgently at Alethea, then looked down at Caesar whose ears he was absent-mindedly caressing. The dog looked up at him plaintively, ever hopeful for a scrap of meat from the table.

'I visited our cousin Mary in Rouen. You know she is one of the Poor Clares in the convent there. She is an exceptional young woman who has renounced all earthly pleasures for a life of devotion. I can see her becoming Abbess one day, not only because of her piety, but also because of her wisdom in public and private managements. She reminds me of you, Thea. There are widows in your position, and many wives during the late wars that ran their husbands' estates in their absence; our own mother was one of them.'

'I am not a nun or a widow.'

William looked at Alethea gravely, holding her gaze for so long she had to look away. From upstairs she could hear the baby crying. Did William know? If Crewe had guessed who she was did he also know it was her and not Ellen who was pregnant? The thought filled Alethea with horror. She hoped her brother would attribute the redness of her cheeks to the heat of the fire.

'In order to carry out my mission in England I have to assume an alias. The name has already been decided; indeed I travelled here under it – Matthew Harcourt. As you know, the life of a priest in England is one of danger and secrecy. Uncle Percy may practise our faith, but I do not believe he would make as honourable a custodian of Measham as you have proved yourself to be. He is a garrulous old man and I wouldn't trust him with my identity; he would boast of his nephew the priest to everyone he met. And of course, I don't want to deprive you of the home you cherish. It would be invaluable for me to have Measham as a place of refuge and also a source of income. Crewe has given me favourable reports and I've seen with my own eyes the well-stocked pastures, the improvements to the gardens and the cottages. He tells me you are noble-minded, that you've gained the respect of tenants and servants alike for your good treatment of them.'

'I'm glad he thinks so highly of me. I did not suspect it.' Alethea fiddled with the buttons on her waistcoat. 'I think I have been fair in the setting of lands and leases, and perhaps I do have a propensity for the managing of estates. I am delighted you are pleased with my improvements. But I have been helped in my work, not only by Crewe, but also by Ellen Liddell.'

William refilled their glasses with wine. 'There was another reason I delayed my return after Crewe informed me you were alive and well.' He studied her for a moment. 'I realised it was exigent that I found you a suitable husband. A man of our own faith, who we could take into our confidence. The friend who first showed me the way, my fellow student at St. Omer, is just such a man.'

'Isn't he a priest also?'

'No, that is not his vocation. But he loves me dearly and will love you too. Not only will he support you in running the estate, he has also agreed to change his name to Hawthorne in order to preserve the family name.'

'Doesn't he care for his own name?'

'He has two older brothers and several nephews; their name is secure.'

'Perhaps I don't want a husband.'

William pulled a locket out from around his neck. He opened it and presented his sister with a miniature of a young man, looking sideways out of the frame, his head tilted over his shoulder, his hand on his hip. His downcast eyes were a watery blue, his lashes and brows so pale they were hardly visible. His bulging lips were parted in a slight pout. His long brown hair hung down to his narrow waist, thick and fluffy, as though it had just been washed.

'His hair is his own,' William said, as if that would impress her.

Alethea sighed and handed William back the portrait. 'I don't think I will make a good wife. I have become too accustomed to being my own master.'

William smiled. He was used to bending her will to his own. 'Lawrence will make a very obliging husband; he will let you have your own way in most things. He understands that you have been living as a man and was as impressed as I have been by Crewe's reports.'

'You told him?'

'Naturally; I have complete faith in him.'

'A third son, willing to relinquish his name; I am guessing that your friend is not a man of means. You might have found me a wealthy husband, William,' Alethea said half in jest. The events of the evening were so surprising she could not take them entirely seriously.

'He is in the middle of certain, rather delicate business negotiations at present, which is why he was unable to accompany me, but we hope he may be about to make his fortune.' William pressed his hands down on his chair. 'It is late and I can see that you are tired. Why don't we resume our discussion in the morning?' He stood up, signalling the end of the conversation.

'Have the servants seen you?'

'Crewe told them I am a cousin come to stay. Only he has seen me at close quarters.' William took Alethea's hands in his own and pulled her gently to her feet. 'Your sojourn in London has created the perfect explanation for Alethea's return. We will say that I heard rumours you had not perished as was thought and went to seek you out. So, I return home triumphantly with my beloved sister.'

Alethea looked at him doubtfully. He was a little taller and broader than she was, and his voice was deeper, but they were still very alike. He was thinner too, but she had been away for a month, she might have lost weight in that time, or rather *he* might have. It would be strange, to have to resign her position and come under her brother's authority.

'The servants will be so pleased to see Alethea return, they'll believe what we tell them. We are only re-establishing the truth after all.' William squeezed her hands. 'One thing I must insist on is that you say nothing of my vocation to Mrs Liddell.'

'I trust Ellen with my life.'

'That is as maybe, but I ask that you do not entrust her with mine.'

Alethea agreed to what she considered a temporary arrangement. She was sure that once William got to know Ellen he would recognise her integrity. They embraced and Alethea laid her head on her brother's shoulder, forgetting for a moment all her fears and doubts in her happiness to have him home again.

Once in bed, however, her mind woke up to her brother's proposal. How could she possibly marry his friend? Should she admit to William she had a son? She did not like the look of the man in the miniature; he seemed a petulant sort of fellow to her. He would let her have her way in most things, William said. What were the other things, the ones that required her obedience? She had wished for a mate and now William had found her one. A complete stranger she was expected to devote her life to. A man willing to take her on her brother's word, without even troubling to meet her in person.

She spent a sleepless night debating back and forth with herself. If she did resurrect Alethea she would be able to confront Margaret Calverton and reveal her duplicity. She could invite Jane to come and stay with her. But what if this Lawrence turned out to be as tyrannical as Roland Sellwood and forbade her having guests? What of Ellen and Robin and Nicholas? William would have to promise they could remain at Measham. Then she considered all she had achieved and all she had planned for the estates. Must she cede control of them too?

As soon as it was light Alethea rose and dressed herself as a man. Then she positioned herself outside her brother's room so she could intercept him before he went downstairs.

'Hello,' William said with some surprise when he finally emerged. 'Still dressed as me then?'

'I must speak with you alone.' Alethea marched into his room. 'I have a different proposition to put to you.' She looked her brother squarely in the face. 'Instead of marrying your friend I continue to live as you.'

William's mouth opened. He tried to interrupt, but Alethea held up her hand to silence him.

'The advantages are manifold. Friends often prove fickle; who knows how Lawrence might change once he has his feet under the table here.' William shook his head and began to speak, but Alethea continued on regardless. 'Believe me, I have some experience of this. Secrets are safest the least people know of them. We know we can rely on each other; there is no need for anyone else to become involved. You said yourself how well I've kept Measham and how impressed Crewe has been by my achievements here. I know nothing of Lawrence or his abilities in estate management, but you have given me the impression he would have little interest in Measham and its upkeep. Well then, I wish to continue as I have begun, with complete command.'

'Lawrence would consult with you before making any changes,' William said, looking uneasy. 'And Crewe of course would continue to act as steward.'

Alethea nodded. 'I work well with Crewe and he is clearly trust-worthy. I am happy to act under his direction.' She gazed earnestly at William. 'You spoke of our cousin Mary the nun, you yourself have decided to live celibate, why should I not wish the same? Only my calling is to this world and not from it.'

'Marriage frightens you,' William said softly. 'I can understand that, but Lawrence is a sweet-tempered man, he will always treat you gently, you have no need to fear him.'

'I am not afraid of him,' Alethea said impatiently. 'I am not negotiating with you, William. I am laying out my terms. I will continue as the guardian of Measham. I will expand the estate and bring in enough revenue to support you as a priest. I will keep you safe here and do all in my power to aid you in your calling, but I will do it as William Hawthorne, not as anyone's wife.'

✦ Chapter Twenty-three ✦

William surveyed Alethea with new admiration. 'I see you have become accustomed to wearing the breeches. You talk like a man, not like the maid I left behind. Well, I am not in any great hurry. We will leave things as they stand for the time being. Why don't you take me on a tour of the estate while I consider your proposal. I am curious to see how you conduct yourself.'

William's horse, Sans Pareil, had reappeared in the stables. They rode out together just as they had done in the past, with Alethea on her old grey mare. She needed to prove herself to William now and hoped to win him over with her enthusiasm for what she had achieved and what she intended to carry out. She showed him the depleted woods and the saplings of oak, beech and ash she had planted in order to build them up again, pointing out that the cultivation of woodland was not only profitable in terms of timber, but also of national importance, given the general shortage of wood for the navy. Not only were woods adornments of beauty to the countryside and pleasant places to hunt, they also provided livings for a great number of people. She had experienced at first hand the protection and bounty of a forest.

William smiled at her ambition and approved her ideas. He was particularly struck with the orchard and her newly acquired knowledge of fruit trees. 'I see you've been reading the books I sent you.'

'What books?'

'The ones Crewe gave you; he bought them under my instructions. I thought, if you were going to play me, I had better make sure you were educated well enough to do my name justice.'

'And have I not acquitted myself reasonably well?'

'Admirably.'

When they reached the lake, Alethea told him about her plans for it and how she intended to consult their neighbour, Sir Peverell, for advice. William in turn explained that at least a hundred acres of what Peverell called his land belonged to Measham. Peverell, being a parliament-man, had been awarded much of the estate after it was confiscated by Cromwell. Their father had tried to buy it back, offering Peverell a good price for it, but he refused to give it up.

'Father never forgave him for it. They had been friends once.'

Alethea recollected then her father's hostility towards Peverell and his complaints about the disputed land. It had been a constant source of grievance, though she had never given it much thought.

'Perhaps I'll have better luck at winning back what once belonged to the Hawthornes,' she told William, partly to impress him and partly because she truly believed it.

Buoyed by William's encouragement Alethea returned home for dinner in good spirits and with a hearty appetite. She felt sure William was going to agree to her plan.

'I must introduce you to young Thornly. He'll explain our designs regarding the livestock,' she told William as they entered the house. She was surprised to see Ellen waiting for them in the hall. 'Ellen,' she said, recollecting herself. 'This is my cousin Matthew. Matthew may I introduce my great friend and companion, Mrs Ellen Liddell.'

Now Alethea had to return to playing William, not only to convince her brother, but also to deceive Ellen. The girl called Alethea was beginning to feel like a former associate. Not herself, but someone else.

They endured a quiet and awkward meal. Fortunately, the children were with the nursemaid.

'Your youngest son bears the same name as William's late father,' William observed to Ellen.

'Yes,' said Ellen looking to Alethea. 'It was William's wish to honour his father.'

'That is interesting.' William also turned to Alethea. 'So, the naming was your decision?'

'I hope that doesn't offend you, cousin.' Alethea picked up her wine glass.

'Why should it offend me?'

'No reason, I'm sure.' Alethea rolled a mouthful of wine around her mouth. It was a sweet, delicate sack. Crewe must have brought out a better vintage than usual in honour of her brother.

'I was sorry to hear of your husband's departure.' William turned back to Ellen. 'William tells me he is believed dead.'

'Well,' said Ellen, clearly in great discomfort. 'We cannot know for certain.'

'Have you left word with friends as to your current abode in case he lives still and wishes to make amends? He would surely like to know that he has another son to provide for.'

'God forgive him, but my husband was a mean rascal. He wouldn't care how many children he fathered.' Ellen gave a short laugh.

'I plan to adopt Ellen's children as my own,' Alethea announced, disliking the nature of her brother's questioning.

'Can you do that without the father's permission?' William's tone was calmly curious.

'I don't know. But there's nothing to stop me from treating them as my own children and providing for them as such, is there, cousin? It's unlikely I'll ever find a suitable wife, given my circumstances, but I don't want to live out my life childless and Measham will need an heir.' Alethea downed the rest of her wine. She could see Ellen looking at her with alarm.

'You plan to make Mrs Liddell's children your heirs?' William sounded incredulous.

Alethea grabbed the flagon and poured herself more wine. 'In the absence of any others, yes.'

'Our Uncle Percy might have something to say on that matter,' he warned. 'You know how litigious he is.'

'I don't see how he can stop me,' Alethea declared, though she was entirely ignorant of her legal standing.

'We are a Catholic family, cousin. Are you going to have these children baptised into the Catholic faith?' William's expression was grave.

'Over my dead body,' Ellen interjected.

'Do you suffer from that general hatred and fear of papists, common in this land?' William raised his eyebrows; he sounded sorrowful rather than angry.

Alethea went to refill their glasses, but they were disappointingly full. She refilled her own just emptied one instead.

'I've nothing against your individual papist,' Ellen said carefully. 'But I have my own religion that is dear to me and I want my children to be sincere in their practice of the Gospel; not to be seduced into idolatry.' She tore at a piece of bread, dropping the crumbs onto her untouched meat.

'Catholics are equally sincere in following the Gospel. We simply believe in the importance of having a well-educated priest to aid us in our understanding.' William laid his knife down beside his plate. 'Look at all the different Protestant sects and the recent wars caused by puritan disputing. Relying on the Bible alone as a source of authority breeds confusion, not certainty.' He brought his fingertips together under his chin, forming his hands into a steeple. 'As to idolatry, well, there is a general misunderstanding of our practices in this country. We do not worship images, God forbid. We make use of images to put us in mind of the originals.'

'I'm not so learned as you, sir, and cannot use your arguments, but I speak from the heart and I can tell you this, we are united by the Holy Spirit and need look only to heaven for our leader, not to bishops, especially not to the Bishop of Rome.' Ellen's cheeks flushed red and her eyes glistened.

Alethea regarded her uneasily; she had not expected Ellen to be so passionate.

'We are all animated by the Holy Spirit, who doubts it? But the Holy Ghost both teaches and governs us interiorly, therefore he establishes pastors and teachers to act exteriorly.' William smiled at Ellen, apparently unperturbed by her heretical views. 'Human creatures, given their spiritual frailty, need a pastor, authorised from above, watching over his flock.' He cut himself a neat cube of meat and chewed on it slowly.

Ellen looked accusingly at Alethea. 'Pastors too can prove themselves susceptible to sin.'

'It is true all persons are susceptible to the temptations of the devil. That is why we need to adhere to the original, true source of spiritual authority, that is the Catholic Church. It's all these wicked sects who undermine the foundations of Christianity.' William seemed to be enjoying this theological discussion.

'I still won't have my children baptised,' Ellen insisted.

'Would you bar your children from the Kingdom of Heaven, leaving them to die like infidels, without hope of grace or redemption?' William demanded, his voice rising.

'Water baptism is just the invention of man.' Ellen gazed down at her plate, pressing a soggy lump of bread into the gravy pooled around it.

'If you don't believe baptism holds any spiritual power then why not allow your children to receive it, for it cannot do them any harm,' William responded more calmly.

Alethea thought this point a fair one, but Ellen refuted it. She would not allow her babies to be bound to a corrupt church by a rite that was generally held to be irreversible.

'So, you do admit the power of baptism?' William probed.

'You're tying me up in knots with your arguing.' Ellen looked on the verge of tears.

'Come, let us not fall out over religious doctrine,' Alethea intervened. 'What do you think of the venison, cousin? It comes off our own land.'

William smiled graciously. 'It is much the best venison I've tasted in a long time. Did you hunt it yourself?'

'Not I no, but it is a sport I intend to take up,' Alethea told him, having decided at that very moment to become an accomplished sportsman.

As soon as dinner was over Ellen hurried off upstairs. Alethea was about to follow her but was stopped by William.

'We need to talk privately, sister,' he said quietly.

Alethea followed him uneasily into the parlour. William stood looking out of the window. The garden was demarcated by a line of hawthorn trees, their branches decked out with creamy blossom. Beyond them speckled white cattle dipped their heads into the grass. A wood pigeon cooed drowsily. It was all looking so perfect, yet what a lot of work it all was to maintain.

'Do you seriously intend to make this Liddell woman's sons your heirs?' William asked.

'Why shouldn't I? I love them as my own and we need an heir to carry on our name.'

'The offspring of a heretic?'

Alethea studied the clouds spread across the sky in layers of white and grey. 'You admired my improvements and plans. Do you not trust my judgement?'

William turned from the window with an earnest expression. 'I've told you Lawrence will take our name. You can provide a legitimate, Catholic heir.'

'I will never become a wife, William.' Even Alethea was taken aback by the steel in her voice.

William took her hands in his. 'I fear Mrs Liddell exerts a malign influence over you.'

'I am master of my own decisions.' She squeezed his hands before gently withdrawing her own. 'You especially admired the orchards, well, the gardener has been showing me how the grafting of old stock onto new can improve the quality of a fruit tree. So might it not be with families? A new scion is grafted onto the old branch and makes it stronger, improving the quality.' Alethea was doing her utmost to construct the sort of calm and reasoned argument that would appeal to her brother's way of thinking.

'That may be true, but you cannot graft a fig or a vine onto an apple tree and produce fruit,' William retorted. 'Otherwise we would have pippin-grapes and fig-apples.'

'Ellen is not so different from me as all that. We are of the same species.'

'She is a schismatic, Thea. A person who would deny her own children redemption.'

'You haven't met little Robin or baby Nicholas. Why, even Crewe has been charmed by Robin. Let me show them to you.'

William sighed. 'They may be angels incarnate, but really I have no interest in children.' He looked up at the portrait of their father that hung above the mantelpiece. 'Why do you favour her sons? Crewe tells me the servants all believe them to be my children. Is this some sort of pact you have with Liddell?'

Alethea turned her gaze away from his and admitted, 'Nicholas is my son.'

He stared at her for a moment before crossing to the fireplace where he gripped the mantelpiece until his knuckles turned white. 'I thank God I've put duelling behind me or I'd have blood for this.' He closed his eyes, breathing deeply.

Alethea said nothing. She thought her brother might be praying.

'And the father?' he asked at last.

'The man does not know he fathered a child and will not trouble us.'

'A woman is not unchaste if she is forced against her will.' William turned to Alethea surveying her with a mixture of pity and sorrow. 'You were left unprotected and have suffered horribly. I blame myself for this; if I hadn't been so intemperate, fighting and killing a man, I would have been here to care for you.'

'Blame the disease that struck, not yourself. If it had not been for the plague I would be your innocent sister still, and father would be here…' Alethea felt suddenly overwhelmed. She sank down onto a stool.

'My poor Thea. When I see you dressed like a gentleman, I forget you are my little sister.' He knelt down beside her. 'You have been abused and left without counsel; no wonder you've fallen in with a woman such as Liddell.'

Alethea straightened up at this. So far, her brother's response had been better than she could have expected. His assumption that his sister could only have conceived an illegitimate child through an act of rape worked to her advantage, but she had to correct him regarding Ellen.

'Ellen saved my life, I would have been utterly lost without her. She has taken on and nursed the child, loving it as tenderly as if it were her own. She's never known any religion other than the one she grew up with. She'll come round.'

William stood up. 'I take into consideration her services to you, but I think you'll find her a more obstinate sectarian than you realise.'

'We will lead by example,' Alethea said, trying to appease her brother.

'Crewe told me about your renunciation of our faith. I understand now that you've been sorely tested and this may have shaken your belief.'

'I lost my path, William, but now you are here, you've helped me to find my way again.' Alethea looked up into her brother's face with as beseeching and sincere an expression as she could muster. She did not like to dissemble but would do it in defence of Ellen. She thought of Machiavelli's teachings, that while it is commendable to live with integrity, it is also sometimes necessary to do the opposite.

William took off his wig and scratched his head with vigorous desperation. 'Now I understand your reluctance to marry. It's a lot to ask of a man, to take on another man's bastard.' He returned to the window, drumming his fingers on the sill. 'We could send the child away. I'm willing to pay Mrs Liddell handsomely for his upkeep. I will even visit the child regularly for you.' He shook his head. 'I can't believe you gave it our father's name.'

'I tell you, William, I'll not part with them.' Alethea felt as though her stomach were turning to liquid and draining away down into her legs. What power had she?

She had kept her bond with her son as tenuous as possible. Whenever she felt a yearning for him rising in her breast she told herself he was not her child but Ellen's. She never cradled him in her arms or kissed his soft head. She had never sung to him or felt his little hand close around her finger. But she kept him close. She watched over him and felt what she told herself was a fatherly pride. He was the only child she would ever bear. Who would she choose if William forced her to it, Nicholas or her brother?

William sighed heavily. 'I cannot deceive Lawrence. He might still take you on out of charity or because he has given me his word. Either way, these are not the best ingredients for a happy marriage.'

Alethea realised that despite their tour that morning and all William's praise and enthusiasm, he had not, until that moment, even considered altering his plans to marry her off. She was glad then that she had told him about Nicholas. She began to speak, feeling her way cautiously.

'Nicholas will of course need careful schooling to ensure he bears no taint of his begetting. I will have to watch him carefully. You can select his tutors yourself, William. And now you are here we can have him baptised. I promise you, he will be brought up to be worthy of his grandparents, an honest gentleman and a Catholic.'

William nodded sadly. 'Perhaps it is just, given my past, that the world thinks I have fathered a bastard.'

'You will let me keep him then?'

'For now. I need to think through the best course for all concerned. I must spend some time in contemplation. I shall retire to my room for the rest of the day. We will talk again tomorrow.'

'Who is this cousin of yours? You never mentioned him before,' Ellen demanded as soon as Alethea entered her room.

'He's a cousin on my father's side. You must understand I have to keep him happy, otherwise we'll have a whole army of relatives descending on Measham, poking around in our affairs.' Alethea hated deceiving Ellen, but it was too dangerous to cross her brother now and besides, she had always been loyal to him.

'I don't like the way he talks to me. No offence intended to your cousin, but he's an odious man.'

'He has a kind heart, Ellen, though you cannot see it now.'

'No, I can't.' Ellen's eyes were red and swollen from crying.

Robin was standing by the bed, holding himself upright by clasping the bedcover with one hand. In the other he held a rattle which he was shaking at the supine baby. Nicholas stared up at the ceiling, blinking occasionally as the rattle swung past his face.

'Careful, Robin,' Alethea warned.

Ellen picked up the baby, driving Robin to swing the rattle more ferociously.

'Where's Abigail?' Alethea asked.

'She's having her dinner,' Ellen said. 'Would you pick Robin up for me? He's being a right nuisance.'

Alethea had hardly acknowledged Robin since their return the previous day. She made a fuss of him now, carrying him around the room.

'I am going to have Nicholas baptised,' she told Ellen.

'I see your cousin has been working his superstitious ribble-rabble on you.'

'There's no harm in it, I was baptised, do you think me a victim of idolatry?'

'I'm not sure anymore. I don't know what you believe in.' Ellen watched the baby in her arms, refusing to meet Alethea's gaze.

'I'm not sure either to be honest, but I won't deny my child this sacrament. What if he should die without any hope of redemption?'

Ellen ran her finger along the baby's nose. 'I know Samuel proved less honest than we thought, or maybe just a weaker man than we believed, but that doesn't mean you should throw out all our faith. It's more than one man. I'm no theologian, but I do have principles I'll not abandon.'

'That's fine, Ellen, I'm not asking you to. But Nicholas is my child and I will have him baptised, if only to keep the peace.'

'I thought you said he was to be my child. I have loved him as such.'

Alethea felt a chasm opening beneath her feet. Desperation made her hard-hearted. She looked at Ellen nursing the baby at her breast. The baby who had come from her womb and carried her blood. She knew what she had promised Ellen, but their predicament had changed. If it came down to it Ellen was just the wet nurse.

'We agreed you would act as a mother to him, but that I would be his father. As his father I decide what's best. You must allow me to be the head of this family.'

'You forget, Alethea, beneath the breeches you are not in truth a man and you are certainly not my husband.'

'To all intents and purposes I am a man; the man in charge of this estate where you reside.' But for how much longer? 'It was Erasmus who said man is his clothing,' she added smugly. What was she talking about?

'I see,' said Ellen, though she had never heard of Erasmus. The baby had fallen asleep. She lifted him carefully from her breast and placed him in his cradle. Then she held out her arms for Robin. 'I'll take my son,' she said.

'Of course, we won't baptise Robin if you don't wish it,' Alethea said uneasily.

'I don't.' Ellen turned to Robin. 'Shall we go out for a walk, poppet?' Robin bounced eagerly in her arms.

'Don't be churlish,' Alethea called out to her.

Ellen bobbed a slight curtsey and left Alethea standing in the middle of the room, her son sleeping peacefully beside her. She allowed herself a brief look, then followed Ellen out, closing the door quietly behind her.

Alethea went up to the long gallery. She could pace up and down there undisturbed. As she was ascending the stairs she encountered Crewe on his way down. He gave her a short bow.

'Crewe, may I speak with you a moment?'

'Of course, sir.' He followed her upstairs.

'So, you knew all along,' Alethea said as soon as they reached the gallery.

'I did, sir, yes.'

She was grateful to him for continuing to call her sir, it gave her hope. 'Well, I thank you for all you have done, for myself and for William,' she said awkwardly.

'My services are always at your disposal.'

'If that's the case, Crewe, I need your help now. William said you reported positively on my progress here. Of course, I couldn't have managed Measham without you. I believe we work well together, don't you?' They walked abreast along the gallery like two gentlemen.

'Indeed, I believe we share a desire for the good of the estate. You have proved a most able apprentice. It has been a pleasure to act as your guide.'

Alethea was taken aback by Crewe's notions. She had not thought of herself as his apprentice, nor of him as her guide.

'I grew up here, you know. My father worked for your grandfather.'

'Is that so?' She stopped and looked at Crewe, but his face remained as impassive as ever. 'So how would you care for a new master, a stranger?'

'These things are sometimes inevitable.'

'The thing is, Crewe, I don't think it is inevitable. I've suggested to my brother that I continue on here, acting as him. I have no desire to marry.'

'You always were a tom-boy,' Crewe noted, bringing Alethea up short again. Despite his demeanour he seemed full of odd disclosures.

'If I were to remain the master of Measham, you could continue to be in charge here. This gentleman my brother wishes me to marry might have his own steward. He might have all sorts of changes and grand ideas in mind for Measham. He won't want the old household here; husbands are always suspicious of their wives' servants. He is, I believe, a man of fashion. He will have all sorts of fancy notions about the laying out of new gardens and architectural improvements. He'll bring a whole French retinue with him. He won't share our vision for Measham, Crewe. He won't care about farming or tenants.'

'I am less concerned about Lawrence Gascoigne's taste in gardenage than his return to his former vice, the card tables.'

Alethea stopped short. 'Lawrence is a table-man? But I thought he took my brother away from all that.'

'He did, but my informant tells me he has recently lapsed.'

'Does William know?' Alethea wondered how many informers Crewe had.

'I think not. Gascoigne could not bear to disappoint your brother, or to lose his affections.'

'Then we must tell him,' Alethea said eagerly. 'We cannot risk Measham falling into the hands of a gamester.'

'Quite so. However, we must tread carefully. It would be best if Master William were to discover his friend's weakness for himself.'

'And how will he do that?'

'I am sure a little moral pressure applied to Mister Gascoigne will be enough to induce a confession.'

Alethea was beginning to comprehend just how deeply she had underestimated Crewe. 'Another thing, Crewe, I understand you may not think very highly of Mrs Liddell, but perhaps you might speak up for her? She is a very good mother and a loyal friend.'

Crewe studied the family portraits for a moment. 'I should like to see Master Nicholas reared here. It is where he belongs after all and if he is to become guardian of Measham his first attachment must be to this house and its grounds.'

'Has William told you?' Alethea stared at Crewe in shock.

'Told me what, sir?'

'About Nicholas.' Alethea paused. 'Being my heir.'

'I have not spoken privately with Master William since your return home, sir.' Crewe gave Alethea one of his rare and enigmatic smiles. 'But I can recognise a Hawthorne when I see one.'

⟶ Chapter Twenty-four ⟵

William remained at Measham for another month. A week after his arrival he arranged for Nicholas to be baptised by an itinerant priest Crewe was in contact with. The man arrived at night with a great trunk containing his robes, oil and holy water. Since there was no chapel at Measham, the priest set up his portable altar in the hall. Most of the household were present at the clandestine ceremony, with the exception of Ellen, though she promised not to speak of it outside the house. William was godfather.

A few days after this William told Alethea that he agreed to her proposal.

'And Lawrence Gascoigne?' Alethea asked.

A momentary expression of pain passed across William's face. 'Not as strong a man as I thought. He has fallen prey to an old affliction, one I don't wish to burden you with.'

And that was the last that was said on the subject of suitors.

Once the plan was decided on, William joined in wholeheartedly, appearing to have complete confidence in Alethea's ability to carry it off.

'Hereafter you are William and I am Matthew,' he told her. 'We have no other names.'

Alethea was kept very busy with the estate. Under Crewe's direction she hired more servants, gardeners and a gamekeeper. She had little time for her son or Robin. Ellen kept to her room and the kitchens, retiring to bed early. Apart from the children, Ellen's main companion was Abigail, the nursemaid.

This time spent with her brother was made all the more precious to Alethea by the knowledge that soon they would be parted again, possibly for several years. The pair enjoyed the house as though they were children once more, let loose to rule in their parents' absence. They moved over the estate with ease, reclaiming once forbidden spaces. They played shuttlecock in the long gallery. William taught her how to ride his horse, familiarising San Pareil with its new master. They opened dusty bottles of their father's best wine and sat up all night beside blazing fires debating the future and the past, their lips stained red with claret wine, their eyes glazed and their words blurring as the sun rose. In the evenings they took candles out into the garden and drank spiced rum on the lawn, the air around them heavy with the scent of flowers. One night a robin, fooled by the candlelight, continued to sing despite the gathering dark.

William pointed to the shadows that fell from the walls of the house. 'See, sister, we are never far from the shadow of death, but if this world is full of misery we can find comfort in the knowledge that we are blessed with saints for protection and angels as guides to defend us against eternal darkness.'

Alethea listened to the birdsong. A slither of moon was emerging in the sky. She remembered Henry Calverton's assumption that, like him, she was not troubled by religion.

'I don't feel them, William. I don't feel their presence and I don't see any evidence of divine intervention in human affairs.'

'My beloved sister, do not become one of those lost and desperate creatures devoid of hope, devoid of morality. A person without faith is nothing more than an animal lacking a soul.'

'And yet animals cause less hurt in the world than humans do.'

'Who can trust an atheist? Look to eternity, Alethea. Our stay in this world is short, as are its pleasures and its woes. Will you see a priest when I have gone? You will save yourself from melancholy if you do.'

Alethea smiled. Her brother knew her well. She hated to be plunged into despondency and would do anything to stop herself from brooding as their father had been wont to do.

William had an intelligent and energetic mind that had been improved by his education in St. Omer and Alethea enjoyed discussing religion and philosophy with him. More important than this, though, was their bond as siblings and as the only surviving members of their family. They were able not only to console each other over the loss of their parents and sisters, but also to preserve those they had lost with their shared memories. She would do nothing to alienate her brother for she loved him more than anyone.

Alethea agreed to seek a confessor, to uphold their faith. William counselled his sister that under hostile interrogation dissimulation was permissible and should not be confused with lying. If she must equivocate to protect his life or save the life of any other Catholic missionary it was acceptable to do so. She might also allow others to think she was a Protestant, so long as she did not actually practise Protestantism. As William Hawthorne she would be providing an invaluable service for him, for England and for the one true faith.

'Remember our beloved mother, how it was her dearest wish to see the Old Religion restored to its proper place in English life. Do not betray her faith,' William exhorted.

He spoke also of the liberation celibacy could bring, the freedom from troublesome passions, the inner calm. 'It is not a lonely life, Thea, as some assume. I have known greater happiness and peace of mind since taking up the life of a celibate than I ever encountered before.' He laid a hand on her arm. 'But you must spend time in prayer to keep you strong. Trust to the Holy Spirit rather than the spirit of the buttery. Cellar physic may help you to forget your troubles but it will not cure them.'

Alethea shrugged. She drank no more than any gentleman and had never allowed drunkenness to prevent her from carrying out her duties. Her brother was clearly preparing himself for the discipline of the Church and its ministry.

At dawn on the morning of 12th June, William left for Spain. Alethea embraced her brother, received his blessing and then went out hunting on Sans Pareil. She did not give herself the opportunity to sink into melancholy at her brother's departure or fear for his safe passage, distracting herself with both business and pleasure.

Remembering her promise to Ellen, she sent for a dance teacher and two musicians from London. She knew she had been neglecting Ellen but did not think the distance that had grown up between them was too great to bridge. Certainly, music seemed to restore a sense of harmony to the entire household and everyone went about in a better humour. Alethea was relieved to hear Ellen laughing again. Ellen became a little flustered at her first attempts to dance and was disappointed she was not as naturally skilled at keeping time as she had imagined she would be. As she persevered, however, she began to improve.

Alethea would have liked to take up the lute again, but she would need lessons and feared her hands would give her away as being too dainty for a man. Sometimes, listening to the musicians play, she was seized by a longing to open her heart in song, to experience the elation of joining her voice with others in the creation of a poignant or uplifting melody. But that skill, which Alethea had once been so commended for, belonged to the past. The girl who sang no longer existed. Besides there were plenty of other more important concerns to take up her time. William could not sit around perfecting his musical skills – he had an estate to run, plans to implement and oversee.

Alethea had become increasingly confident at going out in public as a man. Indeed, she had become so used to being called sir by her inferiors and William by her brother and Ellen, she hardly ever thought of herself as that girl, Alethea.

Not long after William's departure she learnt of another voyage. Ellen received a letter from her sister Lizzie who, along with Jeremiah and Seth, had settled back in London. Lizzie wrote that Samuel Byrd and his wife had set sail for America. God had directed them to take their mission to New England. They would send back word once they were established there so their friends might join them. Lizzie was not sure she wanted to go so far away to a land full of savages, but Dorcas and John were keen to make a new life for themselves in a country that might look more kindly on dissenters.

For a moment, after hearing this news, Alethea hoped Samuel and Rebecca might perish on the long voyage. She quickly castigated herself for such evil thoughts. Still, she was glad there would be an ocean between herself and her former lover. She was free now of any fear Samuel might discover and claim his son.

Summer turned into autumn and Ellen helped Tickell in the kitchens, preserving quinces in apple water, making damson and plum marmalades and quiddony of pippins. The orchards had produced enough fruit to keep them supplied all year. And the gardens enough herbs, gilliflowers, pinks, damask roses and borage for all their household needs. Alethea had collected the creamy heads of elderflowers that filled the hedgerows in early summer and later the clusters of black elderberries, and now they had gallipots full of elderflower cordial and sambucus spirit.

In September they received news of a terrible fire in London that had set the whole city ablaze. Thousands of houses had been destroyed, from the Tower to Fleet Street. The poor citizens had once again been forced to flee for their lives, setting up camp in Moorfields this time, where the King himself had gone to speak to them.

To Ellen's great relief Whitechapel and Stepney had been spared, though the fire had come very close. Lizzie wrote (with the help of her local pastor) to tell her they and their home were safe, though great clouds of ash had descended on them and they could still feel the heat from the burning streets a mile away. Lizzie had never in her life beheld anything like it; standing on their road in the glow of the conflagration, they had heard the crackling of the flames and the screaming of the people along with blasts of gunpowder as buildings were blown up to create fire breaks. It was like standing at the gates of Hell and feeling the devil's own breath on your face, her letter explained. All the livery halls, the customs house and the Royal Exchange had gone, along with hundreds of churches. They said the molten lead from St. Pauls had flowed down Ludgate Hill in a boiling river. This was surely a sign from God to the established Church that such buildings were not loved by Him, nor were the clergy who preached in them. At first there were rumours that the fire had been started by the Dutch, but now it was discovered to be the work of a Popish conspiracy.

'How ridiculous,' Alethea retorted. 'There are plenty of Catholics living peacefully and productively in London; why would they set fire to their own city?'

'They were French sympathisers, Catholic agents acting under orders from Louis XIV. Lizzie says some well-known Catholics were overheard in a tavern discussing plans for a fire weeks before it happened. Now mobs are attacking any foreigners they come across.'

'Ignorant fools,' Alethea said. But Ellen would not be dissuaded from Lizzie's hard evidence.

Despite her bad experiences there, Alethea was sorry to hear of such destruction wreaked upon the capital. Calverton House would have been saved as the fire had stopped short of the Strand at the Middle Temple. She was glad of it, for she had some fond memories of the house. She wondered what sort of new city they would construct out of the ruins.

'There will be plenty of work for carpenters,' said Ellen, ever practical, thinking of her brother-in-law.

In October Measham Hall was searched by an armed militia looking for Catholic priests. Alethea's modest library was ransacked and an inventory made of any books that suggested popery to the eyes of the local constabulary. They checked the house and outbuildings for firearms but finding only hunting rifles left them in peace.

Given the national rise in hostility towards papists Alethea thought it politic to attend the occasional service at their local church. The previous churchwarden had turned a blind eye to non-attenders, but he had been succeeded by a more zealous man who was keen to present a list of all dissenters to the local, as well as the Church authorities. Crewe told Alethea not to worry, the local magistrate had been a friend of her father's and would not press charges, but she discovered in herself a fear of crossing those in authority. Despite her brief period of radicalism in Epping and the religious euphoria she had experienced there, Alethea was not rebellious by nature. She wanted only to be an approved member of the local gentry and as such to be left in peace to continue her life at Measham. Her position was precarious enough and she feared an attack from Margaret Calverton. She felt she must shore up her defences to protect the security of her home. For it was Measham she loved, above and beyond any person or principle. The former had endured where the latter proved themselves to be weak and changeable, subject to mental and physical infirmity. Sometimes, although she loved and missed her brother, she hoped he would decide to remain abroad instead of bringing his mission back to England and putting them all in danger.

'Will you take communion?' Ellen wanted to know.

'We all serve the same God, Ellen, what does it matter if I do?' Alethea was uncomfortably aware that her brother would be as disapproving as Ellen was of her moral weakness.

When it came to matters of religion, she did not have William's courage or Ellen's perseverance. Her faith was not as strong as theirs nor as vital. She would steer a course between their two extremes she decided, navigating her way through gentler, if less heroic, backwaters.

Alethea spent the following spring establishing a friendly relationship with her neighbour, Sir Peverell, whose lake she so admired and began to consult him over the improvement of her own property. She was careful not to raise the issue of the disputed land, gaining his trust and courting his vanity by deferring to his accumulated wisdom. She soon learnt that the old man had no surviving heirs and became even more assiduous in her courting of him. She came to enjoy spending time with Peverell, not only because his poor eyesight and hearing meant she felt secure that he would never doubt her sex or accuse her of effeminacy, but also because his knowledge was useful to her.

She still followed Crewe's advice. He had become indispensable to her, but the mutual animosity between him and Ellen made her feel she had to display some diffidence towards him, at least in front of Ellen. She could spend time with Sir Peverell, however, without any discomfort, especially since Ellen was never present at their meetings.

Peverell approved of much of the work she had done but thought she might do more to cultivate the gardens. She agreed that she had neglected beauty in favour of the more practical deer park, woods and orchards, for these produced food and income.

'The Lord God planted a garden, making trees that were pleasant to the sight as well as good for food,' Sir Peverell said as they strolled around his grounds. 'And what is a garden without flowers?'

Alethea agreed planting up her garden would be a beneficial pastime. She welcomed all occupations that would keep her from melancholy and exhaust her physically, for she was sometimes tormented by carnal desires that came to her suddenly at night or in moments when she was still and made her long for the arms of a lover.

'If you are concerned about practicalities and making your estate more profitable you should look into that area of common land on your Northern boundary,' Peverell told her. 'It used to belong to the Measham estate, I am certain of it.'

'But it's used for grazing by local villagers,' Alethea said uneasily.

'That land is being over grazed, the sheep on it look half-starved. It would be far more productive rented out in plots, the villagers would profit by it. It would make a good source of income for you too.'

Crewe was only too happy to search out the deeds to the land, which it seemed did indeed belong to the Hawthornes, though it had been used as common land for some generations.

'You're not going to rob the people of land they rely on for sustenance?' Ellen demanded.

Ellen would not listen to Alethea's reasoning, accusing Alethea of being no better than the greedy, land-grabbing Normans of old. Alethea had laid aside all her principles as soon as it suited her purse to do so.

'And who do you think pays for your fine dresses and your dancing teachers?' Alethea's anger and indignation were partly fuelled by a guilty conscience, but Ellen's resistance only made her more determined to reclaim the land.

'I'll give them all up before I see peasants starving for my pleasure,' Ellen shouted.

Crewe opened the door for Ellen as she stormed from the room. His eye caught Alethea's for a moment, and if such a thing were possible she might have said he was smirking.

Of all the books that now filled her father's bookshelves, the one Alethea turned to most often was the slim volume of Machiavelli's given to her in London by Henry Calverton. Learning from Machiavelli's examples, she used Crewe to implement the enclosures. So it was he, rather than William, who was associated with fencing off the land and took the brunt of the ill will. Meanwhile she ingratiated herself with her tenants by visiting each family personally, distributing alms. She tried to explain her cause and promised them they would not go hungry. In an attempt to improve her reputation she built a village school and paid for a teacher. In this way she avoided riots; but while she managed to endear herself to some of the people, she did not make herself as popular as she would have liked.

Following Machiavelli's advice that a prince 'ought to take a care for his servant, honouring him, enriching, and obliging him to him,' Alethea rewarded Crewe well for his loyalty. They had reached an understanding about Crewe's piece of property and his farmlands. She gave him some of her best livestock to breed from and shared cuttings and seeds from her orchards and gardens. Secure in the knowledge that his old age was well provided for and that, as the Measham estate prospered so too did his pension, Crewe worked assiduously for a governor he considered to be just and benevolent.

Knowing that Miles and Tickell liked to drink in the village tavern, Alethea called Miles into the parlour one evening.

'Tell me, Miles, what do they say about me down at The Barley Mow?'

Miles stuck his hands into his breeches pockets and shifted his weight from one foot to the other. 'There's many as says you couldn't find a fairer landlord anywhere in England. Sir William, he's a charitable man, they say. And no one could be more just when it comes to poachers. For 'tis known that if a man is forced to take a little game for to feed a hungry family, you won't pursue him.' He glanced uneasily towards the door. 'But don't tell Mister Crewe as I said that.'

Alethea laughed and poured herself another glass of claret. 'And what do the others say? Don't worry, I won't be grieved.'

Miles' protuberant Adam's apple bobbed in his throat. He stared fixedly at the engraving above the fireplace. *'Feare God — Honour the King'* the carved letters warned.

'It's important I hear the bad as well as the good.' Alethea encouraged him.

Miles coughed. 'There are a few, and 'tis only when they're in their cups mind, that complain about how you put up the rents to pay for your fancy arbours and fountains. They say you enclosed the land so you can build new stables and greenhouses. They don't understand that we need these things, see. I do tell 'em.' He shuffled slightly, shifting his gaze to the bottle of wine placed by Alethea's elbow. 'Then there's the rumours of course.'

'Rumours? What rumours?' Alethea tried to smile warmly at him.

'About that trouble you got into in London, back in '64.'

'My duel, you mean?' Alethea nodded with relief. 'I've never hidden the fact I killed a man. But I was pardoned by the King.'

'If you don't mind me asking, sir, what was the duel over? It's just if I knew, I could correct the rumours, see.'

Alethea refilled her glass. 'And what do these rumours suggest it was over?'

The skin on Miles' neck flushed bright red. 'Please don't ask me, sir, I don't like to repeat such things.'

'That's all right, Miles, tell me the worst.'

But Miles only shook his head and looked at the floor.

'It's essential you tell me exactly what they are saying,' Alethea warned.

'Any man called me a buggerer, I'd run him through.'

'They say Fanshawe accused me of sodomy?' Now at last Alethea understood the secrecy and the shame that had always hung over her brother's duel.

'And others say as he was your lover, and that you killed him in a fit of jealousy,' Miles addressed the footstool.

'These are wild accusations. Do these people want to see me executed? I suppose they call me a traitor and a blasphemer into the bargain?'

''Tis only a few men, Sir William, with tongues loosened by drink. No respectable man believes such things.'

Alethea was tempted to ask him for names, but pitying the boy's distress she dismissed him.

'There were some rumours flying around at the time; your father and I thought we had dealt with them,' Crewe said, when she consulted him. 'I suppose your return sparked them off again. I will discover the chief source of them; if they are tenants of yours I'll have them evicted, if not, there are other ways to remove them from the neighbourhood.'

'Find out who they are before taking any action,' Alethea told him. 'We may be better served by taking them into our employment, on the new stables for example. If they have a trade we will support it, if they have a craft let's promote them. A man who is indebted to me will pose less of a threat than one who resents me.'

'Very wise, sir, I am impressed by your prudence.' Crewe bowed. 'Gain their loyalty but maintain your distance. Intimacy erodes respect. Let the villagers see you only on horseback, so that they must look up to you.'

Alethea agreed. She feared she had grown complacent about her ability to act as a man. She must be on her guard always against any trace of effeminacy, even if it was her brother who had been the originator of these rumours. She was tempted to write to him about them. They had developed a code, but even then were careful in what they committed to paper. Too much was at stake for both of them to risk being found out. Besides, she knew he would dismiss these tales as falsehoods. Could Fanshawe have been his inamorato? Was such a thing possible?

'Crewe?' she asked as he was leaving the room. He turned and looked at her inquiringly. 'What was my brother's duel over?'

Crewe stepped back into her chamber, closing the door behind him. 'Your brother is not a sodomite nor has he ever been a sodomite. Your brother has always loved his friends vehemently. But he has learnt how to direct that love for mankind into something chaste and noble.' Crewe looked at Alethea reprovingly. 'Father Matthew is beyond reproach.'

'Watch out, Nickie!' Robin was pointing to Nicholas, who was beginning to climb up the stairs.

Alethea had been watching them from the landing. She ran to the stairs, but before she was halfway down, Ellen had grabbed Nicholas and lifted him into her arms.

'So you can get up the stairs now, can you?' Ellen laughed, and the baby dug his round pink fingers into her neck. Robin resumed riding his cockhorse around the hall. 'Well done my little knight, what a good guard you make,' Ellen told him.

Robin grinned and galloped faster, pulling on the reins of his painted horse. Ellen set Nicholas down on his feet and he walked unsteadily across the hall, holding on to her hands for support.

Alethea's arms hung limply by her sides. Her stomach ached with the effort it took to keep her heart closed. She had trained every sinew in her being to bind her passions so tightly they had become knotted to the sticking place. Eventually she would strangle any dangerous feminine tenderness entirely.

Sometimes she longed for her parents to behold her child. Her mother would have doted on him, she was sure. Mother had cherished all her infants. If it was not for his begetting, her father too might have been proud of his namesake, for he was turning into a fine little boy. Father had always wanted more sons and Alethea had created not only another son, but also a grandson. Would he have recognised either?

Blinking away her tears, she continued to watch the children playing below. She could almost see the ghosts of her little sisters dancing round them. Lucy would have been eight now, and Betty seven. How they would have enjoyed playing with their little nephews. Lucy would lead Robin into mischief no doubt, while Betty would make a pet of Nicholas.

She turned away from the scene and returned to her chamber. Ensconced in her closet she could not hear the laughter or the cries of the children.

When she regarded herself in the looking glass, Alethea no longer saw a woman masquerading as a man; she saw only William Hawthorne, governor of the Measham estates. If she thought of her childhood she thought of herself as a boy. A boy with an unbroken voice, who liked to sing and to roam about the countryside. Who helped his father to plant trees and hedges. A boy who was one of the best horsemen in the county, was nimble at sword-play and liked to hunt. A boy who had matured into a respectable English gentleman. An unaffected squire, who preferred the company of his hounds and the solace of the bottle to the society of other men.

Alethea sat in the parlour after dinner enjoying a glass of claret. It was a bright September afternoon and she felt pleasantly drowsy. She had spent the morning overseeing the harvesting of apples from the orchard and was looking forward to the cider they would produce. They had a fine crop of Golden Pippins and she'd read that the addition of gooseberries could make a cider as strong and pleasing as the best Canary wine. If she could produce half a dozen hogsheads of cider it would reduce her expenditure on wine considerably and save the estate a great deal of money.

She was just dozing off, the sweet smell of apples still in her nostrils, when Palmes knocked on the door. A letter had just been delivered. Alethea eagerly prised open the seal. She did not receive many letters and none so welcome as this, written in Jane's own sloping, childish handwriting.

My dear Mr Hawthorne,

I hope you will forgive my familiarity in writing to you. I have long wished to thank you for the concern you showed for my welfare when last I dined at Measham Hall with my parents. I was struck then by how closely you resembled your sister, a friend whose loss I still mourn, for I loved her deeply. Our shared grief must create a bond between us I think. This, and your likeness to Alethea, make me bold enough to confide in you.

You must wonder at my having allowed two years to pass before writing to you. The truth is, sir, I have had no pen to write with nor no paper to write upon. My husband has kept me, for the most part, under lock and key, with no means of communicating my oppression to any friend who might assist me. His violence towards me grew so extreme that at last his valet took pity on me and got word to my parents. His final outrage was to throw me down the stairs causing me to lose the child I was carrying. This act at least, being witnessed by the servants, meant he was forced to relinquish me into my mother's care.

I have been convalescing at Calverton House for the past few weeks and intend to retire to Castle Rufford in the Spring. I hope my sorry circumstances and the scandal that must attach to them will not prevent you

*from visiting us. It is my dear wish to converse with you upon a subject
close to both our hearts, your sweet sister and my beloved friend, Alethea.*

> *Your humble and most obliged servant,*
> *Jane Sellwood.*

Alethea was dismayed to hear that Jane had suffered so much and for
so long. She remembered the wan creature who had come to dinner.
How misplaced her confidence in the Calvertons' safeguarding of their
daughter had been. Perhaps she should have followed Ellen's urgings
then, but what could she have done? A man's wife was his property; she
could not have broken into Lord Sellwood's house and stolen Jane away.

She walked over to the window and stood staring out, the letter
still in her hand. The hawthorn trees were already heavy with crimson
berries, their leaves a rich amber. At least Jane was free now. The
Calvertons must have secured a separation. She read the last line of
her letter again. Did Jane suspect her, or was she suspicious of her
mother? Alethea would have to tread cautiously, but she would like to
invite Jane to Measham.

A blackbird tugged at a worm on the lawn. A flock of starlings
descended on the hawthorn; she could hear their chatter from where
she stood. She would discuss it with Ellen. They had not spoken much
since the land enclosures and Alethea had been too busy to woo back
her good favour. Consulting her about Jane would make Ellen feel
important. No doubt she would also feel obliged to point out that if
Alethea had done as she had desired, Jane might have been spared two
years of torment. Still, Alethea would happily swallow Ellen's moral
medicine if it healed the rift between them.

When she got to Ellen's room, Alethea saw Ellen's clothes
strewn over the bed. Ellen was bending over a large packing case.
She straightened up when she heard Alethea's footsteps, regarding her
friend with resolute sorrow.

'I would've told you in advance, but there's no talking to you these
days and besides, I won't be dissuaded. Robin and me, we're going
back to London.'

'For a visit?' It was a wish as much as a question, but Ellen only shook her head.

'I've packed what I'll need. Those dresses on the bed I'll leave behind. They're too fancy for the life I'm returning to and besides, their price is too high.'

When Alethea failed to respond, Ellen explained that Lizzie and Jeremiah had a room for herself and Robin. She and Lizzie planned to set up a draper's shop together. Since the King had taken to wearing English cloth, the textile business was doing well. Jeremiah had also found plenty of work in his trade. With the city being rebuilt after the fire, carpenters were in demand and he and Lizzie had been able to move to a larger house. It was clear Ellen had been planning her move for some time, corresponding with her sister without telling Alethea.

'What about Nicholas?'

'Abigail is an excellent nurse and dotes on the child.' Ellen stared down at the clothes she was folding. 'He's fully weaned so has no need of me.'

'But I thought you loved him as a mother.' Alethea felt quite bewildered.

'I'm not cut out for the country life after all. I need to be with my own folk.'

'Have I not treated you well?'

'I can't complain, you've been most generous, but we are not equals here and I don't like to be anybody's servant.'

'Nobody treats you as a servant.'

Ellen merely snorted at this. 'You have your ways and I have mine, I don't belong here.'

'But Robin is so happy here, do you really want to take him back to the filthy, dangerous city? Think of the opportunities I can offer him, the education. Measham is his home.'

'Robin's home is with me. I don't want him growing up a papist.'

Alethea stared at her friend. 'So that is what it comes down to?'

'When we left Epping you had embraced our true Saviour and His lessons. Then, when we got here you said you'd continue to hold to our ways. You said you'd turn Measham into a new paradise. A place where all people could live free and equal. But instead you've gone the way of all men of property, thinking it's your right to make a profit out of others' labour. I said from the start you shouldn't trust Crewe, but you've let him steer you all the way. Him and that cousin of yours.'

'It's true I've had to make compromises, but if you had to manage this place you'd be compelled to do the same. I have a household that relies on the income we generate, if I don't make a profit everyone will go hungry.'

'People *are* going hungry because of your policies. You know there are other principles by which you could manage your affairs, it's just that you like to play the king over this miniature kingdom of yours. We lived as equals in Epping Forest and no one went without, our camp ran like clockwork.'

'Oh hardly, it took days to reach an agreement over anything, no matter how inconsequential. It was Barbara who chivvied everyone into action and Thomas and Samuel who held sway. They were princes too if you want to put it that way. The rest of us followed them and did as they wanted.'

'You are just bitter because Samuel made you his whore.'

Alethea placed her hand against the cold glass of the window. She breathed slowly, allowing the heat of her anger to dissipate. A fat autumn sun shone down on the garden. Robin was playing with a ball while Abigail watched him, Nicholas balanced on one hip.

'You may despise my money and my person, but I would like to give something towards Robin's schooling. You know I have regarded him as my son.'

'I don't despise you. I shouldn't have said what I did, I spoke in haste.' Ellen sounded contrite. 'I'll leave you my address and write to you with our news. If you have money to spare and wish to send it to Robin then it will be received with thanks, but I'll choose his school.'

'Of course. I must extract a promise from you before you go. You cannot tell anyone I am William Hawthorne, not even Lizzie.' Alethea was seized with alarm when she thought of the letters Ellen must have written to her sister. 'What have you told Lizzie?'

'Only that I've been staying with Alethea and looking after her brother's child. I didn't say anything about you being William or who Nicholas' parents really are. I keep my promises.'

'Good. You must tell Lizzie that Alethea is dead, that is why you no longer want to stay here.'

'I don't like telling lies.'

'It is not a lie. Alethea the whore is dead to you.'

Alethea did not stay to see Ellen's expression. She went out to the garden to say goodbye to Robin.

'We were just coming inside, I thought a little fresh air would do them good,' Abigail explained when she saw her approaching.

'That's all right, Abigail. You take Nicholas inside, I'll follow with Robin.'

Alethea chased Robin up to the top of the garden. He laughed and ran as fast as his stout little legs would carry him.

'Come on.' Taking his hand, she led him out through the garden gate and into the meadow beyond. When he grew tired, she carried him up the hill and they stood together looking down at the house below. The sun cast a glow on the red brick walls. The mullioned windows glittered black. The chimneys spiralled up to the sky as if drilling their way into the heavens. Ivy was creeping up the western corner and jackdaws were nesting in the eaves.

Alethea sighed. 'That house is like a spoilt child, it demands constant attention.' She sat down on the damp grass beside Robin. 'You'll be a fine fellow some day and then perhaps you'll seek me out again.' She picked up a fallen chestnut, cradling it in the palm of her hand. 'There will always be a home for you here at Measham.'

She had assumed the boys would grow up together as brothers. That Nicholas would know that greatest, most equal and comforting of bonds, sibling love.

'Measham.' Robin pointed to the house.

His face had lost its infant roundness. His curls were growing darker. Alethea looked into his beautiful eyes, the colour of blue slate just washed by the rain and fringed with long, curling black lashes. It was as though she were looking into Samuel's eyes again. How could she have missed the resemblance? Had she been wilfully blind all this time?

'Come on, it's getting late.' She picked him up roughly and carried him back to the house, setting him down in the hall.

'Willum, Willum,' Robin called to her as he tried to follow her into the parlour.

'I'm not to be disturbed,' Alethea told Crewe and shut the parlour door before Robin could reach her.

She sat for a long time staring into the fireplace, listening to the footsteps running up and down the stairs. Sometimes Ellen's voice rang out, calling to Robin or Abigail. At one point she almost jumped to her feet to chase after Ellen and demand an explanation. But what would she say? 'Is Robin Samuel's son?' She would sound insane and Ellen would treat her with scorn.

It was so long since she had beheld Samuel it could be that her memory was playing tricks on her; she saw a likeness where there was none. Ellen could not have lain with Samuel. But if she had it would explain her husband's desertion of her. Alethea suddenly remembered their first Christmas Night together; Ellen had been about to confess something, a secret she had sworn to keep, when they had been interrupted. She cursed herself now for not pressing Ellen further but there had been so many other matters on her mind she had forgotten Ellen's attempted disclosure.

Eventually she heard the wheels of the coach on the drive and Ellen and Robin's voices as they boarded, but she did not go out to see them off. Instead, she watched from the window as the coach trundled off down the lane. Abigail stood sobbing, one arm wrapped around Nicholas, the other waving until the coach was out of sight.

Alethea turned to the portrait of her father. He stood in front of the chestnut tree, his fowling piece in his hand, leaning against some ancient wall invented by the painter. His spaniel gazed up at him with devoted eyes. He looked strong and stout, a middle-aged man who relied only on himself, his hunting dog and his gun. Alethea was twenty-one, but she may as well have been forty. It was not such a bad thing, to be a man like her father, as he was in this painting with his lace collar and gold brocade, a man who knew his place in the world and guarded it carefully.

She could hear Abigail on the stairs taking Nicholas up to bed, singing him a lullaby. She was a good little maid; he would do just fine under her care. She would now have to make it clear to the servants that, although she had treated Robin like a son, he was not actually hers. They would be surprised no doubt and would miss the little fellow, but she could not help that.

As she walked into the hall, Caesar came padding over to her, his tail wagging. All in all, Ellen's departure was a good thing, for not only did it mean fewer mouths to feed, she could also dismiss the expensive dancing master and the musicians. She would no longer have to listen to Ellen's scolding. She could do as she pleased without Ellen worrying at her conscience. When she needed counsel she had Crewe. She would have to get herself another dog, Caesar was too slow to hunt and she wanted a pup in place before she lost him.

And some day she would have her own portrait painted. The thought of it amused her, William Hawthorne with hounds and firearm. She would hang it opposite her father, so they might regard each other from across the room.

Her footsteps echoed through the empty hall. 'Palmes,' she called to the footman, 'bring me more claret, would you?'

➤ Chapter One ◆

oncealed by ferns, Nicholas sat watching the narrow path
below. He was a good hunter and did not mind waiting.
Having learnt to be both patient and stealthy, he was able
to observe close up the birds, deer, weasels, voles, squirrels and foxes
that inhabited the woodland. He never grew bored, not with these
forest creatures for entertainment. Always happier outdoors than in,
he loved especially the mossy intricacy of the forest, with its twisted,
interlocking branches and hidden dells. This was a better way to spend
his time than parsing Latin epigrams under the critical eye of his
cousin, Father Matthew.

He took a wild plum from the little store he had placed in among
the mushrooms in his basket. It was fat and sweet, bursting pleasantly
in his mouth to release its juices. Hopefully Matthew wouldn't notice
his black fingernails and purple stained palms. Standing up slowly,
he shook out his legs. He would go down to the stream to wash his
hands. It would mean turning his back on the path, but he would hear
if anyone approached.

A branch snapped. He dropped down on his heels. A couple made
their way hesitantly down the path. Nicholas jumped down before
them and introduced himself with a bow. He loved these important
errands, or 'missions' as Matthew called them, imagining himself as a

sort of latter-day Robin Hood, only he was bringing spiritual succour to the people. On this occasion he had been sent out to guide the Caldwells back to Measham Hall for the baptism of their baby.

The young woman, who carried a baby in her arms, yelped with fright, but the man doffed his hat and gave the customary greeting.

'Good morning, young master. What do you be doing out so early on this Sabbath day?'

'I have been gathering toad's bread.' Nicholas held out his basket of mushrooms.

'Have you indeed? We too come in search of bread, bread and water, perhaps you might lead us to them?'

'I know of someone who can provide what you seek,' Nicholas responded. 'Especially for this Holyday.'

The couple smiled, the woman jiggling the grizzling baby on her hip. She was very pretty; her brown eyes were fringed with long black lashes and her plump lips were the colour of raspberries. The only women at Measham were Nicholas's former nursemaid, Abigail, who now helped in the kitchens and with the laundry, and Lady Jane who was a frequent guest. Nicholas wished he could encounter more young maids as attractive as Mrs Caldwell. It was, he thought, like living in a garden filled with shrubs but empty of flowers.

After the baptism of the baby, which Father Matthew officiated over in the parlour, everyone went into the kitchen for a glass of ale, a slice of game pie and a cheesecake.

'Have you put the articles away?' Crewe, their steward, murmured in Nicholas's ear.

Nicholas nodded. Anxious not to miss out on the sweetmeats and Mrs Caldwell's company, he had shoved the family chalice, holy oil and priest's vestments into the chest under the parlour window seat. They were supposed to be kept in a false step in the staircase. He would hide them away properly once the Caldwells had gone.

'We're very grateful to you all for taking this risk on our behalf, especially given the current times.' Mr Caldwell raised his tankard.

'I was sore afraid little Mary might perish afore she was watered by a priest,' Mrs Caldwell said, her large eyes lustrous with tears.

Nicholas watched her as she took a bite out of her cheesecake. The way her tongue curled upwards to dab at her lips reminded him of Jemima, their kitchen cat.

'Everybody's talking about these night riders that've been heard all over the country. People are saying they should confiscate all papists' horses as well as their weapons.' Mr Caldwell shook his head.

Nicholas was glad Father had taken the precaution of stabling their horses at the Thornton's farm. He couldn't bear it if Polestar was taken.

'They think all Catholics are like the Jesuits, after the King's blood.' Caldwell looked at Father Matthew with sudden embarrassment. 'Begging your pardon, Father, I know you wouldn't have anything to do with this plot.'

Matthew smiled genially. 'If indeed there is a plot. I wouldn't be surprised if the whole thing is a fabrication. I've heard reports of this Titus Oates fellow and he sounds like a thorough scoundrel.'

'A chapman at market yesterday was reading out a newsletter what said Titus Oates can prove the Jesuits and their allies design to enslave England to France and the Romish Religion,' Mrs Caldwell said. 'Things like that make everyone suspect us.'

Mr Caldwell tugged at her sleeve and she began to fuss over the baby which lay sleeping in her lap. Nicholas could not help noticing how the nape of her neck had turned red. He felt a sudden urge to reach out and place a fingertip on the downy skin, just to see if it was as warm as it looked.

'I hope we can rely on you both not to breathe a word of the baptism or of Father Matthew to anyone, no matter how trustworthy they seem.' Father, a man of few words, spoke for the first time.

Father did not like allowing strangers into Measham Hall for Mass, but his cousin was adamant. Matthew could not be a chaplain to the Hawthorne family alone, but must serve the needs of the local people. Nicholas thought this very heroic of him, though Father said it was foolhardy.

The Caldwells swore with such earnestness that they would rather be hanged than betray the Hawthornes, Nicholas had no doubts about their sincerity.

Father looked pensive, however. 'The Parish Constable told me he's been ordered to draw up lists of suspected papists and hand it to the nearest Justice of the Peace. Any that refuse to take the Oath of Allegiance will be gaoled.'

Mrs Caldwell looked up at him with alarm.

Matthew patted Father's shoulder. 'We all know what the law says regarding our religion, but it is rarely enacted. Let's not spoil this day of celebration as we welcome little Mary into the one true faith.'

As if on cue the baby woke and began to cry.

Once he had led the Caldwell's back to the forest path, Nicholas took his time returning to the house. At the edge of the wood he stopped to admire some pink and orange berries he hadn't noticed before. He gathered a few to show to Matthew, snapping off a branch complete with leaves as his tutor had told him to.

That afternoon they went through the huge leather-bound herbal kept in the library.

'I think it must be the fruit of the Spindle tree,' Matthew said, pointing to a woodcut illustration. 'It is poisonous so take care with it, don't let it touch your mouth.'

'I'm not a baby,' Nicholas retorted, though he was secretly glad he'd resisted eating any of the pretty berries.

Matthew merely raised his eyebrows. 'It is a good specimen. Take your inks and make a study of it to add to your collection.'

This was a task Nicholas was only too happy to undertake. He loved drawing plants and had a common-place book devoted entirely to his botanical discoveries.

'When I'm grown I'm going to travel to the most distant lands and bring back wondrous fruits and flowers the likes of which have never been seen before. I'll make a present of them to the King.'

'An honourable ambition.' Matthew sounded amused. 'I believe you'll make a fine botanist. Have you shown your drawings to your father yet?'

Nicholas shook his head. 'I don't think they would be of much interest to Father.'

A look of sorrow flitted across Matthew's face. 'William will be impressed by your skilful hand and pleased by your enthusiasm for the works of nature. Why don't you show more interest in our lands here? You know the gardens are your father's pride and joy.'

Nicholas just shrugged. Father hardly seemed to notice his presence and he was convinced he wouldn't want him tagging along as he made his rounds of the estate. He had certainly never suggested Nicholas accompany him.

He suspected it was because he was, what Abigail called, his father's 'natural son'. That meant his mother was a whore, or so the stable-boy, Jasper, had told him. Abigail said Jasper deserved a whipping. Nicholas's mother had been a good, honest woman and always kind to her. She never understood why his father hadn't married Ellen, even if she was below him in station. He'd always treated her with respect and she was lovely to look at, with her flaxen hair and hazel eyes. Nicholas, being dark, was very much a Hawthorne in looks.

He was always being told how fortunate he was his father had recognised him and managed to make him his heir, despite the circumstances of his birth. It was a great responsibility and he must do everything in his power to ensure he lived up to the Hawthorne name. Whenever he misbehaved, Matthew would warn him to be on his guard against the sins inherent in his flesh.

Only Lady Jane never held his origins against him. The King had at least a dozen illegitimate children, she said, the sons had been given titles and many of them had made good marriages. He had no need to feel ashamed; a child was not responsible for the sins of its parents.

'How old are you now?'

Matthew was studying his face in a way that made Nicholas uneasy. He supposed this was one of Matthew's rhetorical questions since he was sure his cousin knew his age, but he answered anyway.

'Twelve, sir.'

'In a couple of years you will be old enough to attend St Omer's College, how would you like that?'

Nicholas almost leapt up from the desk in his excitement. 'I would love it beyond anything.'

Matthew had told him about his own time at St. Omer's; the trips to the countryside, the plays and concerts performed by the students. He said the college excelled at music and drama. Father had also attended briefly, but he never spoke about it. More than anything, Nicholas longed to be among boys of his own age. He would happily endure arduous days in the schoolroom if he could also enjoy the companionship of his peers.

Matthew laughed. 'Well, I will have to persuade your father. I suspect he will prefer to keep you close, but I will see what I can do.' He paused and Nicholas was moved by the warmth and affection with which his cousin spoke to him. 'I didn't know what sort of boy I would meet when I returned to Measham five years ago. If I am honest, I wasn't expecting much, but you continue to impress me, Nicholas. You have an aptitude and enthusiasm for learning and a facility with languages that make you an excellent student. You deserve to be taught by more advanced scholars than myself, especially in natural philosophy and medicine.' He closed the book that lay on the table between them. 'You would not be allowed into the priesthood of course, not without papal dispensation.'

Nicholas didn't care about that. He had no desire to become a priest and the fact that they wouldn't have him made him want it even less.

Matthew gave him one of his wry smiles. 'You will have to come back to look after Measham Hall when your father gets older, but there is plenty of time for travel before then. Perhaps you will bring a Catholic bride back to further the line.'

Nicholas didn't know what to say to this. He couldn't imagine getting married.

'Do you think Father will agree?' he asked anxiously.

Matthew picked at the corner of the book with his slender fingers. 'He wants you to attend Oxford or Cambridge. Presently of course, that would mean taking the oaths and renouncing your faith, at least outwardly.'

'I could never be such a hypocrite as that.'

Matthew sighed. 'When James succeeds to the throne I believe things will change. He will make it safe for us to practice our religion openly again. Catholics will be allowed to hold positions of office and attend university.' He got up, stretched and went over to the window where he stood staring out at the dark November sky. 'That is why so many are stirring up against us; they are terrified England will have a Catholic monarch once more and will do anything to stop it.'

The door opened and Father strode in. 'Studying, on a Sunday?' He nodded at the herbal.

'Your son has inherited your fascination with the natural world.'

'Glad to hear it.' Father looked at Nicholas. 'What about the lute? Have you practised any more on that?

Father had said that if he showed some promise he would get him a music tutor. Though Father did not play himself he seemed to have some knowledge of the instrument and had tried to teach Nicholas a few chords, encouraging him to sing along as he did so. Nicholas had so desperately wanted to impress his father that he had practised until his fingers bled. But he did not have a natural aptitude for music or a good singing voice and Father soon lost interest in coaching him. Nicholas rarely touched the instrument now.

'I'm no good at it,' he said sadly.

'You have to stick at it if you want to improve.' There was an edge of impatience to Father's voice. 'You saw the Caldwells off all right?'

'Yes, sir.'

'Good lad.' Despite his words, Father looked unhappy. He turned to Matthew. 'You will have to lay low for a while, at least until this plot business is resolved and the general panic has calmed.'

'I was about to explain to Nicholas that I might have to disappear for a while. I have been in communication with a Catholic family who have got passes to go to France, they have said I can travel with them.'

'Why on earth would you do that? The ports are being searched and priests arrested. You're safer here; so long as you stop giving communion to every Tom, Dick or Nell that requests it.' Father's sunburnt cheeks looked redder than usual and his high-pitched voice had risen even higher. 'Have you discussed it with Crewe?'

Father and Matthew both deferred to Crewe. He was more like a grandfather to Nicholas than a household retainer.

'Of course. It was Crewe who made contact with them on my behalf.'

Nicholas rushed to Matthew's side, grabbing hold of his sleeve. 'Please, cousin, let me go with you. I won't be a burden. I can be your groom or your servant and when I am fourteen you can send me to St. Omer's.'

Father pulled at his hair. 'What nonsense have you been filling the boy's head with?'

Matthew looked reproachfully at Nicholas. 'I told you I would discuss this with your Father, you are too impetuous. And I cannot possibly take you with me.'

Nicholas was so desperate to convince Matthew he didn't care if he angered the two men. 'I can aid your disguise. We can pretend I am your son.'

'You will do no such thing,' Father snapped. 'You are my son and your place is here. I know how fond of learning you are and am going to great lengths to ensure your entry to one of the English universities, should you wish to attend.'

Matthew held his arms out to them both. 'Wherever Nicholas completes his education, I am sure he will do well.' He bowed slightly towards Father. 'In my opinion the learning at St. Omers is superior, but that is something we can contemplate later. For now, I believe it may be better for all of us if I go abroad.'

→ Chapter 2 ←

It was Nicholas who saw them first. Pursuivants, riding five abreast, galloping down the lane that led to Measham Hall. A rider peeled off from either end of the phalanx, heading towards the east and the west wings of the house.

'What has caught your mayfly mind now?' Matthew tapped on his desk.

'Soldiers.' Nicholas looked up at his cousin, his eyes round with fear.

Matthew turned to the window. 'Find your father. Warn him,' he said before running from the room.

Nicholas raced down the stairs, through the kitchen and out of the open back door, leaving their cook, Tickell calling after him. Hurrying towards the stables, he prayed Father would be on his way home for dinner and he could catch him before he entered the house. As he turned the corner of the walled garden he collided with a leather coated torso. His shoulders were grabbed roughly and he found himself staring up into the large, stubbly face of a soldier.

'Where're you off to in such a hurry?' The man's fingers pinched into his flesh.

'Cook needs some eggs.'

The man's lip curled with disbelief. His eyes roamed over Nicholas's fine linen shirt; it was clear he was no kitchen boy. Spinning him round

291

the soldier marched him back into the kitchen. Tickell dropped the rabbit he was skinning as they barged through the doorway.

'What did you send this boy for?'

Tickell was saved from answering by a thunderous hammering at the front door.

'Let's see who it is, shall we?' The soldier pushed Nicholas in front of him, one hand still clasped around his arm.

Three of the pursuivants stood on the front step. Crewe stepped around the terrified footman, Palmes, to confront them.

'You must have a warrant to enter this house.'

Nicholas was reassured by the steward's measured tone and calm expression. Crewe could handle anything; he always knew what to do.

The captain pulled a roll of parchment out of his jerkin, holding it aloft so that it fell open. Crewe slowly lifted the eye-glasses that hung on a chain around his neck, fixing them onto the bridge of his nose, before extending his hand to take the warrant. But the soldiers pushed past him into the hall.

'The room on the left, that's the one.' The captain pointed to the parlour.

Nicholas's stomach lurched. He felt as though all the blood in his body was draining away into his feet. How did they know where to look? He glanced at Crewe but the old man's face was still as a statue's, his eyes fixed on the opposite wall.

The soldiers, as eager as hounds on the scent of a fox, filled the room with the smell of sweat and mud and leather. It was then Nicholas remembered the chalice and vestments. Matthew's revelations the previous day had distracted him and he'd forgotten to put them back in the concealed step. He bit down on his nails, what were the chances they wouldn't open the window seat?

But the men had moved straight to the parlour walls. They were ripping off the tapestries and knocking on the wood panelling, listening for a tell-tale hollow ring. Nicholas thought of throwing himself to the floor and feigning a fit. Anything to create a diversion, to give his father time to return and Crewe to think up a solution.

One of the soldiers kicked the window seat. He stopped and kicked it again, then pulled the cushions off. Nicholas held his breath. The man felt around the ledge and pushed it up with a creak.

'What've we got here?' He pulled out the vestments and the gold chalice and chrismatory tumbled out of the silk folds of the chasuble.

'Papist trinkets,' the captain said with satisfaction. 'The devil's toys. Put them in the sack.' He nodded to one of his men who held out a hemp bag.

Nicholas couldn't bring himself to look at Crewe. Instead they both watched as the soldier dropped the family heirlooms carelessly into his sack.

'I found it!' The soldier who had apprehended Nicholas gave a cry of triumph as he revealed the small door set into the wainscoting by the fireplace.

'Where's the key?' The captain demanded as his men pressed on the wood frame.

'I have no idea.' Crewe said. 'I had forgotten that cupboard was there. It hasn't been used in years.'

Nicholas imagined Matthew curled up on the other side of the wall, praying.

'Cupboard my arse, it's a priest's hole.'

The captain gestured to one of his men and the soldier pulled a small axe from his belt and began to hack at the door, the wood splintering around the concealed lock. Nicholas clenched his fists, the blood drumming in his ears. What if they hacked right into Matthew? He hoped desperately that his cousin had chosen some other place to hide; that they'd find only an empty space.

Father came into the hall as the soldiers were leading Matthew out, his hands tied behind his back. Palmes had put an arm around Nicholas who was squeezing every muscle in his body in the effort not to cry.

'What on earth are you doing with my cousin?' Father demanded.

'Watch we don't take you away as well. Harbouring a priest is an offence.'

'He's no priest.' Father sounded outraged.

But Matthew looked at Father with a resigned smile and shook his head. Nicholas was shocked to see Father's eyes fill with tears. He had never seen his father cry.

They watched as the soldiers rode off, Matthew slung over one of their horses.

'Someone betrayed us,' Father said as he pulled the door closed.

❖ Acknowledgements ❖

Huge thanks to all my early readers who gave such invaluable support and feedback. I am especially grateful to Colin Teevan, Benjamin Wood, Richard Hamblyn and Susie Farrell for their insightful notes.

Many thanks to my editor Matt Casbourne, copy editor, Catriona Robb, Dominic Forbes for the wonderful cover and to all the team at Duckworth Books.

For my husband, Colin, and children, Oisín and Lily, who put up with me 'living in the seventeenth century' for some considerable periods of time and always make returning to the twenty-first century worthwhile.